D0050173

Also by Maisey Yates

The Lost and Found Girl
Confessions from the Quilting Circle
Secrets from a Happy Marriage

Four Corners Ranch

Unbridled Cowboy
Merry Christmas Cowboy

Gold Valley

Smooth-Talking Cowboy
Untamed Cowboy
Good Time Cowboy
A Tall, Dark Cowboy Christmas
Unbroken Cowboy
Cowboy to the Core
Lone Wolf Cowboy
Cowboy Christmas Redemption
The Bad Boy of Redemption Ranch
The Hero of Hope Springs
The Last Christmas Cowboy
The Heartbreaker of Echo Pass
Rodeo Christmas at Evergreen Ranch
The True Cowboy of Sunset Ridge

For more books by Maisey Yates,
visit www.maiseyyates.com.

MAISEY YATES

Merry Christmas Cowboy

ISBN-13: 978-1-335-60095-0

Merry Christmas Cowboy
Copyright © 2022 by Maisey Yates

Her Cowboy Prince Charming
Copyright © 2022 by Maisey Yates

Recycling programs
for this product may
not exist in your area.

For questions and comments about the quality of this book,
please contact us at CustomerService@Harlequin.com.

HQN
22 Adelaide St. West, 41st Floor
Toronto, Ontario M5H 4E3, Canada
www.Harlequin.com

Printed in Lithuania

MIX
Paper from
responsible sources
FSC® C021394

CONTENTS

To my readers who have been there from the beginning,
this second generation story is for you.

MERRY CHRISTMAS
COWBOY

CHAPTER ONE

WOLF GARRETT *SHOULD* be happy for his older brother. He knew that.

It wasn't that he didn't feel a sense of happiness for Sawyer, and his newfound status in life as a husband and father. It was just that he couldn't say he enjoyed being around it much. He loved his niece. June was adorable. But the problem with all of it was that it highlighted the fact that when it came right down to it, Sawyer was sort of the main character at Garrett's Watch. He lived in the main house, he had his wife and his child, and his happiness was… Well, it was impossible to escape.

Wolf did his best not to wonder about what life he would be living now if things had gone differently. If Breanna had lived. The thing was, it didn't matter. Because there was no amount of what-ifs that would bring a tragically deceased teenage girl back from the dead. And there were no magical remedies for a heart that had broken a long time ago. They said that time healed all wounds.

The one thing he knew for sure was that sixteen years wasn't enough time.

He had stopped waiting for that magical moment a long time ago.

And all of this was a lot more maudlin than he ever cared to get but the fact of the matter was, it reinforced the idea that he needed a change of scenery. At least for a while.

"I had a talk with our cousin the other day," he said, looking around the dinner table.

It was a night when the family got together to have dinner. They didn't do it every night, but truth be told, his new sister-in-law was a wonderful cook, and any time the offer of her making dinner was on the table, he took it.

"Which one?" Elsie asked.

Sawyer and Wolf weren't the chatting type, but even still they tried to keep lines of communication open with the cousins who lived in Copper Ridge. But they hadn't been to visit in years. Elsie seemed to keep tabs on them all with greater frequency, but she hadn't been to visit, either.

"Connor. Had a conversation about the goings-on in Copper Ridge at their operation. They're expanding. They need some help."

"Really?"

"Their spread isn't anywhere near as big as ours, but with Eli's responsibilities as sheriff, he's only able to work on the ranch part-time."

"Well, if you want to do that…"

Wolf knew that Sawyer had no real reason to take issue with it. They had a full staff of workers at Garrett's Watch, and the help was more than enough. Their family up in Copper Ridge, Oregon, just a couple hours north and toward the coast, had a whole different type of spread. A few hundred acres, and a smaller herd of cattle. They specialized in beef they sold at farmers markets and local grocery stores. Whereas Garrett's Watch, part of the broader fifty-thousand acres that made up Four Corners Ranch, joint owned by the Garrett family, the King family, the Sullivan family and the McCloud family, ran massive operations. Beef, horses, hazelnuts, essentially a whole lot of things, making use of as much of the land as possible. It had been in their family for generations.

Of course, the fact was, the oldest sibling in each of those families was always the one making most of the decisions.

And when it came to Garrett's Watch…

Well, Wolf and Sawyer were both take-charge kind of men, and while Wolf had a generally easy relationship with his brother, Sawyer seemed to feel like whatever his word was would be the law, and that was that.

Difficult sometimes, because Wolf felt very much the same.

"Good. I was thinking I'd leave tomorrow."

"Tomorrow?" his sister-in-law, Evelyn, asked.

"Yeah," he said, looking up from his mashed potatoes. "I was thinking."

"Oh," Evelyn said.

"Is there a problem?" She'd said *oh* in that way women said it when there was definitely a problem.

"No," she said. "It's just… Well, June turns six months old tomorrow and I was thinking…"

"He doesn't need to be here for June's half birthday," Sawyer said, speaking of his daughter.

Yet again, Wolf actually had to marvel at his brother's situation. He'd had an accidental pregnancy with a woman who was basically a bar hookup, and had ended up single parenting. Then he'd gone in search of a wife, and had found one through an ad he'd placed online.

Now they were in love, with Evelyn raising June as her own.

Good for him. Really. *Good for him.*

That was Sawyer, though. Whether he realized it or not. Through sheer force of will, the man was always bound and determined to make better a bad situation. And he never failed at it.

Wolf did not have the same touch.

Darker, more intense than his older brother, Wolf certainly had his own manner of success with women. They loved the bad boy. And Wolf was happy to accommodate. Sawyer on the other hand was basically Captain America.

And good for him. Just wasn't Wolf's skillset.

"Well, I'm making cake. That's all. I'm just going to throw that out there."

"*I'll* be here," Elsie said. His youngest sister was always quick to try and shine by comparison.

Little termite.

Granted, he didn't mind. Mostly because he didn't worry all that much about looking good. That wasn't his problem. If people didn't like what he did, they could deal with it. Or not. Wasn't any skin off his nose.

His mother hadn't liked dealing with him, so she'd left. As far as he was concerned, that said it all. If he couldn't keep his own mother around, there wasn't much point trying it with someone else.

An old wound made his heart feel dull.

Breanna had understood him.

When you found something like that, you knew how special it was. He also knew well enough to know you didn't find it again.

"Elsie, are you trying to start a brawl?" Hunter McCloud, part of the neighboring family, and Sawyer's best friend, who often joined them for dinner, said.

"Me? No. I don't *try* to start brawls. If I want one, I'll have one." It was epically funny, coming from Elsie, who was a pint-size horse girl with more mouth than brawn, that was for sure.

"You'd start a brawl and then we'd have to go finish it," Hunter said.

Elsie shrugged. "No one would make you. Your knight-in-shining-armor complex is your problem."

Hunter smiled, slow and mean at Elsie. "Best believe I'm no one's knight in shining armor. I just like a bar fight."

Elsie huffed. "Either way, more cake for me."

"Hey, none of us have been to see them in...ever."

It was true. He'd never been up to their ranch. They had come down to Four Corners a time or two over the years, but it had been at least ten years since he'd seen any of them.

"Well," Sawyer said, "have fun in Copper Ridge, I guess."

"I'm sure I can make some fun." That was part of his goal. A little bit of new scenery. Some new women. Wolf wasn't the kind of guy to do relationships. He liked mystery. He liked fun. He spent a decent amount of time driving to bars in the surrounding areas every few weeks. Looking for girls who liked a good time. The kind of girls who got all excited about guys like him.

But somewhere new? Yeah, that sounded even better.

"Don't do anything I wouldn't do," Elsie said.

"Squirt, if I lived my life that way, I wouldn't do a damn thing."

He looked across the table at his brother, who was now doting on June.

And his heart gave another strange, aching thud.

Yeah. Some time away was exactly what he needed.

VIOLET DONNELLY HUMMED a tune as she took a tray full of cookies from the oven. It joined the cakes, mini pies and quiches already sitting on the counter at her stepmother's bakery.

She had been a little worried at first about the logistics

of splitting her time between her new post as innkeeper at the bed-and-breakfast on the Garrett ranch, and her work at the bakery, but so far everything was working really well. She had a lovely room to stay in, and she got to arrange breakfasts for the guests, and she was still able to do shifts at the place she loved most.

It was strange to think that only six years ago, Copper Ridge hadn't felt like home at all.

She'd been an angry teenager, uprooted from her home in Texas, contending with all sorts of hurt after being abandoned by her mother.

And then she'd met Alison. Alison, who had taught her how to bake. Alison, who had given her purpose and focus. Who had made her feel well and truly cared about. For no reason other than that she did. Because she wasn't a family member, she wasn't obligated to care about her.

Of course, then Alison had met Violet's father…

But actually, it had been the very best thing to ever happen to Violet. They were her parents. And she loved them absolutely.

Of course, now she had a passel of tiny half siblings, which was a little bit weird, considering that Violet was twenty-two. But her dad had been a fairly young father, and Alison was a bit younger than him still. So it was perfectly reasonable.

She sighed with relief looking at all of the baked goods. It turned out great. She wasn't overtaxing herself.

She had been so worried about letting Alison down. She knew that she needed a lot of help at the bakery, what with how much work the little kids were. But Violet had really wanted to take that opportunity that had become available at the bed-and-breakfast.

There had been a few innkeepers there over the years.

While it was still Sadie Garrett's baby, she had less to do with the continual guest care of the place than she had in the beginning. She couldn't live there, and her own children took up quite a lot of time, plus she had gotten back into doing therapy. She had come to Copper Ridge looking for something new, but as she had explained it to Violet, once she had found Eli, and gotten settled, she didn't feel like she had to run from every piece of her previous life.

The bed-and-breakfast was an important piece of the Garrett ranch, but it was just a piece.

Violet had been living at home, well past the time when she should've moved out. But her dad had a fairly large house on the ranch he shared with Violet's uncles, a huge converted barn, and even with the small kids, there was more than enough space for Violet. And given that she worked at the family business… It hadn't really made any sense for her to leave. The bed-and-breakfast was absolutely the perfect opportunity for her to get a little bit more independence, while making sure that she could still help with everything.

She had turned the sign at the bakery to Closed about ten minutes before, and she hummed as she packed away the baked goods into the Tupperware she used to transport, and then walked out the front door. The bell jingled behind her, and she took a moment to look up and down the streets. It was mid-October, with the leaves all around starting to turn. It wasn't quite time for Christmas decorations to be set up on Main Street, but it would happen soon.

She loved that time of year in Copper Ridge. When the deep cranberry-colored buildings across the street were strung with white lights and pine boughs, creating a rich cascade of seasonal color often reefed in fog that came rolling in off the ocean that was just behind the main street.

She couldn't imagine not living by the sea, not now.
She loved it.

She and her dad had lived hours from the coast in Texas, and she had never really considered living in a place quite so different. But that had been one of the things that she had immediately loved about Copper Ridge.

One of the only things.

She frowned as she shifted her hold on the baked goods, wishing she could stuff her hands into her pockets, because the wind coming in off the waves was freezing, and walked toward her car. She had been an entire pain in the ass for her dad when they'd first moved here. She'd just been so wounded, and she had been bound and determined to make her dad feel every inch of the pain that she was experiencing.

She could still remember her big act of rebellion. Seventeen and sneaking out of her house. And her dad had caught her drunk, making out with some boy. It was all horrifying in hindsight. And honestly didn't bear thinking about. She'd changed since then. Her entire goal in life had shifted. Because shouldn't she be more grateful for the parent who had stuck it out? For the parent who had been there for her? And then, she should reserve even more gratitude for Alison, who had *chosen* to be in Violet's life.

Who never made her feel second to the biological children she'd had with Violet's dad.

She was so lucky to have them. And doing the right thing for them mattered.

It mattered a lot.

But she had a new guest arriving at the bed-and-breakfast today. And he would be there by four thirty, so she had to hurry up, and stop musing.

She considered stopping at the coffeehouse to get a

drink, but Asher would probably ask her for a date again, and she just wasn't interested. He was nice. But she just wasn't... She wasn't in a space where she could focus on a relationship right now.

That's what you always say.

It was true, though.

And as much as she didn't have aspirations of dying a virgin, she wasn't in a hurry to change her status either. She wanted to carve out a space for herself at the bed-and-breakfast; she wanted some time to take online classes so that she could get a degree in hospitality. Because she was enjoying this. She was enjoying this life.

It was funny that she'd ended up like this, though. She had been very nearly rebellious. Just the once. But had her dad not interrupted her that night in the barn, it was very likely she wouldn't be a virgin right now.

She had to wonder, if she had gotten it out of the way back then, would sex feel like less of a big deal now? Would she have no problem at all balancing a love life and her goals if she'd...just started earlier?

She didn't know. She *couldn't* know.

Her dad coming for her that night had set her on a whole different path, and she'd changed. She didn't really want to put a foot out of line. That had dictated most of her actions in the years since.

Now that she was twenty-two it wasn't like her dad was going to come after her if she was out making out with some boy. It wasn't a rebellion anymore.

But it was definitely...*definitely* outside of her experience.

Anyway. She didn't want to go on a date with a man she had to...talk herself into going out with. In her opinion, that kind of thing should be blindingly obvious. You should be unable to deny the attraction between yourself and the person who wanted to date you.

In theory, she figured.

Maybe that was another problem with waiting so long. She'd had too many years to build it all up into a fantasy. Now she couldn't imagine having less than that fantasy.

She drove on the winding road that led out of town to the Garrett family ranch. The bed-and-breakfast was a beautiful Victorian that had recently been painted, all deep green and glorious berry colors, honoring the Victorian origins of the home, which had been ordered from a catalog back in the late eighteen hundreds.

It was an oddity, out there on this ranching spread that had otherwise rustic buildings. But it was the original home that had been situated on the property.

Violet loved it. It was just so… It was like a storybook. Parts of her life had been decidedly unlike a fairy tale, so any moment she could grasp that felt magical… Well, she would take it. She walked up the front steps and went inside, admiring the way she had the entryway done up. She was really quite tempted to put up Christmas decorations now, even though it was before Thanksgiving. She wondered if that was too much of a controversial move. She didn't want to be controversial. She didn't think people went to a bed-and-breakfast seeking controversy.

The entryway was lovely and old-fashioned, with a coat tree by the heavy wood door, and a bench positioned to the left for people to sit and put their shoes on. Even though it was late in the day, pale sun still streamed through the green-and-purple glass that was framed in the door.

Violet hummed as she laid out the tray and started to put the cookies on it, arranging them lovingly. She liked for guests to be greeted by ample sweets and a choice of warm beverages. Especially this time of year. Some hot tea. Some coffee. She knew that there were two couples coming in tonight, plus her lone guest, who was related to the family in some way. Sadie had explained it, but Violet had been busy trying to plan out portions and meals and the menu for the next week. She was excited to try some new things. It turned out she was very good at cooking savory foods, in addition to baking sweets, and more than that, she really enjoyed it.

She went into the back to start making coffee, fussing around in the kitchen, which had been transformed into something more commercial, but still smaller than the bakery kitchen, which allowed her to bake quite a few things at once. And then she heard the door open, and hurriedly closed the urn that had the coffee in it, carrying it out toward the entry. And she stopped dead in her tracks. Because she couldn't walk, breathe and take in the sight of the man who had just walked into the bed-and-breakfast.

He was tall. Broad, built like a mountain. He had black hair, and black eyes that looked at her with a piercing sort of knowledge from beneath the shadow of the brim of his cowboy hat. His hat was black. His T-shirt was black. He looked like an outlaw. An outlaw come to kidnap her. Take her away.

She was used to cowboys. She had spent a lot of her childhood in Texas, and happened to be the daughter of a cowboy. Happened to be the niece of several cowboys. And there were a great many ranching families in the immediate area. But she had never seen a cowboy quite like him.

His lips hitched into a half smile. "Afternoon, ma'am. My name's Wolf Garrett."

But what Violet heard was: my name is Trouble.

She could only be grateful that trouble was one thing she was very, very good at avoiding.

CHAPTER TWO

WELL. THE WOMAN in front of him was a sexy little package, no mistake.

He had been thinking that it might be nice to find a little fun in Copper Ridge, but he hadn't anticipated that the fun might actually be in the bed-and-breakfast that his cousin was putting him up in on the ranch property.

"Sorry to just barge in."

"It's a…a bed-and-breakfast," the woman said. "It's fine."

She was petite, extremely cute, with dark brown hair and sparkling brown eyes. She wasn't tall by any stretch, her head coming just to the center of his chest. But she was curvy. And then some. In all the places he liked to see them. "Still," he said.

"I was just… I was bringing out drinks. If you want something other than coffee…"

"A coffee would do me just fine," he said.

He had dinner plans with his cousins tonight, which meant that getting a little bit of fire in his blood would help. Although… The innkeeper was helping with that.

He *really* hoped that this wasn't his cousin's wife.

Though, she looked young. He wasn't the best at gauging age between twenties and thirties; could be anything. People started changing at different rates, after all. But he knew that his cousin's wife was in her midthirties, and this girl did not look near that age.

"You're not…Sadie," he said.

He needed confirmation.

"Oh," she said. "No. I'm Violet. Violet Donnelly. I work at the bed-and-breakfast."

"Oh. All right. I'm kin to Eli, Connor and Kate. I came out to help with their expansion of the operation."

"Right," she said. "Eli did mention that he had a cousin coming. And Sadie reiterated, when she gave me the guest list for the week. I guess… I didn't know what to expect." The way her eyes flickered over his body… The little lightning bolt of attraction that had gripped him when he'd come in… She felt it, too. He wasn't the only one.

It was a damn good thing.

Convenient. Very, very convenient. He could work hard on the ranch all day, come back home and… Yeah, sounded like his kind of a good time.

"Well, very kind of you to put out all these goodies. Did you make these?" Let it never be said he didn't know how to turn on the charm when need be.

For short periods of time, anyway.

She blushed.

The woman *blushed*.

It was the most appealing damn thing he could ever remember, and it had been a long time since a woman had blushed in his presence. He didn't like that sort of thing, not typically. He liked a woman who was bold, who knew what she wanted. It just made the most sense for a guy like him.

"Oh, you're welcome. I mean, I just do it. It's part of my job. And I also work at a bakery. Well, my stepmother owns a bakery."

"You work with your evil stepmother?"

Her delicate brows lowered a fraction. "My stepmother

is not evil," she said. "My stepmother is the most wonderful woman in the world."

He put his hands up. "Sorry. I don't know a thing about good stepmothers. All I know is a thing or two about absent ones. And mothers, for that matter."

Something shifted in her face. "I... Yeah. Well. I know a little bit about that. But my stepmother, Alison, she's wonderful. And she owns a bakery in town. I've worked there since I was seventeen."

"And how long ago was that?" Because there were very important things that needed to be worked out here.

"Are you asking how old I am?"

"Indirectly. Because I'm..." He couldn't even say that he was a gentleman as a joke. He would choke on it. "Because I know better."

"It was five years ago."

"Great," he said.

She was old enough to drink. Barely. So...that was... pushing it. But he was a man neither known for his good decisions nor his good behavior, so *pushing it* was in his wheelhouse.

He picked up one of the cookies from the tray, and took a bite. It melted in his mouth. Damn near the best thing he had ever eaten in his life.

"That's pretty amazing," he said.

And he didn't say that lightly, because while most of his life had been short decent cooking—his dad sucked at it, and the rest of them had never bothered to learn a damn thing—over the past few months his sister-in-law had made it an entirely different experience to be at Four Corners Ranch. She was an incredible cook.

They often had community dinners at Four Corners, and he had to admit that the Sullivan sisters baked some amazing things. Then of course, the Kings were grill masters. So it wasn't like he was a stranger to good food. But he didn't have it all the time, either. And he never took it for granted.

"Thank you," she said, and her blush intensified.

"Violet…"

The door opened again, and two people came in, a woman with short brown hair that had threads of silver woven throughout, and a tall man with a mustache gone white and hair that was still clinging to its original color, whether by design or nature, Wolf couldn't say.

They were both wearing trench coats, the expressions on their faces nearly identical. It was that phenomenon of when couples had been together for a very long time and began to resemble each other. Even their manner was the same. It was something he'd heard about, not something he'd often observed. But these two definitely had it.

"Oh, hello," the woman said. She smiled, looking between him and Violet. "I'm Wendy. Wendy Bertram."

"Ron," the man said, extending his hand. Wolf shook it, because he might have the name of a feral creature, but he'd been taught how to behave. Didn't mean he did it as a matter of course, but he knew how.

"Wolf Garrett," he said.

"I'm Violet," his pretty innkeeper said, and he found it interesting that she didn't give her last name as she had done for him. "I'm the innkeeper. If you need anything, I am at your service twenty-four hours a day."

And while he could see that they were the kind of people who didn't intend to make a fuss, he could also see that they were the kind of people with whom it was dangerous to make such an offer.

They would probably end up making a request for Violet at a very strange time. Likely for linens.

Probably for the aftermath of the sex game. They had a look about them, too. That very khaki suburban sort of look that suggested they went to bed-and-breakfasts to do one of two things. Bird-watch, or get freaky. Well, hell. Maybe not one thing. Maybe both.

It was entirely possible it was both.

"Thank you, dear," Wendy said, making her way over to the cookies and beginning to help herself to the coffee, indicating that she had been to bed-and-breakfasts many a time.

Thus confirming Wolf's assumption.

The door opened again, and in came another couple. This one slightly younger, the man wearing a baseball hat and Carhartt pants, the woman in a flannel and black leggings. It took him all of two minutes to hear that the man was an air traffic controller, who began extolling the virtues of his work and the many benefits of the job without being asked.

The entryway was starting to feel crowded. "I'm just going to take my things upstairs. Do I get the key from you?" he asked Violet.

"Oh." She turned to address the other guests. "A cheese tray will be out shortly," she said. "Along with wine. Just another thirty minutes or so. I'm going to show Mr. Garrett to his room now, and I will be back for the rest of you."

She took a key off the peg and started to lead him up the narrow staircase and down the hall. "Do you want wine and cheese?" she asked, looking at him out of the corner of one of her eyes.

"Oh, no," he said. "I'm more of a beer and pretzels kind of guy. Or potato chips. Or a steak."

She laughed. "I bet I could get you to enjoy my cheese platter." He looked at her for a long moment, and her cheeks went crimson. "It's a real cheese platter," she said.

He held up his hands and smiled. "Oh, I have no doubt that it is."

"Well, you looked at me like *that*," she said.

"Ma'am," he said, "I just met you. I wouldn't look at you like anything."

He grinned at her. She blushed again.

Oh, hell yeah.

"This is your room," she said, stopping at the door in the center of the hallway. "Number six."

"And does the same offer apply to me?"

"What offer?"

"The offer that you will be there for me day and night. Anything I need."

She shrank away from him, but he could feel excitement vibrating from her. "I suppose that depends on what it is you need."

He looked at her for a good long moment. "I'll get back to you."

"I have to get back downstairs."

"That's right. You made grand offers of wine and cheese."

"Yes," she said. "There are menus in the room, and you can order from the restaurants in town, and I can pick food up, or…"

"I'm having dinner at the main house. But thank you."

"Oh. Right. I guess you're not really a guest. I mean, you are. But it's different."

"Yeah," he said. "It's different."

He opened the door and stepped inside the room, and as soon as that barrier was lifted, she scampered off, as if she was uncomfortable at the idea of even being in the doorway of the open bedroom with him.

She definitely felt what he did.

And as he freshened up for dinner, he told himself: *She's*

too young for you. She's clearly a little bit skittish. She blushes.

What man had the time for a prudish fling? There was no point to it.

But still, he couldn't help the fact that he was intrigued by her. And maybe, just maybe, his brain was putting the sexiness of the innkeeper in front of the weirdness of seeing cousins he hadn't seen for more than a decade.

A lot had happened in that time. A hell of a lot.

The last time he'd seen his cousin Connor, he'd been with his first wife, Jessie.

She had been a nice woman. Pretty. And very in love. In fact, he could remember that at the time it had made him a bit uncomfortable. Coming off his own loss, only a couple of years earlier. And since then… Since then Connor had lost Jessie.

And, had gotten remarried.

It did strange things to his chest.

He put on a fresh shirt, stuck his hat back on his head and headed back down the stairs.

By then the entryway had cleared, and people were off chatting in the living room. Violet was giving a history on the furniture in the place.

He didn't really get the appeal of the bed-and-breakfast. But then, he didn't get the appeal of being on top of people like this. Or chatting up strangers. Unless there was potential sex involved. He just wasn't all that into making friends with random people. Or making friends at all. But people did seem to enjoy it.

And you're stuck here for the next few weeks.

Lucky him.

Except, his eyes went straight back to Violet.

And in that regard: lucky him indeed.

His eyes met hers as he walked past, and he gave her a nod, went out the front door. Then he walked down the stairs and crossed the driveway, getting back into his truck. He had directions to the main house, and he knew that it wasn't a very long drive. Just a couple of minutes. The ranch itself was beautiful, very different to Garrett's Watch. It was so much colder here, just a couple of hours northwest, the dampness from the sea seeming to invade everything. And it was green. Aggressive green. Ferns on the floor of the forest, and moss covering the bark of the trees. The rocks.

It was a serene sort of place. Wolf had an appreciation for moments of serenity. In theory. There were many available to a man who wanted to find them at Four Corners. In spite of the fact that it was heavily populated by family and ranch hands, it was so big it afforded big skies and big quiet to anyone who might need it. But then, maybe he didn't find as much tranquility in nature as he might because he also knew that in nature lurked danger. Regardless of the beauty. You could never forget that the earth could easily swallow you whole on a whim if it saw fit. It rightly could.

He got out of the truck after parking in front of the main house, a log cabin that had a much more rustic sort of appeal than the bed-and-breakfast tucked back into the other corner of the property. This was the kind of thing he was used to.

His own cabin at Garrett's Watch was small, just right for one man, and fairly rustic. His brother had gone and updated the main house a bit ago, and he had only ever been able to figure that Sawyer had done that in part to spite their old man, who had been resistant to any change, especially those that could benefit him.

Sawyer was grounded, and a fairly levelheaded sort of

guy. But his anger was there, and you definitely didn't want to provoke it. There was a saying, that one should beware the fury of a patient man.

Wolf was not a patient man.

People should beware of his fury all the same.

After Wolf got out of the truck, the front door opened and two little towheaded children rushed outside screeching, "Wolf! Wolf! Wolf! Is that really your name?" The questions tumbled out of their mouths so quickly, that he couldn't keep track of who said what. But hell, he wasn't going to be able to keep the moppets straight, anyway.

"That's not real," one of them said.

"It's real," Wolf said.

He looked behind them, at a slim blonde woman standing in the doorway. She grinned. "Hi," she said. "I'm Sadie. It's so good to have you."

"Thanks," he said. "Who are the mongrels?"

"Thomas and Sarah." They were exceedingly practical names. No wonder they were so fascinated by his, which was not practical in the least. Not remotely.

Courtesy of his mother. Which seemed mean in his opinion. Dropping a name like that on him and then leaving. Maybe it was common in her circles; he didn't know. That was another thing that bothered him.

"It's my real name," he said to the kids, who gazed up at him in awe. He didn't particularly like kids. But he supposed these ones were his kin. And they were sort of cute.

"Come on in," she said. "I'm afraid there are more children." She smiled. "I can guarantee you a lot more questions."

She wasn't kidding. When he entered the house, it was to a cacophony of noise. There were three small redheaded girls, jumping up and down on the couch in the living room, and there was a dark-haired girl and a dark-haired boy, both a lot more serious-looking.

"The redheads are Liss and Connor's—Mary Beth, Annalee and Jessie Lynn. The brunettes are Jack and Kate's—Carson and Smith."

Between Carson and Smith, he had no clue which name would belong to the boy, and which the girl. He figured it wasn't polite to ask.

The little blond kids joined in the fray, and the other kids didn't seem as interested in him, possibly because they were so busy being holy terrors. Which, in his memory, was what being a kid was about.

"Are there any adults in this place?" he asked.

A beautiful, cheerful-looking redheaded woman appeared, wearing a floral, flowing dress and resting her hand on a baby bump. "Hi," she said. "You must be Wolf. I'm Liss."

He could see this being an evening of introductions. He knew that Liss was Connor's wife, and not just because of the intro to the children. "Nice to meet you," he said.

"The guys are back in the dining room. And Kate."

Sadie laughed. "Always Kate."

He walked back with them and heard a crash behind them, and Sadie and Liss didn't even turn.

"Everything in there's replaceable," Sadie said.

"Except Eli's TV," Liss said. "I mean, I know you can get a new one, but will he be able to watch the Ducks game?"

"He'll be fine," Sadie said. "It would do him good to miss a few games. That team is not what they once were. I used to root for the Beavers just to spite him, but honestly, now I can't even pretend. It's become a long, protracted mourning session every time they play."

Wolf didn't give much of a shit about football himself.

But the rivalry between the two colleges was something sacred in the state of Oregon. You were hard-pressed not to pick a side.

He personally liked to take the opposite side of whatever room he was in.

As a matter of course.

They walked into the dining room, and a fourth redheaded girl blitzed through just briefly.

"Ruby Kate," said Liss. "We have a guest."

The girl acknowledged him with a lift of her stubborn chin. Yeah. She was definitely a Garrett.

Eli, Connor and Kate—who had been barely a teenager last he'd seen her—were all seated at the table. Eli was in his sheriff's uniform, the top button undone on his tan shirt. Connor was wearing a flannel pushed up past his elbows, his dark hair messy, as if he'd just taken his hat off. Kate had her hat on, pushed down low over her eyes, her dark hair in a braid.

There was a man sitting beside her, and Wolf assumed that was her husband, Jack, whom he dimly remembered meeting all those years ago when he'd been out. Jack was Eli and Connor's lifelong friend, who had at some point taken up with their younger sister, causing a minor family scandal. As he remembered it, relayed through phone calls.

They were holding cards, and Kate had an intense look on her face.

"She's ruthless," Jack said. "Don't turn your back on her." He could see that Jack already had his cards folded in front of him.

"Read 'em and weep, Kate," Eli said, laying his cards down.

Kate howled and stood up, kicking her chair.

"Easy there, Badger Cat," her husband said, patting her

on the rear. Which earned him a look from both of her brothers. "That's not good for the baby."

"What?" Connor and Eli asked.

"You knucklehead," Kate said, punching her husband in the shoulder. "We weren't going to tell them yet."

Then silence settled for a minute as everybody seemed to realize that he was standing there.

"Hi there," Wolf said. "Wolf."

"I remember," Eli said. "Good to see you."

"Yeah," Connor said. They made a round of pleasantries, because they were well-trained country folk.

"Have a seat," Eli said.

"Dinner's almost on," Sadie said.

"How was your trip over?" Kate asked.

"Good," Wolf said. "Uneventful."

While he wasn't exactly a people person, there were often changes in staff at Four Corners Ranch, and specifically at Garrett's Watch. It was just the nature of things. He was good at making easy conversation with people who did the same sorts of things he did. He was here to ranch, and ranching was what he knew.

"I'm interested to hear more about this operation, and what all you think you're going to be doing with it."

"Well, we're interested to hear what you think," Eli said. "None of us are experts at expansion."

"I don't know that I'm an expert on expansion, but I'm an expert on dealing with what's already expanded." He started talking about the day-to-day of running Garrett's Watch, and they cleared their money and cards off the table while he spoke. Not long after, a couple of pies appeared in the center of the table, along with a basket of rolls, followed by steak and green salad. The kind of simple stuff you like. They dished up and he gave his compliments to the chef.

"So things are going well at Four Corners?" Connor asked. "And you find that you're more than able to sell off all that cattle and turn a profit?"

"Oh, yeah," he said. "We stay busy. And I imagine given that you're specializing in a more local kind of thing, the demand will be good, and you'll be able to fetch a pretty high price. It'll all be how you manage the land, and how you strategize, particularly as you add employees. You can do this stuff on your own, but it's demanding. And I can see that you've all got your hands full."

The feral children had been sat in the living room, which was quite all right by Wolf.

"Well, we haven't really gotten that far yet," said Eli. "But yeah. We've to balance trying to increase profits with… our lives."

"Which are busy," Sadie said. "Very busy."

"The pies look good," he said as Sadie began to serve them.

"I can't take credit," Sadie said. "Violet brought them from her mother's bakery."

Oh, yes. Violet.

"I met Violet," he said. "I stopped by the house before I came here."

"She's a sweet girl," Sadie said, and he didn't really like the way she said that. *A sweet girl.* Because he was trying to ignore how young she was, because he was so damned attracted to her.

"She seems it," he said.

"And an amazing baker. Honestly, it's not my strong suit. I got to where I can make a pretty passable dinner. But… That was the one thing that I struggled with at the bed-and-breakfast. I had a couple of things that I was good at.

But I wasn't exactly bringing anything special to the table. Fortunately, Violet does that in spades."

"That's an example of hiring people and it working out very well," Eli said. "We had a couple of different innkeepers, and it's been worth it. The bed-and-breakfast keeps bringing in money, but this way Sadie isn't tethered to it."

"Right."

They chatted on a little more, and his mind kept on straying back to Violet. And the pie. It was damn good pie. And the woman had made it with her hands. Expert hands, clearly. He would like to have them on his body.

"In for a game of poker?"

He realized a half second later than he should have that Eli was talking to him. "Sure," he agreed easily.

And before long, they were dealing out cards.

"You gotta watch Katie," Jack said. "She's a very sore loser. And she's mean as all get out when she doesn't get her way."

Kate leaned in and bit her husband swiftly on the side of the neck.

He covered the spot where she'd got her teeth into him with his hand. "Is anyone else *seeing* this?"

"You poke the bear you get the teeth," Eli said. "Seems to me it's your dumbass move, Monaghan."

"And you're the one who married her," Connor reminded Jack. "You knew what you were getting into. You've known her for her entire life."

"I figured she'd domesticate," Jack said, but his tone made it very clear that he had thought no such thing.

"I'm not domesticated," Kate said, dramatically picking her teeth with her pinky finger. "I'm as wild as ever. And not malleable in the least. Motherhood has not steadied me. If anything, it has made me more fearsome."

"And the kids are hellions," Jack said. "Seriously questioning the addition of the third."

"It was not intentional," Kate said.

Connor and Eli shared a glance. Liss and Sadie were in the kitchen, clucking away, and he had a feeling they opted to do dishes to stay away from the family sparring.

"You're happy, Katie," Jack said, "and you know it."

She smiled up at him like the sun shone out his ass. It was a lot of…a lot.

"So this is us," Eli said. "But really, we are glad to have you. It'll be good to get to know each other. Sawyer and Elsie should come out at some point."

"That will depend if you can pry Sawyer away from the land. And from his house he's pretty much nested in with his new wife."

"Well, his wife is welcome to come, too," Eli said. "Connor and I like wives."

"Better only like yours," came a singsong voice from the kitchen that Wolf couldn't readily identify.

"Of course," Connor answered, which made it clear which wife it had been.

They played poker and Wolf lost, Kate ending up with the bulk of the change, laughing evilly as she collected it all. The evening began to wind down, with Liss, Sadie and Jack dispersing to take care of children, while the cousins lingered.

"It's a shame the family's been so splintered," Eli said after a long moment and his third beer.

"I guess so," Wolf said.

He didn't really know how he felt about it. Mostly because he didn't put much thought into things like family. He was squarely around his family—his brother and sister—all the time. And that felt like enough family to him more or less. He wasn't here for any kind of great reunion. It just seemed… It did seem like a good opportunity to get himself out for a while. And he was feeling the need to.

"Yeah. But unavoidable as far as I know. Our dads hated each other."

"And how," Connor said. "The only time I ever heard our dad mention either of his brothers, it was with a curse word beside it."

"It wasn't much better from our dad."

"But you and Sawyer… You get along just fine."

Wolf shrugged. "You don't not get along with Sawyer. That's not how it works. It's his way or the highway. And you can not be there if you don't want."

"You ever think of starting your own spread?" That question came from Connor.

"No," Wolf said. "Garrett's Watch is our legacy. Yours, too, come to that. I couldn't leave it for good any more than I could… I don't know. Settle down and have kids. It's just not part of my DNA."

"Our family had a pretty bad run with romances," Eli said, not even asking why Wolf felt that way.

"Though, Sawyer is working on breaking the losing streak. But he's convinced it's all working out because Evelyn was a mail-order bride."

"A mail-order bride," Kate said, her eyes going wide with wonder. "Now, that's something. I can't imagine marrying a stranger."

"No," Connor said, his voice dry. "You had to marry the man who used to babysit you. And cause us endless grief in the process."

"I can't help it." Kate shrugged. "I'm sexy. He couldn't resist me."

"Sure," Eli said, his tone dry. "But I married a woman I once arrested. Now, that's interesting."

"I quite literally married my best friend," Connor said.

"Well, nice to know some of us are breaking cycles. Others of us just prefer to avoid them." He looked at the digital clock on the microwave. "Right. I better head back to the bed-and-breakfast. Early day tomorrow."

"It will be," Connor said.

"I'm on duty. I'll catch you a different day."

"I'll be at our ranch. But hopefully I'll see you for dinner."

He nodded and said his goodbyes, walking down the front porch and heading toward his truck. Then he stopped and looked up at the stars. The same stars he could see from Four Corners.

And there was a strange sort of aching feeling in his chest at that particular realization.

He had moved. But it was the same sky. And he was the same Wolf.

And he still had the same old grief inside his chest.

It just was.

But at least there would be a different kind of work tomorrow. He would take that.

He damn well would.

CHAPTER THREE

VIOLET KNEW THAT ranchers got up early. Very early. So she made it a point to get up at four and get a special breakfast on just for Wolf Garrett. And she told herself that she was breaking in protocol because he was kin to the Garretts. That was what she told herself. Except deep down she knew that she was obsessing over her hollandaise sauce because he was hot.

"The way to a man's heart is a properly poached egg," she said, whisking the sauce as speedily as possible.

She heard footsteps and her heart jumped up into her throat, and she quickly poured the sauce over the English muffin, Canadian bacon and poached egg. Then she grabbed a mug of coffee and walked out of the kitchen.

She just about ran into him.

He reached out to steady her, and a drop of coffee sloshed over the cup.

"Steady now," he said.

"Oh," she said, feeling flustered.

He looked down. "Bit early to be up having breakfast."

"It's for you," she said.

"Oh, well, that's... I'm headed..." He looked like he was going to decline, and then redirected. "Mighty nice of you," he said. "I think I could eat."

"The dining room is over here." She led the way to a long table with a white lace tablecloth, and he sat down at the head of the table. Because of course he did. The wood-work was ornate, the tablecloth so laughably flimsy… And he just looked out of place. Too big. Too rough. She bet he didn't even eat eggs Benedict. He was probably expecting raw meat and a cup of milk with an egg cracked into it.

"I hope that you like… I hope you like it."

"I'm sure I will," he said.

He took his hat off and set it next to him on the table. Then he took a bite of breakfast. "Wow," he said, pointing at it with the fork. "That's damn good."

She lit up from the inside. "You think so?"

"Yeah," he said. "Where's your breakfast?"

"Oh," she said. "I don't eat with guests."

"Do you eat with acquaintances?" he asked.

"Um…"

"How about people who'd like to get to know you a lit-tle better?"

Oh, Lord. The way he said that. And looked at her. Her mouth went dry and scratchy, like she'd licked a fuzzy caterpillar.

"Grab a cup of coffee."

"Oh… Well…"

"Come on," he said.

And she found herself doing it. Because he told her to. She didn't know where to sit. There was the chair right next to him, but that seemed wrong. The chair all the way down at the end of the table, which seemed silly. She opted for one two spaces down from him, clutching the coffee tightly. Her heart was pounding absurdly. It was so early in the morning and she was being fluttery over a man.

"Did you have a good dinner last night?" she asked.

"I did," he said. "The pie was the highlight."

"I made that," she said, smiling.

"I know," he said.

And then she felt silly. Because he knew. And maybe he'd just been complimenting her on purpose, and maybe he hadn't actually loved the pie, but had wanted to be nice because he'd known that she made it.

She cleared her throat. "Oh. Well. I'm glad that you liked it."

"You're an amazing cook."

"Thank you. I… So… Your cousins… You don't see each other very often? I felt like Sadie more or less implied that."

"I haven't seen them in about ten years."

"Oh," she said. "Wow."

"Yeah."

"Well, I didn't see my family for a long time. But then my dad and I moved here. I'm the oldest of all my cousins, though. By quite a lot. At least the cousins I know of."

"Is that so?"

"Yeah. My dad… He got married really young. And he moved to Texas to get away from here. To get away from his family. The Donnellys are a whole thing. Their dad… He was difficult, and he left town years ago. And their grandfather—as I understand it—was sort of hard, too. But when their grandpa died he left the ranch to all four of his grandsons, split equally. Didn't go over well with my uncle Finn, who had been there the whole time working. But it meant something to all of them. So…my uncles Liam and Alex came to the ranch for their share, Uncle Finn was already there, and then me and my dad came from Texas. I was not thrilled about it."

"I guess not. You were seventeen you said."

"Yes. But… As much as I hated leaving Texas, I… needed the change."

She became very conscious of the lingering twang in her voice when she said the name of her home state. She did miss it sometimes. But mostly, Copper Ridge was her home.

"What happened to your mother?"

The question was bold, blandly spoken.

"She left," she said, returning boldness with boldness.

"Hmm," he said. "So did mine. Sucks when they do that."

She hadn't expected that.

"She did?"

"Yeah," he said. "That left just us and our dad. But she wasn't the only woman to leave my dad. Sawyer and Elsie are my half siblings. My dad had a pattern."

"Oh," Violet said. "Well. My dad just got left the once."

"That means the problem was likely her. In our case… the problem was…everybody."

"Oh."

"And the Garrett curse."

She leaned in, her hands wrapped around the mug, the warm liquid inside warming her. "What's the Garrett curse?"

"For generations no women stayed at Garrett's Watch. That's the ranch that I have with my siblings. Not until my grandmother. My grandmother was not my grandmother by blood. My actual grandmother ran off. Just like all the others. But then my grandpa married a woman that he ordered by mail."

"No kidding," Violet said.

"Yep. And they stayed married. That's how my brother got it in his mind to get himself a mail-order bride."

"You're making that up," Violet said, smiling. "There's no way."

"No," Wolf said, a grin stretching across his handsome

face. "It's absolutely true. And I have to tell you, they're so happy it's almost nauseating."

"Well, good for them."

"It is."

He looked at her, and she felt the burn of those dark eyes all the way down to the pit of her stomach. And it was absurd. It was four thirty in the morning. And she was staring down this guy like he was a dinner date. While she had coffee, and he ate the breakfast she just made. And he probably would think she was crazy if he had any idea what she was thinking.

"I better head out." He put his hat on his head, tipped it, and her stomach flipped. "I'll see you later, Miss Donnelly."

And as he walked out of the dining room, she would be damned if she didn't just sit there and stare at his ass.

He was the best-looking man she had ever seen.

She was still thinking about it when she went into the bakery later that morning.

"You seem distracted."

She looked at Alison. Her stepmother was looking at her with a curious gaze. Alison was only about fourteen years older than Violet, so as the years had stretched on, the gap between them had shrunk. She was definitely a mother figure to Violet, but she also had an easy time confiding in her, too.

The problem was she was also an open valve to Violet's dad. Which Violet could understand was all about them having healthy communication, and she was glad for it and everything, but she didn't really need her dad to know everything about her life.

Not that there was much to know.

"Oh, I just had an early morning," she said.

"Lots of guests?"

"Yes. And… Well, one of the Garretts' cousins is staying there. And he's helping with the ranch, so I wanted to get up early and get him some breakfast."

"I see," Alison said, a little bit too keenly. She started to wipe at a spot on the counter, then paused. "A handsome guest?"

"You're being nosy," Violet said.

"An understandable amount of nosy," she said.

"Says you," Violet said. "I think it's invasive."

"You only think it's invasive because he's hot," Alison said.

"Tell me about your Christmas cookie plans," Violet said, changing the subject.

"Oh, I have plans," Alison said. "They involve so much royal icing."

The subject happily changed, Violet made it through the morning smoothly.

"Are you sure you're all right with me leaving?"

"I'm fine," Violet said, waving her hand as her stepmother started to depart around two o'clock.

"It's just you got up so early…"

"I'm fine," Violet reiterated.

She set about to making the quiches for the next day, and a few minutes later her aunt Clara walked in. Clara really wasn't like an aunt. Clara was her best friend.

Clara was only four years older than Violet, and that gap really didn't matter now. She had married Violet's uncle Alex a few years earlier. Alex seemed young, but he was also a full ten years older than his wife. Something his brothers liked to give him a hard time about.

Violet was grateful for her.

Sugar-loving Clara was one of the best people to be around, in her opinion.

"Good afternoon," Clara said. "I am seeking a sugar fix."

"Where are your adorable children?" Violet asked.

"With their equally adorable father. They're getting food for the family dinner Sunday. So that I don't have to. And thank God."

Everybody contributed their own piece to the Donnelly family dinners one Sunday a month. It was massive, and there was always way too much food.

"What a guy," Violet said.

"He is. But I would like cookies and a hot chocolate, please."

"Coming right up."

"Sure."

Violet started making the hot chocolate, which she always put a little extra vanilla in to suit Clara's tastes.

She served the cookies warm. Clara sat down at one of the tables by the window, and since the bakery was otherwise empty, Violet joined her.

"How long can you keep working at both places?" Clara asked.

"Well, the inn isn't a full-time job," Violet said. "I mean, I guess it could be. But right now I do all right kind of squeezing it all in. I bake in the morning there, and do all the straightening up in the evenings. I'm there in time for check-in, because the bakery closes."

"You work all the time," Clara said.

"I don't have anything else to do," Violet said, shrugging.

"Spend more time with me?"

"I enjoy that," Violet said. "I do. But… I dunno. I like this, too. I can't quit the bakery. Alison needs me. I can't even cut back."

"Alison can hire someone else. I know that she can."

"I don't want her to have to do that."

"Why not?"

"Because having a senior employee allows her to keep bringing women on that don't have experience. You know she's still doing that. Hiring women who have been in abusive marriages and training them. To bake, to start their own businesses. I don't want anything to interrupt that."

"It's not really your responsibility, Vi."

"I guess not. But it's…my contribution. It matters to me."

"One of these days, you're going to have to do something for yourself."

"All of this is for me," Violet said. "I love it."

"And are you going to live here forever, working at your stepmother's bakery and running the bed-and-breakfast just down the road?"

"What's wrong with that? You live on the same ranch you grew up on."

"I know that," Clara said. "But it's my ranch. And… I… I love it here."

"I love it here. Alison really gave me…so much. I can't even explain everything that her being in my life has done for me. It's… She gave me the skills that I needed to even have the job I do at the inn. I don't want to just leave her."

"There's a certain amount of leaving that's just normal," Clara said. "You know that, right?"

"I do," Violet said.

"I just worry sometimes that you're so obsessed with being perfect that you try to do too much, and you don't leave yourself any time…for you. Everything you do is for other people."

"That isn't true," Violet said.

"When was the last time you went out?"

Violet laughed. "Where would I go out here? Ace's bar, sure. But…it's all the same old people."

"Yeah, the same old people. That you went to high school with. Maybe you could make friends with them. Go on a date with someone."

Violet pulled a face. "Profoundly not interested."

"Look, I know all about being stuck."

"Again, you're still here, Clara."

"I mean… After my brother died I was stuck. Emotionally. And I know that I'm in the same place now, physically, but I'm not emotionally. So I'm just telling you I'm responding to something that I see in you that's…emotional."

"That doesn't make any sense."

"Well, it does to me. Because I've been through it. Okay?"

"Okay," Violet said, but she still didn't understand.

She stood up and nearly tripped. Because there he was, walking down the street, next to Eli. They were talking, and Eli was gesturing to the buildings, as if he was explaining something.

Clara's gaze followed hers.

"What are you looking at? Eli Garrett?"

"No," she said. "It's just… That's his cousin that he's with. My… He's one of my guests."

"Oh," she said. "Oh. He's… He's *attractive*."

"It's *not* that," Violet said.

"Would it be so wrong if it was?"

"He's not from here. He's ridiculously handsome. He's older than me."

"All things my husband is."

"Well," Violet said. "I'm not in the market for a husband, and even if I was, he does not have husband material written all over him."

"But does he have *good time* written on him?"

"Clara," Violet said. "Are you advocating that I… I…?"

"I am advocating for you to have a little bit of fun."

"Says the woman who has never kissed a man other than her husband. I know too much about you."

"Hey," Clara said, loftily. "I went on a date with Asher."

"You *did*?"

"Did I not tell you about the terrible date I had with him before Alex and I...well, before Alex gave me my first kiss?"

"See? It was a date with no kiss. Your only kiss is your husband, which was my point."

"While I am limited in variety," Clara said, "had I not reconnected with Alex when I did, I think I might've enjoyed a fling or two."

"You would not," Violet said. "You didn't kiss Asher even though you went on a date with him, so what makes you think you would have wanted to make out with other random guys?"

Clara grumbled, taking a sip of her hot chocolate. "Fine. No, I wouldn't have. But whatever."

"I don't know that I'm a fling sort of person," Violet said, still staring at Wolf.

He was making her consider it.

You couldn't ride a roller coaster forever, but that didn't mean it wasn't fun.

Fun didn't need to be forever.

"You won't know unless you try," Clara said.

Violet narrowed her eyes. "It seems a good dangerous thing to try out."

"But you *could*," Clara said. "Because you're a grown woman, and you don't need anyone's permission to do anything. And you are not going to disappoint anyone."

"He's a guest," Violet said. "On top of not knowing if he's interested... I can't just like show up at his door and try to proposition him. It would be unprofessional."

"But it would be a story I'd like to hear later."

"I do live to entertain," Violet said. "But maybe not on that score."

The door opened and a customer walked into the bakery, and they had to stop talking about propositions.

Clara stood, draining the rest of her hot chocolate and lifting her cookie in mock salute. "I have to go, or Alex will put the food in the wrong spot, and the wrong things will touch. I can't have onions flavoring up anything."

"What will you even eat at Thanksgiving?" Violet asked.

"Mashed potatoes are all right. Turkey breast. Black olives."

"How do you even teach your kids to eat healthy?"

"They like broccoli," Clara said, looking genuinely distressed. "They might be changelings."

"Don't worry," Violet said, her tone mock-comforting. "A lot of successful people have liked broccoli."

"A lot of serial killers, too, I bet," Clara returned.

"It's probably not what makes them serial killers," Violet said.

"You don't know that," Clara said. "No one can know that." And with that, she smiled and exited the shop.

When Violet looked out the window, Wolf was gone. And she tried to keep herself from checking continually over the next hour. He had moved on. Whatever he was doing, he was done with it now, and she needed to let it go. She really did.

She served customers and kept looking out the window, trying to get a glimpse of him. And she kept thinking about what Clara said. About doing something for herself.

She felt disloyal, immediately, even having that thought. However briefly. She was so lucky. She was so lucky to have her dad. And so very lucky that he had found Alison.

Because everything else they'd had was just difficult. And if she had a dad that was any less... Well, she knew exactly what would've happened. The night that she'd gotten drunk at that barn party in their first few weeks in Copper Ridge was the evidence. But her dad had gone out looking for her. Her dad had come after her. And she'd been angry, and humiliated and embarrassed at the time. But now she realized. Now she understood.

What he'd done had been the ultimate demonstration of love. He had come to get her. He had come to rescue her, in a way. Even though it had been from herself. Her father cared for her. He was willing to make her angry, willing to risk her hating him, in order to keep her safe.

And she'd realized since then what a profound love that was. How sacrificial it was, truly. And all she wanted to do since then was pay him back. Pay him back for being there. For being two parents to her. And then for giving her another parent who was just as supportive. Just as loving.

So yeah, she felt...guilty thinking about the things Clara had said. About just how much she did for everyone else. And she knew why. She was afraid. She was afraid of not being enough. She was afraid of not adequately being able to pay them back.

And maybe... Maybe that was the problem. That no matter how wonderful the people in your life were, it was just very difficult to erase the fear that the kind of profound abandonment issues you got when your mother left you entrenched in you.

She frowned.

The other thing Clara was right about was that she was old enough that nobody had to know. She was not a rebellious teenage girl. Her father did not need to storm the barn, so to speak, to stop her from making a drunken mistake.

She realized just then that she had put an extra egg into her batter. She growled and scooped it out the best that she could. Then she finished mixing, and popped the cookies into the oven.

And right then, the door to the bakery opened.

It was Wolf.

"I wondered if this was you," he said.

She felt all hot and flushed, her cheeks tingling. She had only seen him this morning, and she still felt…giddy.

Had it been this morning? It had been ten hours ago, so it felt like longer ago. The day felt very long.

"It is," she said. "The bakery."

"Is your stepmom here?"

"No," Violet said. "I'm here by myself."

"When do you close up?"

"Oh, in just a half hour. And then I usually go back to the bed-and-breakfast to make sure that no one needs anything."

"Anyone checking in today?"

She shook her head. "No."

"Could you spare a few minutes to show me around town?"

"Oh," she said. "Isn't that… Weren't you just with…?" Then she started blushing; she could feel it, because she was admitting that she had seen him outside the window, which made her feel just a little bit flustered and uncomfortable.

"He was showing me his office. Gave me a little bit of a brief overview. But I'd like to see some of the things you like."

"Oh," she said. "Well… I don't have any customers." Guilt rolled over her. But she didn't have any customers. And if she closed a half hour early today it wouldn't be that big of a deal. And it would let her get back to the bed-and-breakfast in plenty of time.

"If you're sure it's not a problem."

"Not at all," she said. "But you have to help me get the cookies out to the car."

She indicated the stack of freshly baked cookies that she had earmarked for the bed-and-breakfast.

"Of course."

He grabbed all the trays and grinned. "Point me in the right direction."

And with butterflies in her stomach, she did. She locked the door to the bakery behind them and walked down the covered sidewalk toward where she parked. She unlocked the car, and he put the cookies in the back seat. Then she straightened, standing and facing him, her stomach turning flips. She was ridiculous. But honestly, she couldn't remember the last time she had talked to a man she was attracted to.

Sure, she'd had crushes in school. And yes, Asher was interested in her. If she wanted to get flirted with, she could pop into Stim—the coffeehouse Asher worked at—anytime. But it wasn't the same. It could never be like this.

And with Clara's words still echoing in her head, it all felt… It all felt something. She didn't really have the words for it.

Maybe it was to do with the bed-and-breakfast. Maybe it was to do with the fact that he didn't live here. But there was a dangerous sort of edgy freedom that seemed to be firing along her nerve endings. She didn't often feel hemmed in. But the reality was… She was. It was a small town, and everyone knew Cain and Alison Donnelly. By extension, everyone knew her. Anything she did was going to make it back to her family. There were too many Donnellys.

Copper Ridge was lousy with them. There were connections all over Logan County, and it was completely inescapable. And it wasn't that anyone would care; it wasn't that. It was just that she was very aware that whatever she did was going to have an audience. But tucked away at the bed-and-breakfast...

Of course, you're about to walk down the street with him.

It was true. But when people asked around, the answer would obviously be that he was from out of town. That he was a Garrett. All of those things would lend validity to the fact that she was playing tour guide. And give it undertones that were not actually nefarious in any way.

Not that anything she felt around Wolf seemed like it was nefarious.

"Well, I assume that cutesy kitchen stores, seasonal decor stores and the like are not up your alley," she said.

"I told you. I just want to have a look around."

"Have you had lunch?"

"No," he said.

"Well, you don't live near the ocean, do you?"

"No."

"Come on, then."

They walked down Main, and she took a right, headed toward the ocean, and toward the fish shack that was right there on the wharf. "Fish," she said. "And the sea." She gestured toward the ocean.

"So it is." He walked over and looked at the menu. "What do you want?"

"Oh," she shook her head, "I don't need anything."

"Come on," he said. "You brought me over here. You must be thinking about food."

"I really don't..."

"I'm not eating again while I watch you sit there with nothing. It isn't happening. Halibut and chips?"

"Sure," she said, liking the way that he bulldozed her

protestations in order to make sure she was taken care of. She didn't know why she liked it. Only that she did.

She never had a man do that before. "You want a Coke?"

"Okay," she said.

"Go ahead and snag us a picnic bench. I'll bring the food over."

She obeyed, going over to the bench and watching him while he placed the order. Paying with cash. It was such a funny, antiquated thing. But there was something essentially timeless about Wolf. And it couldn't be denied.

You have a crush on him. He appeared yesterday, and you have a full-scale crush on him.

It felt like such a childish thing to think, and there were bigger feelings attached to him that seemed a lot less innocent than that word implied.

But on the surface… Well, she did. She had a crush on him. It made her grin, made her feel a little bit giddy. Because when was the last time she had felt anything quite so… fun? So carefree. She was always trying to do better. Always trying to serve the people around her. Always trying. And this felt completely separate from that. This just felt… It felt good. She was enjoying it.

He turned around, two white cardboard boxes in his hands, and a Styrofoam container on top, and a couple of Coke bottles tucked under his arm. He arrived at the table and laid everything out. The bottles were glass, and it only added to the sense of being out of time. He popped the tops off on the edge of the table and handed her an open one.

"I thought we needed some clam chowder. I don't mind sharing."

He held up a spoon, and she realized that he intended for them to use the same one. It made her feel warm.

What was wrong with enjoying this? She had never…

done this. Just casually hanging out with a guy like him. It wasn't like she hadn't gone on dates. She had. It was just… They were all guys she knew from high school. Guys she knew from town. It was different. This was exciting. He was a stranger. It felt full of possibilities. It felt new.

And she hadn't realized how much she wanted something new. How much it meant. How exciting it was.

"All right," she said. "If you insist."

He took the lid off and took a bite of the chowder. Then passed the spoon to her.

She did not like clam chowder.

She didn't like it at all.

But she wanted to use the same spoon as Wolf Garrett, and if it was weird… Then she was weird. She took a bite of the chowder, and she really didn't like it, but she felt warm and emboldened. She realized that she was staring at him, and she looked down, feeling a blush heat her cheeks again. And then she felt the press of his thumb against her cheek. She startled, looking up, and he grinned. "You're very pretty, do you know that?"

Oh, she wasn't imagining it. She actually was not imagining this at all.

He lowered his hand, but the impression of the brief touch remained.

"I… I don't know what to say to that."

"Say yes, I am very aware of how beautiful I am, and the effect I have on men."

She laughed. "But I'm not."

If she didn't know better, she would say that he looked a little taken aback by that. "Well. That's going to have to change. Because no one as pretty as you should be in the dark about it."

She took a deep breath, trying to stabilize herself.

And suddenly, she was very upset that they were eating fish. Because really, that wasn't sexy. Everyone's breath was going to be bad.

She considered not eating it, but when he opened the carton of his own food, she knew that she needed to. She started munching on fries, not really sure what to say next.

"What are you thinking about?"

She nearly choked. "Hmm. Well. I was actually wondering if we were flirting."

"Oh, we're flirting," he said, smiling.

"Oh. Well, that's good to know. I just… I wanted to be sure."

"If you're not sure, I think I'm slipping."

She laughed. "No, I think I'm just very bad at it."

"You're not bad at it. It's certainly working on me."

All her breath left her body in a gust. "Well," she said.

Silence lapsed around them for a moment, and the only sound was the ocean. And then she suddenly realized that she had lost track of time. She took her phone out of her pocket and checked it.

"Oh, shoot," she said. "I forgot that I have to go. I have to get back."

"Is there anything I can help you with?"

"No. It's fine. I'll… I'll see you back at the bed-and-breakfast."

"Yeah," he said. "See you there." And then he started cleaning everything up at the table. And he walked her back to her car. She felt a little glow spark and expand inside her chest. He was flirting with her. And she had a crush on him. And maybe Clara was right. Maybe this was what she needed. Just a little harmless something. A little something that felt this indulgent and wonderful and a tiny bit selfish. Because what was wrong with that?

What was wrong with enjoying a little bit of male attention?

He wouldn't be here that long. And whatever happened... Once he was gone, it would all go back to normal. And she tried very hard not to think about how her normal was starting to look a lot like monotony that stretched out in front of her with infinite sameness. Because she had chosen the sameness. And she was not going to listen to Clara. She was not going to internalize Clara's nonsense.

She had chosen to be here. She was happy with her life.

And yes, Wolf was a slight diversion from the usual. And that was a good thing. Proof, maybe, that she could have her cake and eat it, too. That she could flirt—so to speak— with adventure—and then get back to her everyday life.

It was harmless. Just a little harmless flirtation.

He might be trouble, but he might be exactly the right kind of trouble.

CHAPTER FOUR

HE ENDED UP going back to his cousin's place before returning to the B and B, which meant that he didn't actually see
Violet again as quickly as he thought he would. He didn't
quite know what game he was playing, and while it was
normally women who asked him that question, he asked
himself that a few times. Because there was only one game
that Wolf Garrett even played with women. And that was
of the one-night stand variety. Violet was... She was a nice
woman.

Not only that, she was linked to his cousins in a really
specific way, so it was entirely possible that getting involved
with her—his manner of getting involved—was a very bad
idea. Still, he had not resisted when the temptation had arisen
to go into the bakery. He had not resisted when he'd gotten
the idea to try to get her to knock off work early. He had
not resisted the urge to buy her lunch, or touch her, or any
of the other extremely bad behaviors that he had engaged
in this afternoon. And, dammit all, he wasn't even sorry.

Dinner had been another excellent affair, this time at
Connor's place. Jack and Eli were running the kids around
in the house, and the ruckus that was coming from inside
the house suggested they might actually be learning to ride
bulls in there.

Connor was kicked back on the chair next to him, drinking a beer.

"Relaxing," Wolf said.

Connor smiled. "Yeah. Very. Honestly, I don't mind."

Silence settled between them, the knowledge of everything that Connor had lost. Wolf had noticed that one of his daughters was named Jessie.

Jessie Lynn.

And he knew exactly who she was named for. It struck him as a little bit odd considering that Connor had gone and gotten remarried. But he knew that Liss had actually been a friend of theirs. Connor and his wife's.

"I never thought I'd have it," Connor said as if reading his mind.

"I bet not."

Connor looked at him out of the side of his eye. "You seem pretty resolutely set against it."

"Yep," Wolf said. "Not for me."

"That's interesting," Connor said.

"How is it interesting?"

"Oh, I'm just always fascinated by what we're so certain of. Until variables get thrown in our paths. There's a whole hell of a lot we don't know. About ourselves. About the world. Hell, I didn't ever think that I would have four little redhead daughters. I didn't think that I would ever be able to fall in love again."

"Yeah, well. I'm happy for you," Wolf said.

"You know, the thing about this sort of thing is... None of it's magic. You make decisions. Because you can try to give meaning to tragedy all you want, but at the end of the day it's about what you decide to take away from it. Or what you don't. So if this is your takeaway...well, that's it."

"It's not that simple," Wolf said. "I don't want to sound dramatic or anything like that, but Garrett's Watch is cursed. You try to sidestep that, and it just comes for you. Somebody ought to burn it down and salt the earth."

"Except your brother seems fine enough?"

"Yeah, well, you don't know Sawyer very well. He's... He gets what he wants. And he'll make it work. Because it's who he is."

"What about you?"

"You deal in agriculture."

"Lightly. Not sure that I would consider cows agriculture."

"Then you understand how it all works. If the seed is bad, you're not getting a good crop out of it, are you?"

Connor looked at him for a long time. "With seeds, sure. But people aren't seeds. People get to choose."

"Not everybody," Wolf said, thinking of Jessie. Thinking of Breanna. They hadn't chosen their fates, nor would they have.

Nobody would.

"All right, you don't get to choose everything. That's what makes the things you can choose all the more special." He tilted his beer bottle back toward the house. "Like all that in there. I'm real glad that Liss helped me be brave enough to choose it."

"Again, mighty happy for you," Wolf said. "I'm not looking for that kind of change. It's good to see. It's good to see Garretts doing all right. It gives me hope. For Sawyer. For Elsie."

"Not for yourself?"

He raised his beer bottle so that it covered up the sinking sun. The light poured through the brown bottle, but it diluted it. Making it so it didn't hurt his eyes. "Hope for me is just waking up to ride again. To see about my business. Work the land. Maybe go out, get laid. That's hope to me. I got nothing beyond that. And I don't want anything beyond it. You know, there's something to be said for that. For just accepting what you have."

"Oh, sure," Connor said. "You might be the first man in existence to actually do it."

He knew his cousin didn't believe him. Well, fuck him.

"There are probably a lot of us," Wolf said. "We just don't run around talking about it." He drained the rest of his beer. "I might call it a night."

"Have you met Violet?"

"Why?"

Connor's gaze became far too astute. "Well, because you seem antsy to get back to the place. You mentioned this morning that you had a nice breakfast before you went out to work. Unusual, considering the hour. I figured it was Violet. And also, you didn't just say *yes*, which means what I suspect to be true is likely true. You sweet on her?"

Wolf snorted. "I don't do sweet."

"You see, somehow I was sure that you'd say that." His expression got deadly serious. "Violet is a sweet girl."

"I know," Wolf said. "I can see that."

"And you don't do sweet."

"Are you warning me off of her?"

"Consider yourself lucky that it's me. Her dad and her uncles don't have a reputation for being the nicest guys. And they're no older than I am. They could kick your ass."

"Her dad is no older than you?" He was mildly horrified by that.

"Well. Her dad might be. A little bit. But her uncles are young. And can kick your ass."

"I don't want my ass kicked."

He said that because Connor would think he'd listened.

But he wasn't deterred in his pursuit of Violet. And as he left the house that night, he stopped his truck in the middle of the road and asked himself why. Not because he cared about getting his ass kicked. That didn't scare him. But because what Connor had said was true. Violet was sweet. The kind of sweet that men like him shouldn't mess with. And he knew better than that. He didn't do sweet. He really didn't. He liked a good-time girl, and it was clear enough that Violet wasn't that. The way she had blushed when he touched her cheek…

Yeah, she was not the kind of girl whom he should be messing with. But he was absolutely and completely drawn to her. Confounded by the attraction that existed between them. Normally, his attraction wasn't specific. He liked beautiful women. And there were a lot of them. So one was pretty much like the next as far as all that went. Didn't much matter. But she was weighing heavy on his mind, looming large in his consciousness all the time. And he didn't feel guilty about it.

He had to wonder if this was rock bottom. And then he wondered if he even cared.

If Breanna were still alive, she wouldn't love him now. Of course, he might not have become this if she were still alive. He certainly wouldn't have been thinking about seducing another woman.

His veins felt like they were full of ice by the time he pulled back into the bed-and-breakfast, because the thought of Breanna's disappointment in him wasn't even enough to make him feel deterred from the path that he was set on.

When he walked into the bed-and-breakfast, it was warm. Enough to thaw out his veins. And even though he'd just eaten at his cousin's house, his stomach growled when he saw the goodies that Violet had set out on the table by the door. There was warm apple cider. And he couldn't remember the last time he'd had something like that. Evelyn would probably make it. Evelyn had brought all that kind of softness into their house. All kinds of things that had never been there before.

But he didn't want *hers*. He wanted Violet's.

He stopped and grabbed a little white paper cup, and began to fill it up with cider. And then he heard footsteps. He looked up and saw Violet looming in the doorway of the hall. "Hi," she said.

"Hi," he said. "Sorry. I had dinner with my cousins tonight. And it was late by the time I got back here. Didn't realize that I'd…" He lifted his cup. Didn't finish his sentence. Why was he apologizing to her? Why was he explaining himself?

"It's fine," she said. "You don't… You don't owe me anything." Music to his ears. His favorite thing to hear a woman say. And yet…

"I haven't had cider since I was a kid," he said, taking a sip of it, unprepared for the nostalgia that hit him. Wolf was not one who was given to nostalgia. He didn't like to think about the past. There were too many people in the past that weren't in the present, and everything about it felt thorny. But there he was. A little kid, out on the hayride after going to the pumpkin patch. And his mom was there. His dad, too. Along with a smile, which he hadn't seen on the man all that often.

She smiled. The smile lit up her face, and he focused on her smile, which was uncomplicated, and not tangled around thorny memories.

"I love it," she said. "I didn't for a while. I mean, I mentioned that my mom left. I was really angry after that. And I… I pulled away from my dad. I pulled away from everybody. My friends. I didn't want to do things like have holidays. It seemed…sad. And empty. I couldn't understand why she left. Why she would leave me. I guess you know something about that."

Damn. Why had he told her any of that? This was the problem with talking to women. And earlier it had seemed like a good idea because it gave them something to relate to each other on.

Seemed like less of a good idea now.

"Sure," he said. "But I was only six."

"I was thirteen. I remember it. And I was… I was very angry. And I really noticed the difference."

He sure as hell noticed the difference. But his brother had been right. He'd told him then that there was no use in crying. There wasn't. It didn't change anything. It didn't bring people back. Ever.

"Well. I'm glad you found your way back to holidays."

"Me, too," she said.

And he was done talking just then. But she was an interesting thing, Violet Donnelly; she wasn't his typical woman. Not his usual type. He couldn't approach her exactly the same way he would have a woman in a bar, and he knew that. But he couldn't just stand here doing nothing, either. If it was a woman in a bar, he'd say something shocking, something dirty. Make her giggle. Make her come to him.

But with Violet, he just moved toward her, and her eyes went wide. "The cider is good, but what I really want to taste is you."

He reached out, wrapped his hand around the back of her head and drew her to him. And she went, willingly, up on her toes. Then he brought his head down and kissed her. All the air went out of his lungs. The minute their mouths touched, it was like fire. She tasted so sweet. Better than cookies, better than cider. She didn't taste like restraint, or good decisions, or being a decent guy.

Yeah, she didn't taste anything like that.

She tasted like she wanted more. Like he wanted to drown in this. Drown in her. He moved his hand down to the center of her back and wrapped his other arm around her waist, drawing the length of her body up against his. And he let her feel what she did to him. He didn't have words. He didn't have anything beyond need. Feral and pulsing through his veins, and quite unlike anything he'd experienced before.

Because this wasn't like a bar hookup. It was nothing like that. Because it mattered too much that it was her, this woman whom he had known for going on two days, who had occupied his thoughts ever since. He'd been warned off her, and it shouldn't matter. He should just walk away, because he knew, he full-well knew, that she was the wrong woman for him to be messing around with, but he wanted to.

When they parted, they were both breathing hard, and she looked up at him, her eyes bright.

"Well," she said. "I…"

She was tentative, hesitant, and he shouldn't like it. He shouldn't be interested in her obvious inexperience. But he was. And the way she was looking at him, all shy and hesitant, but clearly hungry for more… That should not appeal to him, either. But hell and damn it did.

"You are so damn sexy," he said. Just to see what she would do.

She sucked in a sharp breath, her eyes going wide. "I am?"

He laughed. "Yes. You're about to make me lose my mind over here."

She bit her lip, and he wanted to return the favor. "Could you kiss me again?"

"You don't have to ask me twice."

He closed the distance between them, wrapping his arms around her again, and consuming her mouth. But this time he didn't go slow. This time he didn't give any quarter.

He kissed her until neither of them could breathe. Until he couldn't tell the difference between her breaths and his, the beat of her heart or his. It was all the same. It was all frantic. All desperate. She clung to him, her fingernails digging into his skin through his shirt. He backed her against the wall, the pictures rattling, and she startled.

"I don't want to wake anyone up," she said.

"Do you think they're asleep?"

"Well. Everybody retired to their rooms."

"They might be doing something other than sleeping."

She blinked at him, looking mystified.

He decided to let that go. Instead, he leaned in and kissed her gently, on the mouth first, and then across the forehead. He was so turned on he couldn't think. So hard that it hurt. She was so beautiful. So beautiful and just so… She wasn't for him. That was the thing. She felt ill-gotten. And he liked it. He couldn't deny it.

"I… I have some things I better finish up."

"All right," he said.

"I'll… I'll see you later."

Lust kicked him in the gut. She knew what room he was in. And he was looking forward to her paying him a visit.

"All right."

He kissed her one more time, then went up the stairs to his room, closed the door and didn't lock it. Even though he had a feeling she had another key, he didn't see the point in adding any unnecessary barriers. He was ready for this. Ready for her. But he waited. And waited. And his promised visitor did not appear.

CHAPTER FIVE

VIOLET WAS STILL buzzing the next morning as she made a very early breakfast for Wolf. She had kissed him. Well, he had kissed her. And it had been amazing. She had never felt a kiss like that before. Of course, she never like, full-on made out with anyone before. That was… Well, it had been amazing. She wanted to kiss him again. She couldn't wait.

She had the table set with his breakfast by the time she heard his footsteps on the stairs. She ran out to greet him. "Good morning," she said, smiling.

He raised his brows and looked her up and down. "Good morning."

"What?" He looked… She couldn't quite pin down how he looked.

"Oh, nothing. Just surprised that you're here serving breakfast is all. I thought maybe you'd run for the hills."

She blinked. "Why would I do that?"

"Because you…" His forehead lowered. "Because you didn't come to my room last night."

"Oh," she said, her heart slamming against her breastbone. "Was I supposed to *come to your room*?"

"You said you'd see me later." His brows were drawn together, and he didn't look angry, so much as mystified, but the confusion was definitely apparent.

"Oh, I… Well, I mean we don't even know each other. It

didn't occur to me. We only kissed the once. I mean, multiple times, but the one incident."

He looked at her long and hard. "Violet... I... Hell. I don't know what to say. I think we're working off of two separate scripts."

She didn't like that. She didn't want that to be true. She wanted to be working off the same script as he was. Because she really liked him, and...

She realized how silly that sounded.

What do you think this is, Violet Donnelly?

She couldn't like him. She didn't know him. And sure, it wasn't every day that she met someone who had experienced the exact same sort of trauma she had in her childhood, but they didn't know each other. It wasn't that she liked him particularly more than any other person she had met recently. It was that she was attracted to him. Very, very attracted to him. And what the hell did she think that meant between two adults? She was just so... She was so aggressively inexperienced and limited in this kind of thing. That for her it had meant to kiss. And for him it had obviously meant sex. And how could she be that foolish not to realize it? She felt small and young. And stupid. And ridiculously out of her league with a man like Wolf.

"I'm sorry," she said. "I feel...really stupid. I..."

"Don't," he said, frowning. "I made some assumptions. You never said you wanted that. And I would never... Hell, I would never pressure you into anything."

And now he was apologizing to her.

Great.

And she felt bereft.

Like she had missed an amazing opportunity. But it was an opportunity she wasn't sure she was ready to take. She knew that was what Clara had meant when she said have some fun. She knew that deep down. She knew that her friend did not mean having a nice little lunch by the ocean and sharing a couple of kisses. And she knew that a man like Wolf wasn't built for dates and hearts and flowers.

He was built for sin.

It was just that Violet wasn't entirely certain if *she* was. And that complicated things.

It was just that she had been wounded a lot. And if she was honest, that was the real issue. It wasn't that she was too busy. It wasn't that she was a prude. It wasn't that she didn't like men; she did.

But the problem was she had a feeling—she had always had the feeling—that it would be too easy for her to feel too much too quickly. That it would be far too easy for her to get emotionally involved—way more emotionally involved—than the person she was with. And she had just been hurt enough. She had been left one too many times.

By her mother.

Which meant that once was enough. And she just didn't have it in her to expose herself to that kind of pain ever again. And that was what scared her about something like this. She already was trying to think in terms of liking him. Having a crush on him. All the soft things that were wrapping up the truth in something fuzzy. Something a bit more connected than it should be. She swallowed hard.

"You're not pressuring me. You aren't. I'm just… I made you breakfast."

"Thank you," he said. "Looks good."

"I hope so."

"Do you have any for yourself?"

"You still want to have breakfast with me?"

He arched a brow. "Yes."

She felt warmed. She scurried into the kitchen and

grabbed the plate of quiche that she had put on for herself. Just in case. That was of course prior to realizing that there had been a misunderstanding between the two of them.

"Would you like me to take you out to dinner?" he asked.

"I… Why?"

"I'm trying to figure you out, Violet Donnelly. I'll be perfectly honest with you. I am used to a different sort of… A different sort of dynamic."

"What dynamic is that?"

He took a breath. "Okay. So I'm going to be as honest with you as possible. I like to go out. I like to look around the room, see which woman catches my eye. And then I like to approach that woman, make some quick conversation and get her back to my place. That's what I like."

"Oh," she said, feeling deflated.

"But meeting you was different. I walked in, and there you were. I wasn't looking for anything, and there you were. I felt attraction to you instantly. So if I have to work a little harder…then I will."

It was not a romantic thing to say. Not at all. It wasn't a crush, and it wasn't *liking*. It was frank. Physical. It was probably closer to the truth of what her body wanted. It was just that she didn't have the vocabulary… No. It wasn't even that. It was that she was ashamed. Because she was still trying to be good. And she was trying to reshape and redistribute all of this until she could find a way to make it okay. But Wolf Garrett didn't live here.

He wasn't going to live here.

He had a ranching spread. And sure, he had family here; he might come back and visit. But there was no possibility of a future between the two of them, geographically if for no other reason. Wanting him—she was going to go ahead and try to be honest with herself—was futile. It either had to be about right now, or she had to go ahead and nip it in the bud. But he was not the kind of man you just kissed in a hallway and left it at that.

He wanted something more from her.

And the truth was she wanted the same thing from him. Even with sex being as fuzzy and theoretical to her as it was, she knew what he wanted. It was just she had to decide if it was something that she could do. Emotionally. If that was how she wanted to…have her first time.

"How long are you going to be here?"

"Two weeks."

Two weeks. Two weeks.

It scared her.

Two weeks.

"Okay," she said, taking a bite of her quiche.

"Okay what?"

She let out a frustrated breath. "I don't actually know. I don't know."

"It's okay." He got up and walked over to her end of the table. "Thank you, for breakfast." He pinched her chin between his thumb and forefinger, tilted her face upward, and she felt herself get all hot. Because his body was so close to her, and she could imagine him naked. She could imagine him putting his hands on her. She could imagine climbing on top of him. And it made her want to cry, because it was all so intense. But that raw freedom that she had experienced when they were out by the beach came back to her, too.

These rules that she was grappling with were self-imposed. She had put them up to protect herself. She had decided they were reasonable because she had wanted to keep herself safe. But was she really going to live this way for her entire life? She couldn't see it being practical.

"Better get to work."

And he left her sitting there, breathless and unsure. Of what she was going to do next. Of all that she could unlearn in the next space of time.

And whether or not she would hate herself more if he broke her heart, or if she never took the chance on having this experience.

And she had a feeling that this was not something she was going to solve over quiche.

She had a bad feeling it was something she wasn't going to solve. She was just going to have to make one choice or the other and deal with the consequences.

And she didn't like that at all.

WOLF WAS GRATEFUL for the physical labor that afternoon. Grateful that he had the opportunity to do some real, punishing work. Building actual walls to hold up a new barn. Swinging a hammer until everything in him ached. Because he had a lot of shit to work out, and he would much rather just exhaust himself.

Realizing that Violet hadn't... That she had not been propositioning him, had been something else. Because the woman wanted him; he knew that. He knew what it looked like when a woman wanted him, after all. But... Well, she was clearly a much more traditional type of woman than he was used to. And that was... Well, hell, that was potentially some kind of problem. It was a sign that he needed to listen to what Connor had told him last night. It was a sign that he needed to figure out how to get in touch with his damned conscience. But what had he done? He'd offered to take her to dinner. Whatever she needed. Whatever she needed to make sleeping with him okay, he was willing to do it.

He had never… Hell, he never worked this hard to get laid in his life.

And he didn't know why he was doing it now.

He also didn't know why he couldn't access any kind of regret about it. But he just didn't have any. "Damn glad for your help," Connor said, straightening and breathing hard.

Wolf really hoped his cousin couldn't read his mind.

They were all hands on deck today; Kate, Jack, Connor and Eli all out working.

Kate reminded him a lot of his sister, Elsie. Spunky and more than willing to jump in and do all the work the men were doing. Not just to prove that she could, but because she wanted to. Because it was in her blood. Sadie and Liss were not ranchers by nature. Or by any other token, as far as he could tell. They were just women who had married into the family. But they were still here. A damned miracle as far as Garretts went.

"Not a problem. The expanded facilities and silos should be helpful for you. But you're going to have to finish all that with a crew. You can't do it all yourself. Not given the scope of the expansion you want to do."

"Understood," Eli said. "Anyway. I've got too many responsibilities with the sheriff's department."

"Is Logan County really that big of a mess?"

"Same problems everywhere else has. Domestic violence and drugs. Kids getting into trouble. And then every so often you get something you really wish you didn't have to deal with. Not typical. But this isn't a fairy tale. You have things like kids disappearing. Hate crimes and things like that. You don't like dealing with it, but at the very least… Hey, I can try to do something about it. People around here… I imagine they are much the same as they are in your neck of the woods. Community minded, and it can be a very good thing. But sometimes they get insular, and they don't want to help law enforcement. Not when they'd rather keep to themselves and keep their heads down. They feel… Well, I think they feel like they can mind their own business. Particularly when you get into the smaller, unincorporated areas. Very unfortunately, there's just always work to do."

"People are people," Wolf said.

"Damn sure are."

"But Eli is the best sheriff this county's ever had. That's why he keeps getting reelected," Kate said proudly.

"Good for you. I can't imagine a Garrett getting elected to law enforcement out in Ponderosa County. Our reputation is not so great there."

"You mean your dad?"

Wolf grinned. "And me."

"You don't have warrants, do you?" Eli asked. "Because that would be inconvenient for me."

"No," Wolf said. "I toyed around with misdemeanors when I was a minor."

"Hell," Eli said. "So did my wife."

"Unfair," Katie said. "Sadie isn't here to defend herself. She did not commit any misdemeanors. The bonfire was an accident."

"Regardless," Eli said. "I still had to arrest her."

"Please tell me this was not last week?" Wolf asked.

"It was not last week," Eli said. "She was seventeen. But still. I'm just saying. I don't have an issue with that."

"Right." Everywhere he looked it seemed like his family was trying to make the point that people could change. He didn't know why they were so wedded to it. Well, except they were like him in the sense that they were.

Good for them.

Good for them.

"You want to go out drinking tonight?"

It was Jack who asked that question.

"Hell yeah," Wolf said.

"Really?" That came from Kate.

"I do," Connor said.

"I have to keep my drinking private," Eli said.

"I have to check with the wife," Connor said. "Since we've been gone all day, I want to make sure she's not pulling her hair out."

"Your cousin's visiting," Jack said. "Seems reasonable to me."

"Yeah, she has your monsters, too," Connor said. "She's probably just about done."

"I can take the monsters. Yours included," Kate said. "I don't mind. Tell Liss to have the night off."

"Great," Connor said. "It's settled. We'll go out to Ace's tonight."

"What's Ace's?"

"Only the best bar in town."

"The *only* bar in town," Jack said.

"There is a mechanical bull," Kate said. "You can show your chops on Ferdinand."

"No, thanks," Wolf said. "I try to keep making an ass of myself to a minimum."

He thought of this morning. He made a pretty decent ass of himself then. Actually, what he should do was see if there were any women that he found particularly attractive down at the bar tonight. Maybe that would cure him. Maybe that would give him something else to focus on. Surely, there was a motel or two in town. He didn't even have to bring the woman back to the B and B. Hell, he wouldn't. He wasn't that tacky.

But he could rescue Violet from him and his evil intent. There. He wasn't a terrible person. He had a plan all sorted out to save her. From him and his untrustworthy cock.

"Guess we better wrap it up and go get cleaned up a bit," Jack said.

"Guess so."

And Wolf felt satisfied with this. All right, maybe it meant he wouldn't get quite what he wanted. But he could deal with it. And whether or not he actually felt some kind of prick in his conscience, it didn't really matter. He was going to do the right thing. That ought to count for something.

CHAPTER SIX

THE PROBLEM WAS that Wolf didn't come back to the bed-and-breakfast. She waited, and waited, and he didn't appear. She tried to be friendly and engaging to all of the guests over wine-and-cheese hour, and remember the local history, and all of that so that she could make them feel like they were getting the full experience. But she was distracted. By the fact that she had finally decided to do something, and the man had not come home. She waited. She waited and waited, and she was beginning to think that this was revenge for last night.

Finally, in a fit of rage, she called Clara. "I want to go out."

"You do?" Clara asked.

"Yes. I want to go out. Let's go to Ace's."

"I have to get the kids to bed."

"Well, tell Alex to do it."

"Will you be the designated driver so I can promise him I'll come home tipsy and easy?"

"Aren't you always easy?"

Clara laughed. "Well. Yes. But he does like me tipsy. Hell, I like me tipsy. It's fun."

"Fine. Unless…unless something happens. Then I'll pay for a taxi for you."

"Violet," she said, sounding scandalized. "What could possibly happen?"

"Maybe I'm in the mood. In the mood to make some things happen."

"Like and such as?"

"I don't know. Maybe I thought it was time that I had a little adventure."

After making arrangements to swing by to get Clara in twenty minutes, Violet raced to get ready. She didn't have anything all that sexy. She had a pair of jeans that were pretty tight, and a crop top that she didn't hate that went with it. She put on makeup, quickly. She didn't bother with it every day, but she did like it, and had a small collection of eyeshadow palletes that she wore maybe once a month. She looked at herself in the mirror and was reasonably satisfied with the level of anger-motivated attractiveness she had managed to get into place.

She went down the stairs and got in her car, and started to drive toward the Donnelly ranch. She waited in front of the old farmhouse, and Clara came out, and Violet saw as Alex reached out, grabbed her around the waist and pulled her back in, kissing her before releasing her again. Clara stumbled down to the car, looking flustered.

"He's in a mood."

"It doesn't look like it's a bad mood."

Clara looked smug. "Oh, it's not. But I owe him something when I get back."

"Yeah. Looks like it."

It was funny, because there was always going to be a little bit of awkwardness given that Alex was her uncle. But at the same time... She had been older when she'd gotten to know her uncles, and she essentially didn't know him that well separated from his relationship with Clara, who was a good enough friend that she did share things about her love life. Just like Clara was keeper of the embarrassing knowledge that Violet was a virgin. It was one of those things that felt easy enough to compartmentalize. Because her friendship with Clara was so specific. And the relationship just didn't feel like the one they actually had through marriage.

"So what's going on?" Clara asked as they headed out toward town.

"Nothing."

"Something is clearly going on. You are acting like you had a fire lit under your ass."

"Well, maybe I did. Because maybe you're right. Maybe I've been overcautious for a very long time. Maybe I am stuck trying to earn my dad and Alison's love and affection by trying to be perfect. And maybe I need to stop that. Because they didn't put it on me. I did."

"That's a lot of sudden realization to be triggered by nothing."

Violet realized she wasn't getting out of this without some explanation. "Wolf propositioned me."

"I see."

"And I didn't realize it. He thought I was going to come to his room. And I just thought because we had kissed for the first time we were several steps away from that."

"Oh. Honey. Bless."

"I didn't know. And so I thought he was going to come back tonight, and I had made the decision that I was going to… But he didn't come back. He didn't come back to the bed-and-breakfast. For all I know he's out whoring it up right now."

"Did you just call him a whore?"

"It is my understanding that he is a little bit of a whore. So maybe I should be one."

"I hate to break it to you. But I don't think going and hooking up at a bar is going to make you a whore."

"Well, then maybe I'll stand on the street corner and charge for it."

"You could. But that probably would make your dad mad."

"Well, I don't want to do that. But…"

"I didn't know you were self-destructive when you were thwarted," Clara said. "That's concerning."

"I'm not being self-destructive," Violet said. "But I am working to dismantle the rules that I have built around my life that were imposed on me by no one other than myself, and do not serve me."

"Well, that makes going out to a bar to get drunk and hook up sound almost worthy."

"I'm nothing if not worthy," Violet said, feeling testy.

The parking lot of Ace's was already full, lines of trucks parked beneath blue security lights. Her stomach did a little flip. Because what the hell was she even doing?

"I'm gonna ride that bull," she said, gripping the steering wheel tight.

"Oh, don't ride the bull," Clara said. "It seems like a good idea when you're going through a crisis, but it only ends in embarrassment."

"Maybe it'll be sexy. Maybe some guy will think it's sexy."

"Violet," Clara said. "No. Also, the guy that thinks it's sexy is maybe one you should avoid."

"Why can't I make a bad decision?"

"You *can*," Clara said. "I'm not saying you can't. It's just… Don't make a really bad decision. Make like a slightly questionable decision. One that won't scar you for life, or leave you with a disease."

"I am given to understand that's what condoms are for, Clara."

"Indeed. But condoms don't help with herpes of the soul."

Violet narrowed her eyes. "What does that mean?"

"I think it's self-explanatory."

"It is not. It is *not* self-explanatory. I do not know what it means."

"Well, I'm not going to explain it to you."

The two of them got out of the car and headed into the bar.

"I want to get a fancy drink," Clara said. "Something with like eight cherries and a cup of sugar."

"Isn't that…the only kind of alcohol you ever drink?"

"It's why I rarely drink. I can't stand beer. And wine is disgusting."

"That must go over well what with the fact that your sister-in-law owns a giant winery."

"Yeah. Well, there's a lot of very nice free wine that is wasted on me."

They walked into the bar, and Ace, the owner of said bar, was behind the counter. Ace had once been one of Copper Ridge's most notorious bachelors. But he'd settled down since. Didn't mean he wasn't still incredibly good-looking, though.

"What can I get for you?" he asked, smiling broadly.

"I'll have… I'll have…whiskey."

Yeah, she would have whiskey. So there.

"Something really sweet. With cherries."

"Can I get you a Shirley Temple, Clara?" he asked.

"No, I want something with booze."

"Do you, though?" Ace pressed.

"Well, no. Especially now that she ordered a whiskey. You were supposed to designated drive," Clara said.

"I know. But it's my emancipation."

"Fine. I don't want alcohol, anyway," Clara muttered.

When Clara's drink arrived, it was fizzy and pink from the juice of the cherries, and she didn't look the least bit sad. Violet herself felt a bit uncertain about the whiskey. She had very little experience drinking on this level. But it felt like a night to be bold.

She brought the shot glass to her lips and basically just touched the amber liquid to them. She licked them, and gasped. "Oh. This is…" She coughed.

"You don't sip it," Clara said. "Or so I have observed."

"I can't take a shot of it. I will die. It will set my esophagus on fire. I can't pick a guy up if I have a burned out esophagus."

"Might help with your gag reflex."

"Why would that…" Suddenly, she got an image. Of herself, on her knees in front of Wolf. "Oh."

"Yes," Clara said. "Indeed."

"Well, that's…disgusting in the context of this conversation."

"It's not disgusting. In any context."

"Well. *Well.*" She looked around the bar. There was an array of cowboys. There always was. People drinking hard to prepare for the endless work that was ahead. There were no weekends when you were a rancher. There was always something to do. She'd known that all of her life. Because her dad had done it. He loved the life. Took it very seriously. As far as she could tell, it was a life you pretty much had to take seriously. Which was probably why it attracted this sort of work hard-play hard philosophy.

She was familiar with it, and yet she still felt like she was on the outside looking in. Unable to take that shot of whiskey. Unable to drain it.

Then she saw a figure, in the shadows. He moved. And she felt something shift inside her. The man had a cowboy hat drawn low over his face, and when he emerged from the darkness, her heart caught in her throat. It was Wolf.

Looking every inch the predator that his name implied he was. And he was stalking toward her.

Her heart fluttered, and all she could do was stand there. A sheep waiting to be eaten. By the big bad Wolf.

"And what the hell are you doing here?" he asked.

"I might ask you the same question."

"Well, do you want an honest answer?"

She looked over her shoulder and saw that Clara had lifted her glass up, and was sipping it through a straw, her blue eyes wide and pinned to both her and Wolf. She turned back to Wolf. "Well… I came here to…"

Clara swirled her straw around in her glass and made a loud clanking sound. Then she tipped the glass to her lips and captured some ice between her teeth, crunching noisily. "She's here to find a man," Clara said, setting her glass down on the bar. "Since the one that she found ended up being a disappointment."

"Clara," Violet muttered.

"I'm helping," Clara said in an obvious stage whisper that Wolf could clearly hear.

"You are not." She turned back to Wolf. "But yes. I am here to find a man."

"Are you?"

He did not sound at all interested. In fact, he sounded irritated.

"Well. *Well.* Like Clara said, it's only that I thought that I had found one, and then you didn't show up. You didn't come back to the bed-and-breakfast, so I figured… If I was in the mood to have a little fun, I might go out and find some by myself."

"Is that what you thought? You. The woman who did not come to my room last night after she kissed me like she was thirsty and I was water?"

She looked back over at Clara, who was watching this with far too much interest. "Can we go over here?"

She stepped away from Clara, whom she could still feel watching. "Why didn't you come back tonight?"

"Because I was trying to do the right thing," he said. "Look, you're a nice girl."

"And you seem like a nice man. So I don't see the problem?"

"That is the problem. I'm not a nice man, Violet. I play one for short periods of time. And I did a pretty good job playing one with you. But the fact of the matter is, I have one decent thing to offer a woman. And that is a good time in bed. I figured we were on the same page. Last night, when you didn't come to my room, and when you explained it this morning, it became clear to me that we weren't. The last thing I want is to get involved with something that I can't do right by. Because that's not who I am."

"Some bad boy then," she said. "Isn't leaving a swath of destruction in your wake and not looking back supposed to be…the whole bad-boy thing?"

"I guess if you're all about an image. I'm not a bad boy, Violet. I'm a little bit of a bad man, though. And I think you need to be careful about that. I'm not sure that you have the respect for that that you should. Because I've been nice to you." He stuck his hand out, dragged his thumb over her lower lip, and she shivered. "There's only one way this ends, though. I don't change. And sex sure as hell doesn't change me. I'm not that kind of man. I don't have transformative experiences in bedrooms. I just rock worlds and walk away. So here's the thing, sweet girl. I came here tonight to rescue you. To find some other woman who knew the game. Because I don't have it in me to teach you the rules."

"Then why did you… Why did you cross the room to come to me?"

"Because dammit all, you're the one that I want. That's the problem. I told you… I like to go to a bar and see if there's a woman that catches my eye. But it never matters who she is. I don't give a fuck. I've slept with women I wouldn't be able to pick out of a lineup the following day. No skin off my nose. This… I don't like this. I want you. And I can't seem to shake it. And maybe I would've had a hope in hell of picking up one of these honeys in here, but not when you're in the room. If my family hadn't gone home, you'd be safe right now. That's how I know this is wrong. I'd never have come over here if they were still here to see it. But they're gone, and here I am. So you have two choices as far as I'm concerned. You take your friend, and you leave. Or you stay, and test my word. See if I'm telling you the truth about who I am. I guarantee you I am."

She shivered, his promises echoing inside her. She couldn't square off the Wolf that she had spent time with over the past couple of days with this one. Who seemed darker, edgier and more intense.

But this one seemed… He did not seem too good to be true. He seemed too sexy to bear, but he didn't seem like a fantasy. And that made her think that this really was the truth. And that it would do her well to listen.

But earlier, she'd already made her decision. She wasn't going to know if she could handle this until she tried it. She wasn't going to know if it would break her heart until she took the risk. But he was clear. It was sex, and it was only sex. And it couldn't be anything else. So maybe if she knew that, if she believed it, she would be able to handle it.

"Maybe I'm not what you think I am," she said.

"I'm afraid you are."

That made her feel hot all over, because that made her wonder if her inexperience was quite so obvious. If you looked at her and saw big virgin stamped across her forehead.

"Well, all right," she said. "Maybe I am. But you want me just the same. So maybe… Maybe you like what I am. And maybe it's because you think you shouldn't have me. Did you ever think of that? Maybe… For a man who's given himself all the things he wants over the last few years… Someone like me is forbidden fruit." She liked that idea. She liked it a lot. That as much as he was a departure for her, she was one for him. As bad of an idea as he was for her, she was a problem for him.

"Maybe so," he said.

"I won't stop at kissing tonight," she said.

"Good," he responded.

"I got a shot of whiskey," she said, sniffing. "I'm not that safe."

"Have you ever taken a shot before?"

"No."

He walked across the space between her and the bar, grabbed her tumbler of whiskey and knocked it back.

"Hey," she said. "That was mine."

"And if you want to have sex with me tonight, you're not drinking it. Because I don't want you compromised in any way."

"Well," she said, "you drank it. What about your…your consent?"

"Please. A shot of whiskey isn't enough to get my blood hot. You'll have to do it for me." He turned and walked away from her. "See you tonight."

"Yeah," she said.

She went back to Clara. "I think… I think I'm going to… I think I'm going to sleep with him tonight."

"Well, I would love to warn you off of him," Clara said. "Because he seems like very bad news. But I know that look on a man's face. And he is intent on getting what he wants. Not that I think he would do anything you didn't want. It's just that… Any red-blooded woman would take him up on that."

"I am only human," Violet said. She sounded as helpless and turned on as she felt. "It goes without saying, but please don't tell my dad and Alison?"

"Absolutely not," Clara said. "Those are things that do not need to be shared. Sexy cowboys are your business and your business alone."

"Thank you," she said.

Clara suddenly looked worried. "Do you need a primer?"

"Do I need a… A what?"

"Like you know where everything goes, right?"

"Oh, my gosh, yes, I know where everything goes."

"It's just that I know you haven't done this before."

"Did anybody give you a primer before you… With Alex?"

"No. But the whole thing with Alex was… Alex was there to take care of me. And the situation with us was very complicated. He was sort of… I mean, what I'm trying to say is Alex had an emotional connection to me. Even though it wasn't the kind of connection we have now. He was not a bar hookup. He was my brother's best friend. He took the responsibility for taking care of me after he died really seriously. He knew me when I was younger. He… He knew my life story. He knew me. And in some ways… He was the person teaching me? Giving me the talk? I don't know. It's hard to describe. But the point is, Alex knew.

And unless I'm mistaken, your hot dude does not know that you've never…"

"Well, he might've guessed."

"Maybe. But… I'm just… Condoms. You need condoms."

"I'm sure he has them."

"Well, you need to use them. And tell him if you like something. And tell him if you don't like something. And make sure that he makes you come first."

"How do I make sure of that?"

"I don't know. Just…tell him you want to."

"I'm *not* telling him that."

"You can't be all shy about it. If you're going to get naked with a guy," Clara said, "you need to be able to say what you want."

"I don't know what I want."

Clara winced. "That's not a good sign."

"I don't know what I want except I want him. I have never felt this way about another person before. I've never wanted to… I have been contorting to make it something different, to make it something more important and more… acceptable since the moment I met him. But the fact of the matter is, I want to take his clothes off of him and lick his body everywhere."

Clara sighed. "Okay. I release you. I'll take you home. Because obviously it is time for you to get prepared."

"I can drive," she said. "I ended up not having anything to drink."

"You are heavily under the influence of Wolf. So I'm thinking that I should probably drive."

They left the bar shortly after that, and Clara drove to her home, then they swapped seats, and Violet drove the rest of the way to her house.

And the whole way, she was questioning herself.

But it was fate. It felt like fate. Because somehow she had ended up in the same bar as Wolf tonight. And he had been trying to forget her, the same as she had been trying to forget him. And that… That mattered. But of course when she got back home, she was worried about her outfit, and if it would be too hard to take off. The idea of him having to peel off her jeans didn't really appeal. She changed her underwear five times. She changed into three different dresses. But a dress felt like something that would be easy for him to manage. She debated whether or not she should put on some lipstick. But it seemed like it would just come off. Then get everywhere. Which…didn't seem like the best idea.

Her hands were shaking, and her stomach was tight. Making a sex appointment was a really bad idea. She should have just gone up to his room after they'd kissed in the hall yesterday. It would have felt more spontaneous.

She heard the door downstairs close.

And she froze. She knew that it was him. She came out of her room, padding quickly down the hall, and meeting him at the top of the stairs. She was breathing hard, her whole body on high alert.

Then he wrapped his arm around her waist, hauled her up against him and dragged her right into his room.

He closed the door hard, locking it behind them. Nerves threatened to completely overtake her, but she took a breath, gazing instead at him, and not thinking ahead.

He was so beautiful. His eyes were almost as black as night, his skin brown. His hair was black, cut close to his head, and the way the cowboy hat highlighted his angular features gave him a dangerous appearance. She had thought earlier that he fit his name perfectly, and it was true. He did.

She wondered how he had ended up with that name, and

figured he probably didn't know. Because it probably had something to do with his mother. Who had left him when he was six, and Violet knew all about things like that. All the questions that you wish you would've asked, but you didn't. The relationship that you would like to have had, but couldn't. The absolute unfairness of it. The gaping holes surrounding your personal history because the person who had brought you into the world hadn't stuck around to see it through. Hadn't lovingly placed you in the care of someone who could give you that same sort of life. Had just left. Just abandoned you.

Those thoughts crumbled when he took another step toward her. He was so beautiful, broadly muscled and intimidating. But she liked that. Maybe it was why Asher had never appealed.

He was a handsome guy, nice enough, too. But what she loved about Wolf was the difference in them. He was like a completely different species. The masculine to her feminine so extreme that it couldn't be denied. And she loved that. Loved the impossible solid breadth of his body. Loved the immensity of his form, which made her feel small and delicate.

Danger.

She had been good for so long, and standing this close to danger was electric. This close to rebellion. She was incandescent with it.

And then he kissed her, his rough hands dragging along her jawline, and she sighed, folding into him.

"Condoms," she said against his mouth.

"Yeah," he growled. "I have one."

"Good," she said.

There, she had been responsible. Clara couldn't be mad at her now.

The kissing intensified, and he moved his hands over her curves, down beneath the hemline of her dress, pushing his hands upward, cupping her butt. She wiggled against him, feeling the hard length of his arousal against her stomach. He was so… She couldn't even think of the words. She couldn't think of anything. Need pulsed through her like an insatiable thing. And suddenly…none of the labels mattered anymore. Good girl, bad boy. Virgin. Whore. None of it meant anything. Because there was only them. There was nothing outside this room. Nothing at all. There couldn't be. Because her world now turned on Wolf Garrett's kiss, on the touch of his hands. The masculine grip that he held her in. The orbit that kept her enthralled.

He kissed her neck, his whiskered jawline teasing her, tantalizing her. He moved down to her collarbone, gripping the neckline of her dress roughly and pulling it down, his lips brushing against the top of her cleavage.

"So pretty," he muttered. "I want you. I want you."

And the way he said that left no room for her to wonder whether that was significant or not. It was. That he wanted her meant something. It made her shiver. Made her ache.

"I want you," she said, stretching up on her tiptoes and kissing him on the mouth. Softly at first. But then it began to intensify. She felt like she was caught up in a storm, encircled by a cyclone of desire that pressed them against one another, impossibly. Inseparably.

He jerked her dress up over her head, leaving her in nothing but her lacy underwear and matching bra. She was very glad she had chosen the underwear she did, because the banked fire in his eyes leaped higher, an incalculable need that she felt echoed inside herself.

He was breathless. Over her. Because she was his forbidden fruit, and she was glad. Because she was as singular to him as he was to her. And she was going to cling to that. Desperately, maybe. But who could blame her? She couldn't have forever. But she wanted him to remember her. Remember this.

And what he told her? That he'd slept with women he couldn't pick out of a lineup. But she always wanted him to know who *she* was.

Maybe that was small and silly. Maybe it was the reasoning of a virgin. But she would always remember him. Because he would always be her first. Not just the first man she'd ever slept with, but the first man that she'd ever wanted to. Even if she hadn't actually slept with him, that would've been true. He would've been the one she wanted. The only one she had ever wanted like this. And it mattered.

He pushed his hands beneath the waistband of her panties, his hands large and rough on the globes of her rear, and she gasped. She had never given a lot of thought to the realities of being touched so intimately. She liked it, she was surprised to discover. She liked it a lot. She wiggled against him and kissed him harder, then she pulled her mouth away from his and whispered against his ear, "I like that." Because Clara had told her to do that.

He growled, squeezing her tight as he walked her back toward the bed. The bed. Her heart leaped. And at the same time, a pulse beat between her legs, hard and insistent. Spurring her on. Giving her the confidence to know that this was exactly what she wanted. And there was no mistaking that.

You want him.

She did. She really did. The consequences of it be damned. The aftereffects be damned. If it left her burned up, then it did. At least she would be burned up by the passion between them, and not by the bitter ashes of regret.

He deposited her on the center of the mattress and stood back, wrenching his shirt up over his head.

Her jaw dropped. Literally dropped.

He was huge. Thickly muscled, his body the perfect specimen of masculinity. Hard, defined lines that showed deep cuts in his abs, his chest thick and deep, sprinkled with dark hair.

He was like a sensory overload. Beautiful and deadly to look at all at once.

"Don't look at me like that. Or it's going to finish before it starts."

She didn't really understand what that meant. "Oh," she said, nodding.

"Violet, do you know what I mean?"

"Yes," she said while simultaneously shaking her head.

"It means that if you keep looking at me like you want to eat me alive I'm going to end up coming a lot faster than either of us wants me to."

Her heart tripped over itself. "Oh. Well. Then you shouldn't be standing there looking like that. It's hardly my fault."

He laughed. Actually laughed. The deep, husky sound sending a devastating friction over her body. She felt like she'd been scrubbed raw with it.

"Sorry. I'll try to take it down a notch." But she had a feeling that he couldn't. She had a feeling there was no way. Because he was too much. All of him. Every piece.

And when his hands went to his belt buckle, her eyes went to the bulge just beneath. Yes. She had a feeling he was quite a bit too much.

"You're not listening."

"Neither are you." He undid the buckle on his jeans at the same time as he kicked off his boots. Dispensing with all of his clothes in the next thirty seconds and leaving her both slack-jawed and breathless. His body was breathtaking. His masculinity thick and intimidating, standing away from his body. He wanted her. He really did. There was no earthly way that he could be faking that.

"Your turn," he said, coming over to the bed, reaching around her back and undoing her bra. Her panties went next, stripped away quickly and discarded on the floor with the rest of their clothes. And for the first time in her life, she was naked with another human being. She waited for there to be nerves, but there weren't.

She remembered what else Clara had said.

To ask for what she wanted, because this was about her pleasure. There wasn't any room for embarrassment, not given that. And the thing was, if he was really only going to be here for two weeks, if this was really all she was going to get, why should she be repressed? Why should she give in to any flutter of nerves? Why should she give in to anything but her own desire? She should have exactly what she wanted and no less. She should have everything she needed. Absolutely everything. Emboldened by that, she got up on her knees, wrapped her arms around him and kissed him, allowing her bare breasts to press up against that gorgeous, impressive chest.

He groaned, deep and long into her mouth, and she made a similar sound in response. He felt so good. He was hot and rough and perfect, and he made her feel wicked. And free. Most of all, he made her feel free. There was no one here to tell her what to do. No one to tell her to stop. She was her own woman. And this was her own life. She had nothing to prove to anyone, nothing to earn, not here. Because Wolf was the object of her desire, and there was no potential for permanence, and yes, there was part of her that should feel sad about that, but most of her felt… Most of her felt liberated by that. Because this could be all about Violet. What she wanted. What she secretly wanted. Not about proving herself; not about earning anything… Just about her.

She arched her back forward, pressing herself even more brazenly to him. He gripped her ass, bringing the very heart of her up against his hardened arousal. She squirmed. Whimpering as need built inside her. She was wet. Absolutely slick with her need for him, and she felt hollow inside. Desperate to be filled by him. And it was going to hurt. She knew that. It couldn't not. He was… He was huge. But she wanted him enough that it didn't matter. She felt reckless with that want. And it felt good. Because if there was one thing Violet Donnelly never was—not anymore—it was reckless. And this wasn't rebellion. She had experienced rebellion. She had gone to a party to get drunk and fool around with a boy just to be rebellious. That was about other people. About showing them. About defying them. This was about her. Surprising herself, defying herself. Breaking the barriers that she herself had built up in her own soul. That was what this was about. It was bigger, deeper. More. It was essential to everything that she was. And it was wonderful.

His hands moved from where they were, dipping between her thighs, feeling her wetness, her readiness for him. She gasped as he pushed one finger inside her tight channel. It was unfamiliar, the invasion, but she knew she had to get used to it. And it didn't take long for her to find that she enjoyed it. That it felt good for him to do that. He lifted her up slightly off the mattress, gripping her thighs and wrapping them around him as he laid her back, opening her to him. Then he began to stroke her there, his thumb moving in a circle over her sensitized bundle of nerves, his fingers working at the entrance of her body, until he finally pushed one deeper inside her, then another, and she squirmed, wiggling against him, arching her back in a desperate bid for more.

And he delivered, working his fingers in and out of her in an expert rhythm as he continued to stroke her right where she was most desperate for him. She was panting, tension inside her building and building until she didn't think she could take it anymore. And then finally, it broke. And every thought in her mind went blessedly blank. As if it had vanished on some cloud of pleasure. Her internal muscles pulsed around his fingers, and when the storm passed, all she could think was that…

She hadn't had to ask.

He made sure she came first without her having to ask.

He leaned over her, kissing her as he continued to stroke her lazily. She jerked beneath his touch. She was so sensitized she could hardly stand it. And then suddenly, she was desperate for him. Any satisfaction she felt in the moment evaporating as need began to build inside her again. She pushed her way upward, running her hands all over his body, his chest, his abs. What if this was the only night they had? What if it was the only chance she had to explore him? She practically knocked him back onto the mattress, kissing him all over. His chest, his stomach, and then she paused, when she got down to his…

She did not know what she was doing. But suddenly… she completely agreed with Clara. It was not gross. Not at all. She wanted to do this. She wanted him. She just had to figure out how to approach it.

She decided with an experimental lick. From base to tip. He swore, sharp and hard, pinning his head back to the mattress, his hand going to the back of her head. And she figured she must have done something right. So she licked him again, then kissed him, and his hips bucked up off the bed. She changed the angle of her approach, taking him into her mouth. And suddenly it felt…at least a little bit intuitive. What to do. Because his responses were so clear. His need so obvious. And it fueled her. Aroused her. Made her ready for more.

"Stop," he said, his voice hoarse. "I can't… I can't take any more."

Then she found herself being lifted away from him, up toward the top of the mattress, and he brought his head down between her thighs, licking her like she was a dessert. He pinned her there, looping his arms over her legs and holding her down to his mouth. Pushing her until she climaxed again, until she had shattered utterly and completely.

And then he brought her down to the center of the bed, settling himself between her legs. He grabbed a packet she hadn't even seen him get, and tore it open, rolling the condom down over his length. And she couldn't be nervous. She was slick with need, and aching for more. Yes, she had peaked twice, which she would've said was impossible, but she hadn't had what she really wanted. Which was him. In her. As deep in her as he could be.

He positioned himself at the entrance of her body and thrust inside. In one swift stroke.

She gasped, a tearing sensation suffusing her with hot pain. She really hadn't expected it to be that bad. Yes, she'd known there'd be some level of pain, but she had thought that the degree of arousal she'd built up inside her would do something to cushion it.

If it had… Good Lord.

What would've happened with a less expert lover?

She was panting, panicking slightly.

"Hush," he said, holding her to him, shushing her like you would a horse. "It's all right. It's okay." He froze there, holding her against him. "You want me to stop?"

"No," she said. "Please don't stop."

After a moment, the pain began to fade. After a moment, she felt calmer. After a moment, she could feel her arousal starting to build again. Feel her desire becoming more apparent.

And as if he sensed that change in her, he began to move. Slow, steady strokes at first that took her breath away, and then the rhythm began to increase. Harder. Faster. And words began to tumble from her lips that she never said in her life. She urged him to go harder. Faster. More. She was out of her mind with it. He made her into something she didn't recognize. Something she didn't know she could be. And she liked it. She liked this Violet, who somehow knew innately what she wanted. Whose instincts were right, and not wrong. Who didn't have to police her behavior to make herself acceptable, because…here, it was good. Here, this very particular sort of bad was just right.

"Come for me," he whispered against her mouth. "One more time."

He moved his hand between their bodies, rubbing his thumb over her again, and she shattered. She arched against him, clinging to his shoulders, and then he thrust into her one last time, growling his own release as he pulsed deep inside her.

It only took a breath for him to withdraw, moving away from her. He went into the bathroom and closed the door behind him. She felt stunned. Completely rocked by what had just happened, and cold because he had moved away from her so fast.

She tried to catch her breath. Took a moment to orient herself to her surroundings.

She was no longer a virgin. So there was that.

She looked down at the sheets, and saw blood. And she cursed. Because she was the one that was going to have to clean that up.

Of course she was going to be one who bled. Because that just made it all the more…medieval.

He came out of the bathroom a moment later, the protection dealt with. "Why didn't you tell me?" She noticed then that he had a washcloth in his hand.

"Why didn't I tell you what?"

"You know full well." He came over to where she was on the bed, and much to her horror, pressed the warm washcloth between her thighs. When he pulled it back, it had some blood on it. He winced. "Are you okay?"

"Yeah," she said. "I'm fine."

"Dammit," he said. "You really should have told me. I would've been a lot more gentle with you. I knew you were inexperienced but…hell."

His words were scolding, but his movements were tender, and she blinked back tears as he soothed her.

"Have a lot of experience with this?"

"No. It's been a hell of a long time."

"How long?"

"Not since I was a virgin myself, thank you." There was something that passed over his face. Something regretful. Something sad. But it went away as soon as it appeared.

She wanted to ask about it. But he was gone again, back into the bathroom. He left the washcloth there.

"You know, I'm the one that has to do the laundry."

He shook his head. "I don't know what to say."

"Nothing. There's nothing for you to say. I knew. It's not like I'm surprised."

"Well…"

He couldn't seem to form any words. "Look, it's just that I knew I shouldn't. You're too young for me."

"Am I?"

"I'm thirty-two."

"Oh. That's not so bad."

"Isn't it?"

"I don't know."

He sat on the bed and looked at her for a moment, and then he pulled her into his arms, and underneath the covers. "You know, I don't *sleep* with women."

She grinned against his chest. "Is that your way of saying you're going to sleep with me?"

"Hell yes," he said.

She clung to him, and she felt ridiculously pleased with herself.

"Are you mad at me?"

"Yes, I'm mad at you," he said. "You really do need to warn a guy."

"Well, next time someone takes my virginity I'll make sure to let them know that's what he's doing."

"Very funny. I told you that you were a sweet girl. Not for the likes of me."

"Yeah. Well. I feel very sullied. So. I guess you were right."

"I'm only here for two weeks."

"I know," she said, feeling unspeakably sad. "You did say that already."

"I know. But I'm making sure you realize that. And that this doesn't change anything."

"I already told you. You were the one with the missing information. Not me. I made my decision."

"Well, as long as we're clear."

"Very clear. Don't worry. I'm not going to start romanticizing it." She turned and pressed her face against his bare chest, suddenly feeling…giddy. She had done it. She was lying there naked with a man. A beautiful man. The most beautiful that she had ever seen. And she didn't feel sullied. Not at all. She felt…happy.

She hadn't imagined that she would feel this after sex. Well, she hadn't really imagined what she would feel. She had a lot of strange hang-ups around it, and she knew that. But she also hadn't stopped to examine any of them at great length. It had never really felt like there was a reason to. And it turned out there wasn't. Because when it had been right, it had just been right. He was right.

It was only two weeks. Just two weeks.

"I do expect, though, that I will receive a thorough education over the next couple of weeks."

"Do you?" he asked, tightening his hold on her.

"Yes. Because if two weeks is all we get…"

"Two weeks is all I've got."

"Right. Well, I don't want to jump straight into a life of promiscuity. But the thing is I'm still desperately curious about all there is to offer."

"Don't knock a life of promiscuity until you've tried it," Wolf said. "I myself find it extremely medicinal."

She stared at him, at the hard cut of his jaw, the sensual set of his mouth. "I don't think it's for me."

"She says, having had sex once."

"Well, I don't. I went to Ace's tonight thinking that I might pick someone up. But I don't think I would have. Or, if I had, I think I would've regretted it."

"It's not about the number of partners you have," he

said. "The thing is there's no point sleeping with one person when you want another."

She lay flat on her back, looking up at the ceiling. "You were going to sleep with someone else, though. Even though you wanted me."

"Yeah. I was going to give it a try. But I have a lot of practice wanting what I can't have."

She wanted to ask. Because that same deeply sad look crossed his face that she had seen momentarily a few days ago, and she was curious what had put it there. But she didn't ask. She didn't say anything. She just lay there with him. Because that felt like the right thing to do. And her instinct hadn't failed her so far. She was sort of impressed with that. She hadn't thought she had an instinctual sensuality, but what had just occurred between her and Wolf made her think that she might.

She started to fall asleep, and she worried that maybe she wasn't supposed to. But he didn't tell her to leave. And she tried very hard, as she settled into that peaceful sleep, to tell herself that this was just the beginning of two weeks. And nothing more.

And that she was okay with it.

CHAPTER SEVEN

WOLF WAS DISTRACTED. Not that he needed to give his full concentration to expanding a fence line. He could fix the fence in his sleep.

But he should not have done what he did last night. Still, distracted though he was, he wasn't as regretful as he should be, either.

He had tried, for two seconds, to be a good person.

It hadn't worked out. And now all he was thinking of was the fact that he wanted to see her again. That he wanted to get her naked again.

This wasn't typical behavior for him. Two weeks was actually a damn long time for him to go conducting an affair. It wasn't in his repertoire, not generally.

What he liked was a good one-night stand. Nothing quite like it. It took no strings to a new level. And he certainly didn't like to share a bed with a woman all night. But he hadn't been able to send Violet down the hall back to her room. It was… Well, especially after the revelation of her virginity. Maybe that was it. It was a novelty for him.

At his age, and the kind of circles he ran in, there was just no expectation of finding a virgin. Not that he would've wanted to. He would've said that he had no particular interest in such things. But she was an eager and incredibly sexy student. And he couldn't deny that her saying she wanted to learn everything there was to learn over the next two weeks was a hell of an aphrodisiac.

He was only a man, after all.

"Here comes the meal train."

He looked out the direction that Connor was staring, and saw a truck coming up their way.

"Who's that?"

"Sadie," Eli said. He had joined them today. "She likes to bring lunch out when she can."

"Nice of her."

But he realized that in the passenger seat was someone he was a lot more interested in than his cousin's wife.

It was Violet. His body went hard, instantly, and the last thing he wanted to do was telegraph his reaction. He didn't need his cousins knowing that he had started messing with the sweet proprietor of their inn.

The truck stopped, and Sadie got out, her blond hair flying in the breeze. Then Violet got out of the passenger side, and his stomach went tense. Eli walked up and gave Sadie a kiss on the mouth, and he found that he wanted to do the same to Violet. A little display of possession.

Hell.

That wasn't his style.

She started talking about a life of promiscuity last night, and he had considered it his sovereign duty to pretend that he was absolutely fine with her pursuing other lovers if she wanted to. Because he wasn't going to stay. So obviously the woman couldn't be celibate forever with Wolf as her only sexual experience.

He also couldn't deny that the idea of that gave him a sort of deep, savage satisfaction.

Their eyes collided, and her cheeks went pink. If anybody was paying close attention to her—and in Wolf's mind she

was the center of the damn universe so how could they not—
they were going to see that there was something between
them. Though it seemed that Eli, Connor, Jack and Kate
didn't particularly notice what was happening between them.
However, he caught a sly look from Sadie. Who had driven
over with Violet, clearly, so that made him suspicious about
the content of the conversation that had occurred on the way.

Sadie went around to the back of the truck and grabbed
a large folding table and much to his surprise, set it out
right there in the grass. Then she and Violet began to un-
load dishes of food.

"What's this?" he asked.

"Well, I don't know how to do anything halfway," Sadie
said, smiling. "So if I'm going to bring lunch, I bring lunch."

She set out a glorious feast: bread and meat and cheese,
beer and all kinds of fancy spreads. He put every single
one on his sandwich. Along with all of the meat. "Delicious," he said.

Violet ducked her head. "I made the bread."

"Good," he said, barely able to keep the edge from his
voice.

"Violet is pretty amazing," Sadie said, her gaze a little
bit too incisive.

Kate took a bite of her sandwich and wrinkled her nose.
"My taste is off," she said. She pulled the cheese off, and
tried again. "Better. Man, I'm so hungry I could eat an entire horse." She turned and looked at said creature. "It's an
expression. Don't worry. But I never know what's going to
actually taste right and what's going to taste funny. I love
cheese." Her expression went mournful. "But at least I have
energy. I could do all the same work I've been doing. Not
like with Carson. I could barely get off the couch when I
was pregnant with her."

His cousin was an odd, forthright creature. But he had a feeling it was exactly how Elsie would handle a similar situation. She really did remind him of his sister. And he thought—not for the first time—that it was a shame they hadn't had the chance to be closer. Particularly for Elsie's sake. It would've done her good to have a slightly older cousin around, a strong woman who was so much like her. Who would probably make her feel like she was a little bit less of an odd bird than he knew Elsie sometimes felt.

"Sorry, Kate," Sadie said. "Did you need some kind of special cheese?"

"I don't think any cheese is going to work. This baby hates me. It's a very bad sign."

Jack grunted. "It's a bad sign for me."

"It probably is," Kate said cheerfully. "I can only imagine all the abuse I'll hurl your way in the next few months."

Jack grinned. "I'm the luckiest man in the world."

But Wolf had a feeling the guy meant it. That he really did feel like the luckiest man in the world, even sitting with a feral, hormonal wife.

It was such a strange thing. And something Wolf just couldn't access. There had been a time in his life when he'd dreamed about it. About breaking the cycle. About being one of the happy Garretts. Which was just such a rare thing that he… That he hadn't imagined it was possible, not really. Until he met Breanna.

He didn't want to think about her right now. Not here.

They finished up lunch, and the men helped pack away all the lunch gear. "We're pretty much done here," Eli said. "If you want to head off."

"I came to help," Wolf said.

"Yeah," Connor said. "But if you want to spend some time checking out town…"

He laughed. "I'm not really a checking-out-town kind of person."

"Suit yourself."

He turned to Violet, and in spite of himself, caught her arm. "Did you want to take a ride?"

Her eyes went wide. "A ride?"

"On my horse."

"I…"

He could feel his cousins looking at him. "You mentioned that you wanted to. Sometime. And that you hadn't had a chance."

"Right," Violet said. She seemed to suddenly catch hold of his drift.

"Well, then," Connor said, his gaze cool. "Enjoy that."

"See you for dinner?" Wolf said.

"Yeah," Connor agreed.

He set about to ignoring his cousins, and helped Violet get up on the horse. Then he threw his leg over the back, getting on behind her, fitting himself snugly behind her body. "You hanging on?" he whispered in her ear.

"Yes," she said.

"Then let's go."

They started riding up toward one of the trails he had noticed earlier, taking her deep into the woods.

"You know they know now," Violet said.

"They don't know anything."

"They *know*," Violet said.

"Well, I don't know what you and Sadie talked about on the way over, but she clearly knew."

"I didn't tell Sadie," she said.

"Well. She knew all the same. She was giving me a dead eye."

"Her dead eyes were not my fault."

He swept her hair over her shoulder and leaned in, kissing her neck.

She jumped. "We're riding a giant horse."

"I thought you grew up on a ranch."

"I did," she said.

"You're from Texas," he said. "Sometimes I can hear it in your voice. I like it."

"I don't like it," she said. "I've been trying to get rid of that drawl for the last six years."

"Why is that?"

"I decided that this was my home. I couldn't go back. I don't want to go back."

"Angry at your mother?"

"Not anymore."

"No?"

"No. There's no point. I was at first. I was thirteen and she left me when I needed her most. My poor dad had said... Well, all the girl things were up to him. And he was wonderful. But... She threw him in the deep end. I feel too sorry for him, and too grateful to him to waste a minute being upset about her."

"Liar."

"I'm not a liar," she said.

He didn't know why he was pushing this conversation. Except they were out here in the woods, and it would only be two weeks. And he... Well, he didn't talk to all that many people he didn't already know. He was doing a lot of that these past few days. With his cousins, and now with her. But...there was something fascinating about talking to a woman he'd slept with. He never did that. He'd gotten to know Violet a little bit first and it was... Well, it was producing a hell of an interesting dynamic. And if Wolf was one thing it was a glutton.

He'd found the best way to drown out unwanted echoes of emotion and memory was to cover them up. With layer on layer of everything that felt *good*.

He liked new physical experiences.

And there was something about this that seemed to be heightening the physical connection between them. He was all good with that.

"People leave," he said. "It's terrible forever. And look, you can decide that you shouldn't care. Doesn't mean you won't."

"You're still upset about your mother?"

"*Upset* isn't the right word. I'm angry." It was easy enough to talk about this. Because he was angry. It was true. It wasn't so much a nest of snakes and hurt as it was just rage. He was pretty comfortable with rage. He had a damned lot of it. At his mother. His father. At the universe. At God, if He was out there. "I already told you about the family curse."

"But you don't actually believe…"

"At Garrett's Watch, the women don't stay. My older brother, Sawyer, his mother left. Then mine. Then my sister, Elsie's. My grandmother left my grandfather. It was only when he got a mail-order bride that he got a woman to stick around. That's what my brother, Sawyer, did. His wife, Evelyn. And that's why he did it. He thought that was the only way to break the curse."

"What about you? Do you believe in a curse?"

"No. I just believe in selfish people doing selfish things. You see it all the time. You see it all around you. It's nothing more or less interesting than that."

"Selfish people doing selfish things," she repeated. "I don't know. The older I get the more I think…something must've been broken inside of my mother."

"Yeah?" he asked.

"I can't imagine leaving my child."

Her words sent a strange sharp spike through his chest. "I can't imagine having a child."

"Really?"

Once upon a time he'd thought maybe. But then he'd been reminded who he was. "I told you. Family, commitment, not really my thing."

"But your brother did it."

"My brother had a baby. And…like you, he couldn't imagine doing anything but stepping up."

"Well, good for him."

"Yep. Good for him. I've always thought so." Silence lapsed between them. "You shouldn't hate your accent, though."

"I shouldn't?"

"I like that drawl. Sounds like a slow lick to me, and I can imagine where I'd like that."

She shifted against him. "You can't get sexy with me on the back of a horse."

"Oh, honey, I can get sexy just about anywhere."

She went stiff for a moment, then pliant, and leaned back against him. "Well, I guess that does fall under the header of teaching me everything there is to know."

He moved his hands to her waist, then let them hitch up slightly, until his fingers were skimming the undersides of her breasts. "I think so."

She made a deep, satisfied noise. "Is this part of my lesson?"

"Hell yeah."

He started to kiss her neck again. "I'm supposed to be taking in the view," she said.

"Hell," he said. "I'm the tourist. But I think you're the only view I'm interested in."

She turned and looked at him, her eyes wide. And he realized his words did sound a little bit more serious than he'd intended. A little less like a fling, a little more like something else. And he rationalized it. Because back at home he'd been…unsettled. Things were different. And he was damn grateful for Evelyn. He was. His niece deserved a mother. Sawyer deserved to be happy, and if this was what made them happy, then more power to him. Wolf could be as cynical about things as possible, but he did believe in love. He believed in its power to change, transform and destroy things beyond reparation.

He would be the last person on earth to ever doubt that his brother was truly, deeply in love.

But believing in it and wanting it for himself were two different things. Also, knowing he didn't want it for himself, and being all right with being around it, were also two different things.

And he had a feeling that… The way that left him unsettled, to be around his brother, all settled and happy and having things that at one time Wolf had thought would be his… Well, it was messing with him. So a little affair at a time, something different. Something that may indulge that part of him that was living in the past in a way that was more bittersweet than usual…

Well, he was leaving. That was the thing. It was temporary, and it was only going to be temporary.

They rode on in silence, and he continued to stroke her body, keeping it light, not taking it too X-rated in the outdoors, not that he was opposed. He wasn't at all. But he didn't know his cousins' ranch well enough to know where all the boundaries were, and who he might run into. He knew exactly where he would take her at Four Corners. Exactly the place he could lay her down in the grass and…

He shook his head. She would never see Four Corners, so it didn't matter.

But when they finished the ride they went straight back to the bed-and-breakfast. And there were no guests around, so he dragged her right up to his room, stripped them both of their clothes and had her the way he'd been fantasizing about all day. They lay there spent and breathless, until she looked at the clock. "I need to... I need to put out cookies and coffee. And I have someone checking in." She rolled out of bed.

"You look like you've just been had," he said. "Thoroughly, I might add."

She scrambled over to the mirror, and began to smooth her hair. "Well, I need to look less...that."

"Who cares," he asked, leaning back and watching her as she collected her clothes. She had a damn fine ass.

"I care," she said. "I need to be taken seriously and not..."

"What makes you think being a woman who has a sexual relationship will keep you from being taken seriously?"

"The *everything* about the world?"

He shrugged. "Okay. But what is it you want? Why is it important to be taken seriously?"

She stopped. "I don't know. I... I have to do something. So I should be good at it."

"I didn't realize that innkeepers were required to be chaste."

"I just don't want... I don't want anyone to say anything bad about me. I don't want... I don't want to cause trouble."

An odd expression crossed her face, and she finished dressing and ducked out of the room. His impulse was to go after her, but they didn't have that kind of relationship, and they weren't going to. It was easy to feel like...

He had a nice afternoon with her. But it didn't need to be more than that.

Hell, it couldn't be more than that.

TIME WAS MOVING by too quickly. Violet hated it. She was trying to will the days to move slower, but even as she did that, she knew that it was… Well, it was a mistake. Time needed to pass, and she needed to… She needed to be okay with it. Because on the other side of this two weeks was a future without Wolf.

Wolf, who filled up her days, and her nights.

Wolf, who was every thought in her head. She actually burned a batch of cookies, which she hadn't done since she was seventeen years old. But she was thinking about him constantly. Even while she was talking to her stepmother, her dad, everybody, she had a running montage of him in her head.

She was being deliberately distant from her family, and she knew she was beginning to mystify and irritate them. Only Clara knew.

And Clara gave her a warning glance every time she got a faraway look in her eye. "Just be careful."

She lost track of the amount of times Clara had said that to her.

Which was ridiculous, because Clara was the one who had told her to indulge. Clara was the one who had told her she deserved this.

But she also understood why Clara was getting concerned about her.

Violet was getting concerned about herself. Because it was beginning to become something of a giddy obsession, and while it seemed fair enough on the one hand…it was also potentially ruinous. She knew that. She did. Except being with him was so much better than…thinking about being without him. And glorying in what they had… Well.

He was an accomplished teacher, she would give him that. Except, she couldn't really think of it as lessons. Because when she was with him…she just got lost in him. It was like shattering every time he took her to the point of release. Like being broken apart and put back together again. But slightly different each time. As if each and every time she came apart in his arms she was then remade, a slightly different version of herself. And each and every time she felt like pieces of him seemed to fill the cracks. And that was perhaps the biggest concern of all. But… What was to be done? She was in too deep already. He was staying at the bed-and-breakfast; there was no question of cutting off their affair while he was within arm's length.

She was committed. Committed to the heartbreak. And she could see it coming. Like a truck barreling down on her and her lying on the straightaway. She could see it coming, but there was no way to stop. She had no brakes. And if she swerved she would just hit a tree. Pain now, pain later. It was all pain. So she was seeing it through to the end.

Even though it made her melancholy.

The last thing she expected that day was for him to come in right when she was closing the bakery. But he did. Big and broad and standing in that space, and making her heart beat just like the first time she'd seen him. Except now…there was this intensity between them. This deep connection. Except now…she felt like she knew him in ways she didn't know another person, after only knowing him a week and a half.

"What are you doing here?"

"I thought we could take a walk."

He helped her close up the bakery, and when they left,

her hand slipped effortlessly into his. And her heart jumped into her throat. They walked down to the beach, and she took his hand, lacing her fingers through his and letting him take her down to the edge of the water. She leaped back as a wave encroached, and then sat down, the damp sand soaking through her jeans. She shivered. But took her shoes off, anyway, rolling her jeans up. "Come on," she said.

"It's fucking cold," he said.

"I know," she said.

But he still didn't take his shoes off, and didn't join her splashing in the water. So she shoved him. Right to the edge of the waves, and one of them went directly inside his cowboy boot.

"Woman," he said, his voice a warning, "you're asking for trouble."

"Maybe I am." She remembered thinking he was trouble. When he walked into that bed-and-breakfast. The kind of trouble that missed her. But here she was, right in the middle of all that trouble. Bathing in it.

So she grabbed hold of his broad shoulders and used all her weight to pull him forward, and the two of them fell, right into the shallow surf, the soft sand giving way around them.

She screamed, because it was freezing.

And she found herself being picked up, held in his strong arms, but then unceremoniously laid back down into the water and dunked.

He laughed, and she looked up at him, breathless, giddy. Because Wolf was playing with her. And she was playing with him, like they were kids. Like they'd never been abandoned. Like they weren't going to be separated from each other in a couple of days.

She chose not to think about it. She chose not to think

about anything but how wonderful it felt to be cradled in his strong arms. Against the heat of his body, even while the water was frigid around them.

He lifted her up, held her against his body, and she started to shake. And ridiculously, wanted to cry when even a moment ago she'd been laughing.

"It's too cold," he said, scolding.

"Yeah, but it's the ocean. It's always cold."

"Your pretty little ass is going to get hypothermia," he said.

"I will not. Because we're going to go straight home and get in bed, right?"

"Don't you have guests?"

"There's no one in the house today. They checked out this morning. And no one's checking in tonight."

"Well," he said, his voice a growl.

They went home then, stripping as they went through the door, locking it behind them. They got into a hot shower, and made love with an intensity that nearly left her destroyed. Then they ate dinner together, on the floor of the living room, both of them in robes. Then they made love again by the fire. By the end of the evening, there wasn't a room in the house they hadn't christened.

And she knew that forever, always, she would walk in here and it would be him. His words from a few days ago came back to haunt her.

It's a stupid idea to be with someone when you want someone else.

A life of promiscuity was always going to be out of her reach in that case. Because she was never going to want anyone else. Nobody but him. Nobody but Wolf Garrett. And then what? Because he didn't want anything to do with permanent. He didn't want anything to do with… With her. Not after the end of this two weeks.

She pushed that thought aside, gritty as they climbed into bed together. And she slept.

And over the next three days, she barely saw him. They were together at night, but that was it. No more visits to the bakery; no more rides on his horse.

He was separating from her. Except for those desperate couplings all through the night. When they were somewhere between asleep and awake; somewhere between sane and crazy.

And on the last day he got up, that bag he'd had on when he arrived slung over his shoulder.

"I'm going to go out and work, and then I'll be leaving straight from there."

"You don't have to go," she said, her throat thick.

She had sworn she wouldn't do this. And the look in his eyes accused her of that very thing. Of going back on her word. Because she'd said she understood, but now that he was leaving she felt like she didn't understand at all. She felt like she didn't understand anything. Like the world was suddenly upside down.

Like everything was wrong.

Including her.

Because Wolf had made her into somebody different. It wasn't about becoming a woman; it was just that every time he touched her...

She found some new dimension of herself. And now he was just leaving. And she didn't know who this new Violet was apart from him.

And she was suddenly terrified, because she wasn't even sure that she wanted to know.

"I do need to go, though. I have a life. I have a ranch. It's been great to be here, great to visit family, but it's time for me to go."

"You are a grown-ass man, though," she said, tears spilling out of her eyes. "So you could stay. If you wanted to."

His face turned to stone, and she knew she was doing the very worst thing. She was crying. She was breaking apart, but she didn't have the shield of pleasure as an excuse. This was just her being broken apart, bit by excruciating bit. Not by desire, not by the touch of his hands.

By his words. By the horrible, flat look in his eyes.

By her own breaking heart.

"I wish you would stay."

"I can't. It was a bad idea, Violet, and I'm sorry. But I told you… I told you. If I had known you were a virgin I would never have taken you to bed."

"You didn't have any trouble taking me to bed about a hundred times since then. Which is pretty damn impressive for fourteen days."

"It wasn't a hundred. Either way… Look, I never said I wasn't a bastard."

"No. You actually told me with your words that you were. But everything that you did… Everything that you did says that's a lie. I choose to believe what you did."

"You shouldn't have. You just… You just thought it was good sex. And good sex makes you a little muddled. You'll get over it. Start on that career of promiscuity." And then he winked. Like it was… Like it was a joke.

"You're honestly okay with that? You're okay with me going off and sleeping with someone else?"

"You're not mine, Violet. Do what you want."

And then he turned, putting his black cowboy hat on his head and walking out the door.

And Violet felt like he'd taken something of hers that she would never be able to get back.

CHAPTER EIGHT

It HAD BEEN a month since Wolf had left. Violet still wasn't smiling. Not ever. She was also struggling to get any of her work done. Struggling to function at all. She felt like such an idiot. She was a bad stereotype of everything virgins were in these situations. She was pathetic. She was pathetic and she was… She was depressed. She was more than depressed.

She couldn't even smile over Thanksgiving dinner.

"Violet," Clara said. "We really are going to have to talk about this."

"There's nothing to talk about."

"He's been gone a month."

"I know," she said, looking around the room at her family. Her uncle Liam and his wife, Sabrina, her uncle Alex, Clara's husband, her uncle Finn and his wife, Lane. Plus everybody's assorted children, including her two little half brothers, who were currently sword fighting with turkey legs.

There were so many kids at this point it was difficult to keep track.

And there was Violet, sort of the odd one out. More peer almost to her uncles and aunts, than her own half siblings or her cousins.

But they still saw her as a kid; all except Clara. A kid who wasn't really a kid. Not like the little ones running around all over the place.

"Bo," her dad said, walking over and pulling her into a hug. "I've barely seen you the last few weeks." She looked up at her dad and tried to smile. "Are you honestly grimacing at me over the nickname?"

"No," she said. In the grand tradition of nicknames, her own had very little to do with her actual name.

He had once called her Violet Beauregarde the Blueberry, a nod to Willy Wonka. Over the years it had been shortened to Bo. And it had never fully gone away.

"Then to what do I owe the scowl?"

"She's full of scowling," Alex said, walking over to them. "I think she's working too hard."

"*She's* standing right here," Violet said. "And she is twenty-two, and not a baby. And fully capable of managing her own schedule."

"But anybody that can frown that hard over a cheese platter—especially cheese from her own family—is not in the best frame of mind."

She rolled her eyes, doing her best impersonation of herself at seventeen, and grabbed a stack of different cheeses. Her family owned the biggest dairy in the area, and they had gourmet cheese, among other things. And truly, it was usually one of her life's great delights. She took a bite of one of the cheeses, and her throat pushed back on it. She spit it out on her plate without thinking.

"That's gross," she said.

"It's smoked cheddar," Alex said. He grabbed a piece off the tray. "It's good." He shoved it into his mouth as if she required a demonstration.

"Well, thanks, Alex," she said. "I think it's nasty."

Something tickled at the back of her brain, and she chose to push it to the side. But then she caught Clara staring at her, and she couldn't quite banish the thought.

Of Kate Monaghan picking cheese out of her sandwich.

"What?" she asked Clara, as horror made her stomach hollow out.

"Why does the cheese taste bad, Violet?"

"I just don't want cheese," she said, because it wasn't possible. There was no way. There was absolutely no way. Because they had… But not all that careful sometimes. Especially that night… That night in every room. The shower… It had been intermittent. And she hadn't been willing to admit it to herself. That they'd made some very serious condom mistakes sometimes.

And she also had been ignoring her period. Or lack of it. But she felt terrible the entire time, and so she put it down to hormones being impacted by emotions. But…

"I'm not," she said.

"You're sure that you're not?"

"I'm not bleeding right this second if that's what you mean."

"Have you at all? Since he left?"

"I… I've been under a lot of stress."

"Yeah, do you know what kind of stress makes you not bleed after you engage in a torrid physical affair?"

"Clara…"

"That would be a baby."

"Please don't," Violet whispered. "I can't handle this right now."

Not in the living room with the whole rest of her family. Just not.

"You have to take a test," Clara whispered, fierce now.

"Not now," she said.

And all the denial that she'd been holding back over the past few days started to knock at the door.

"Then when?" Clara asked.

"Give me a few days. Maybe I'll start my period."

"I think we both know you're not going to."

"Maybe I will."

"Oh, Violet," Clara said. "I'll do whatever you need me to do. I'll support you…"

"Then you can support me by not talking about it. And getting me mashed potatoes, because the cheese is going to make me throw up."

Clara scampered off and returned with a plate full of mashed potatoes, and she ended up having a Thanksgiving that looked a lot like Clara's.

Beige.

And when she drove past the grocery store that night, and saw that it was open, she considered stopping and getting a pregnancy test, but she just couldn't bring herself to do it. So she went back home, and went to sleep instead.

The next day, she drove to the store and sat in the parking lot with her hands gripping the steering wheel for a full twenty minutes before she went back home, empty-handed and completely gutless. Two days later, she fell asleep on the couch in the middle of the living room, and nearly missed guests at check-in. Sadie ended up waking her up, coming in like a tornado, and Violet had never been so embarrassed. Not only had she been napping in the middle of the day, she had also shirked her duties, and she could only apologize to Sadie profusely, who had been almost weirdly sympathetic.

"Can I get you something to eat?" Sadie asked.

"No," she said. "I don't feel very well."

"Honey," Sadie said. "If you're sick, just let me know. I can always take a few days over here."

"No," Violet said. "It's not that. It's not… I'm fine. I didn't realize…"

When Sadie came by the next morning Violet was dragging around, and had to run out of the kitchen into the bathroom. When she returned, Sadie was staring at her.

"Violet… Is there something you want to talk to me about?"

Violet smiled, and shook her head. "No. I just…can't shake this stomach bug."

"I see," Sadie said.

Violet went back to the grocery store. But she went home without going inside again.

WOLF WAS IN a foul mood, and he had been for the past month. And it was not going unnoticed by his siblings, or by Hunter McCloud, who was making a nuisance of himself by hanging out, as always.

"Shut up," Wolf said as Hunter commented yet again on what an asshole Wolf was. "You're not exactly a prize turkey yourself, McCloud."

"Yeah, but at least I'm charming. You're a straight up dick."

Yeah, well. He knew that was true. He'd been…well, shit, he'd been having feelings. He didn't like it. He felt like some little betadouche asshole.

Feelings might be too strong of a word.

He missed Violet's body.

He was pissed with himself for having told her to go off and screw another guy.

He was enraged he'd made her cry.

He couldn't do anything about any of it, and he hated that.

"Just settling back into being in your charming presence every day. Maybe I preferred the other ranch," he bit out.

"If you did…maybe you should go back for a while,"

Sawyer said, unbothered as he usually was these days, which was just annoying.

Wolf missed *Violet*. Not just her body. That was the problem. The undeniable, unacceptable problem. She was supposed to just be a fling. He was an expert at flings. So damn good at them that it was never a concern. Never an issue. And yet, he couldn't stop thinking about her. Couldn't stop dreaming about her. He had gone over to the bar and tried to find himself a hookup; he didn't want to do that. His own damned words haunted him. That it was a dumbass thing to do to sleep with somebody when you wanted someone else.

Well, what he wanted, always and forever, was Breanna. He couldn't have her. So… So there. Except, he could hardly picture her, because all he could see was Violet. And that just pissed him off.

Suddenly, he heard the sound of pounding horse hooves, and he looked over to see Elsie, flying across the field with dirt clumps going up behind her horse's hooves. By the time she got to them, she was breathless. "Wolf Garrett," she said, her voice coming out like an epithet.

"Yes?"

"I just got off the phone with Sadie."

"Yeah?"

"She said that the girl at the bed-and-breakfast you stayed at is knocked up." There was no missing the outright accusation in his sister's tone.

A chill went down his spine. "What?"

"She called looking for you, because she said that the girl who works at the bed-and-breakfast is *pregnant*." Elsie's cheeks were bright pink, her eyes glittering with outrage.

Everything in Wolf went still. "What exactly did she say? And why did she tell you?"

"Oh, she's fit to be tied. She said that Eli had to stop her

from coming down here and castrating you. Because she's
sure it's you." Beneath Elsie's rage, he could see fear. Like
she didn't want to believe it. And his stomach went sour.

"*Why* did Sadie call?" he asked.

"She said she went over to the bed-and-breakfast this
morning, and…the girl, Violet, was sick. And she won't
admit it. But Sadie thinks she's pregnant."

"So Violet didn't say she was pregnant?"

"It was you, wasn't it?"

He could feel Hunter and Sawyer staring at him. He
looked over at Sawyer. "Shut your fucking mouth," he said.
"You don't have any right to make a comment to me."

"I didn't say a damn thing," Sawyer said, raising his hands.

"I will," Elsie said. "Sadie said she's twenty-two."

"I…"

"Is it yours?" Hunter asked. "I mean, did you sleep with
her, Wolf?"

He looked at the round of judgmental glances he was
getting. "Yes," he said. The world was spinning now, and
he couldn't quite find the right of it. "But she should have
called me. She would've called me."

"Did you leave her your number?" Hunter asked.

"*They* have it," he said.

"So you went and stayed with our cousins," Sawyer said,
"who put you up in the bed-and-breakfast, and you went
and got one of their friends pregnant."

"She's not really their friend. She works for them. And
she… I don't have to justify myself to you," he said to Sawyer. "You knocked up some girl that you slept with at a bar,
and had to find a wife to help raise your daughter, because
you didn't even know the girl well enough to make a relationship with her."

"You have to go back," Elsie said.

Everything in him denied it. Just for a moment. Because he couldn't imagine…

She couldn't be pregnant. It wasn't true. That was what he landed on. That was what he decided.

"Sadie's wrong," he said.

"So there's no way she could've gotten pregnant?" Hunter asked, his gaze direct.

"These things can always happen," Wolf said, his tone flat. "But it's unlikely." And even as he said that, he was damn sure it was a lie. Because he'd done his best to have amnesia about some of the things that they'd gotten up to… But…the fact remained, he hadn't been as responsible as he was with… Well, anyone else.

You were careless with her. You were careless with Violet Donnelly, even though you knew that you had to be extra careful with her. She was young, she was a virgin and you the hell know better.

"I'll go. I'll go and I'll talk to her." He wasn't going to call. He wasn't going to call and say that Sadie Garrett had called him in a fit of pique and told his sister on them. No, he sure as hell wasn't going to say that.

"You better get your ass out of here right now," Sawyer said.

He looked at Elsie, who was giving him a stubborn look. "Men are disgusting," she said.

"You can be mad at me all you want, Elsie, but she was there, and she wasn't mad about it."

But he was currently furious with himself.

And he turned his horse right around and galloped back to the house. And before he could even think about what he was going to do next, he was in his truck driving toward Copper Ridge.

CHAPTER NINE

SHE HAD FINALLY done it. She had finally gone into the store. And now she was slinking into the back entrance of the bed-and-breakfast, hoping to get a little bit of time to herself to actually commit to taking the test, which would tell her something she already knew at this point. She was more than just a little bit late. And on top of that, she had taken to throwing up every morning.

She was still in denial, though, and actually taking the test would badly damage that denial. So… So…

She paused in the kitchen, looking around and slowly setting her fabric bag down on the counter. She began to get the items out.

A can of soup.

She didn't want a can of soup.

Maxi pads, just to keep people on their toes. A meat log, which she had bought because it was at a display by the counter. A bag of Hershey's Kisses, which she had bought for the same reason. The pregnancy test. The only thing she had actually gone into the store for. And she had looked around furtively the entire time she had used the self-checkout.

Normally, she didn't like a self-checkout. She liked having a casual conversation with the person working the register. She didn't like having to scan her own items. But she was being shifty, and she was hiding things, so self-checkout really suited her.

She let out a long, slow breath. And then she heard the front door to the bed-and-breakfast open and close.

She wasn't expecting anybody. She took a breath, trying to deal with a new wave of nausea that swept over her. At this hour it wouldn't result in vomiting. It was just that she felt horrible. Most of the time.

Ridiculously, her eyes started to water, tears threatening to fall. She didn't have time for them. She didn't have time for tears; she didn't have time for…anything, really. Not anything but just dealing with this.

And now someone was here. So she had to.

She took a deep breath and plastered a smile on her face, walking out toward the entryway.

Where she froze.

Because there he was. Black cowboy hat, black T-shirt. Looking every inch the trouble that she'd known he'd be from the first moment she'd seen him.

She started to look around for something to throw at him.

"Is it true?" he asked.

"Is *what* true?" She couldn't actually figure out what the hell he was talking about.

"Are you pregnant?"

She felt like she was the one who'd had something thrown at her. And that it had hit its mark true. She just stood there, gaping at him. How could he be here for that? She hadn't told anyone. Yes, Clara suspected but Clara wouldn't say anything to anyone, and she didn't even know how to get in touch with him.

Had someone seen her buy the test? How would they know to call him? And how would he get there so fast? "I don't know," she said.

"How do you not know?"

"I didn't… How do you know?"

"Sadie called my sister," he said.

She shook her head. "I didn't talk to Sadie."

"I know. She said you weren't acting right."

And Violet Donnelly, who did not put a foot out of line, who did not cause trouble, who did not make waves, let out a howl of rage that vibrated her entire body.

"She had no right to do that. She had no right to call your sister. You shouldn't be here. I am dealing with some things. You left. You left and you have nothing to do with any of this."

"Did you go out and get laid the night after I left?" he asked, his voice hard. "Because if not, then I have everything to do with this."

"You don't want a baby," she said, her throat suddenly going painfully tight, to the point where she felt she had a crimp in it, one that ached and burned.

"That was different. You can't use a theoretical conversation against me."

"I can do whatever the hell I want, Wolf Garrett. I asked you to stay. You didn't stay. You didn't want anything to do with me. You didn't want any part of this. You just took right off. And you know what? I don't need to accept you back. I asked you to stay, but it was not an open invitation. The offer is rescinded. Get your ass out of my bed-and-breakfast."

"Last I checked, it was a bed-and-breakfast. Therefore, not a private residence."

She crossed her arms. "But it is a private business. And I happen to know the town sheriff. And I will have him arrest you for trespassing."

"He's my cousin," Wolf said.

"And believe me, he will side with me."

That successfully made Wolf shrink back slightly, and she figured, she was probably right, and he probably knew it.

"What do you mean you don't know if you're pregnant?"

"I bought a test. I haven't taken it."

"Take it," he said.

"No," she said. "I will take it when I'm good and ready. You don't get to decide when that is. You don't get to stomp in here and make demands."

She was ready to take the test. But she wasn't going to do it just because he said. And he was here... He was here and she wasn't sure that she wanted him to know. She didn't think she wanted him involved. He didn't have any right to be involved. He had said he didn't want children. Unequivocally. Didn't want a wife, didn't want kids. He had rejected her. Coming back just because she was pregnant...

"Look," she said, "you can't do a trial run with kids. We both know that. If you don't want kids, you shouldn't be standing here. Not even for a minute. I know what it feels like to be abandoned by a parent. And I will never do that. I never will."

As she said those words she felt them resonate deep inside her soul. And she knew it was true. She hadn't really thought about it. Hadn't thought about what she wanted, hadn't thought that far ahead. But she knew it, as soon as she spoke those words. Knew that she was going to be here for this child. If she was really pregnant... Well, it was a nonnegotiable thing.

She was going to be the best mother. She was going to be there for this baby.

Suddenly, she wanted to weep. Because this was her

chance. This was her chance to be everything her mother could've been and wasn't.

And she really didn't want to be having that epiphany standing there in front of him. Because he didn't get to have any more of her emotions. She had already broken down and wept. Begged him to stay. Begged him for no other reason than that she… Well, she wanted to see where this thing between them could go. Because she cared. Because she…

Well, she had thought that she felt something that clearly didn't exist between them. She had been an idiot virgin. Fine. But she wasn't now. This whole hard five weeks with him gone had taught her a lot. A hell of a lot.

She wasn't the same girl she'd been when he left her. And that was his own damned fault.

"I don't intend to do a trial run of anything," he said. "Take the test."

"It's my body," she said. "If I don't want to take a test right now, I don't have to."

"I don't know what gave you the idea that I was enlightened or some shit, but I'm not. And I want to know the answer. While I'm standing here."

She growled in a fury. "I'm going to do it! But only because I want to know." She turned on her heel and walked into the kitchen to get the test. Because honestly, locking herself in the bathroom for a few minutes was infinitely better than standing there looking at him.

She grabbed the test off the counter and went upstairs. She didn't care if he didn't realize what bathroom she was going to use. He didn't need to follow her.

She locked the door behind her for good measure, then opened up the box with shaking fingers. She'd never taken one of these before. Obviously.

And for a minute, she felt dizzy. For a minute, she felt completely overwhelmed.

How was she going to tell her dad?

He wouldn't be angry. That wasn't how he was. He would get that look on his face, kind of resigned, when he realized that he had lost a battle. It wasn't very often, but there were things in the world that you couldn't control, and Cain Donnelly was a pragmatist.

Alison would be supportive. So supportive. And it made her feel like her chest was going to break open. Because they would be good to her. And she would always wonder just how disappointed they were. That she had done one big irresponsible thing and she had gotten herself in trouble.

You're not in trouble. It is not 1950 and you are not fifteen.

No. She was twenty-two. She was a twenty-two-year-old woman who was only just now figuring out what she wanted from her life. That was the honest truth. The stark truth. And the things that Clara had said to her suddenly came home to roost. Maybe she was stagnant. Maybe she was stuck in a little bit of a time warp because half of her goal was to make sure that she was still wherever her family wanted her. Pleasing them. Doing what they wanted.

Making up for the fact that her dad had… That he'd had it hard raising her by himself. That he'd been stuck in a marriage that wasn't any good in the first place because he was trying to be a good father. And that Alison had chosen to be there for her. That Alison had chosen to be the kind of mother her own had never been.

"The test isn't going to take itself," she muttered. She managed—with much struggle—to tear the test open. And after reading the instructions four times, she was able to complete the task.

While she waited, she listened. Then she heard heavy footsteps outside the door. Pacing the hall. Back and forth.

"Knock it off," she shouted.

"Did you get the answer yet?"

"No," she said. "And listening to you pace isn't helping me relax."

"This may shock you, but I don't really care about your relaxation."

"Well, it may shock you, but I don't care about your nerves."

"I'm not nervous," he said.

"You're nervous," she said.

"I'm not," he said.

"Are, too," she shot back.

"Are you having a baby or *are you a baby*?"

"Fuck off," she said. And she had never said that to another person in her life.

She walked back over to the test and stared at it. There was a faint pink line beginning to darken. She looked away quickly, unwilling to see if there was a second one trying to appear.

"I will not have a kid out in the world and not be involved," he said.

"Weird," she said. "Because you seemed pretty much in the opposite camp when last we spoke of this topic."

"No," he said. "I said I didn't want to have kids. That's different than…one being inevitable."

"Did I say I wanted it?" she shouted.

"You do," he said.

And she hated that he knew that. Hated that somehow, even though he had managed to blindside her in spite of having told her exactly who he was from the very beginning, she didn't surprise him at all.

She looked back over at the test, and it was unambiguous. There were two glaring pink lines. Pregnant. Absolutely pregnant.

She let out a long breath, and a tear slid down her cheek. She wiped it away and threw the test in the trash. Then she walked out of the bathroom. "Yeah, congratulations," she said, pushing past him, out of the bathroom, into the hall.

"You're pregnant?"

"Yes," she said.

He walked into the bathroom, where she heard him moving around for a minute, and then he came out holding the test.

"Don't pick that up," she said, grimacing in horror.

"I wanted to see it." He stared down at it, his face grim and forbidding as the side of a cliff.

She ripped the test out of his hand and walked back into the bathroom, throwing it away again. Then she came back out.

"So," she said. "That's that."

"I'm not going to ask how it happened. I know how it happened." His dark eyes collided with hers. "I'm sorry," he said.

"You're *sorry*?"

"I'm the one with experience. And I don't… I use condoms. I swear to you. Every time. But I didn't with you. I just… I wasn't thinking. That's it. Plain and simple. And I owed you more thought than that. I owed you better than this."

Of all the things she had expected, it wasn't that. And actually, it infuriated her.

"You owed me better than a lot of things," she said. "Protection being the least of it. Honestly…you apologizing for… For the presence of our child… I… I don't want you involved, Wolf. I think that you should do the right thing. I think that you should walk away and let me deal with this. Because you don't want it. You want to…go on with your life. That's what you want. I know it, because I asked you to do something different and you wouldn't. You didn't want to be with me. You didn't want to stay here. You didn't want to try something new. So… So don't. Go back and forget that this happened."

"Right. Forget that it happened and…have my family come chase me down and string me up the nearest tree?"

"Look, I can't speak for what your family's going to do to you, but at the end of the day, it's no more their problem than it is yours. This is… I don't want you involved."

"Too damned bad."

He looked at her, and she saw… Well, she saw a lot of bitterness ahead. A lot of ugliness. She didn't like it, but she didn't see another way around it. Because he was… He was going to be exactly who he'd said that he was. And he might be filled with adrenaline right now; he might be filled with…even good intentions.

Except, last time he told you. He told you unambiguously exactly who he was and what he was going to do. He told you. He didn't pretend. Why would he pretend now?

She shoved that voice off. Because she was angry, and she wanted to be angry. And she wanted Wolf to be an enemy; she didn't want to make him into anything else. She wasn't in the mood. She didn't want to be giving. She wanted to be furious. He had broken her heart, and he had changed her life in ways that she hadn't asked for.

"I don't put my mind to something and then not see it through," he said. "You'll find I don't put my mind to a lot of things. I don't commit to a lot of things. Hell, I don't commit to a damn thing. But you know what I'm not? I am not a deadbeat. And I will be damned if a kid of mine is raised without knowing me. Grows up knowing that I'm out there somewhere in the world and I didn't give a shit about them. No. I won't do that. Because I lived that. And I'm still pissed off about it to this day. You know it. You're no different. You honestly want that for your kid? You want them to know that I walked away? Even if it was because you asked me to? How would you like that? How do you like it? Knowing that one of the people who made you didn't have the wherewithal to commit? Hell. You and I both know that doesn't lead anywhere good."

"Right. It doesn't lead anywhere good, so… I guess, as a result you and I aren't that good. How are we going to… functionally raise a child? And don't you think the end result is just going to be what we both experienced? A broken home?"

"Seems to me there's nothing to avoiding a broken home other than…not breaking it. Seems to me it's a choice."

"Yeah. But…you're a human being, so surely you know how that works. It's like going on a diet. It seems really easy until this plate of cookies is in front of you. Salad is fine when it's theoretical. Sugar is what you pick if you have the choice. It seems simple, then you have to do it. You don't know how to commit to anyone, and I…"

"But you know there's nothing else for it. We have to get married."

"I just… I'm sorry, what?"

"We have to get married," he said. "And you know there's no other choice. I can't have a woman out there pregnant with my child. I can't have a child and not marry its mother. I wouldn't be able to set foot back on Four Corners property. And you… You think your dad and your stepmother would just be fine with you…having a baby with no father in the picture?"

"This isn't about other people," she insisted.

"The hell it's not. What in your life doesn't have anything to do with other people? Other people are all tangled the hell up in mine. As much as I like to consider myself a man who does what he wants, I understand what commitment is. I understand what responsibilities are. I work a family ranch that is dependent on every single person to get all the work done that needs doing. I'm dependent on them. They're dependent on me. That's how it is. It's the way of it. Four Corners is basically a town in and of itself. And my father… My father didn't take care of his kids. Yeah, it was our mothers who left, but it had to do with how he treated them. It had to do with what he wouldn't do. And you know what he never did? He never offered marriage. My mother wasn't having any of that. She left. She left because he wasn't holding her there."

"That doesn't make any sense," she said, her throat going tight. "You don't want me. You don't want to stay with me. You made your choice already and you…"

"I made my choice based on a different situation than the one we're in now."

"You don't want to get married because of me."

"No. I'm also man enough to know that when things change, you gotta change with them. You grew up on a ranch, Violet. You can make all the plans you want, but when the weather turns, you've got to go with that. You can't argue with the earth. You can't argue with nature. And neither can we. This is real. It's happening. So we're happening."

When he looked at her, his eyes were like fire. "You need me to speak with your father?"

"You're not done speaking with me," she said.

"I am. It's done. We both know it."

Her heart fluttered. "No. I don't want to talk to my dad.

I'd… I'll tell you what. I will… Let's… I'm in my first trimester. And that's… It's kind of the danger zone. I don't see the point of us getting married if…" Her head was spinning. The problem was… The problem was he wasn't really wrong. They were both part of incredibly small communities, and even though he had never been a significant factor in Copper Ridge, he was related to people who were. Their lives were strangely, inadvertently tangled around each other.

"What if we wait? What if we wait a few months? I just… Oh, my family. What are they going to say? I just… I can't. And I'm sick and I can't handle all of this. I just can't."

"Come to Four Corners."

"What?"

"Come to Four Corners with me. For a bit. See the place. Because I will tell you, I can't leave."

"You can't… You can't leave Four Corners?"

"No. Garrett's Watch is part of my family legacy, and I have to carry it on. It's what I have for my child. For our child. I was working it, all this time just for the legacy. But now there's actually a reason. And I want… I want the kid there."

"But Copper Ridge is *my* home," she said on the verge of tears now. "It's where I… It's a place where I found myself. It's the most important place to me. I…"

"Violet," he said. "This is important to me. I spent time with you here. Come back and see Four Corners. Meet my family. Hell, they already know about you. Does your family know about me?"

"My aunt does. My… It's complicated. My aunt is basically my age. She's my best friend."

"Right," he said. "Well, tell her not to tell anyone else. Give yourself some time."

"I would like some time," she said. "I don't really know

how to explain that I'm leaving right around the holidays. I can't leave," she said. "I have this job."

"We'll talk to Sadie."

"I can't… Wolf, I can't just walk away from my life."

"We have to figure out how to deal with each other. We have to figure out how to build a life together. And exactly what that's going to look like."

Well, she was fairly terrible at her job right now, anyway. She was falling asleep everywhere; she didn't feel very well… The idea of going off to his ranch and…well, lying low for a while appealed.

Except…

Did you forget that you're angry at him?

She looked at this man. The object of her first heartbreak. Her first sexual experience. The biggest, most frightening change she had ever endured.

This wasn't a small thing. Wolf had been something from the moment he walked through the door of that bed-and-breakfast, and she'd known it. She called it trouble then, but that was a small word for what he actually was. An entirely new phase of her life. She had been here, and only here. And now she was faced with this massive change. And maybe she did need to leave, just for a while. To think.

"You and I can't… We have to…"

"Agreed," he said, which was good, because she hadn't even been able to get out the sentiment. But what she actually wanted was a little bit of time to reflect on this away from her family. The fact of the matter was she wasn't doing a very good job of hiding the pregnancy. She hadn't even known about it and Sadie had guessed. Clara was on pins and needles waiting for her to take a test.

Clara.

She was going to have to talk to Clara.

And she was going to have to figure out her story to tell her family.

"I need to go to the bakery," she said. "I have some things to take care of. And then I'm going to have to talk to Sadie."

"I'll talk to Sadie," he said. "And I will put her and everybody else under strict orders not to tell anyone. It's a small town. We know how things spread. We need to keep it under wraps. It's important."

"Thank you," she said.

This man had been her enemy a few moments ago, and now he was her ally. Out of necessity. Because he was the only one who knew everything. Who knew the whole story. Who knew how they got here, and well, he was the only person she was going to be able to figure out where they went from this moment with.

She moved past him and went down the stairs. Then she stopped and texted Clara.

She would meet her at the bakery. And she would kill two birds with one stone.

Because she couldn't be miserable and inefficient.

So she would just settle for miserable efficiency. It was the best she could do.

CHAPTER TEN

WOLF FOUND HIMSELF staring down a crowd of very judg-mental family members only twenty minutes later. But he had told Violet he would handle this. So he was going to.

"Look, Sadie," Wolf said, "I like you. But your med-dling has caused a little bit of a problem."

"My meddling is the reason you're here," Sadie said. "And if I didn't…would she even have told you?"

"Fine," he said, holding up his hands. "Fair enough. But you need to keep it quiet. All of you."

"None of us are gossips," Kate said. "Well… Sadie is."

Sadie shot her sister-in-law an evil glare. "I would *not* gossip about this," Sadie said. "I swear we will keep it quiet."

"She's coming back to Four Corners with me."

"But…" Sadie looked aggrieved.

"It's fine," Eli said. "We'll get somebody on a short con-tract basis to take her place. That way…if it doesn't work out, she has a job to come back to."

If it doesn't work out.

That meant if they couldn't stand each other, or she lost the baby.

The idea made him feel grim.

But then, there was nothing to feel but grim about the whole thing. He hadn't asked for this. He wasn't an opti-mist. Why the hell would he be? Life had never given him a reason.

He hadn't wanted this, but he had known the minute he walked into that bed-and-breakfast and seen her there that she was pregnant.

She was ashen; she looked... Well, she was so beautiful, but she looked terrible. And he had also known that there was no question about whether or not he would be involved in the child's life. Also, Violet needed someone to take care of her. She looked like hell. And he had caused it. And that meant that he was going to step up and do what a man needed to do.

On that, he completely understood Sawyer.

Sawyer had immediately stepped up taking care of his child; he had made a decision. He had done what needed doing. Because their old man had been incapable of that. He'd been a wishy-washy leader on the ranch who had failed at the most basic of tasks. The cattle had thinned, the fences gone into disrepair. He hadn't innovated. He hadn't figured out how to weather different issues, because it all required thinking on your feet. Moving with the times. He hadn't been able to do it, because it had required doing. And he just hadn't *done*.

It was the same thing with Sawyer's mother. With Wolf's mother.

With Elsie's mother.

Women who had all been pregnant with his children, and he hadn't even made a commitment to them. He had brought them onto the ranch and just...let them sit there. He'd had affairs; he'd cheated as the opportunity arose. And even that was lazy as hell. None of it was decisive. None of it was being a man, in Wolf's opinion, and he just wouldn't be that.

He'd always known that.

But he had seen to making sure it didn't happen by always being scrupulous and careful in his sexual encounters. But he'd failed Violet. He had utterly failed, and it was his own damn fault. And he would face the consequences. And he wasn't going to hem and haw about what the right thing to do was, not when it was so clear.

He would marry her. Assuming it was a healthy pregnancy.

He wouldn't expose her to any kind of censure. He wouldn't get her kicked out of her family's home. All things that he knew his own mother had faced. And then she'd had to make a decision. Be stuck there forever, be a single mom on her own out there in the world, or leave Wolf and go back home. She had chosen to go back home. Gone back to her parents, the only way that they would accept her.

She had chosen family over him. Even though he'd been family.

He would never put Violet in that kind of a position, or his own child.

He would do what he needed to do to make it right. He would do what he needed to do.

"I'm going to marry her," Wolf said. "I'm not going to make this difficult for her. I swear it. My father was no kind of man. I know that we suffered a bit from that in this family. But I'm a better man than that. I'm not perfect. Obviously. But I care about her. I care about what people think about our kid. I'm going to do the right thing. You can count on that."

Connor stood up and shook his hand. "Good for you."

"I don't offer my hand to men doing the bare minimum," Kate said, giving him an evil eye.

"Fair enough," Wolf said.

Eli just nodded at him. And he had a feeling getting a woman pregnant out of wedlock was just not something Eli could be cool with. He had that same bearing about him that Sawyer had. He believed in right and wrong, and he believed it was all black-and-white. Connor, on the other hand, had seen some shit. He'd been through things. Not that Eli hadn't, but it was different.

He wrapped things up with his cousins and headed toward the door. Connor caught him on the porch.

"You're doing the right thing," Connor said.

"I know."

"Life is complicated," Connor said. "You lost your girlfriend, and I know you loved her a lot. Believe me, Wolf, I feel that. I loved Jessie. I loved her so much. And I had to learn how to feel again. How to want something new. How to accept that my life was different, and how to want that life, and let me tell you, there is nothing easy about that. I'm not going to tell you that everything is going to be okay. Because I don't know. But I will tell you that you can have something different than what you think. You can have a different life than the one you've decided to have. This is evidence of that."

"Yeah, life kind of made the decision for me."

"So life is only going to make a certain amount of those decisions for you. And the rest is up to you."

"I decided to marry her."

"Bare minimum," Connor said.

And he realized his cousin was a little more rigid than he had maybe thought before.

"I'll be good to her," he said.

"You better be. Or the whole trio of us will hunt you down and kick your ass."

"Don't worry. I have a feeling my own brother will do it."

He walked back to his truck, and when he reached the driver's-side door, he stopped. Because he realized he was going to have to do a lot of thinking about what being good to someone else even meant. And he hadn't thought in a long time. Even longer since he'd felt.

And he didn't quite know what he was going to do with that.

"I'M GOING TO leave for a while," she said.

"What happened?"

She was standing behind the counter, using it as a shield, and she had invited Clara to come down to the bakery. Because it seemed like a neutral place to talk. It was closed, so no customers would walk in, and her parents were occupied. Also, if she went to Clara's house, then Alex would overhear. It wasn't like Clara wasn't going to tell Alex; it was just that she couldn't stand to be a part of it.

"I took the test."

"Oh," Clara said.

"You already knew."

"What are you going to do?" Clara asked.

"Well…" She picked at an imaginary sticky spot on the counter. "He wants to get married."

"That's stupid," Clara said. "You can't get married just because you're having a baby."

"Can you think of a better reason to get married?"

Clara blinked at her. Not the blink of a woman with dry eyes. The blink of a woman who thought if she cleared her vision enough times Violet might suddenly appear to be less stupid. "Love."

"Sure," Clara said. "But really… This is permanent. It's…" She blinked. "We won't get married until after we're sure."

"Right," Clara said. "So what are you doing?"

"I'm going to… I'm going to his ranch for a while. For Christmas. I'm getting to know his family."

"That's almost romantic," Clara said.

Violet laughed bitterly and grabbed a cookie. Which she hoped that she wouldn't throw up. "It was not romantic. Nothing about it was romantic. I am so angry at him. He really…"

"He broke your heart."

"He did," Violet said. "And I know that's ridiculous but…"

"Not ridiculous," Clara said. "You slept with him. You gave yourself to him. And you asked him to stay."

She felt tears threatening to fall again. "I know. It's just… I wish I didn't have to feel that. I wish I didn't feel any of that. I wish that I was just okay with everything. I wish that I could push it aside and be rational. Because he's not… He's not who I wanted him to be. For me. He's everything he said he was, and I harbored a fantasy that maybe he would… That he would magically transform into a man with feelings when he warned me he wasn't one. And you should see the way he is about the baby. It's intense. It's not happy. It's not…"

"Well, you're not really happy about it, are you?"

"No," she said. "I'm not happy. But I…" This time tears did start to overflow. "Clara, I want this baby. Really, really badly. And I'm aware that it might be just because I want to prove that I can be a better mother than my own was. That I want to stay. That I want to…" She let out a long, hard breath. "I want to have a relationship like that. A mother-child relationship. Alison is wonderful. She has been the best mother figure to me. She is my mother, really. Calling her my stepmother is… It's not enough. But there's still this hole. Because whoever Alison is to me, I was left. By the woman who gave birth to me. By the woman who promised to be there. And she never thought about me again, as far as I know. She never called me again. She never came to see me. She never… She never went hey, where did you go? Why aren't you in Texas anymore? We moved to Oregon, and I don't even know if she realizes that. For all I know she still thinks we live in that same house. And she just never…"

"Nothing that you're feeling is wrong," Clara said softly. "It's not. I've lost so many people that I've loved. And they didn't choose to leave me." Violet felt a stab of guilt. Because of course. Clara's mother and father had died, and then her brother had been killed in Afghanistan. Clara had really and truly been left on her own. She knew all about loss. Deeply.

"And you know what," Clara said, "I have been really angry about that loss. And they didn't even choose it. I… You don't just get over things. It doesn't matter how long it's been. When somebody isn't in your life anymore, the hole it leaves behind is so big, so devastating. Believe me, I know."

"But Alex helped with that."

"Yes," Clara said. "Alex… Alex changed everything. But even more than that, Alex's love did. That's what I worry about, Violet. You deserve to be loved."

And then she realized something very sad. That the first response she wanted to give to Clara was that as far as she could tell, not everybody could be loved. And maybe she was one of those who wasn't destined to be.

Yes, her father loved her. He loved her deeply. So did Alison. So did all of her siblings. She didn't doubt it. It was just that…

There had always been a piece of her that had felt inadequate. Because you could add all kinds of new people to your life, but it didn't take away… It didn't take away the damage her mother had done. Not entirely.

"Maybe it's a gift," she said softly. "Because I can actually make this decision with a little bit more rationality. I understand what's important. I will be there for our child. And I think it's important that he is, too. Because he is right. If our child knew that he was out there and was fully capable of taking care of him, but wasn't… That would hurt. And we don't want to cause that kind of hurt. We want to do the right thing. We want to do the best we can."

"Violet, your feelings do matter."

"I know that," she said. "But…they aren't going to be how I make this decision."

Feelings could be incredibly selfish, and what she'd said to Wolf was true. She wasn't even always angry at her mother. She did think a lot, though, about how a person rationalized that decision to themselves. That decision to walk away. How they cast themselves as the hero in that decision. And it had always made her feel sad. Wary. Because it had made her believe, deeply and truly, that you could never trust you might find yourself in that same position. Twisting and turning reality until you could justify doing whatever it was you had already decided you were going to do.

"His mom left, too," Violet said softly. "He wants… He wants a family for the baby and I feel the same way. We don't want our child to experience the same thing."

Clara's expression shifted. "Oh…well, dammit. That makes me hate him less."

Violet laughed. "Yeah. Me, too."

"What will I tell everyone?" Clara asked.

"Tell them that I got invited to stay with a friend."

"And when they ask me if that friend is a man?"

They would ask. Because it was weird and Violet knew

it. And she felt bad enough asking Clara to conceal things at all.

Violet nodded. "You can tell them. Look, if I were to lose the baby, I would end up telling everyone about it. It isn't that I want to lie to them forever. It's just that I want to be by myself while I get used to this. I love everybody, but this family is so big, and everybody has opinions. I love them so much. But I just… I need some time. And what Wolf is giving me is time. A little bit of time to myself. A little bit of time to be somewhere else. Weren't you the one saying that maybe I needed that?"

"Touché," Clara said. "Way to use my reasoning against me."

"I'm just winging it," Violet said. "And hoping that I'm not making a terrible mistake."

CHAPTER ELEVEN

As SHE GOT into Wolf's truck the next morning with one bag full of her belongings, she was certain that she was making a terrible mistake.

"It's not a terribly long drive," he said. "Only about two and a half hours."

Great. She was going to be stuck in this vehicle for two and a half hours with a man whom she alternately wanted to strangle and make out with. That seemed about right.

"Good," she said.

She took a sleeve of saltine crackers out of the bag and started to eat them as they pulled away from the bed-and-breakfast. She felt unaccountably sad. And like a coward, because she had entrusted Clara with telling everybody what she'd done sometime today, because she didn't want to have a conversation with her dad or with Alison, or with anybody for that matter, and they were going to be upset and they were going to be concerned. It was only just hitting her how weird they were going to find it. And how obvious it was that she was going off with a man. Because if she was going off with one of her female friends she would have clearly just told them what was going on. It was so obvious that something shady was happening...

"You're thinking louder than you're chewing," Wolf said.

"What do you care what I'm thinking?" she asked, shoving an entire cracker into her mouth and being sure to crunch as loudly as possible.

"It may surprise you to hear this, but I actually don't want to be your enemy."

"No," she said. "*Enemy* is a bit too decisive of a feeling for you. Too much commitment."

"Look," he said, "I am who I am. I never pretended to be otherwise." He looked at her. "What about you? I actually don't know much of anything about you."

"Yes, you do," she said. "My mother left me when I was thirteen. I moved from Texas to Oregon when I was seventeen. Until about a month ago I was a virgin."

"Is that all there is to know?"

"It's as much as I know about you. Your mother left when you were a kid. You grew up on a ranch. You were *not* a virgin."

"Fine. Were you good at school?"

"Yes," she said.

"I wasn't."

"Could you be more of a stereotype?"

"Maybe if I said 'howdy.'"

"Skip it," she said. She watched the scenery go by and tried not to be entranced by it. She was too angry to enjoy the beauty in front of her. But she was never going to be immune to the beauty of Oregon, no matter how irritated she was. The dense, green trees, the thick moss and ferns that grew all over. The mountains in the distance.

"Did you always want to work at a bed-and-breakfast?"

"No," she said. "When I was a kid I wanted to be a research scientist. Because I like the idea of pouring things in and out of test tubes. And then I found out science was more difficult than that."

"That's like a metaphor for life, isn't it?"

"I guess so. My first job was at my stepmother's bakery, and I loved it. It's a lot like being a scientist. Except you're trying to make baked goods instead of chemical weapons."

"Did you really want to research chemical weapons?"

"No," she said. "I just wanted to make things blow up in a lab."

"I'll bear that in mind," he said. "And try not to make you mad."

"Oh, it's too late," she said. "You already made me mad. Very mad."

"Yeah. I got that."

"Did you?" In the mood to belabor the point, he said, "Because I'm not sure that you fully understand."

"You're here with me now. Why make a thing out of it?"

She took a deep breath, her chest feeling tight. "Well, what else do we have to do except make a thing out of it?"

"I went to school in a one-room schoolhouse," he said.

"Well, that's an interesting piece of Wolf Garrett trivia." She gritted her teeth, and she tried not to wonder about it. About what that had done to shape the man that he was now. About…anything. Because it was just annoying.

What's the point of staying angry? You agreed to go back with him.

She swallowed hard, her throat feeling scratchy.

"That's all I am," he said. "Interesting bits of trivia. For your enjoyment."

"Except when you're not," she said, popping another cracker into her mouth. "Except when you decide to leave."

"Yeah." He cleared his throat. "Well, now I want you to stay."

"Tell me how you think *that's* fair," she said, staring at him full-on now, and he kept his eyes fixed on the road.

"Do you hear yourself? I'm supposed to stay, but it was okay if you left. How is that fair?"

"None of this is fair. It's not about fair. It's about doing what's right."

"And right now, in your eyes, what's right means I have to do what you say. Because I have to now get on the Wolf Garrett Experience. At least, that's my understanding."

"Hate to break it to you, sweetheart, but a lot of women want on the Wolf Garrett Experience."

"I doubt that," she said. "I think what they actually want is the idea of you. You're a handsome son of a bitch, Wolf Garrett. And when you're focusing all your attention on a woman it feels pretty amazing. But your follow-up game is shit."

"I never said it wasn't."

He wasn't fazed. Not by her anger. Not by what she said to him. He wasn't fazed by any of it. And she hated that. Because she was…

Her thoughts went back to the moment he had seen the pregnancy test. It wasn't that he wasn't affected by this. He was. He was absolutely as affected by this as she was. It was just that whatever all this was… This kind of bland small talk, this implacable brick wall. It was his defense against it. But she honestly couldn't feel bad for him, or even curious. Because she was just too…

And you're going with him. So it doesn't really matter what you feel, does it?

"Tell me about your family," she said, blinking.

"That's a change."

"No, you're right. I might disagree with you. I might think it's ridiculous that I'm the one making all of the compromises. But I did choose to come with you. So there's no point. There's no point rehashing what happened. All that stuff…" A deep sadness welled up in her chest. "We have to pretend that it didn't happen. We have to pretend that this is…a fresh start. Because we need to be able to think. We need to be able to deal with each other. And I need to not be angry. And I'm angry, Wolf. Make no mistake. But I can't afford to be. Because I have to think about something bigger than myself. More than you. I know that's difficult for you to grasp."

"Fine," he said. "I can play this game if you want. Strangers. I don't know you. You don't know me. But if we are going to play this game, then you need to understand something. You don't know me. You never did. So don't go making proclamations about how you think I see the world and everyone in it. Because you don't know."

For the first time he sounded bothered. For the first time he sounded angry with her.

"I already told you about my brother and his mail-order bride. So you'll meet Sawyer and Evelyn, and their daughter, June. Then there's my sister, Elsie. She's around your age."

Violet blinked. She didn't really know what to make of that. That she was the same age as his… His younger sister. "Actually," he said. "She's older than you."

She laughed. She couldn't help it. It was a bitter, strange sound, and she didn't recognize her own voice.

"What?" he asked.

"Oh, nothing," she said. "I just find it mildly hilarious. All of it. Really."

"Get it out," he said. "Before our fresh start hits."

"You know, there's really nothing," she said. "You're right. I was foolish. I romanticized things that happened between us because I was inexperienced. Because I hadn't been with anyone else. I did that. It was…not my best move. But I did. I got caught up in the moment. I got caught up in the fact that we had really great sex. And I thought it felt nice to be carefree for a little while. But that came back and bit me, didn't it? It bit me really hard. And I feel… I feel small, and I feel embarrassed. And I hate the fact that my family is going to know that I…"

"What do you hate that your family's going to know exactly? That you're a human being? Doesn't really make much sense to me that you were a virgin, Violet. Not when you clearly like sex as much as you do."

She didn't know what to think of that comment. Didn't know what to make of it. Did she like sex a particular amount more than other people? Than other women? She hadn't really given that any consideration. But then, she hadn't *not* had sex because she wasn't interested in the idea, or anything like that. She just hadn't met anyone who had made her want to do it.

"Seems like repression to me," he said.

"Well, you're the one who slept with me," she said, the words like acid. "Did it feel repressed to you?"

"Hell no," he said, growling, in a way that made her feel more satisfied than she ought to.

She looked at the clock on the truck dashboard. And she felt aggrieved that more time hadn't passed.

She reached out and turned the radio on. It was country. Which she enjoyed, so that worked. She cranked it up, enjoying music over their conversation.

He didn't say anything; he just kept on driving. And she found herself getting sleepy. She let her head fall back against the bench seat. And when she woke up, they were pulling onto a dirt road.

"This is it," he said. "Four Corners Ranch. Garrett's Watch is just to the left here. About four miles down that way is the beginning of McCloud's Landing. Just across the way to the right is King's Crest. And four miles down from that on the right is Sullivan's Point."

She yawned and tried to wipe the sleep from her eyes. "I'm never going to remember that," she said. Except she knew she would. "I was sound asleep."

"You were a lot sweeter when I first met you. I'm afraid I've already ruined you."

"Starting over," she said. "Thank you for the information."

She was about to ask some more questions when they turned onto a narrow driveway that carried them back into the grove of trees. And there was a massive house that overlooked a river below. Built into the side of a mountain. All craggy and majestic.

"That's my brother's house. But I figure you don't want to go there first." He kept on driving, past the backside of the house, and then took a left turn deeper into the trees. The road narrowed, became rockier and even more impassable. And buried there in the trees was a cabin. A narrow smokestack stuck out of a shingle roof covered in moss. The roof pitched down and sloped, covering a porch that looked dangerously like it might collapse at any moment. The shutters were painted dark green, and each had a pine tree carved into them. Which she found odd. It was just such a homely little touch. Something kind of out of sync with the general...

This was it.

"It's rustic," he said.

"Yeah," she said. "I feel like I wasn't warned."

"Sorry," he said. "It's just home to me. Hell, my brother's house is pretty nice. I guess you could bunk there if you get really sick of me."

"Please tell me you have more than one bedroom."

"I do," he said.

Her heart was fluttering, somewhat wildly. Which was ridiculous. There was no call for that kind of nonsense. She didn't wait for him; she got out of the truck and she stopped. The air smelled different here.

Different than it did in Copper Ridge.

It wasn't damp with salt and ocean spray. But there was a heaviness to the air. Wood and pine. The ground was soft, soft dirt, pine needles all over. There were ferns around the bases of the trees. Fallen logs back in the timber with plants growing all along them. A shaft of light broke through the trees, spilling over the ground. Only in certain places. Everywhere else it was dark.

And she hated it. Because she didn't hate it.

Because there was something that felt a little bit magic about it. Because there was something that felt mysterious and otherworldly, and part of another time, much like Wolf, and no matter how much she knew she should look at him and see an enemy, see somebody she hated, there was a part of her that still lived in hope. A part of her that still sparked.

He started to head toward the house and she followed, finding herself gazing down at his ass, as she had done many times back when she hadn't been angry at him, and then hadn't committed to starting over. She looked away resolutely. His boots were heavy on the porch, and it didn't give way, so she followed him with a little more confidence than she felt when she just looked at it. He pushed the door open and held it for her. The expression on his face was rueful, as if he knew as well as she did that he was no gentleman, and it was just a gesture.

She walked in, and stopped. The furniture had to be as old as the house. Wood framed with ancient, shabby cushions on the couch. The cabinets were painted the same green as the shutters outside, with little pine trees carved into them.

"Oh," she said.

"Yeah, it's modest," he said.

She looked at him, and she just… She didn't know what she'd been thinking. She had been naked with him. Intimate. She thought that she had feelings that… Well, honestly, she realized they were impossible. There was no way for her to have the kind of feelings that she'd been sure she did. Because she didn't know this man. She thought she did. She had convinced herself that she did. And then she'd been angry at him for not wanting to uproot his life—a life that she didn't even know anything about—and stay with her.

Really, she just hadn't known a thing about him. How had she tricked herself into thinking that she did?

"It's fine," she said. "Can I see my room?"

He nodded. He led her down the hall, and the floorboards creaked under her feet.

"I'll have to fix that," he said.

"I… It's fine."

"It's just that I don't usually have guests," he said.

"Is that what I am?"

"Don't know what else you could be."

"Well. I don't know. I'm sure there are choice words for it."

He shrugged. "You're the one with the hang-up about it, not me. Remember, I'm not the one who was a virgin."

"I think you have plenty of hang-ups, just maybe not that."

He chuckled. "Fair enough."

"So what… What now?"

"I have some work to do," he said. "Gotta get out and pull my weight. I had a building project I was working on."

"You… You build?"

"We're all handy with whatever might need doing in a place like this. There's no reason to hire someone when you can just get the job done yourself."

"So you're sort of a…general…handyman?"

He winked. "I'm a cowboy."

She found that annoying. Because it was harkening back to when they had first met. When he was all charm and none of this other stuff. When it was all fun, with none of the hurt. They were supposed to be starting over, but she couldn't look at him now and see the same uncomplicated thing she'd seen before. None of the sharp things. The hard things. She couldn't start over, not clean. And honestly, it would be foolish. To forget. To forget what she knew now.

She wasn't the sweet, innocent Violet that she'd been a month ago. She had been badly wounded, and she had first-hand evidence of the consequences of this kind of thing. Of the fact that it was not carefree fun.

A fling that would be temporary.

Nothing about this was temporary.

It was all… It was all a little bit too real. A little bit too heavy.

She blinked, and took a breath. "What should I do?"

"Whatever you want. Take a rest."

"A rest?"

"I know you haven't been… Well, you haven't been well."

She could have easily mistaken his tone for concern. But she didn't actually think Wolf was concerned. She looked at him, hard, and tried to read some emotion behind his eyes. Honestly, she wasn't sure what was there.

What had she seen before?

Nothing, nothing but a handsome face.

He was funny and sexy, charming when he wanted to

be. But there was nothing behind it. It was terrifying. She had seen what she wanted to see, and he was the sort of man created to let a person do just that. To let you fixate on his looks, to let you fixate on that easy manner he could affect. And he was good at hiding whatever was really happening there. So good at hiding himself. All that openness. All that easiness. It wasn't real.

He wasn't real.

"Yeah. Maybe I'll rest. I've been working two jobs the whole time. It's not easy."

At this point she was just saying that to get rid of him. She didn't actually want to stand here and have this conversation with him. She wanted an escape. A reprieve.

"I'll be back come sundown."

And for a minute, she thought she saw something in his eyes. She remembered then, the sadness she'd seen there. He had feelings. He just buried them so deep it was almost impossible to see them. She wondered if he even felt them most of the time, or if he was adept at hiding them even from himself.

"All right. See you then."

"See you."

He walked out then, and left her standing in the cabin. She walked down the hall, toward the bedroom that he had indicated would be hers. It was small. The furniture in it was as old as the rest of the place. That same rough-hewn wooden frame, and a warm blanket that had definitely seen better days.

She turned a circle in the room and looked up and saw a small square painted over in the ceiling. That was definitely an attic access. Okay, maybe she wasn't going to rest. Maybe she was going to do something. Because why not? Why not get something done. If she was going to stay here

for the next little bit, then she might as well turn it into a
place she could stand.

*You're Snow White. You moved in with Grumpy and now
you're cleaning his house.*

No. She had moved in with The Beast. But there was no
enchanted rose to be found. Pretty sure the monster had
always been a monster.

She would explore the attic later. She was definitely intrigued. And sure, there were probably spiders or whatever,
but she had grown up on a ranch. First in Texas, and then
in a converted barn in Oregon.

She wasn't bothered by any of that.

She walked down the hall, back into the kitchen. And
she started to open cupboards. There wasn't much to speak
of. It would've been nice if she could have retained a vehicle so that she could maybe find a store. Not that she was
incredibly hungry. She dug around and found some basic
dry ingredients, which surprised her. Canned tomato sauce,
some spices. Beans. She could make something out of that.
She could make chili. She opened up the freezer and found
some ground beef. She would have been very upset had
she gone to a cattle ranch and not been able to find beef.

So that was the first thing. She would get food going.
She was angry about the lack of onion, but found dried
onion powder and figured it would do. She found a large
stockpot shoved into one of the small cabinets, and set
about to cooking.

She found a broom, and once the chili was on, she started
to sweep. And then she scrubbed. And by the time it was
all done, the little kitchen was looking tidier than it probably had in more than a decade. The layers of dirt she had
found practically told the story. You could carbon-date it.

She found cornmeal, eggs and oil, and decided to throw

together a cornbread, as well. Then she went into the bedroom and looked at the blankets critically. She opened the
door to what she assumed was his room, and saw a much
larger bed that was... Well, it was a lot nicer. She frowned.
And a very mean idea occurred to her. She began to dismantle her small bed, taking the mattress off, and finding it full of dust. Then she grabbed the blanket and took
it outside, draping it over the railing and beating it with a
stick, watching the dust fly.

She took the mattress out to the porch and did the same
thing. After a little more hunting, she found a basic tool
set and started to dismantle the bed. Then she went into
Wolf's room, and started to do the same thing. He could
have his room. But she was taking his bed. She was pregnant with his child.

She deserved it.

It was a little bit trickier moving Wolf's bed. It required
a lot of assembly, and the song and dance to move the mattress had been epic.

She'd had to scurry from one end to the other, alternately pushing and pulling, the whole way down the hall.

And it was big. It basically went wall to wall in her bedroom. But she didn't really care. She lay on it for a moment,
and was perturbed to discover that it smelled like him. It
made her eyes prickle with tears.

She hated that.

She swallowed hard and rolled over onto her side, scoot-
ing to the end of the bed, and got up again. Then she looked
up at that crawl space. She got back on the bed, standing,
and pushed at it. It was essentially painted shut, but she was
able to jimmy it to the side, and then she looked around the
room. Looking for something to get her a little bit higher.

After feeling around for a moment, she found a ladder,

rope and wood slats, and she was able to pull it down. Then she grabbed her cell phone and climbed up into the space, shining the flashlight on the phone into the darkness. It was tiny. She couldn't stand up. But there were boxes.

And in them were linens, Christmas decorations, dishes. Plates.

All kinds of things that were not actually stocked in the little house, but spoke to the fact that a family might have lived here at one time. With great eagerness, she began to cart the boxes down, dispatching any spiders that crawled out from the depths of them. Some things were chewed, suggesting a rodent presence. But that was just life when you lived in the country.

Violet accepted these creatures as part and parcel to the deal. It didn't really perturb her.

She took the box of dishes into the kitchen and began to unpack it, cleaning each and every one before she put them in the cupboards. Then she went back into the bedroom and examined the other items critically.

She hunted around until she found a washer and dryer, stashed into an alcove in the hall, covered by an accordion folded door. She stashed as many of the linens in as possible, then started to look at all the Christmas decorations.

They were clearly old. All yellow-gold tinsel and aluminum stars. Perfectly preserved houses and a blanket of snow, that seemed to make up a village. They were made of slim cardboard with glitter pressed to the outside, and small colored cellophane windows. And she decided then that if she was going to be away from her family for Christmas, she would have some retro Christmas cheer. And so the next bit of work was something a bit more arduous, but she found an axe and put on a stocking cap, then wandered into the forest, hunting around until she found a scraggly tree that would be easy for her to manage. She cut it down, the axe moving through the spindly trunk with only a few blows.

Then she began to drag it back toward the house. It got hung up on a few rocks, and once between two trees, but otherwise her journey was smooth enough.

She hefted it up the steps, and then dragged it inside, making sure to turn it the correct way so she didn't strip the branches on their way through the door.

She dug out the rusted tree stand and managed to prop the tree in it, turning the screws as tightly as she could. And when they wouldn't go tight enough around the tiny tree, she wedged some washcloths in there to brace it.

She stood back and surveyed it, feeling pleased with her work. She pushed it to the center of the living room. There was no TV. So might as well make the tree the focal point. She spent the rest of the afternoon digging through the ornaments and procuring a nice little set for the tree.

The smell of the chili and cornbread filled the house now, and she was exceptionally pleased with everything she had done.

Are you auditioning to be his housewife?

She scowled at herself. No. It was just that she wasn't going to sit in unfestive, nonseasonal squalor simply because he was happy to do so. And maybe, just maybe, she was picking at him a little bit.

It was beginning to get dark outside, which was perfect. She plugged in the lights and was thrilled to see that they all lit up. They were large, brightly colored, bold, and they added to the exceedingly midcentury appeal of all the decor.

Just then, she heard heavy boot steps on the porch, and she felt her heart jump up into her throat.

Oh, she really was ridiculous.

He opened the door and stopped. And Wolf Garrett

looked shocked. It was the second time she'd seen that look on his face. The other time had been when he had seen the pregnancy test.

"Merry Christmas," she said.

"It's November," he said.

"But Thanksgiving is over. And I am in a festive mood. If I have to be away from my family, then I'm going to have some Christmas cheer." She said the same thing to him that she had said to herself. Because it was true. It was all true.

"What the hell did you do?"

"It's fairly self-explanatory. But I also made you dinner."

"Thanks," he said.

"What would you have done for dinner?"

"I don't know. Usually I just dig something out of the freezer."

"Right. Well, I'm not going to do that. That's not how I eat. It's not how I live. So. There you are."

"You're very tentative about the whole arrangement, but have no trouble coming in and making it all yours," he said.

"No," she said, feeling a bit evil now. "Not at all. But then, you had no trouble walking into my life and telling me exactly what I was going to do, and the only things that made sense. Which were all things that made sense to you, and all things that you wanted. Asking me to change everything. So if I change a few things around to suit myself, then you're going to have to deal with it."

"Where did you get all this?"

"From the attic."

He frowned. "There were things in the attic?"

"Yes. They literally look like they have been up there since the sixties or seventies. Or at least, most of the things are from that time."

"Weren't there…spiders?"

"Yeah," she said. "Why would that bother me?"

"It bothers most people, Violet."

She wondered if spiders bothered him. Maybe she'd put one in his boot.

"Nothing is going to happen," she said. "Anyway, even if a poisonous one bit me, as long as I got treatment I would be fine."

"You're pregnant," he said.

She winced. Because she hadn't really thought of that. She was just focused on the fact that she actually had some energy. She wasn't really thinking that perhaps moving around industriously wasn't the best thing to do. Although, Kate Garrett was pregnant and she was still working the ranch like it was nothing. Whatever she had done before, she continued to do. So it seemed reasonable enough. She wasn't going to start training for a marathon or anything, but she knew her body.

Spider bites notwithstanding.

"I didn't get bitten," she said. "Besides, I don't like sitting around. I intended to rest, but it's not something that I really get a lot out of. I like to be useful. And in this case, I was being useful to myself. So here we are."

"I'm not a big fan of Christmas," he said.

"I am," Violet said. "I love Christmas, and I'm going to miss Christmas in Copper Ridge, so I'm going to have some Christmas cheer here."

"I really don't like it," he said.

"Too bad," she said, unwilling to back down. Because there was a whole host of things that she didn't like, and he hadn't consulted her on them.

"Doing really well on the starting-over thing."

"How am I failing? I gave you every chance to come in here and be grateful for the fact that you have chili and cornbread waiting for you, and that I cleaned your house and put up this beautiful Christmas tree, and you're being a grinch."

"Thank you for the food," he said. He crossed the space and went over to the stove, lifting the lid on the pot and looking inside. He looked over at her, and something flickered across his face. Shock? But it was deeper than that.

"What?"

"Nothing," he said.

"No, sometimes you look... Sometimes you look like there's nothing inside you. And it scares the hell out of me, Wolf. Because I met you, and I looked at you and saw someone charming. And sexy. And I think those were the things I *wanted* to see. After you left I thought I'd made it up. That what I saw in your eyes was a trick of the light. And that's how you like it. But then sometimes you look like that. And I don't know what's going on in your head. And sometimes you look sad. You just look really sad."

"Can I eat my chili without psychoanalysis?"

He grabbed a bowl and started to pile it high, then took two thick pieces of cornbread. There was no table in the little cottage, so he sat down heavily on the couch. Violet got a bowl of chili and sat down in the chair opposite him.

"Psychoanalysis is the cost of my chili," she said. "If we are going to live together, then I want to understand some things about you. And mostly... I want to know... Why exactly do you want to be in this child's life? I mean, really. Why do you want this? Because I just can't... I can't figure you out. You do look sometimes like the kind of man who doesn't care about anybody. But none of this suggests that's true. And I also can't... I can't figure you out. Bottom line."

The corner of his mouth quirked upward. "Many have tried. None have succeeded."

"And then there's that. You just go right to that. Wolf Garrett. Push everything off."

"The alternative is sitting in it," he said. "And I'm not sure that's any better. Are you?"

"What are we sitting in? Reality? Because you know, that you have to deal with. You have to deal with the people in your life."

"I think I'm the one that just told you all about the ways that I'm connected to people. And why I have a responsibility to…"

"To what? To perform at a certain level? To pretend you're a good person even if you don't feel like being one?"

"I want to be here for this child because I will be damned if I caused the kind of pain that my own parents did. Okay? Is that good enough for you? It scars you. And I don't want to leave any scars like that. The one thing that I ever wanted… I don't want much, Violet. I let go of a lot of things a long time ago. But what I want is to not salt the ground that kid is going to walk on before he ever takes his first step, okay? Because that's how it was for us. Everything was harder. From the beginning. We grew up with a dad who didn't care about us. Mothers who abandoned us. We didn't know what functional family looked like except staring out at the other people that live here. Thank God we got to see it. But then I always wondered why we couldn't have it. Why it wasn't for us. I don't ever want that. Not for my child."

"Will you love him?" That question stuck in her throat.

"I love my family, Violet. I'm capable of love."

"Oh. I thought you were sort of… Didn't believe in it."

He laughed, and the sound was so bitter it pierced her soul. "I believe in love. It's real. It can kill you. It can save you. It's a hell of a thing. Not wanting to have a child in my life because I didn't want to have to care that much is not the same as not being able to."

"Oh," she said, feeling like all the air had been squeezed out of her lungs.

"Does that satisfy you?"

"I don't know."

Because it was clear that there was more to his story than he was telling her. It was clear that there was more to Wolf than she had realized. The answer was in those eyes, and she knew it. And it hurt. It burned.

He wasn't going to tell her. That was the thing. He wasn't going to give her any information that he didn't have to. That much was clear. Wolf Garrett didn't want to be known.

And she didn't know if she had... She didn't know if she had the emotional wherewithal to try and push through all of this. Because she didn't know what she would find on the other side. She didn't know what lay at the depths of who he was. And she felt... Well, every inch a decade younger than him and short of a lot of experience.

She hadn't felt this gap. Not when things were light and easy and she was getting to know him. Not when she was kissing him. And not today when she had been cleaning the house. Switching their beds. No, then she had felt industrious. She had felt responsible. She had felt like she had everything under control. But right now she just felt... like she was at sea.

"It'll have to," he said. "For now. Thanks again for dinner. I've got to wash up and get ready for bed. Morning comes early around here. As you know. You don't need to get up and make me breakfast."

"Don't worry," she said. "I wasn't going to."

"You don't have to make dinner, either. We'll probably go to my brother's house tomorrow."

Violet didn't know if she was ready for that. She didn't know if she was ready to meet his family. She wanted to hide here. She wanted to hide here and figure out her own emotions, and she had no idea what they were doing, quite frankly.

"I guess." She would wait and see how she felt tomorrow. There would be leftover chili, and she could have that if nothing else.

He walked out of the room, leaving her to her own devices. A few minutes later she heard the shower turn on, and she tried not to imagine him. Naked with the water pouring down his body. She didn't have a right to picture him that way. Because they were starting over. They were not the people who had shared those intimacies.

Not anymore.

They were not the Wolf and Violet who had gotten themselves into this situation. They had to be the Wolf and Violet who can actually handle the situation, and that was going to be difficult. But it was better. Because those people hadn't known what they were doing or how to proceed. Those people hadn't known they were going to have to deal with each other long-term. She had been naive, far too naive to deal with a man like him. And he had been fake.

That was the bottom line. He hadn't been truthful with her. And he could say that he was, that he had told her that he was going to leave, and then did. But he had also played the part of lighthearted charmer, and he wasn't that at all. There was a quiet intensity to him that she couldn't pin down. Emotion that ran far deeper than he was comfortable conveying. She was going to have to be strong enough, savvy enough, to handle that. And he was going to have to drop his guard eventually. Because the alternative was... Well, it wasn't awesome.

She sat there on the couch, holding her bowl of chili until he got out of the shower. She heard the door close to the bathroom, heard his footsteps down the hall, then heard his bedroom door close. She closed her eyes.

"What the fuck?"

She heard his voice muffled through the bedroom door.

"I made some changes," she shouted.

She heard the door open, and he charged out. With a towel wrapped around his lean hips, his broad chest bare and just as appealing to her as he had been back when she had been new, innocent Violet, who had thought that the two of them were embarking on an incredible, sensual journey, not this rocky road through their own personal hell. Unfortunately, she just couldn't be unaffected by him. It was very irritating.

His face was like thunder, and still handsome. "You stole my bed."

She smiled broadly. Sweetly. Meanly. "I didn't think that I should be the one to have to sleep on *that*."

"So you… You moved it?"

"Yes." She looked down at her hands as if she was examining her fingernails. "There was a lot of assembly required. It was a ton of work."

He gestured toward her. "You're crazy, do you know that?"

"I don't know. I think you're crazy. You expected your pregnant…whatever I am, to go sleeping on that threadbare mattress, using that dusty comforter. At least I cleaned everything for you."

"I'm a big man," he said. "My feet are going to hang off of that."

"Well, I suggest you come up with a solution."

"Or we share," he said, his eyes going molten.

"No," she said. "We cannot share, and I think you know

that." Except her voice had gone high, and her throat was dry. Because he was half-naked. Actually, he was all naked. Just with a towel covering the fact up.

Well, if you're going to use that logic, then you're really both naked, because your clothes are covering you up, and you're just halfway to...

She shoved that to the side. "We are being adults. Or at least, one of us is."

"You did all of this to bug me," he said.

"Yes. I made you dinner to bug you."

"Not the dinner, the tree and everything else. And you know *that*. So stop acting like butter wouldn't melt in your mouth."

"Butter melts in my mouth just fine. On fresh delicious cornbread, which I made. So there."

"You don't want to start a war with me, Violet Donnelly."

"Why not? What would happen? What is it that you fight for, Wolf Garrett? Perhaps I do want a war. So I can see where you stand."

"I stand in the middle of my house, plenty pissed off that I'm being put in a kid bed."

"Well, you were more than happy to put me in it. So now you see how it feels. And maybe you'll be a little bit better about thinking of others. Now that you have to sleep a night on my mattress."

"See you tomorrow."

He walked down the hall and slammed the door behind him, and Violet sat there, and then a smile spread over her face.

She had lost a couple of the battles in the past few days, but she had just won a very petty war. And if she couldn't stop herself from desiring his body, then she would take that. Yes, in the end, she would take that.

CHAPTER TWELVE

"You WENT AND got her?" He was sitting around the break-fast table at his brother's house the next morning, taking on a hard stare from Hunter, Elsie, Sawyer and Evelyn, in equal parts. It was Elsie who had asked that scandalized-sounding question.

"I did," he said.

"You hauled her up and threw her in the back of the pickup?" Hunter asked.

"Well," Elsie said, looking at Hunter and then back to Wolf. "Did you?"

"She came of her own volition."

"You're going to be a father?" Sawyer asked.

The words sat uncomfortably in Wolf's stomach. And he wanted to deny it. Wanted to reject it. What he wanted was to pretend that this wasn't happening at all. But he couldn't. Because Violet was in his house, she had stolen his bed and there was a Christmas tree in his damned living room.

And provided that everything went fine in the next couple of months, odds were, he was going to be a father.

He didn't like that word. There was nothing good tied to it, not for him. He didn't like parents. Not the entity or the word. Nothing. He hated every single thing about the idea of being involved in that kind of domestic life. He hated all of this. He just really did.

"I guess so," Wolf said.

"Congratulations," Sawyer said.

He looked at his brother's steady gaze, and he honestly didn't know how to respond. He knew Sawyer hadn't been thrilled when he discovered that the woman he had slept with was pregnant, but Sawyer had done what Sawyer did. He had decided a path forward; he had decided to be involved, and so he was. He had decided that it would all be okay, and it had been. That was just the way his brother saw the world. It was sort of glorious and black-and-white, and Wolf had never really envied him that before, but he did now.

Because Wolf couldn't see the bright side. Wolf couldn't see it working out. He couldn't see it at all. He just couldn't even picture it. He couldn't muster up a feeling of warmth or excitement. Not anything but the fierce, terrible need inside him to make sure that Violet was with him. Where he could see her. It wasn't a comfortable feeling. It was… It was sharp, and it was angry. Like his namesake had woken up inside him and decided that he was in control of a pack that he needed to protect. But if there were supposed to be warm, paternal feelings, or a sense of anticipation, a magical influx of wisdom, and softness, that had skipped him.

"You look…angry," Evelyn said.

He hadn't known his sister-in-law for that long, but she had the benefit of being an outsider. Which really bothered him. She didn't ignore a lot of the things that they ignored about each other. Because they were used to the way each other behaved, and saw no point in calling it out. Evelyn called them all out regularly. She called Hunter on his smart-ass mouth; she called Sawyer stubborn—rightly—and she made sure that Elsie knew it was feral to put her boots on the table. She circled Wolf, though. She didn't often get right up in his face. But he had felt her keen blue gaze on him more than once, and he didn't really appreciate being the focus of Evelyn's laser-like assessment.

"I'm not happy."

"Why?"

He blinked. "Because I am in the middle of the situation I did not want or plan."

"Okay. I guess that's fair. But… I mean, why are you doing it?"

"Because it's the right thing to do."

"Says who? Is it the right thing to angrily parent a child? June's biological mother decided she didn't want to do it, because she knew herself. I can admire her for that. For knowing it was the right thing for her."

"Are you advocating for me doing the same thing?"

"I'm not advocating anything. I'm just asking you why you're doing something you clearly are enraged by?"

All he could see was red. Anger. And the hot, sharp need to possess.

"Because I can't let her go."

"I see."

He hated that. Hated it as an answer because it seemed to imply that she understood something he didn't. And the thing that made it worse was he was almost certain that was true. That she did understand something about himself that he didn't.

Violet was a little bit like that. The way she looked at him last night… The way she'd talked about his eyes.

He didn't like that.

"So what are you going to do?" Sawyer asked.

"I'm going to marry her," Wolf said as if his brother was the biggest idiot on the planet.

"Has she agreed to marry *you*?" Sawyer asked.

"No," Wolf said. "She wants to wait until she's sure

everything's going to…you know. Until she's sure nothing is going to happen with the pregnancy."

"So you dragged her up to your cabin—which to be clear looks like it couldn't comfortably house a family of raccoons—and now you're sitting at my breakfast table scowling," Sawyer said. "The woman hasn't agreed to marry you necessarily, and you're demanding it like it's your right. I have a little bit of advice for you. Try being nice."

Anger licked at Wolf's veins, because what right did Sawyer have to tell him to do any damn thing?

"I'm nice," Wolf said.

They laughed. They all laughed. Every single asshole sitting at that table.

"I am," Wolf said. "At least I don't go out of my way to be a dick like Hunter. I don't have the energy for that."

Elsie snickered. "Fair." She cleared her throat. "You are not nice, Wolf."

"I can behave myself."

"Wolf, you're not used to answering to anyone but yourself," Sawyer said.

"And you," Wolf said. "Because you're always on hand to tell me what you think I ought to be doing."

"Sometimes you need it. But anyway, you don't listen. You don't listen, so what difference does it make if I tell you what I think you should do, or I don't? You do exactly what you want no matter what."

"And you're different?"

Evelyn nodded. "You're not different," she said to her husband, patting him on the forearm. "Although, to his point, Wolf, you are not friendlier. You are, in fact, deeply unfriendly."

"Friendly enough that I got her pregnant in the first place," Wolf grumbled.

"That's not friendly," Evelyn said. "That's something else."

He drained the last of his coffee and stood up. "I'm done with this bullshit. Let's go do some work."

They all stood, with the exception of Evelyn, who kicked back in her chair and tipped her cup to her lips. "Coming to dinner tonight?"

"We'll see," he said.

Violet had seemed hesitant when he'd talked to her about it last night. But then, she had known that she'd switched the beds, and that he hadn't seen them yet. So maybe some of it was that. That she had been anticipating his reaction.

They all walked out to their respective trucks, and as he opened the driver's-side door, Sawyer turned to him. "Do you need anything? Is there…some older brother thing I should be doing to help you through this?"

"You want to tell me to quit crying and just get on with it?"

He had meant it to sound like a joke. A reference to what had happened after his mother had left. And hell, it wasn't like it was Sawyer's fault. He'd been eight. And he hadn't known how to be sensitive. Hadn't known what to do with his crying little brother. He wasn't mad about it.

Sawyer looked down. "I'm sorry about that."

"Don't be. You were a kid. And hell, at the end of the day, you're right. There's no point crying."

"But a kid is going to cry when his mother leaves. I was just angry because I'd already been through it and I didn't want to feel bad for you. I still felt bad for myself. I was just a selfish asshole, Wolf."

"You were eight," Wolf said. "You were not a selfish asshole. You were a child. And if anything makes me deter-

mined to be part of my kid's life, it's that. The fact that we…
Look at how we talk to each other. About our childhood.
You think you should have done better by me. Your mother
doesn't think she should have done better by you. Same as
mine doesn't think she should have done better by me. Our
dad probably still thinks he's a damned hero. For not letting
us starve. Which was the bare minimum. And if there was
a bare minimum, you could be sure that he was going to do
it. I'm not going to be like that. I don't want my kid to be
standing around talking to his cousin asking why the hell
his dad left him to his own devices. And you stepped up."

"Yeah," Sawyer said. "I did. I love Bug. She's the best
thing that's ever happened to me. And with it, Evelyn. But
it was a life I decided I was ready to have, Wolf."

"Yeah. Well. I'm not ready. Not for any of it. But it's
happening. So what's my excuse?"

"People find them. You know they do."

"I'm not going to," Wolf said. He started to get in his
truck, then stopped. "She disassembled my bed and moved
it into her room."

"She *what*?"

"She didn't like the bed in her room. So she didn't move
into my bedroom. The varmint disassembled my bed and
moved it into her bedroom, and moved the little twin bed
into mine."

"When do I get to meet her?" Sawyer asked, smiling.
"Because I think I like her."

Wolf grumbled as he got into his truck, and when he
started the engine, he had to admit to himself that he liked
her, too. And that was one of the very annoying things.
He liked her an awful lot. And he wouldn't have chosen
to put the poor girl in his path. Not on a permanent basis.
Connor was right. She was sweet. But she was more than

that. She was feisty as hell. And he didn't want to be part of breaking that.

Breaking her.

"Too late for guilt," he muttered to himself.

He hadn't felt any when it counted. When he could have turned back. So he wasn't deserving of it now.

And he would do well to remember that.

VIOLET SPENT THE day baking bread. She had decided that she would go to his family's house tonight to meet them, after all. But she would be coming with bread.

She stuck her finger into the ball of dough that had been sitting on top of the fridge for the past couple of hours, and tried to gauge whether or not it was proofed enough. It seemed good. Her phone started to buzz on the counter, and she looked at it from the chair she was standing on, and carefully got down. Wolf would probably growl at her. But then, when was Wolf not growling?

She answered the phone. "Hello?"

"Are you going to explain what the hell is going on?"

Great. It was her dad.

"Hi, Dad," she said.

"Clara said something about you taking off for the holidays?" He tried to keep his tone neutral but she could hear concern and deep suspicion in his words.

He was not neutral. Not at all.

"Yeah, I... It's just..." There was no way to play this off. "I wanted to go stay with a friend. At a ranch?"

"It's him, isn't it?" Her stepmother's voice came over loud and clear.

"Alison," Violet said, her tone filled with irritation.

"You went off with that guy," she said.

"I didn't... I didn't go off with him. I..."

"Where are you?" Cain asked.

"Dad," Violet said. "I'm not seventeen. I am not drunk at a barn party, and I don't need you to storm in and rescue me. I made a decision. I *am making* a decision."

"What decision are you making, exactly? To blow your family off to go stay with some… I'm going to kill him. I'm going to kick his ass."

Her dad didn't even know she was pregnant and he was already threatening ass kickings. Great.

"I needed some time… It's not… It's not like that. I'm not *with* him." Except that she kind of was. But she wasn't actively sleeping with him. So there was that.

"You're not *with* him?" her dad said, his voice deadpan. "I don't believe that, Violet."

"I'm twenty-two," she said.

"Oh, I'm well aware," her father said. "But this is out of character. And that's what worries me. It is not like you to take off without talking to us. It is not like you to blow off the holiday. What about the bakery?"

Guilt lashed at her. She hadn't even thought about the bakery. How had she managed to overlook that?

"I'm so sorry," Violet said. "I just… I handled everything with the bed-and-breakfast…" Wolf had. She hadn't even done it. She had been a coward. A coward who was absolutely and completely invested in her own misery. "I haven't felt very well over the last couple weeks and I…"

"Tell me what's going on," her dad said. "I need you to tell me what's going on. Even if you aren't lying, you're leaving things out, and I can tell. This isn't like you, Violet."

"I am telling you what's going on," Violet said, feeling angry with herself, because she didn't know how to talk to her dad when she knew she was going to disappoint him.

"As best as I can. I don't want you to be angry with me. I really need you to not be angry with me."

"I can't guarantee that," he said. "Because I don't know if you're going to tell me that you went off to start a meth lab or you had some kind of a nervous breakdown. One of those things is going to make me angry."

"It's not a meth lab. And it's not a nervous breakdown. But there are so many people in our house. So many Donnellys. Everywhere. And I love you. But there are some things going on, and I need to sort it all out for myself. I just have to. I have to try and figure this out on my own. Because if I don't, then…"

"Tell me," he said. "Otherwise I'm going to call the police."

"And tell them what? That your twenty-two-year-old daughter who is perfectly fine went somewhere of her own free will?"

"I will still call them," he growled.

And Eli Garrett knew exactly where she was and why. So if her dad called the police, he was going to find her. And he was going to be angrier. Actually, if it escalated to that point…she couldn't trust Alex and Clara to keep her secret. That was the problem with all these sticky family connections.

"I'm pregnant," Violet said. There was absolute silence on the other end of the phone. "And I didn't want to tell you. Because I'm afraid of what… I'm afraid. Because I made a mistake. And I've never made a mistake. Not since you came and rescued me from that barn party, Dad. I did my very best to be good. To be good for you. And to not cause you any trouble. Because I know you've been through enough. I just didn't want to disappoint you. I didn't want to disappoint you again."

"Are you okay?" he asked.

That was all he asked. If she was okay. He didn't yell; he didn't judge. Nothing. He didn't scold her; he didn't…

He just asked about *her*.

And it made her heart feel bruised.

"I don't know," she said. "I mean, if you mean… He's… complicated?"

"What do you need from me?"

His tone was grave and low, and it was worse than she had imagined. Because he wasn't yelling. He wasn't being wildly supportive or anything like that. But he was… He sounded so emotionally affected that he couldn't even hide it. And he was still being good to her. In spite of the fact that it was clear he wasn't pleased.

"I don't know what I need," she said. "That's why I came… When Wolf suggested that I come to Four Corners with him while we sorted everything out, I thought it was a good idea. Because I can figure out… We can figure out what we're going to do."

"Wolf?" His dad's tone was completely flat. "His name is Wolf."

She closed her eyes. "I promise you, he's a human man."

"How many tattoos?"

"None," she said. "This is why I don't want to be home right now."

"I'm sorry," he said. "Having a hard time wrapping my head around this."

"Violet, you can come home," Alison said. "You're right, you're twenty-two. This is your situation. It is not ours. You're not a child and…"

"She's *my* child," her dad growled.

"I'm fine," Violet said. "I'm not in trouble. I'm not in danger. He is a good man, who has a ranch. And I am stay-

ing on it. With his family. He has a big family. He's... He's
a Garrett," she said.

"Is that so?" Her father's voice sounded deadly.

"Yes. And if you ask Eli about it, he can tell you. Wolf
is his cousin."

"You can bet I'll be having a talk with Eli."

"Please don't do anything silly like come find me."

"Bo," her dad said, his voice suddenly going hoarse.
"That's all I want to do. I just need to give you a hug. I
need to... Honey, don't you understand that I held you in
my arms for the first time twenty-two years ago, and I still
feel like I should be holding you? Especially now."

Tears burned her eyes. "It's not about you, Dad," she
said. "This. Me needing to be away. It's not about you. It's
about me. Because I have to decide if..."

"If what?"

"Well, he wants to get married."

She swallowed hard, and the sound of that swallow was
all she could hear. Her dad had gone completely silent.

"Dad?"

"He'll have to ask my permission first."

She had a lot of thoughts about her dad's insistence on
that but now wasn't the time to voice them.

"I'll have him do that."

"He really asked you to marry him?" her dad asked.

"Yes. He thinks that it's the right thing to do."

"Didn't expect that from a guy named Wolf..."

"Well, it's what he thinks is best."

"You don't *have* to get married," he said. "Don't get me
wrong. I'm not... I'm just glad he thinks that way. That he
has a sense of responsibility. But I don't want you married
to somebody that you don't want to be married to."

"I won't. I promise that I will think everything through. But that's the thing. I have to do it by myself."

"How old is he?" he asked.

"Thirty-two."

"Fuck," her dad said.

"What? It's not like…"

"Just…"

"It's going to take him a while to process this," Alison said. "Please, call us every day."

"I don't know if I can do that," Violet said, feeling guilty. "I can text you. And I will call. But this has to be… I was so stressed about it. I couldn't even bring myself to take a pregnancy test for a couple of weeks, even though I did… I suspected it."

"Thanksgiving," her dad said. "You spit the cheese out."

"Yes."

"Clara knows, doesn't she?" His tone went hard.

"Yes. But please don't be mad at her or Alex. She's my friend. And she's been my friend this whole time. And she was highly concerned with my safety, believe me. She…"

"She knew about him, too, did she?"

"Don't be mad at Clara," Violet reiterated. "Frankly, Dad—" she steeled herself to say the next words that were about to come out of her mouth "—my sex life isn't any of your business."

He practically gagged.

"Well, you had me when you were younger than I am now," she continued. "So you're not really in a position to lecture me. On age or responsibility or anything. You know these things just happen sometimes. And I'm at least old enough to sort out how I want to handle it on my own."

"She's not wrong," Alison said.

"I just didn't want you to have to have it hard like I

did," he said. "That's all. You want what's best for your kids, and you want better than you had for them. I was… Your mother was stuck with me. We… We did our best, but we didn't do a great job. Our marriage wasn't good. And I don't want that for you. I don't want you to get married quick because you're going to have a baby. I don't want… What I want for you, Bo, is for you to fall wildly in love, and have a life that you choose."

"How many of us get to have a life we choose, Dad?" she asked, tears filling her eyes. "Mostly we're just trying to get by."

"I want better than that for you," he said, his voice rough.

"Well, I have what I have. So that's it."

She hung up, feeling… She didn't know. It was a relief that they knew in some ways, but in another way she felt absolutely defeated.

She worked the bread, and then set it up for a second rise. Going over the phone call with her dad the entire time. And by the time she took the bread out of the oven, Wolf was home.

"Hi," she said, affecting a faux cheer to her words. "I got to tell my dad I am pregnant. How was your day?"

"I had to get a calf out of barbed wire, but I think you win." He stood there for a moment. "Is he going to kill me?"

"If you were in proximity, I have a feeling he might try."

"Right. Well. Give me the phone."

"What?"

"I want to talk to your dad."

"You *do not* want to talk to my dad."

"I do."

She had absolutely no idea what to make of that. She took the phone and handed it to him, unlocking it as she did. "Last call. Good luck."

She could only stare. Why did this man... Why did he just make no sense to her at all? She had no clue what he was thinking half the time. None at all.

He tapped the bar with her dad's number in it and waited.

"Hello?"

He put it on speaker.

"This is Wolf Garrett," he said.

"What?"

"I told Violet I wanted to talk to you. She gave me her phone. She told me that she talked to you today."

"Yeah," her dad said. "She did."

Wolf didn't know her dad well enough to hear the outright murder in his voice. Violet heard it. Violet knew that if Wolf were in front of her father right now he'd be down for the count and not getting back up anytime soon.

"I just wanted to let you know that I intend to do right by her. Whatever that is. Whatever it looks like," Wolf said.

There was a long silence. "Look, son, I already know you didn't *do right by her.* That's the problem. You can see how I have a little bit of an issue accepting that you're going to do any better moving forward."

"I agree. Violet is a nice woman. Reports on my niceness are mixed. But I believe in being responsible. And I sure as hell believe in doing the right thing. If she'll have me, I'd like to marry her."

"Are you asking permission?"

"No," Wolf said.

"I suggest you do."

Wolf shifted. "If it gets to that."

"You have a lot of balls."

"Yeah. Well, that's never been my issue. But I do believe in being up front. So now that she's told you, I wanted to make sure that I spoke to you."

"I don't know whether or not I admire that."

"You don't have to decide now," Wolf said.

"No man wants to accept that his child is grown. But I have to. So. All I can say is this. I myself am in possession of a predug six-foot hole and a very large bag of lime. I will make your ass disappear."

She was almost sure she saw Wolf's expression shift to one of...respect. "Noted."

He hung the phone up.

"Was that necessary?" Violet asked.

"Yes. I'm not particularly a man of honor, Violet, but I am not a man who hides."

"I don't believe that," she said. She looked into his face, and tried to figure out what he was thinking. And couldn't.

"Believe what you want," he said. "The bread looks good. Ready for dinner?"

And before she could answer practically, she found herself bundled into his truck.

"I really should've brought my car," she said. "I need to be able to go and get supplies from town."

"There's not much of a town."

"Can I buy groceries?"

"Yeah," he said. "Why don't you let me take you the first time?"

There was a protective note to his voice. And she... She knew it wasn't a put-on.

"Okay."

The main house came into view, and her stomach turned over. She didn't know how he did that. Just grab the phone and talk to her dad. She felt...terrified to meet his family. And honestly, her dad was much scarier. She was confident in that.

The lingering anxiety from the whole situation with her dad and Alison was still chewing at her, too.

"I'm just really upset that he's disappointed in me," she said when the truck stopped.

"You think he is? I think mostly he just wants to skin me."

"It's just… I know this isn't what he wanted for me. He was really young when he had me. And I know he doesn't want me to go through the same hard thing. Especially because he and my mom were in love."

"Yeah. Well, let me tell you something. My dad didn't even bother to marry the women that he knocked up. And it's not better."

"You don't think?"

"No. I always wondered… If you would have married my mother, if she would've had some security here. If you would have been a decent husband. Well, maybe she would have stayed. But you know, I can never know that. She might've just missed her family."

"She couldn't see her family here?"

"They cut her out of their lives. She had to choose. That's why I wanted to talk to your dad. I don't ever want there to be a burned bridge between you and your parents, Violet. Because that just about killed my mother. She couldn't stand to be here. She had a big family, one that she was close to. And I just… I don't want that for you. I made some mistakes. I shouldn't have… I shouldn't have messed with you. I knew that. I did. Because I know who I am. Whether you believe it or not, I know who I am. And I didn't want any part of breaking you."

"I'm not that easy to break, Wolf. Don't worry about me."

"Well, no matter how awkward, I'm going to make sure that's clear to your parents. And I'm also going to make it clear you don't deserve their judgment, and if there's an issue, I'm happy to go speak to your dad face-to-face."

"Wolf, that really is a nice thing."

"See, I'm nice," he muttered as he got out of the truck. She got out, holding the bread. And they walked up to the door. He just went right in, without knocking, which she supposed stood to reason, since it was a family home. She shrank behind him, embarrassed slightly that she was quite so...awkward about it all. That she felt quite so...intimidated by the entire situation. But she did.

"Violet?"

A blonde woman with clear blue eyes and a sophisticated sense of style that didn't look like it came from anywhere around here, greeted her.

"Yes," she said. "I brought bread."

"Excellent," she said. "Bring it into the kitchen."

She almost immediately ushered Violet straight through the expansive living room before she could get a good look at it, and into a shockingly modern kitchen.

"You have a beautiful house," Violet said.

"Thank you. I can't take any credit for it. Well, I can take credit for the organizational aspect, but not for the decor. That's all Sawyer. But he remodeled the place a few years ago." She laughed. "I'm Evelyn. I'm Sawyer's wife."

"I've heard about you," Violet said.

"Surprising," Evelyn said, fixing a look at Wolf.

"Is it surprising?" Violet asked.

"Yes. I never can tell what's going on in Wolf's head."

"Oh, so it's not just me?"

Wolf walked past them both, muttering something about betrayals, and he began to dig through the fridge to get a beer.

"Everyone else should be here in a second."

And then as if on cue, a parade of other people came into

the room. Well, not a parade. Just two more. A girl who had the same sort of cocky bearing as Wolf, but very different coloring, and a tall, broad man with a beautiful face, dark hair, blue eyes and an easy smile. He was stunning. Prettier than Wolf's rough appeal. And Violet could see how he was the kind of man who would pick up the first choice of girls in the bar every time. But Wolf still got to her most.

"You must be Violet," the man said. "I'm Hunter. Hunter McCloud. But I bet Wolf hasn't mentioned me."

"He hasn't," Violet said.

"You're so predictable," Hunter said, looking at Wolf in mock disgust.

"I'm Elsie," the small woman said. "Wolf's sister."

So this was Elsie. The younger sister who was two years older than Violet herself.

"Hi," she said, feeling shy, because she had a feeling that Elsie was the person she would have to work hardest to impress. And that Elsie was the person she wanted to impress the most.

"Sorry that my brother's an asshole," Elsie said.

That surprised her.

"Oh," Violet said. "He's not."

"You don't have to lie for him."

Elsie sat down at the table and propped her boots up on it. Evelyn went by and smacked the bottom of the boot with a spoon. "Knock it off."

"Rude," Elsie said, slinging her feet from the table and leaning forward. "I don't know how you got mixed up with him."

"The same way all women get mixed up with him," Hunter said. "I may not understand it. *You* may not understand it. But he attracts them like flies to hon—"

"I don't need your help," Wolf said. "I thank you to not bring up my past in any regard."

"Fine."

And then, as if by magic, a large amount of food appeared. Roast chicken, mashed potatoes, green beans, and suddenly her offering of bread felt meager.

"The bread is perfect," Evelyn said as if she sensed that Violet was feeling insecure.

"Oh. I…"

"We know you're pregnant," Evelyn said. "Because there's not a secret contained in this entire family. We all live on top of each other. So don't feel awkward about that. And, we already dragged him over the coals for it."

"Oh," she said, really not sure what to do with the frank line of conversation.

"Can you guys not scare her?" Wolf asked.

Elsie shrugged. "I'm just being myself."

Midway through dinner, a baby started to cry, and when Evelyn left the room, and appeared with the most adorable little girl Violet had ever seen, her hormones did something very strange. Her whole face got hot, her entire body feeling unsteady.

"You want to hold her?" Evelyn asked.

"Oh, I… I probably shouldn't. I…"

But she found the baby being dumped into her arms, and she could only stare at her, as the little girl with wide blue eyes stared back.

"She's beautiful," Violet said, meaning it.

She had a lot of experience with babies. After all, she had younger half siblings. And so many baby cousins. But… she had never been pregnant while holding a baby before. And imagining that in just a few months' time, she herself could be a mother.

"Oh," she said, touching the baby's downy cheek, and feeling it all settle in, very real. Very intense.

"Her name is June," Evelyn said.

"Hi, June," Violet whispered.

After a minute the infant got fractious, and she passed her back to her mother, thankful to have a slightly less intense moment to exist in. Dwelling on the reality of the situation was only acceptable for a few minutes at a time.

When they finished they adjourned to the living room, with plates of dessert. And Violet, feeling like a coward, stayed at the kitchen table. It surprised her that it was Elsie who stayed behind.

"So you've been just staying in my brother's cabin?"

"For the last couple of days."

"Are you in love with him?"

The question sent a streak of horror through Violet. She wasn't ready to think about that, let alone talk about it.

"It's complicated," Violet said.

Elsie nodded, her expression thoughtful. "Yeah. Well. Wolf is tough."

So it wasn't just her who thought so. It made her feel... Well, validated if nothing else. If his own sister thought he was tough, then maybe there wasn't something wrong with her that she couldn't just magically understand him. "Well, he's tough but he is kind," Violet said, feeling defensive of him.

Is he kind? When exactly has he been kind to you?

The whole situation with her family. That demonstrated how deep he did care, even if he had difficulty conveying it.

"He's... I mean, he really loves all of you," she continued. "He says we're about the same age?"

"Yeah," Elsie snorted. "You're younger than me."

"Oh. Yeah. I guess so."

"I can't believe you're having a baby. I'm not ready for anything like that."

"I don't know that I'm ready..." Violet said.

"Well. I have a lot to do before I could consider it."

"Is Hunter your..."

She suddenly looked horrified. Stricken. "Is Hunter my *what*?"

"Your boyfriend?"

"Oh, hell no," Elsie said. "He's like my... He's like another brother to me. It's not like that at all."

"Is it not?"

"No."

"Sorry," she said. "It's just that I assumed."

"No. Not at all. Not even remotely at all. He is...the biggest pain in the ass that I have ever known. Except for maybe my brothers. Who are actually the worst."

It felt a little like protesting too much to Violet, but what did she know?

"Why are they the worst? I feel like I have a right to know. All things considered."

Elsie frowned. "They're not the worst. I shouldn't have said that. They took care of me. Wolf and Sawyer. Wolf's not... I dunno. I'm sure you've noticed. He's hard to know. He doesn't really like to share a lot about himself. But that's fine. We're not really great at talking about our feelings. Suits me just fine. Honestly. It's our parents who were the worst," she said.

She was echoing what Wolf had already told her.

"They really... They left us to handle it. They left them to handle it. My brothers. And they were... Look, they've been good to me. Even Hunter has. He's all right."

She nodded. "Yeah, he's told me a little bit about your family. I... My mother left."

"Really?"

"Yes," she said. "That's...something that he and I have talked about."

"You got Wolf to talk to you? I think you're a few steps ahead of the rest of us, then."

Violet sat in that for a moment, her heart beating a little bit faster. Wolf did talk to her. He'd shared quite a few things with her. She wondered if…if that meant more than she'd realized at the time.

Wolf walked into the room then, his dark eyes burning on hers. Everything slowed down. Stopped. Maybe she had to reevaluate the way she was thinking about this. The way she was thinking about him.

What do you want?

Her whole conversation with her dad was resonating in her. He hadn't wanted a life for her that wasn't happy. Hadn't wanted one she didn't choose. But the more she thought about her life and Copper Ridge, the more she realized she hadn't exactly chosen it, either. She had been swept up in it. That was the thing. She had stayed because she wanted to make her parents proud of her. Because she was so afraid of disappointing them. So here she was, sitting in—not a worst-case scenario—but sitting in a pretty rough scenario, and while her dad wasn't thrilled, he hadn't disowned her. And at the end of the day, she had never really believed that he would. Because he wasn't her mother, and she knew that. She had always known that. So it had to be something else. She wasn't protecting herself from their abandonment.

Maybe she had just been protecting herself. Not trying anything. Not going too far from home. Not going from the absolute safety that her father and Alison represented.

She hadn't asked to have a revelation sitting there in Wolf's brother's house, but she was having one.

She had always told herself she just wanted to make them proud, but…she knew that she made them proud. They had never been stingy with their praise. She had always known that they loved her. She had always known that they would support her. No, what she was afraid of was failing. Being hurt. Being thrust back into that place that she'd been at when she was thirteen. Feeling like she just wasn't good enough. Because how could she be good enough, if her mother had left her. How could she be?

What was wrong with you when your mother left you?

But here she was, in a house with three people who had been abandoned by their mothers. And none of them seemed broken. Wounded, maybe. Because how could you go through something like that and avoid being wounded? But it wasn't… It wasn't like she had always thought.

And yes, she was afraid. She was afraid of being hurt. But the question that resonated inside her, the one that she really needed to think about, was what did she want her future to look like?

Because she had always known she didn't want to be alone. She had intended to go on dates. She had intended to kiss men. She had intended to have sex. She had intended to fall in love and get married and have children. But something had always stopped her from taking the next step. Fear. It was that simple.

Wolf had been terrifying, from the moment he had first walked into the bed-and-breakfast, but Wolf was also too compelling to ignore. And that was… It was a gift, in many ways. Because it had propelled her into something new. Into something different.

She blinked, her eyes feeling scratchy.

What did she want?

She wanted to be a mother. She might not have wanted to do it now, but she did want to do it.

And she wanted to be in love. And the simple truth was,

she couldn't actually imagine being in love with anyone but Wolf. She didn't love him right now.

That was... It would be silly to love him now. After the way he had hurt her. But... Well, that was the thing. She didn't want a loveless marriage. And she couldn't really imagine any outcome beyond marrying him.

Unless she lost the baby.

The idea made her feel devastated. Absolutely, completely devastated. She didn't even want to entertain the idea. That would mean leaving here like they had never... Like he hadn't changed who she was.

He didn't change who you were. He just thrust you into the exact thing you've been protecting yourself from and made you start to face things.

"Are you ready to head back?" he asked her.

"Yeah," she said. "I am tired. It was really nice to meet you, Elsie," she said.

"Yeah," Elsie said, "surprisingly nice to meet you."

Violet wrinkled her nose. "Surprisingly?"

"No offense. But you know, when it comes to women my brothers get tangled up with... Well, let's just say they're not my kind of person to hang out with. You seem okay." Wolf scowled, and Violet couldn't help herself. She laughed. As far as she could tell, Elsie just enjoyed harassing Wolf, and given that he was formidable, unknowable and all those other adjectives they had just spent the past fifteen minutes or so applying to him, it was genuinely amusing.

"You know how siblings are," Wolf said as they got into the truck.

"Not really," she said.

"Don't you have any?"

"I do. I have two half brothers," she said. "But they're... you know, five and four. So I love them. To pieces. But they're not like brothers. Not really. I mean, I tickle them, but I don't give them a hard time. Not like that."

"So you were basically an only child," he said.

"Basically," she said. "But it's fun to see you with your siblings. But you know, they think you're mysterious, too."

She was pushing. But after the thoughts she'd been having…she figured why not?

"I don't know. We're not…a big family of sharers."

"Yeah, Elsie said the same thing." And yet he'd shared with her before.

"It's hard to describe our dad," Wolf said. "But the older I get, and especially as I'm thinking about actually having a kid, the angrier I get at him. You see, he didn't leave. Not outright. So of course I was angriest at my mom for a long time. Because she was the one that abandoned me. But as you get older, and you get a little more perspective… She was just a person. It made the situation pretty difficult for her."

He was continuing to share with her. Maybe it was his family. Maybe he couldn't share with them.

Maybe she mattered more than…more than she'd realized.

"She went away from her family. Her culture. Everything, to come live with him. To try to figure out a life."

"Her culture?"

"She grew up in Karuk Tribe Housing. Not a reservation really, but in designated housing. The community was tight. And very connected to their heritage. She lost all that when she left for my dad. And I just think she could never… She could never find her place."

"She left you."

"She didn't have a choice."

"And you grew up here."

"Yeah. I don't know that I could fit in my family if I wanted to. I mean, it's not something I spent a lot of time thinking about. It's not... My mother was young. Very young. Much more than my father. That's one reason I... I don't feel the best about all of this. I can see the similarities."

"But like you said, you handled my family."

"Yeah. At least I tried. I'm not about to isolate you. I swear that." He looked ahead, at the road. "I'm just trying to do a little bit better. And I made a mistake. But I can see all the ways my dad failed, and I don't want to fail you. I don't want to fail our kid."

"Wolf," she said. "I... I was really afraid of hurting my parents. Of them being disappointed in me. But that's not who they are. And I know that. I know it's not who they are. And so I'm left with the question of what I actually thought I was doing. And I just think I was trying to protect myself. You want to know why I was a virgin? I told myself a whole lot of stories about how I wanted to be good. And yeah, I knew that... I'm sure that if pressed, if forced to think about it, my dad would've thought that I'd already been with somebody. It's not even that. It's just that I... I... I was afraid."

"For good reason, it turned out. Your taste in men is shit."

She laughed. "Yeah, it turns out. I didn't really think I was the type to go for brooding bad boys."

"Everyone goes through that phase, I hear."

"You're not a phase, though, are you?"

No. She was having his baby. And for some reason, that made her want to...connect with him. She reached across the truck seat and put her hand on his. Then she curled her fingers around the edge of his hand. He didn't move away. And she just sat. Like that. She heard him take a breath. Deep. Steady. But they didn't say anything else as they drove to the house.

She let go of his hand when he parked the truck, and they

got out, walking up to the front, and he opened the door for her. And for the space of a moment, she wondered if she would kiss him. And she genuinely didn't know if she would. She didn't know what she would do. But then he moved away from her, and the decision was made.

"You know, I'm going to want my bed back."

"Well, if I leave, you can have it back. If I end up staying…" Fire arced between them. Because if they got married… Well, presumably they wouldn't be keeping separate rooms.

"Good night," he said.

She didn't follow him down the hall; she sat on the couch until he was no longer moving around. And then she took a shower and went into her room. She lay across the bed that still smelled like him, and she tried to ignore the cascade of images moving through her mind.

The what-ifs. The potential future. The one where everything changed. Where she married Wolf, and spent the rest of her life trying to navigate this relationship that had never been intended to be permanent. But the alternative, in the current arrangement, meant going back to a life without him.

She didn't want that. That was it.

So what did that mean?

It meant making a decision. Not waiting for nature to take its course or not. It meant deciding what she wanted. Because her dad was right. She didn't want to be stuck.

Violet Donnelly had been a coward for an awfully long time.

It wasn't kissing that had made her brave. It wasn't sex.

It was this moment.

And she had to seize it.

CHAPTER THIRTEEN

"WELL, I LIKE your woman," Hunter said.

Wolf's hackles rose. "Do you consider it your solemn duty to hit on every woman Sawyer and I bring home?"

"I didn't hit on Evelyn," Hunter said.

"You did," Sawyer said.

He lifted his beer to his lips and shot Hunter a sidelong glare.

They had finished up a particularly rough workday early, and were sitting on Hunter's porch at his cabin over at McCloud's Landing, marinating in the hurt they'd put on their bodies. The echo of labor ran down straight to his bones.

Hunter's cabin was right on the river, easy access to fishing, which they often enjoyed. Elsie had gone over to the Sullivans' after work, because she and Alaina had plans for an endurance ride, and they were getting all of their gear together and making plans for what route they would take.

Elsie had been working with Hunter today, getting familiarized with the ranch. It was strange; no one from the families had ever crossed over to working at one of the different branches. But Elsie was invested in horses. And while it might ultimately end up that she brought more of an equine spin to Garrett's Watch, it was going to be linked to the McClouds. So she was starting with work there.

"It's just because Evelyn is a particularly beautiful woman," Hunter said. "And you were very uncertain with what you were going to do about all this at first. If you re-call. The angriest I've ever seen a man be about being at-tracted to a lady."

"Because it wasn't that simple," Sawyer said.

"Sure," Hunter said. "What about you?" He directed the question at Wolf. "You mad about Violet being pretty?"

"She's too young for you," Wolf said.

Hunter snorted. "She's too young for *you*."

"I'm two years younger than you," he pointed out to Hunter. "And anyway, no, I'm not mad about it. I'm just waiting her out. Waiting the situation out. I know what I'm going to do. I'm going to do the right thing."

They lapsed into silence, nothing but the sound of the rushing river, the creaking wooden chairs and the clink of beer bottles. "What is the right thing?" Hunter asked after a while.

Sawyer laughed. "I think in our case it's basically the opposite of whatever happened in our family. Because that seems about right. Probably the best you could do."

"Damn straight," Wolf said, taking a swig of beer. "I think if we don't look anything like our parents, we're prob-ably doing okay."

"You okay?" Sawyer asked, directing the question to Wolf.

"What do you mean am I okay?"

"Look. Hunter and I never wanted this. Never wanted the marriage and kids thing. You did, though."

Wolf gritted his teeth. "I'm not thinking about that. Got nothing to do with anything."

"It does, though. Because as far as I can tell she has a lot to do with how you live your life every single day. So how can this be separate from it?"

"Because it is. I have to do right by Violet. No. I wouldn't have chosen this."

"And you're not in love with her."

Wolf shook his head. "No."

"Okay," Sawyer said.

They didn't say anything, again.

"Are you going to tell Violet what happened? Because eventually, someone's going to tell her. Town hall is in the next couple of days, and you know someone's going to mention it."

"Not a secret," Wolf said.

"But you don't talk about it. You don't talk about it like it is a secret."

"It's not a secret. I'll tell her. I don't give a shit."

Except he did. That was the problem. He just didn't want to bring the past into the present. And he…

It was sacred ground. That was the thing.

He could talk about his mother. He could talk about all his anger at his father. But he didn't talk about Breanna. Not unless he had to.

And sometimes he did. He put Brody and Hunter in their places a few weeks ago when they were badgering Sawyer about Evelyn. He had no problem with that. But they knew the story. They'd all been here. It was part of Four Corners. One of the tragedies. That was the thing about a property like this. A place like this. A place that had been around for so long. There had been births on this land, and there had been deaths on it.

It just was what it was.

Except, for him, it would never be that.

For him, it would always be the lesson he had to learn, whether he wanted to or not.

"I guess we're all adults now," Sawyer said.

"Not me," Hunter said. "You guys go quietly into this good night. I will not be."

"It's not like we chose it," Sawyer said. "And you have higher odds of getting a woman pregnant on accident than either Wolf or I had."

"Nope. You're clearly a lot sloppier than I am."

"I wasn't sloppy," Sawyer said. "Condoms have a failure rate."

"*I* was sloppy," Wolf said, gritting his teeth.

"Were you now?" Hunter asked. "But you're not particularly affected by this woman."

"She's hot," Wolf said. "I was out of town. I was blowing off steam. Blew off a little too much."

"You play, you pay." Hunter grinned. "So my father used to tell me."

"Since when did you listen to him?"

"Never," Hunter said. "But I do like to spite him."

The three of them kicked their boots out, leaned back and finished their beers. And then Wolf got in his truck and started down the road back toward Garrett's Watch, and his place.

It was impossible not to think about the grim connection he had to the land. Hell, the grim connection they all had to each other. Life had been harder than it was good for the McClouds and the Garretts. That much was true. And they hadn't always been better people for it.

He pulled up to the house and saw that there were lights strung along the edge of his porch.

Be nice.

Sawyer's words from the other day echoed inside him. Maybe it wouldn't kill him to be a little bit…

He knew how to be charming. He didn't know why it was difficult with her now. He had managed at first.

But she was in his house, and it was just different. He wasn't trying to get her into bed. He'd already done that.

Well, that's sad damn commentary.

He didn't know how to charm somebody if he didn't want something from them.

He got out of the truck and slammed the door shut, walking heavily up the front steps. And when he walked through the front door, Violet was standing there by the Christmas tree.

He froze.

Because there was something different about her.

Her hair was all tumbled around her shoulders, something tousled and suggestive about it. She had some smoky, glittering eye makeup on that enhanced how large her eyes were. Made it impossible to look away.

Her lips were red.

She was wearing a figure-hugging dress that matched the lipstick. A dress.

"Well. Hi," he said.

She crossed the space, wrapped her arms around his neck and pushed his cowboy hat off his head as she stretched up on her toes and kissed him.

And he was…

Hell.

He didn't stop to ask why this was happening. He didn't stop to ask what the game was. He just wrapped his arms around her slender body and held her close. Lost himself in the kiss. In the rhythm of it. In the sweetness of her mouth.

Her mouth was *so sweet*.

There had never been another mouth like it.

Not in all his vast experience. There had never been a woman who got to him like this. Not ever.

He forgot himself when he was with her. And better still, he forgot the past.

It was like there was nothing. Nothing but her hands on his body, her soft skin beneath his palms.

And she fitted against him so perfectly.

He groaned. And they could talk later. He could ask why the hell this was happening; maybe he could even find his way back to charming.

You weren't charming. And she's still kissing you.

That made him feel guilty. Made his chest feel like it was cracked. Because he didn't deserve this. And he was going to take it, anyway. And wasn't that the story of his entire relationship with Violet. He didn't deserve her sweetness. Her trust or her honesty. He didn't deserve to put his dirty hands all over her sweet, angelic figure, and yet he was first in line to do it. No hesitation. Nothing.

Shouldn't he have learned something by now? Shouldn't he have cultivated some resistance?

But there was none, and he wasn't going to start trying now.

He growled and deepened the kiss, taking control of it, backing her up against the wall. He reached around behind him, took hold of one wrist and pinned it on the wall above her head, then grabbed the other, holding them there with one hand as he explored her figure with the other. As he continued to devour her.

"You have no idea," he said. "I've been haunted by you. I've been haunted by you for the last month."

He wasn't going to talk. But this kept spilling out of him. And he wasn't a man who... He wasn't a man who engaged in casual confession. Wasn't a man who revealed much of anything, not if he could help it. And he could always help it.

But he told her everything.

"I haven't even wanted to touch another woman. Haven't even been able to think about it. You ruined me." He growled against her mouth. "You made it so I couldn't want anyone else."

She blinked, her eyes glistening, but she said nothing. His Violet, who always seemed to say exactly what was on her heart, exactly what was in her mind, didn't speak. She just listened. And then she kissed him. Kissed his throat. And bit him there. Like she was the predator. Like she was the beast.

He grabbed the straps of her dress and yanked down, revealing her breasts, glorying in the fullness of them. Her body hadn't changed, not yet. It was novel and familiar all at once. That body that had haunted his dreams every night since. And he'd been consumed by this whole baby thing between them. But this… This was still the biggest thing. Still the truest thing.

He couldn't imagine being a father. But he didn't have to imagine this. It was real; it was right in front of him. It was everything.

He pushed the dress the rest of the way down her hips, and thanked God that her feet were bare, because there was something about the sight of her in nothing more than that scrap of red underwear she was wearing, in her bare feet, that undid him. He pushed his hand between her thighs, stroked her, teased her over the filmy fabric. And she arched against him. And for the first time she spoke.

"Wolf."

Just his name. Whispered. A plea. And he wanted to answer it. He pulled the fabric to the side and found her wet and slick for him. And he was reduced to shaking. Because he was… He was undone. That she wanted him. That she wanted him still. When he had… He had abandoned her. He had abandoned her, then he had dragged her back here.

He had been an ass about her decorating the house for

Christmas. He had been… Well, he had been not awesome, and she still wanted him. Was desperate for him, if the feel of her body beneath his fingers was any indication. He grabbed her thighs, lifted them up off the ground and pulled her core hard up against the ridge of his arousal. He ground against her, against the wall, still pinning her there. He was… He was not in a space to handle this. He couldn't be gentle. He couldn't be… He couldn't be better. He could only be him. But she seemed to want him. So maybe that was okay.

It had to be. Because he didn't have anything else. Couldn't be anything else. Not in this moment. He just wanted her. And that was it.

He kissed her like that until she was panting, until he could tell by the way she held her body that she was on the verge. He released his hold on her wrists.

She bracketed his face with her hands, kissed him, clinging to him. And he pulled her away from the wall, taking her down the hall to her room, where his bed was.

He laid her down on the mattress and stared at her. At her pale silhouette against the dark comforter. The rise and fall of her plump breasts, that lace that barely covered the part of her that he was so hungry for.

He started to strip, slowly, only because if he went too quick, he was going to be inside her before he could breathe again. And he wanted to give her something a little bit better than that. Wanted to give her something a lot better than that, actually.

"Please," she whispered.

And he didn't have to be asked twice. He kicked his boots off, pushed his pants and underwear down and stripped himself naked. He grabbed the waistband of her underwear and jerked them down, tearing them as he pulled them away from her body. And she gasped. He gripped her hips and lifted them up off the mattress, positioning himself at the entrance of her body, and pushing into her in one slick stroke. She gasped, arching against him, and he was lost.

All of his good intentions.

He gritted his teeth, trying to go slow, trying to make it good for her. Taking the time to tease her, where he knew she needed it. He lowered his head, pulling her nipple into his mouth and sucking hard. And she gasped. He said a prayer that all his hard-won skill wouldn't fail him now.

He lifted her thigh and hitched it up over his hip, opening her up to him more, grinding himself against her. She shuddered. And he knew he was on the right track. Except it didn't come from a vast array of knowledge of women.

But just wanting to please Violet.

Wanting to give her everything she deserved. Everything she should have. He was her only experience. And he could see now that… Well, there was no way in hell he was ever letting her have another one. There would be no other man for her. He couldn't allow it. What he'd said to her when he left…when he told her to go find someone else. A lot of someone elses…

It was nonnegotiable. It wasn't happening. Not now. Which meant he had to find a way to be the best. To be everything.

She shuddered beneath him, and he kissed her. Kissed her until they were both mindless. Until he lost his cool. Until he lost his rhythm. Until he was just at the mercy of this thing, a storm, tossed by it as she was. She trembled beneath him, and then she shattered. Her internal muscles clamping around him, pulling his own release from him. He gripped her hips hard, thrusting into her wildly, then freezing as his climax gripped him like a beast. Tearing his throat out. Leaving him spent and gasping for breath.

He rolled away from her, and she went with him. Clinging to him. Burrowing her face in his chest.

He curved his arm around her, pressing his palm between her shoulder blades.

And maybe this was…just the reality of it. That no matter how many times they started over, no matter how many times they hit reset, they would just end up back here. Maybe for them this was inevitable. Maybe for them, this was Groundhog Day.

No matter how many times they started, this is where it would end.

"Stay," she said.

"Yeah," he said. "I'm not in a hurry to get back to the small bed."

She nodded against him.

And he waited for her to say something. Because she always did.

Because she was the one who seemed to lead the conversation, and it was… It was something he was used to with her. But she hadn't been talking. And he had no idea why she'd done this.

Why do you even care?

That was a good question. Why the hell did he care? It was only that he did.

"To what do I owe the change?" he asked.

The words felt dragged from him.

"I had to make a decision," she said. "And be honest with myself about what… What I wanted. And I want you, Wolf. All of this is just pretending that we don't. We're just dancing around it. I want you. And we're pretending that that isn't going to be something between us. That we can… That we can somehow manage it. We've been walking on eggshells around each other, trying to pretend that we know what being adults looks like. Like we know how to handle this. Like somehow not having sex is going to make it better." She sniffed loudly. "Not having sex was not better. I missed it."

He laughed. He couldn't help himself. "Well. Yeah, agree with that."

"I think I want to marry you," she said softly.

The words sent a streak of terror through him. Which was ridiculous. Because he'd already decided that he was marrying her. He had unequivocally decided. But hearing her say that she wanted it, rather than it being an edict coming from him, well, that was different for some reason. It just was.

"After…"

"No," she said. "I think I want to marry you."

Yes. That was the answer. The certainty inside him.

"I can't go back," she said. "No matter what happens. Not now. I can't pretend that this didn't happen."

"All right. We'll get married. But I'm going to have to go talk to your dad."

She nodded. "Yeah. Thank you. He'll… He'll appreciate that."

"I'll drive to Copper Ridge tomorrow."

She swallowed hard. "You don't have to do that. You can call him."

"No," he said. "If a man is going to marry his daughter, I suspect your dad needs the question to come in person. I'm not about to get on his bad side. Hell, I am already."

"I'll go with you," she said.

"No," he responded. "This is something I have to do."

CHAPTER FOURTEEN

THE NEXT MORNING he found himself leaving a warm, sleeping Violet in his bed, and getting on the road, going straight to Copper Ridge without stopping.

He had gotten her address last night, and had found his way easy enough.

It was possible her father could be out working, but he would wait.

He pulled up to the house, which was a large barn that had been converted into a dwelling. There were Christmas lights strung around the outside, bright and cheery, the way that she had made his home. This was what she had come from. Yes, she'd been abandoned by her mother, and he knew that hurt her. He knew it hurt her badly. But she had...this. He did not have that.

He got out of the truck and walked down the path to the front door. Then he knocked.

A pretty woman with red hair answered.

"Can I help you?" she asked.

"Yeah. I'm looking for Cain Donnelly."

"And you are?"

"Wolf Garrett."

Her eyes widened fractionally. He assumed that this was Violet's stepmother. She looked only a few years older than Wolf himself. But Violet had explained the situation, so he expected as much.

"Oh," she said. "Well. Is Violet with you?"

He shook his head. "No."

She stepped away from the door. "Come in."

"Cain," she shouted. "There's a young man here who wants to speak with you."

Wolf shoved his hands into his pockets and stood, just waiting in the entryway. Alison didn't offer him an alternative. She just looked at him, and waited. And when Violet's father walked into the room, he knew that what Connor had said to him was true. He was in very grave danger of having his ass kicked. Cain Donnelly was a big man. And very much looked to be in his prime. He also very much looked pissed off.

"Wolf Garrett," he said. "I assume."

"You assume correct."

"What is it you want?"

"I'm here to ask you permission to marry your daughter."

"Is that so?"

"Yes."

"I thought you were waiting on that."

"I was going to. But I decided I want to marry her."

He fixed a hard look on Wolf. "Do you love her?"

He couldn't lie to this man. Not staring him down, straight in the eye. But he could sidestep.

"I don't know her all that well. Just being honest. She doesn't know me all that well, either. But this is something that she wants. And I told her… I told her that I would do the right thing by her. That I would talk to you because… you know, you're the most important person to her. She wants your approval. And if I'm going to ever have Violet's approval, I know I need to have yours right along with it."

"I'm not sure that I can give approval to a man who

doesn't know my daughter all that well but managed to get her pregnant, anyway," he said, that gaze never wavering.

Wolf did wonder, briefly, if his life was in danger.

"It's fair that you don't have a lot of respect for me. I don't have a lot of respect for myself. Violet is too good for me. And so I'm going to have to figure out how to be someone who deserves her even a little bit. She came to my house and cleaned it and cooked me dinner. She decorated for Christmas. No one's ever done that for me before. I might not be great at feelings, but I have land. And I keep my word. I'll stay with her as long as she wants to stay with me. As long as she will have me. I'll never hurt her. I'll never betray her. I'll be a good father to our child. At least, I'll do my best to figure out what that looks like. I can't say that I had a great example. But I know enough to know that the example I had was bad. I don't expect to impress you, Mr. Donnelly," he said, the *Mr.* strange, all things considered, but he figured he had to work overtime to show this man the kind of old-fashioned respect he wanted, since Wolf had kind of failed at one of the key aspects of it. Namely, getting his daughter pregnant before marriage.

"Violet said it's what she wanted," Wolf said.

Because in the end, it was the only real compelling truth.

"You're sure about that?" Cain asked.

"She told me last night. So the first thing I did today was come to ask you."

"You were waiting for her to say it?"

He nodded. "And in the grand scheme of things, I wouldn't, probably. I would do it when I knew it was right. But all things considered, I thought I should wait until she felt comfortable."

He didn't offer his hand. He didn't smile. He rocked back

on his heels, his glare hard. "You have my permission. If you hurt her…"

"Six-foot hole," Wolf said. "Bag of lime. I believe it."

"Do."

Then he turned and walked away from him. Alison showed him the door.

She put her hand on Wolf's forearm, her manner infinitely softer than her husband's. But he saw a light burning behind her eyes just then that let him know she was made of steel.

"You listen to me, Wolf Garrett," she said. "I myself am a fan of a hardheaded cowboy. I married one of my own. I'm also a woman who knows how cruel men can be. Cain's not my first husband. I managed to get myself safe. And I did it without being a vigilante. But that was me. If you ever lay a hand on my stepdaughter in anger, it may not be her father you have to worry about."

"I've never hurt a woman," Wolf said, making eye contact with her. Offering her all the sincerity that he had in his being. "Not like that. And I would never hurt Violet. I'd hand you the shotgun if I did."

"I'll take that."

"Also, best believe, Eli Garrett would help you get away with that murder."

"Oh, I do," Alison said. "Eli was pretty instrumental in helping me. And so was his wife, Sadie. I respect your family a great deal. Without them, I don't know that I would be where I am today. And it's because of that respect that I believe you're probably a good man. I hope you dig in and figure out how to be the best one for Violet. Because she is very dear to me."

"I can promise you that."

He tipped his hat and went back to the truck. And then

he started driving toward the Gold Valley. He'd seen there was a store there that sold jewelry. It was a little place on Main Street, occupied by a friendly-looking woman with blond hair that looked like a halo, and a white dress that added to the angelic effect. "What can I help you with?"

"I'm looking for an engagement ring," he said.

"Okay," she said. "I have a few things that can work with that. I'm Sammy."

"Wolf," he said.

"What's your fiancée's name?" she asked, fixing her clear blue gaze on him.

"She's not my fiancée yet," he said.

"I'm sure she will be. Especially if we find the right ring. Her name?"

"Violet," he said.

She closed her eyes, like she was doing some kind of weird transcendental meditation thing. "I have just the thing for her."

She took out a tray and set it up on the glass top. "I make these," she said. "And this is a moonstone. It's not traditional, but it's very pretty. You have all these colors reflected there, including violet, of course. Set into rose gold with eternity knots around the band. For forever."

Forever.

His.

He had never been sure forever existed. Four Corners was forever. And it was work.

Well, if it took work to make it forever, if it took a ring, he'd do it.

"I'll take it," he said.

"Do you know what size ring she wears?"

He frowned. "They come in sizes?"

She laughed. "Is her hand about like mine?"

No, Violet's hand wasn't like this woman's. Violet's hands were hers. And they were perfect against his skin. Fit right around his cock. He couldn't look at another woman's hand and try to compare them.

"Her hands are like *hers*," he said.

Sammy laughed, and he didn't know what the hell was so funny. "Well, if she needs it sized feel free to bring her back here. I'll do it for free."

He walked out of the place, holding a little paper bag, and then got back in his truck. He decided to stop at the bakery around the corner and get a box of treats. The woman there suggested sugar cookies with purple icing, and he was happy enough to go with that. And that was how he found himself walking toward his house with a large pink box, that small paper bag and a grim sort of determination.

He opened up the front door to find Violet standing up on a chair dusting the top of the cabinets.

"What the hell are you doing?" he asked, crossing the room, wrapping his arm around her waist and lifting her down from the chair. "You have to quit climbing all over everything like a spider monkey."

Her face was pale, breathless. "You scared me to death," she said.

"Sorry. But you looked like you could fall."

"I wasn't going to fall. Though I might have, given that you gave me such a fright."

"I caught you," he said.

He had the box in one hand, along with the bag, and her in the other.

She looked up at him, her eyes wide. "How was… How was Copper Ridge?"

"Good. I met your dad."

"Oh," she said. "Well…" She patted his chest. "I don't feel any bullet holes."

"No bullet holes."

She tried to laugh. It seemed to get caught halfway up her throat.

And then, he couldn't help himself. Because she was in his arms. And he was about to make her his.

He kissed her. Just kissed her. Simple and sweet. Or maybe it would have been sweet if he were sweet. If he wasn't instantly imagining her naked beneath him. If he wasn't filled with a sense of primal possessiveness that overtook everything else.

He carried her over to the couch and set her down on his lap. He put the box and bag next to him, and she stared at him, saying nothing.

"I stopped and got you something," he said.

"What?"

"Cookies," he said, pointing at the box. "And this." He opened up the bag and pulled out the little ring box that was in there.

He paused for a second, and realized the strangeness of the moment. Because actually… Though he would never admit it to anyone, it was something he'd thought about. When he'd been young, and he'd been in love… He'd just been waiting.

Waiting to be eighteen, waiting until he could buy Breanna a ring. He'd started to save up. Money that he got from working the ranch, because he wanted to buy her something great. He hadn't had to save up for this, because he wasn't a sixteen-year-old boy, he was a thirty-two-year-old man. He had his own money. But he'd still had to go talk to the girl's father.

He thought about how he'd take her out somewhere

fancy. Maybe even drive to Eugene. Have her get all dressed up. And then he'd get down on one knee. That had been the best thing he could think of then.

All he'd had to do was wait a little.

All he'd had to do was be sure she felt the same.

And it had all ended too soon.

That fantasy and this moment were not the same.

He opened up the box. "I asked your dad. He said as long as you want to do this, you have his blessing. We have his blessing. So will you? Will you marry me?"

"Oh," she said. Her eyes filled with tears, and he instantly wondered if he had made a big mistake.

And he felt for a moment like the bottom had fallen out of his world.

"Is this not what you wanted?" he asked.

"It's just… It's *more* than I expected."

And that didn't restore the ground. No, instead, it made him feel like he was falling.

"I'm sorry," he said. "I'm sorry you didn't even expect a ring from me."

"Don't be sorry. It's just the whole thing has been inside out."

"She said there are sizes? I don't know anything about that."

She took the ring out of the box and slid it slowly onto her finger. It seemed to fit.

"It is perfect," she said. He could feel her retreating into herself, and he didn't understand why. But then, he didn't understand a whole lot of what was happening right now.

She put her hands on his face and kissed him. And this, he understood. This, between them, he understood. And he wondered if this was when he should tell her about Breanna.

If he needed to have the conversation now. But it seemed wrong. And it just didn't… It didn't matter.

He just kissed Violet, because she wanted to kiss him. And as long as they were kissing, everything was fine. When they had their clothes off, things seemed easy. It was when they had them on that it all seemed harder.

It was when he didn't know what to do.

And Wolf Garrett never didn't know what to do. There were certain things he chose not to involve himself in, and he could see now that maybe he didn't live a life of absolute certainty so much as he lived a life absent of some very specific things.

Connecting with people being the biggest one.

Hadn't his own sister said to Violet that he was difficult that way?

That he kept things to himself.

But it didn't matter now. She was in his arms; she was wearing his ring. She was his. It was that simple.

He took her to bed and made sure to affirm that. Over and over again.

And when it was over he felt resolute. In that at least.

CHAPTER FIFTEEN

"THE TOWN HALL meeting is later today."

Violet looked up when Wolf walked in and said that as a greeting. She had been distracted all day. Staring at the ring on her finger. Luxuriating in the fact that she had spent the whole of the past two nights making love with him again. In some ways, things felt right. In other ways...there was a tenor of uneasiness that seemed to wind between the cracks of their interaction, but she chose not to dwell on that.

"What's the town hall meeting?"

"It's more of a potluck. It's a bit chilly out, so we're having it in the barn down at the McClouds'."

"Oh," she said. "It's all the families?"

"Yeah."

"I'll get to meet them," she said.

"Yeah. As my fiancée."

She flushed with pleasure at that, and really hoped that he didn't notice.

There. There was the uneasiness. Because she wanted to hide how much this meant to her. Wanted to hide her response to it. Wanted to hide how deeply she was affected by it. She wanted to pretend that she was right with him on this. Not any more invested, not any more emotionally involved. He was resolute, certain. But it wasn't the same as being...happy.

She had never seen Wolf happy. Not particularly. He

seemed settled right now. Seemed content. But it wasn't the same as…

She did not feel settled, not really. She didn't feel content.

She was something else altogether, and she was loath to examine it too deeply.

"I can bring some food," she said.

"There is going to be food. Tons of it. The Sullivan sisters always go overboard. It's part of their charm."

She was nervous. And spent too long choosing what to wear. She hadn't been to the McCloud property yet, and it took several minutes going down the winding dirt road to get there. When they pulled up, there were already trucks parked out front in a line. So many trucks.

And cowboys everywhere.

There was a parade of women in fluttery floral dresses carrying food, and that she assumed was the Sullivans. One of them was gesturing broadly and directing some of the men to carry things, unloading the back of their truck, and the food seemed endless.

She saw Elsie, standing with them, dressed in her jeans. When the car stopped, she got out, and went over to her future sister-in-law. "Hi," she said.

"Hi." She looked down at her hand, her gaze zeroing in on the ring. "Oh, my gosh," Elsie said. "He *proposed*."

"Oh. Yeah," she said, putting her hand behind her back.

"This is Wolf's fiancée," Elsie said. "This is my friend Alaina. Alaina Sullivan. And those are her sisters, Fia, Rory and Quinn."

The other girls smiled. "Wolf's fiancée," the one who she thought was Quinn said. "Well. That is something. Good for him."

There was something strange and grave about the way that she said it, and she felt certain she had missed something. But she didn't have time to ask, because Wolf joined her then, putting his hand on her lower back. "I see you met all of them."

"Yes," she said.

There were a lot more men than women, and so the women stood out. There was one group that seemed a little bit aloof, even standing there in front of the barn. And there was a woman with them, with long, curly chestnut-colored hair, and her lips set down into a frown. She was very cowgirl chic. Rhinestones and studs all over her jeans.

"Who are they?"

"The Kings," he said. "They're a whole thing."

"As far as I can tell every single one of you are a whole thing."

"Well, they're the most of it."

She was then introduced to the McClouds. Angus, who went by Gus, and had scars covering most of his face. Lachlan, Tag, Brody and of course she already knew Hunter.

They went inside the barn, and she was dazzled. The place was lit up completely, lights strung from the ceiling, and draped down the walls. There were long tables set up, and all the food had gone there. Everyone took their seats—they all seemed to know exactly where to sit, and she found herself seated with the Garretts, and most closely to the McClouds.

It was Gus McCloud who took the lead of the meeting, talking about his expansion efforts with his equine facility. Up next was—she was informed by Elsie—Denver King, whose voice was deep, and his presence commanding in the same way a black hole was. It sort of just sucked you in, whether you wanted to be or not.

He was talking about quarters and profits. About new

crops. He was fascinating even though the topic wasn't. Not to her, anyway.

It seemed to be resonating with everyone around them. The meeting part was over very quickly, and then the food was unveiled, and the beer came out.

It was chaotic, but not in a bad way. And there was music, which she hadn't expected at all.

"It's basically an excuse to have a hoedown once a month," Wolf muttered.

"Everyone seems to be enjoying themselves," she said.

"A lot of it's for the employees. They… They deserve it. They work hard for us."

"You all seem like you know how to have a good time. Well, okay, some of you do."

Other than Gus, who held himself slightly apart from the group, the McClouds seemed happy enough to get in and dance and flirt. Particularly Hunter, who exuded easy charm.

But Wolf didn't. And he didn't seem to enjoy the social aspect of…anything.

"Were you always like this?"

"Was I always like what?"

"Just… You don't seem to like this. You don't seem to like things like this at all."

"Pretty much. I was always like this."

He got up from the table then, went to get a beer and didn't come right back. She noticed that he was talking to one of the Kings; she was fuzzy on who was who.

It was Quinn Sullivan who took the chair next to her. "So are you going to live here?"

"I guess so," she said, her heart sinking.

That actually did make her sad. Because she had just been thinking about how much she loved Copper Ridge.

How much she loved the ocean. And the idea of living a couple of hours away from her family was… Well, it was foreign and unsettling.

"You haven't talked about it?" Quinn asked.

"It was kind of sudden."

"Oh. That really does surprise me. I mean good. Good for you."

"Wolf is… I know. I know that he's…" She thought of his earlier words in regard to the Kings. "A whole thing."

"He's a good guy," Quinn said. "At least, as far as I can tell. He's hard to get a read on. He's always been intense. For a while he was… He tried to sort of get along with everyone, but then he changed."

"He did?"

She had just been asking him about this very thing, and he hadn't said anything. She had given him a chance to explain whether or not it had always been like this for him or if he had grown to hate social gatherings, if he had become closed off. But then, she guessed people who were closed off were never going to take the first opportunity to tell you why.

"Well, yeah. After Breanna he was never really the same. But I guess…it affected all of us."

She nodded slowly, and she didn't want to look like a fool, not understanding who Breanna was. But it wasn't even a name she had heard. She had heard a lot of names when they pulled up. She had heard a lot of names over the past few weeks of knowing him, but she had not heard that one.

"He just… I was really worried about him for a while. I didn't know he would ever… If you ever pull out of that funk, but he did. It's just that once he did he wasn't the guy he used to be. Sawyer has always been serious. You know Sawyer."

She nodded.

She *sort* of did.

"He's a great guy. But he's very much the oldest. Wolf was never like Sawyer, except in his desire to do what was right. He was never the most outgoing, or talkative, but he was… Well, he was sweet."

Violet laughed. "I don't know that I'd call him *sweet*. But he's… He is a good man."

Quinn cleared her throat. "Now, if Arizona King can find somebody to love her exactly the way she is…then there really is hope for the rest of us."

Arizona was sitting by herself, scowling and drinking a beer.

"What's her deal?"

"No one knows. Something happened, and she got… feral. And it's been so long that whatever it was, she really should be over it by now. But it's like it broke something in her. I guess that's how grief is sometimes. Whether it's death or…something else."

Death.

Breanna.

She was going to ask Wolf about that. She was going to wait. She wouldn't do it here. Because she had sense enough to know that if it hadn't come up, there was a reason. Because Wolf was nothing if not utterly and completely protective of himself and his emotions.

She had a feeling she didn't want to know exactly where this line of questioning was going to lead. But she did want to know Wolf. And she wanted to know Wolf a hell of a lot more than she wanted to be comfortable.

You're not comfortable. That's the thing. Because you

know there's more to him, and he's just not telling you. You know there's more to him and you also have to know that it isn't going to be a happy story or he would be a happier person.

And maybe that was just it. Maybe caring about him was going to mean being brave enough to face all of that.

But she was going to have to pry it out of him with a crowbar.

But everybody here knew. It wasn't fair that she didn't.

That thought brought her up short.

Fair?

What was fair and not fair about this entire thing?

Sure. Maybe if she was his real girlfriend. Maybe if she was what everyone here thought she was. What Quinn seemed to believe that she was. Maybe if she was actually a woman whom Wolf had fallen in love with. An unexpected bright spot in a life that had clearly been difficult. But she wasn't.

She was just a woman he'd gotten pregnant. And the one thing that was very clear about Wolf was that he would have proposed to any woman he'd gotten pregnant.

He played like he was a bad boy, but he was traditional. It was clear. In everything he did. And the fact that he'd gone to visit her father. The fact that he'd gone to get her a ring. And she had allowed herself to believe that it might be romantic. But it was just…

She looked across the barn, looked at that man. And she tried to make sense of him. Because who had taught him to be so traditional? He had a mother who left him, and a father who didn't seem to care. So where did this core of honor come from? It was there, and she was grateful for it. He was good; that was the thing. It was inarguable. Maybe it came from Sawyer. That would make sense. Maybe it was his relationship with his older brother that spurred him to be like this, but Sawyer had it from somewhere. She just… She just wished she knew. And she didn't know that it mattered. Maybe it didn't matter at all. Maybe she needed to come to her own conclusions without having those answers.

Well, you're in luck, because you're not just going to get them easily.

But fairness wouldn't be a part of it. Because he didn't owe her anything.

She wished that he did. But all of this, the entire time, was… It was her own traditionalism, actually. She had been so sure that she was careful and protecting herself. But she had met a beautiful man she wanted to believe in, and she had ignored everything that he'd said to her, cast off all of her misgivings and jumped right in, telling herself that she knew exactly what it was. Telling herself she could handle an affair, all the while secretly believing that she would get to keep him. To the point where…after two weeks of sex she had asked him to stay.

She was still doing it.

Romanticizing every gesture.

Inserting herself into the space she wanted to be in. She wanted to be special to him. She wanted… She wanted to be special, and in the absence of that, she was feeling pretty content exploiting his traditionalism, and his willingness to make a commitment, and she knew that meant that more decision-making was ahead for her.

Because with all this revelation, with all this self-honesty, came the need for her to do something about it.

Whether it was sad or not, she wanted to be here. She wanted to be with him. She was drawn to him like she had never been drawn to another person. And she was fascinated by this place. By the possibility of this life around her.

And if she left tonight, it wouldn't change the fact that Wolf was the father of her child. But he was the first man she had ever wanted, which was much more important than his being the first man she had slept with. He was the first man she had even wanted to be with. He was the first man to take those feelings in her and make them something irresistible. And he had broken her heart. But without saying he loved her, without giving her any kind of emotional anything, he had started to piece it back together with his actions.

Wolf represented security. She could see that clearly, right then.

And security was actually what she wanted. More than anything, it seemed, because she was willing to contort and twist to make this work in the name of security.

But what did he want? And how did she give it to him? Maybe it didn't matter. But it felt like it did. It felt like it mattered an awful lot.

He came back and sat next to her, and she tried to smile. "What?"

And that simple question made something warm filter through her body. Because he noticed that something was wrong. And it did seem like he cared.

"Is everybody being nice to you?"

"Everyone is being very nice to me," she said. "This is a wonderful place. I can see why it means so much to you."

She thought back to her earlier revelations about him. And he would do his duty. It mattered to him. Because at his core he was no rebel at all. Because he was a man who worked the family land even though his family legacy had never been anything for him but pain. Because he was a man who stayed. At least, when he needed to be.

They stayed a while longer. Then they got into the truck

and started driving back home. It was dark, and the headlights of the truck provided the narrow beam of illumination. On the next curve. But nothing farther ahead. And that was much how she felt her whole life was at this moment. She could get just to the next curve. But what lay beyond that, she didn't know. And it could be something lethal, or something easy.

"Wolf," she said. "Who's Breanna?"

CHAPTER SIXTEEN

WELL, HELL. SAWYER HAD told him. He had warned him that he needed to give her the story or somebody else was going to do it for him. And maybe part of him hoped someone else would.

He just didn't have any practice telling it.

Tell yourself that all you want, but you know that's not why.

No. The beast inside him turned circles around this particular truth, snarled at anyone who might get too close. The beast inside him wanted to protect this wound like it was a living thing, and it paced around it in a slow circle, snarling at him.

Because this was his most cherished pain.

That prize trauma that had turned him inside out and finally changed him.

The one that had made sure he knew that there was no happiness for him in this world, and believing it when he had already been shown that it wasn't to be by his parents...

Well, it was foolishness. And he had been a fool. He learned his lesson since. And it was that lesson he guarded with such ferocity. Because it was more than a lesson.

It was a human being.

It was a sweet girl who'd had the misfortune of being on the receiving end of his overly intense, obsessive brand of desire.

But there was no reason to not tell her. She deserved to

know. She did deserve to know. Because to be with him was to share space with this. Hell, he'd been doing it for the past sixteen years. He was comfortable with it. As these things went.

"Breanna was my girlfriend," he said.

"I see. I had it on good authority that you didn't have girlfriends."

"Yeah. Not after her."

"She must have hurt you really badly," she said.

"She was the daughter of one of the workers here. Really pretty. I… I didn't have a chance. She showed up, joined our little one-room schoolhouse when we were fifteen. I was a goner. She was really good friends with Nelly McCloud—Tag's wife. Who wasn't his wife at the time, but you know. Anyway. She… She played like she didn't notice me. Like she was too good to have her head turned by the likes of me. I wish she had been. No. Just like…"

And he realized, she was the first girl, so it wasn't just like those girls always were, not to him, not then. But it was what he had learned. Later.

"I fell for her hard. And we were young, with very little supervision. So…" He remembered taking the trucks out in the middle of the night, parking somewhere, laying a blanket down in the back, and the two of them… They'd get lost in it. In each other. They'd been each other's first time. And a whole lot of other times after.

He'd been in love. Head over heels. He hadn't wanted another woman, not ever.

"I wanted to marry her. And I never wanted to get married. Because I never saw it go very well. But I knew that the two of us, we couldn't fail. Because there was never anything like that. And there never would be again."

"What happened?"

This was the part he didn't have any practice with.

"It was summer. We went out swimming. It was dark. We used to horse around by the dock. And we were… We were talking. She… She slipped off the dock, I guess. I thought she was jumping. But she wasn't. She didn't come back up. It was dark. I couldn't see anything. I jumped in the water. I couldn't feel her anywhere. I couldn't… Couldn't see."

And he just didn't want to tell the rest of the story. Because it didn't end well. Because it was a whole lot of images that haunted him. That made him feel broken inside. And that beast in him was snarling. Telling him to keep it safe. There were certain things that didn't need to be shared. There wasn't a reason for it. It didn't fix anything. Didn't bring back the past.

"She drowned. The best they can figure she hit her head, knocked herself senseless enough that she couldn't find her way back to the surface. And it was dark. It was dark and we were idiot kids that shouldn't have been out in the lake."

"Wolf…"

"It's really awful. But I don't need you to take that tone of voice with me. But that's Breanna. And that's… That's it."

"You said you believed in love," she said softly.

"Yeah. I do. I can't deny it. I've been in love."

"Right."

He hated to think about it. He hated to think about the days following that. Her parents were angry. They'd blamed him.

Hell, he'd blamed himself.

He'd been there with her. They'd been out there in the dark. He'd upset her.

It would've been the better thing for him to drown saving her. But he dived down deep, and then he'd come up to the surface. Every time. To breathe. And in the end, when her body had come up without her soul in it, he had wished that he'd stayed down there.

Maybe they could have found each other. Maybe then…

It wasn't that kind of grief, not anymore. Not the same as he felt that first six months after, when he just wondered why he bothered to take another breath every time he did. Because it felt like there could be no happiness, no nothing on this side of heaven, not without her.

No, that grief had faded. But somehow, everything else had faded along with it. And it had left him who he was.

"That must've broken your heart," she said.

And it was such an obvious thing to say. Because of course it had. But at the same time, he didn't recall anyone ever addressing that. In fact, he didn't think he'd ever thought of it in those terms. Mostly because he hadn't deserved for it to be a heartbreak. It was a loss, for sure and certain. But didn't he have a stake in that loss? How did he deserve to be broken by it?

"Yeah," he said. Because whether or not he felt it was deserved, it was honest. And it made a certain kind of sense. His heart had already been damaged, but just… Just enough that he could still love. And then after that, it had been broken. Putting it back together hadn't been a simple thing. But he found a way to go on. But he'd never been the same. It had never been quite the same way. Not since.

"Yeah," he said. "I expect it did."

"I'm sorry that happened. I'm sorry that happened to you."

That hit him all wrong. "It didn't happen to me. It happened to her."

"You're the one that's left dealing with it."

"And her parents. Her brother. I hardly have the monopoly on this one."

She said nothing. Not for a long moment. The sound

in the truck was nothing more than the engine, the slight rasp of tree branches on the windows as they drove down the narrow, rocky road, and his own heartbeat in his ears.

"Do you still love her?" she asked, finally.

He thought about that. Because sometimes he couldn't see her face, not clearly anymore. And his clearest memories were reduced to snapshots rather than moving film. And her voice, thinking about what she might want him to do, had gotten him through quite a bit over the years, but hadn't been enough to keep him away from Violet. But still.

"Yeah," he said. "I do."

"Okay."

"Sawyer said I should have told you earlier. Because it was going to come up when people met you. I don't know how to talk about it, though. So I didn't. That wasn't fair to you."

She shook her head. "No. It's fine. Wolf, I made the decision to be with you before I knew anything about why you were the way that you were. I'm not changing it now. Not now that I have more information. That we need to make this work isn't going to change."

The beast inside him calmed down, because it seemed that this was going to be the end of the conversation. And he had to wonder what he'd expected. Maybe for there to be more emotion. In himself.

No, he didn't like thinking about it. So he didn't.

But it was a marvel, the detachment in his soul. And even he recognized it. And every so often, that beast seemed to rise up and take him over completely, not snarling in the distance regarding old wounds, but roared to life. It had done so when Violet had stripped her dress off for him in the living room. Hell, it had done that when he'd first met her. But now it stood apart. Comfortably away from him. Comfortably circling all the things inside him that he wanted left alone. He managed to tell the story without touching the wound. And that, he supposed, was a victory.

They pulled up to the house then, and for some reason, it was surprising that she walked up the steps with him. She had been staying with him now for a week. It shouldn't be a surprise that she was coming inside with him. And yet, there was something about it that jarred him. Perhaps that he was used to being alone. He didn't usually have to navigate other people. Especially not when he didn't want to. But she was there.

And he walked in, and the Christmas tree was there, too, and he couldn't deny that things were different because he was sharing a household with Violet.

And he realized right then just how solitary he typically was. Particularly when he was on the verge of having an emotion.

It was pretty early yet, and not quite time to call it a night. He tried to think of what he would do with the time if Violet weren't here. He might have stayed longer at the town hall. Might have had another drink with Sawyer and Hunter. He just sat on the couch, though, right in front of that Christmas tree. And Violet sat next to him. She didn't say anything. She just sat there.

He wasn't thinking. Not really. But there was a strange sort of disquiet in his body. An anxiety that he didn't like. That he wasn't used to. Like he was on the verge of disaster. But it was just that memory.

A desire still to do something about it. To fix it. A hatred of the helplessness that he'd felt in that moment.

Violet reached out and pushed his hair off his forehead. He looked at her, and the corner of her mouth hitched up.

"I think I'll head to bed," he said.

"Okay," she said softly.

She got up along with him, and he walked ahead of her down the hall, turning toward his room.

"You're sleeping in your room?"

He huffed a laugh. "Not really in the mood."

She looked hurt. He might as well have stabbed her. But it was in service of the being alone thing, which he was feeling the need for pretty hard, and didn't want to admit it.

"I don't need you to be in the mood to share a bed with me, Wolf."

He clenched his teeth together, his jaw tight. He didn't really know what to do with that.

"You really want to sleep in that tiny twin bed?"

He grunted, moving to her room instead. She undressed slowly, and he turned away from her, taking his own clothes off with swift efficiency before getting under the covers. When she joined him, she was wearing a nightgown. A nightgown that could have almost been considered virginal.

Usually, time in bed with Violet was sexual if they weren't sleeping. They made love, and it drowned out all thought, all feeling. Everything. But instead, tonight, they just lay under the blankets, a healthy amount of mattress between them.

He flung his forearm over his eyes and let out a long, slow breath. And then he felt a tentative touch on his chest. He moved his arm and looked down, and in the dim light, saw Violet snuggling up to him. Her palm pressed more firmly on him, right over his heart. And her cheek pressed against his shoulder.

He froze there like that. And the beast in him growled. But he didn't move away.

Then she kissed him. Right there on his chest. And a soft sigh escaped her lips.

She was sleeping within a few minutes, and Wolf had a feeling sleep wasn't going to come for him for a long time.

CHAPTER SEVENTEEN

VIOLET FELT TENDER the next day. And she wasn't really enjoying being alone with her thoughts. Wolf went out and worked all day, and she toiled away in the tiny cabin, trying to find things to do.

Really, she should get some books and lie around.

She was supposed to be on some kind of vacation figuring herself out. And really, she did need to figure herself out. That was the bottom line. But after last night she was even less certain of what she wanted.

No. She knew what she wanted. She wanted both her and Wolf to magically be undamaged so they could figure out a way to be together. To be wildly…happy. She wanted to be with him. But she wanted to figure out a way to make it easier. Knowing that he was in love with somebody else—a girl who had died tragically in her teens—she didn't know what to do with that. Because she couldn't compete with it. She couldn't possibly compete with some idealized lost teenage love. And maybe it had been amazing.

Maybe it had been deep, true love.

She didn't know.

She didn't have a great love in her past.

She had him.

And it made her feel lonely and isolated to realize that. That there was somebody in his heart and there was no one but him in hers.

She let out a growl of frustration that echoed around the cabin. Because she was truly driving herself crazy.

Her phone buzzed on the counter, and she saw that it was Clara. "Hello?"

"You are a really annoying friend, do you know that? I can't believe how little you've been in touch with me. You don't even answer my texts."

Violet winced. "Well, I'm going through stuff."

"That is literally what friends are for. To go through stuff with you." And Violet knew she didn't really have a great excuse for that. Because yeah, she had been kind of sticking to this idea that she wanted some time to herself, that she wanted to be alone, but then she found herself rattling around the cabin driving herself crazy with nothing to do.

"I'm sorry," Violet said. "I'm bad at this. I am good at living my normal, sedate life in Copper Ridge and having nothing going on, and hanging out with you and eating cookies. I am not good at big changes and figuring out how to sort them out, and looping people in my life in on them."

"I know he came to ask your dad if he could marry you."

"Yeah. He did do that."

"So…" Clara let the first word linger. "You want to marry him?"

She didn't even have to think about that. "Yes," she said.

"What are you doing today?"

"Laying around the cabin feeling sorry for myself?"

"Excellent. Sounds like the perfect thing to do to celebrate your engagement. I'm on my way to Pyrite Falls."

"You cannot be on your way to Pyrite Falls," Violet said, shocked.

"But I am. I want to see you. It's only a two and a half hour drive. I'm about an hour and a half away. Give me directions or I'm going to end up somewhere in the middle of the woods. Probably eaten by a pack of rabid voles."

Since she didn't want Clara to end up in the woods—and she had absolutely no doubt her friend was serious, and would call her from the middle of the woods, pretending to be victimized—she gave her directions. When Clara pulled up to the cabin, she immediately opened the door. "Hi," she said.

"This is rustic," Clara said. "I like it. I particularly like the Christmas decorations."

Violet laughed. "He doesn't. Like really doesn't. Watching him try to cope with it is kind of hilarious."

Clara walked up the steps, and then pulled her in for a hug. "I am really glad to see you. And I'm really glad to see that you look better than when I last saw you."

"Did I look bad last time?"

"You were pale. And you were very unhappy. It actually… It really helps to know that you're this much happier just being with him."

"Well. I…" She frowned. "Is that sad?"

"Is it sad that he makes you happy?"

"I feel like he shouldn't. I mean… That's stupid. What I mean is I feel like given the way things are between us, I should be more cautious about it. More cautious about him."

"If you're happy being with him, why worry about it?"

"I don't know," Violet said. "I don't have enough experience with men to sort that out."

"Show me around. And then let's adventure a little bit."

"That sounds like a great idea," Violet said. "I really need to grocery shop, because his stock of food is pathetic, and I don't have a car."

Clara frowned. "We'll have to fix that. I can drive you

back to Copper Ridge, and we can pick your ride up. Maybe this weekend?"

"Oh. That might be good."

"Are you still avoiding everyone? Because your secret is epically out."

"No. I'm not avoiding everyone." It was interesting how now that she was resolved and knew what she wanted to do, she really didn't feel as avoidant as she had before. "I just hadn't thought about going back. But... Yeah, that's a good idea. I should get some more things. It's kind of impractical looming around here with nothing."

"Indeed."

"Yeah. That sounds good. Sounds like a plan." And it would defuse some of the intensity between Wolf and herself. Last night they had slept together. Just slept. It was the first time they'd done that. The focus of the two of them sharing a bed had been sexual from the beginning. And just sleeping had been... Well, there was something heavy about it. About all of it. But then the entire revelation about Breanna was heavy.

She thought about bringing it up with Clara, but she didn't really want to talk about it. She just wanted to enjoy the day with her friend.

They got in Clara's car, and drove off the ranch property.

"I have no idea where to go," Violet said. "I've been staying here for almost two weeks and I have no idea where anything is."

"Well, the ranch is pretty," Clara said.

"From the map it doesn't look like there's a lot in the town."

"He said as much. He didn't really want me combing around by myself. Though, I kind of wonder if it has more to do with the fact that everybody knows who he is, and if they knew that I was here with him there was sure to be commentary," Violet said.

"There's always commentary when you live in a small town. And this makes Copper Ridge look like a booming metropolis."

It didn't take long for them to arrive at the town. Which, as far as they could sort out on the map on Clara's phone, was this collection of buildings on either side of the highway. There was a general store, a small restaurant, a bar. An ice cream shop. All small, wooden buildings with shingle roofs and rustic wood siding.

"I say we start with lunch," Clara said.

They went into the tiny diner, called Becky's, and waited to be seated.

A woman with short curly gray hair greeted them, and led them to the table. She was not effusive at all.

The tables were full, except the one they were seated at, with what she assumed were locals. People in work clothes and flannels, mostly eating soup. Which stood to reason, as it was a soup sort of day. She also took that as her lead when placing her order. The chicken and dumpling soup was served with ample rolls, and she gave thanks that she was able to eat and enjoy the flavor of the food. And that nothing seemed off. She had been feeling much better really since she arrived here.

"Have you been to the doctor yet?" Clara asked.

She shook her head, tearing her roll in half and dipping it in the soup. "I just was waiting. Really, I've been waiting for everything. Except…"

"Except you did decide to marry him."

"Yes." She made a study of her soup. "But what's the other option?"

"There are many other options, Violet," Clara said.

"Moving back home. Moving somewhere else. Moving into the forest and beginning a life as a raccoon."

"I just mean... I don't marry him, and we live in separate towns and have to work out a custody arrangement? I don't marry him, and something goes wrong with the pregnancy and I go back to pretending that I never met him?"

"Right. Okay. So basically, you can't see a way around having your life be fundamentally changed by knowing him."

"I don't think I want to," Violet said. "Does that make me a cliché? Am I a cliché virgin?"

"Yes," Clara said. "But hey. Me, too. I fell for Alex so hard, so fast. Being with him... It changed me. It reordered my priorities. It made me realize how lonely I was."

"That's it exactly," Violet said. "It made me realize that I was lonely. That I was holding myself back from things I actually did want. Just protecting myself and not fully realizing it. I've been sorting through that. And..." It hit her then that part of the reason this entire thing with his revelation about Breanna affected her was that it made her want to protect herself again. Made her want to take a step back from the initial decision she'd made. To push forward. To go all in. He was in love with someone else. And that was different than his feeling emotionally unavailable.

He had given his emotions to someone else.

"Do you love him?" Clara asked.

It was a question she didn't want to answer. Why would she *want* to answer it now? Why would she want to answer it now that she knew he loved someone else? And how small and obnoxious was it to be irritated that he loved someone who had died? It wasn't the same kind of love. Because it wasn't active.

"You don't have to answer that," Clara said, taking a

bite of her plain hamburger. "I'm sorry. I am prying. And I didn't come here to pry. I didn't come here to make you regret having a friend."

"I don't regret our friendship," Violet said. She sighed heavily. "Actually, what I'm realizing is that I'm not as normal as I thought I was. It's easy for me to look at Wolf and see how damaged he is. By the different things that he's been through. And to think that maybe I'm the person that needs to heal him. But I'm just kind of…turning over all the ways that I need to figure out how to heal myself."

"Well, the unfortunate thing is I think it's pretty hard to heal yourself," Clara said, wrinkling her nose. "I think it usually involves other people."

"That sounds messy," Violet said.

"In my experience life is. Relationships are. I know we do our best to kind of compartmentalize the fact that you are related to my husband, and I never really want to creep you out, but also I'm your friend. And I'm not sure that we've really gone into just how messy things were with Alex and me in the beginning. I'm younger than him. I'm his friend—not just his friend, his military brother in arms's younger sister. The guilt that he felt over all of that… It was pretty intense. And the thing with us… It started as attraction. But I think it wasn't that simple. It never was. We wanted it to be. We wanted to believe that we could sleep together and not get emotionally involved. But I don't think we ever could. I think that from the beginning the emotion was there. And that's what fueled the sex, and I don't know any other way to explain that. Except we had a connection that was real and deep and pretty quick. And all of our stuff got sorted out…messy. And often naked."

"Well, thanks for that," Violet said.

She tried to pretend she was horrified, but instead, she

was just thinking. About the fact that she and Wolf were pretty good at the naked part. But there was a lot of clothed interaction that they seemed to struggle with.

"Was Alex a human wall?" Violet asked.

"He was pretty messed up. Yeah. Kind of like a wall. I thought of him as a piece of iron sometimes. He was hard, and he was especially hard when he was running away from forever. Because it became clear pretty quickly that things were going to be forever between us, and he was trying to figure out a way to make it...not that."

"Well, Wolf and I have already decided to get married."

"That's its own unique challenge, I would think. He's already got you. So what incentive does he have to change anything?"

That was a sobering question. "I don't know," Violet said.

She didn't know, but she also didn't want to hold marriage or uncertainty over his head. But it was... It was a very good point.

They paid and left the diner, then walked over to get ice cream, in spite of the chill. The ground was damp, covered in pine needles, and Violet kicked them to the side as she took a bite of her strawberry cheesecake ice cream cone.

"Tiny though it is," Clara said, as they walked next to the gigantic pine trees, in front of the modest buildings, "this is a pretty adorable town. I suspect you could be pretty happy here."

"Definitely," Violet said. "Possibly."

"I didn't mean to fill you with doubt. That wasn't the point. I just... I just wanted to... I wish I could help. I wish I could give you a guidebook. But I don't have one. My relationship with Alex... We went into it thinking temporary."

"Well, so did Wolf and I. Even more temporary than you and Alex were thinking, I imagine, considering he didn't actually know me. Not the way that you and Alex knew each other."

"True. But we also didn't end up pregnant until later. Until we already decided."

"I think I'm just using the pregnancy," she said softly. "Because I wanted to be with him, anyway."

"Do you feel bad about that?"

She shook her head. "No. Should I?"

"No. When you know, you know, Violet."

"That's just it, though. I don't know. Except that I want him. Intensely. Wildly. And I feel like I will be absolutely devastated if I lose him. But I also feel like staying with him could be its own sort of devastation."

"Well, yeah. That's what being in a relationship with another person is. You can't care about someone, or something, without there being fear and bad feelings just on the other side of the horizon. When something matters a lot to you, you want neutral. The idea of losing it is horrible. The alternative is unthinkable. That's just how it is."

"Oh. Maybe that's why I've spent so much time not building extra connections. My family is enough." She meant it as a joke, but it wasn't a joke. It was true.

"No, Violet," Clara said, squeezing her shoulder. "I wish there was an easier path. But I think it's only easier before you've met the person. Then you can commit yourself to a life of isolation. As it is…you're already at risk. You could turn away now, but it wouldn't fix anything. Because you already know what it's like to be with him. You'd miss him. Your heart would be broken."

"Ugh. Stop being right."

"Can't," Clara said. "Trust me. It bugs Alex, too."

They went into the general store and were pleasantly surprised by a small selection of local produce, plus a great many quirky things. Clara insisted they buy bags of old Halloween candy and a tabletop Santa holding a bowl, which she said they could put the candy in, and it would also increase Wolf's annoyance.

They decided on hamburgers for dinner, even though Clara had had one for lunch. And when Wolf returned home, they had a whole spread on the counter waiting to allow all three of them to build their own burgers. They had also made oven fries, and some cookies.

"Your ring is pretty," Clara said as they arranged everything on the counter.

"Thank you," Violet said, looking down at it. "He did a good job."

Just then, the door opened, and Wolf came in.

"Oh," he said. "I didn't know we had company."

"Wolf," she said. "This is my…my friend Clara."

"Who is also her aunt," Clara said, smiling. "So you're Wolf Garrett. I've heard a lot about you. From Violet, which was nice. And also some things from her dad. Not so nice."

He grunted. "I bet."

"Clara is going to stay here tonight," Violet said. "I offered up the twin bed."

He nodded slowly. "Okay."

"And I'm going back to Copper Ridge with her tomorrow."

"Okay," he said, asking absolutely no follow-up questions.

She stewed on that, all through dinner. Clara made conversation about beekeeping, and bison, asking Wolf if they had ever considered taking on either animal.

"No," he said.

"Why not? Bison really are great animals to raise. I mean, once you figure out how to keep them in the fencing. Those upgrades are a little bit of a headache, but it's very popular meat."

"I'm honestly fine with just standard cow," Wolf said. "You can't beat a good beefsteak."

"I dunno," Clara said. "As a fan of bison, I have to disagree."

"The Sullivans have bees," he said.

He went on to explain the layout of Four Corners, which Clara asked incisive questions about, and Violet was suddenly irritated at herself for not being more astute about ranch work. She learned more about what Wolf did in a day from Clara's making conversation than she had in the past two weeks from her own line of questioning. And it was talking about ranching that actually got Wolf...talking.

She was going about it all wrong. She wanted to know all these intimate things about him, but she hadn't started with the easy things. She hadn't started with the surface things. The things that he found simple to make conversation about. And that was shortsighted of her. Not entirely brilliant.

When they got into bed, she rolled over and faced him. "I'm not leaving you."

"Good to know," he said, his gaze fixed on the ceiling.

"I mean, I'm going back to get my car, and to do Victorian Christmas with Clara and Alison and my other aunts."

"Good," he said.

"Were you worried?"

He looked at her out of the corner of his eye. "I don't do worried."

"Well. Just in case. Just in case you randomly decided to do worried when I didn't come home for two days and it finally sunk in that I might have left you."

A grin lifted the corner of his mouth. "You're not going to leave me."

"So confident."

He rolled over, quick as a mountain lion, and pinned her down to the mattress. "Confident in some things."

"Clara is just down the hall."

"So she is."

He looked unrepentant and unconcerned.

"She surprised me today. I mean, she was halfway here when I found out that she was coming. So I couldn't have told you."

"I have one of those things called a cell phone. And I do believe you have my phone number."

"Well, all right. We went all around town today and…"

He kissed her neck. "Very interesting," he said.

"You don't sound interested."

"Maybe I'd just rather do other things."

He was so different tonight. Different than how he'd been last night. As if he had managed to go away and re-group and get into a space where he could pretend that the revelations of the day before hadn't happened.

And she decided to let him. Because the revelation of earlier about the fact that she never talked to him about light and easy things was stuck there inside her. Maybe she needed to let him have this moment. This moment of retreat. Maybe it was just as important as the pushing. The moments where she didn't push. She just let him take what he needed. And she got a whole lot out of it herself.

And when it was over, she lay against his chest. And she smiled.

She didn't have to solve any problems right now. She didn't have to answer the question of how she felt. Maybe right now she just needed to be with him.

CHAPTER EIGHTEEN

"Violet went back home for a few days." At least, Wolf assumed that she was gone. He had been up before the sun, and out before Violet and her friend Clara.

"Back home?" Sawyer asked, fixing him with a hard gaze. "I thought she was living here now."

Wolf shrugged. "You know what I mean."

Sawyer gave him a long look. "I guess."

Wolf swung his axe down hard, splitting the log in two that he'd just set up. He was trying to get a good stock of firewood going for the cold weather that was up ahead. He wanted to make sure that Violet stayed warm.

Of course, he didn't know if she had any clue how to start a fire. But given how game she was dealing with rodents and spiders, he imagined that she could get a wood-stove going.

"You aren't worried she isn't coming back?" Sawyer asked.

Damn his brother, honestly.

He gritted his teeth. But she'd told him not to worry last night.

I'm not leaving you.

"She said she was coming back."

Violet would keep her word. That much he knew.

He ignored the disquiet in himself. The fact that he had been worried about it. The fact that he'd taken her proclamation about going back to Copper Ridge on board and done his best not to react while inside he'd been questioning whether or not it meant his time with her was over. And the beast inside him had roared. But he'd managed to keep it easy. To keep a smile on his face. But then when they'd gotten into their room…she'd said she wasn't leaving him.

So he believed her.

It was clear that Sawyer didn't necessarily. But Sawyer didn't know her.

"She wants to go do some Christmas thing."

"Without you?"

He arched a brow. "Weird, because I'm known for my sparkling, glorious personality that is obviously geared toward holiday celebration."

"I'm just saying, did she *want* you to go?"

The way his brother said that made him wonder, and he didn't like that. He didn't like being uncertain at all.

"She would've invited me," he said.

Sawyer laughed. "Okay. Granted, I've had a wife for like four months. But… No. She wouldn't necessarily have asked."

"Why not?"

"Because it's a test. Because you're supposed to prove your love by offering, even though she didn't indicate that she needed you to do that. There are a lot of reasons. I don't know all the reasons. I just know that there are reasons."

"I think she wanted to spend some time with her friend. And with her family." But he had doubts now.

"She probably wants you to come after her."

Wolf sighed. "I don't know how to do this."

"You did," Sawyer said, fixing him with a hard look.

"That was different. I was sixteen when all that started. And it just happened. There was no… There was no baby. There was no marriage. There was no…"

"You mean, there was no *life*? Yeah. This is being an adult and navigating relationships, I guess."

Wolf snorted. "I was excited to be in a relationship back then. Because I was an idiot."

"Maybe you should try to think a little bit about what *idiot* you would have done. Or actually, just think about what you actually want. Do you want to be away from her for a few days?"

The beast responded with a resounding *no*. "I like being alone."

"You're alone too much."

"Define that. I think that I need time alone. I'm used to it."

Sawyer's expression became far too serious. And given that his brother was serious by nature, that it could get even more so was saying something. "Wolf, you manage to be alone in rooms full of people. It's your superpower. But it's not a particularly great one."

"We're different people, Sawyer. We don't need the same things."

"Going back to Breanna, I think that suggests we do need the same things. I thought I didn't need that. I thought I didn't need to be in love. You think you had it. And that's it. But you had a lot of life to live in the meantime, and…"

Wolf cut him off.

"And I know enough to know what I'm not doing again. Thanks, though."

He stared off into the horizon and took a breath. Then he brought the axe down on the next log.

"That's fine," Sawyer said. "Don't listen to your brother who successfully fixed his life."

"We both know *Evelyn* fixed your life."

He chuckled. "Yeah. I guess so."

When Wolf went home that night, the house was empty

and dark. And it felt empty and dark. There were leftovers in the fridge, though, which was all Violet. Because without her, there wouldn't have been anything. He heated them up, and sat on the couch in front of the tree. Did she want him to go to Copper Ridge?

He ate his burger and leftover oven fries and tried to find the same sort of relaxation he usually felt when he was in his house by himself. It was how he had lived for a long damned time. And he should like it. But the house felt empty and his bed felt empty. And he was irritated at Sawyer for introducing the idea that maybe staying here wasn't the best idea.

You're good at being alone in a room full of people.

Yeah. He was. That was true. But the fact that he felt alone so profoundly right now...

He didn't do alone when Violet was here. Not in the same way. She demanded more engagement from him. She demanded more of him...in general.

He plugged in the damned Christmas tree. Because the room seemed dark without it on. But then he discovered the Christmas lights didn't really help.

It was too dark without Violet here. That was the bottom line.

And when he went to bed, it was too empty.

VIOLET AND CLARA made light conversation in the car the whole way back to town, and Violet made it her mission to point out each and every decoration on the main street of Copper Ridge as they drove to the Donnelly ranch. Because she was trying very much not to turn all of this into conversations about her love life. "Want to head out around one?"

"Sure," she said. Clara dropped her at the front of her

house and then drove off. Probably thinking it best to give her a little bit of time alone with her parents.

Her car was there, in front of the barn, just as Clara had promised it would be.

She felt so oddly relieved. There was something so familiar about it, and she had been awash in unfamiliarity for a long time.

She hitched her toiletry bag up her arm and walked to the front of the house. The door swung open before she could knock.

"Oh, my gosh," Alison said, pulling her in for a hug. "You're *here*."

"Who's at the bakery?" Violet asked.

"I hired a woman who had some previous experience. It's fine."

"Oh."

So apparently, they could get along without her. And Alison wasn't mad.

"I'm so glad that you're here," she said. She put her hands on Violet's face. "Are you okay?"

"I'm fine," she said. "I'm just visiting. Clara came to see me, and I decided I wanted to spend the weekend doing Victorian Christmas."

Alison grabbed her hand and looked at it. "That is a very nice ring."

"It is," Violet said, not able to keep herself from flushing with pleasure. "He did a good job."

"Well, I'm glad to hear that. He seems very… He doesn't seem nice, actually. But he seems…"

"Good? Honorable?" Violet suggested.

"He's good-looking," Alison said.

"Well. I *know* that," Violet said, rolling her eyes. "That's why I'm in this mess in the first place."

Alison laughed, and Violet was relieved.

She heard heavy footsteps in the doorway and turned, seeing her dad standing there, his hands shoved in his pockets. Her face got hot. She hoped he hadn't heard the last thing she'd said. Although, it wasn't like he didn't know. "Hi, Dad."

There was a pause. Only a breath.

"Get over here," he said.

She wrapped her arms around him, pressed her head to his chest and let him hold her for a second like she was a kid whose every issue could be fixed by a hug from her dad.

"I'm just back for a couple days," she said, her voice muffled, trying to ignore the tears that had leaked out of the corners of her eyes. She took a breath and tried to steady herself as she moved away from him. "You know how much I love Victorian Christmas."

Cain cleared his throat. "So everything is fine with... I'm not going to say his name."

"Dad," she said. "Everything is fine with Wolf."

"Great."

"You don't sound like you believe that," she said.

"I do," he insisted. "I want you to be happy."

"I know that you're mad at me..."

"I'm not mad at you, Bo," he said, holding on to her shoulders and looking down into her eyes. "But I will kill him if he hurts you. And I'm a little on edge about that. Because I don't exactly want to go to prison for the rest of my life."

"No need," Violet said. "He's actually just really great."

"Well, I'm pleased to hear it."

"Clara and I are wanting to go into town today," she said to Alison. "We were hoping that Sabrina and Lane and you could join us?"

"I can," Alison said. "I can check with the rest of them."

They ended up all being able to go, and they met in town, at the end of Main Street. Lane had an employee for her shop, and Sabrina was able to get her shift covered at the winery, and that meant they could all shop freely on the little Main Street, which included antique stores, little boutiques, Lane's specialty food item store and a new candy store that offered samples on just about everything and smelled like a Clara trap.

They ended up at The Grind, ordering croissant sandwiches and coffees for lunch.

And Violet felt…a little more part of it than she normally did. Not like a kid tagging along. It was just that the dynamics of her family were often so strange, and she was such a weird outlier in the whole thing. Right now she felt… She felt like an adult in the group.

"So when is the wedding?" Lane asked.

"Oh," Violet said, wrinkling her nose. "We haven't really talked about that."

"I hear congratulations are in order twice," Sabrina said.

"Yes," she said, brightly.

At least, she was trying to be bright, and not embarrassed. She knew no one here was going to judge her; she really did. But that didn't mean she didn't harbor some… Well, a little bit of shame over the fact that she'd been caught up in passion and gotten pregnant after sleeping with a man she barely knew.

She had known that her pregnancy was public knowledge in the family. But still, acknowledging it just at the moment was a little bit of a whole thing.

"So the wedding should be soon," Lane said pragmatically. "Or later. But you hate to catch it right in the middle."

"I think we should give ourselves enough time to plan

something really wonderful," Alison said. "You don't need to rush into anything."

"Maybe she wants to rush," Sabrina said. "When you've found the one that you want to be with, why wait?"

"They *didn't* wait," Clara said, cheerfully.

"Hey," Alison said. "I sincerely doubt any of you were pure as the driven snow."

"Obviously, your father and I were," Alison continued, turning to Violet, her face overly grave.

"Ha! Liar," Sabrina said. "All it takes is a glass and a half of wine and you are full of stories of your decidedly unchaste behavior. I once heard a story about you, Cain and a certain table in the bakery..."

Violet blinked rapidly. "No!" she said. "Please don't tell me this."

"You're an adult now," Sabrina said, putting her hand over Violet's, her expression vaguely mocking. "It's time you learned the facts of life. And the truest fact is that you don't have the monopoly on losing your head and getting physically involved with a cowboy. We're basically a support group for that."

"*No*, I want to go back to the kids' table," Violet said.

"Too late," Lane said cheerfully.

Once she got over the horror of having to know that her dad and stepmother had...on a table in the bakery, it was... It was incredibly soothing to be with this group of women and not feel judged. Or like she was an idiot. Or any of the other things she'd said to herself several times over the past couple of months.

By the late afternoon, Lane, Sabrina and Clara had all gone back home. It was just Alison and Violet still wandering around the shops.

"Dinner?" Alison asked. "We can go to the fancy place on the wharf."

Violet felt…light. Both younger than she had for weeks, and older. She was home, which felt soothing. But she also felt alien in it, because Four Corners had become part of her life, her story, too. But one thing she knew, she didn't want her afternoon with Alison to end. "Sure. That would be nice."

Alison hastily texted Cain, and the two of them went down to the restaurant on the wharf, getting a table for two.

"Get something really fancy," Alison said. "You deserve it."

"I'm getting the filet mignon," Violet said, "since it's on offer."

They made casual conversation over cheddar bread while they waited for their food to arrive, and once it did, Alison cut one bite of her food, and suddenly looked thoughtful.

"Violet," she said. "I just wanted to say to you, absolutely and sincerely, congratulations. You're going to be a really great mother."

Violet's throat suddenly went tight. Tears pushed against her eyes. "Oh. Don't do that. I…"

"I was so afraid to step in and try to be your stepmother after everything that had happened to you. And after everything that I'd been through I wasn't sure that I could do a good job. I was really scared when I got pregnant with Jonah. I was sure that I wasn't going to be a good mother to a boy. To a young child. I have felt doubts every step of the way, actually. And I just want you to know that."

Violet looked down. "I would never have known," she said.

"I know," she responded. "So I wanted you to know that it wasn't smooth sailing so that when you had your own doubts you didn't question yourself. So that when you had your own doubts you didn't think…but my parents always knew what they were doing. Because we didn't. We don't."

"That actually does help."

They ate in silence for a while, and Violet listened to the sounds of cutlery and conversation around them. Her eyes felt scratchy.

"You have grown up into a wonderful young lady," Alison said. "And the fact that I just said that makes me feel a hundred years old. And you know we are here for you. Whatever happens. No matter what. You don't have to earn your place with us, honey. It's secure."

Her throat went tight.

She sniffed, a tear sliding down her cheek. "That's exactly what I needed to hear," she said. "Really."

She ate more steak, until the question in her breast started to burn. But she had Alison here and now, and they had honesty, so she might as well ask.

"I have a question," Violet said, her lips suddenly feeling cold. "I don't know… I don't know what to do. Because he told me something about his past. And I don't know… I don't know what I feel about it."

"What?" Alison asked, looking concerned.

"It's nothing bad. I mean it *is* bad. He didn't do anything bad. It's… He was in love. He was in love with a girl. And she died. And it's something that he's never gotten over. He told me that… I mean… This is awkward. Because… You know. But he told me up front. When I met him. When I decided to… To be with him. Physically."

"Violet," Alison said. "I understand that it's awkward, but I did in fact hook up with your dad on a bakery table. I'm not actually a prude."

"Okay," Violet said, lifting her hands for a second, realizing she was literally about to cover her ears. "All right. I won't be prudish about it, then. But I thought…that I could have a fling with him. And I thought that it would be fun. And he told me that that's all it was. He told me that was all he did. And I… I said that was fine. I told myself it was fine. And then when he left I begged him to stay. I actually begged. And I was devastated. And then I found out I was pregnant, and then he came to get me because he found out I was pregnant and…"

"What are you saying, Violet?"

She closed her eyes, and the air in her lungs suddenly felt too big to occupy the same space as her battered, bruised heart. "He has warned me at every stage that he isn't going to fall in love with me. He's ready to do the right thing. And he treats me really well. It isn't that. But there's a part of him that is not available to me. And it's incredibly obvious. I know why now. But I don't know what I should do about it. I don't even know what I want to do about it."

"Hearts don't stay closed forever," Alison said. "Believe me. If they did, I wouldn't be married to your dad."

Violet let out a harsh breath. "He was pretty messed up after Mom left."

"It wasn't him. It was me." She cleared her throat. "You know my first marriage was bad. My ex-husband hit me. Abused me. Made me feel small. Like I'd never be able to stand on my own. And then I found out that I could. And my independence… After I got it back it was the most important thing to me. I didn't want to fall in love. I didn't want to get married. I didn't want that life. I convinced myself that the part of me that could love was broken. I wanted it to be. I wanted it to be broken because it meant that I would be protected. From ever… Ever going through what I did with my ex. And your dad… He was so wonderful with me. He was patient. And I was *cruel* to him."

Violet couldn't imagine Alison being cruel. "You probably weren't…"

"Oh, no, I was. I was that wounded animal backed into a corner, fighting to protect myself. And he loved me first, Violet. At least, he said the words first. He admitted it first. He went to bat for me, and if he hadn't, I don't know that I would be sitting here. So what I can tell you is this, hearts can heal. Especially when there's a reason for them to. Especially when someone is there, ready to be everything you need. When you're ready to admit what it is you want."

"So… I'm just really afraid. And I realize that I knew that you and Dad would never disown me or anything. But I use that fear to keep myself safe. Because it was easier than putting myself out there. And now… I feel like…"

"You love him?"

She felt like her heart had been grabbed, squeezed. "I have from the beginning, I think."

"And you're afraid of getting hurt."

"He warned me," she said. "I mean, he really warned me."

"I know," Alison said. "I can't guarantee you aren't going to get hurt, Violet. But that's what happens when you start playing with big emotions. That's what happens when you grow up. And this is a lot. This isn't just getting to know each other. It's not just getting to take it slow. You jumped into the deep end."

She laughed, but she didn't find it funny. "I did things backward."

"You're human. You met a man who made you feel things that no one else ever had, and you jumped in without realizing what the consequences of it would be. And actually, even though your dad didn't get me pregnant, and even though I wasn't twenty-two, and even though he wasn't my first boyfriend, it's not any different. I met him, and I didn't realize what it would mean for me. I didn't realize where it would lead. You always feel like you're in over your head when you're falling in love."

"Clara told me that it's messy. And there's nothing you can do about it. I feel like I was sold a bill of goods." She tried to laugh. "Aren't modern relationships supposed to be simple and enlightened and…and happy?"

"Sure," Alison said. "They can be. But big emotions are messy. And broken people don't give in easily."

She tried to laugh. "Yeah. I sure can pick them."

"Honey, we are *all* broken people." Violet felt exposed. Like Alison had shone a light on the jagged pieces in her she tried to hide. "That doesn't mean we can't love or be loved. Fight for it. Fight for love as hard as he fights to stay safe. One of you will have to win."

"What if it's him?"

"I would like for you to be with someone who can give you everything that you want. But the question is, do you want some pat version of love you've been told is out there? Or do you want him? His love. If so, you might have to be willing to wade through the mud to get there. You might have to be willing to get dirty, to get your knuckles bloody, fighting for the man you want, the love you want, the life you want. And figuring out how best to love him, even if it's not exactly on your terms. Relationships aren't a one-way street. It can't just be about your fantasy. You have to find out what he wants, what he needs, and be willing to meet him there, too."

"Maybe that's what I always knew," Violet whispered. "Maybe that's why I always stayed away from this kind of thing. Because I knew it would cost this. Because I knew it would take a fight."

"Because you always knew that what you wanted was

something big. Something real. You didn't want what your parents had."

"No," she said. "I want what you and Dad have."

"Then don't give up. Love isn't fifty-fifty," Alison said. "Love sometimes requires that you carry the person that you want to be with through hard times. And they should do it for you when you need it. But it's not about keeping score. In the end, when you find the person that you're supposed to be with, you hope it's a whole lifetime. And if you plan on keeping a scorebook for a whole lifetime..."

"You can't," she said.

"No," Alison said. "Not and be happy."

"I'm also starting to think maybe you can't be happy without being sad sometimes."

"That's the other side of joy," Alison said. "It's just part of being human. If you're comfortable, if you're protected, forever, then I guess it means you don't love anything enough to be afraid of losing it."

They finished their meal, and Violet pondered that, all night. Pondered it in her empty bed.

She missed Wolf. She wanted to be with him.

And she was afraid. Afraid of what it might cost. Afraid of getting hurt. But she was more afraid of what a future would look like without him. And she supposed that was where it started. She supposed that was what made the risk worth it.

She supposed that was where love met the edge of fear, and dove off into the abyss of it.

Because the risk became worth it. Because not taking the risk became unthinkable.

And she didn't know if that brought her an intense amount of joy, or an intense amount of sadness.

And she had a feeling it would be the question she was asking herself a lot from now on.

CHAPTER NINETEEN

SHE SPENT THE next morning doing puzzles with her brothers, and enjoying the simplicity of the moment. She had plenty of things to worry about, but she was still going to be here through tomorrow, and she was bound and determined to enjoy her time at home, rather than letting Wolf consume all of it. She was also pondering the edge that she felt over her thoughts about him. And wondered how good it would feel to be back in his arms again. If this would make it all the sweeter. But then, she didn't know if she could handle being with Wolf being any more intense or any more sweet. It was a little bit much already.

"Violet!"

Her dad's voice had her scrambling up from the floor. "What?"

"I think you have a guest."

She walked over to where he was standing at the front door and looked out. Wolf's truck had just pulled into the driveway, and he was getting out.

"Oh," she said.

And she couldn't stop herself. She opened the front door and ran out to the driveway. She wrapped her arms around his neck and kissed him, and he held her on the hip to steady her. When she stepped away from him, she felt her face flush. Felt her embarrassment. Because she knew her dad had seen that. And that she hadn't played it cool at all.

And she just… She didn't really care. Not after the discussion with Alison. Not after…

She just wanted to *touch* him. All over.

"What are you doing here?"

"Hell," he said, looking at her like he'd just been hit over the head with a two-by-four. "I guess Sawyer was right."

"What?"

"Don't worry about it. I thought… I can stay with my cousins. But I thought I might come and see a little bit of the town at Christmas since it's something that you love so much."

She flushed with pleasure. All the way down. "Oh. That is so… Thank you. I… But you don't have to stay with someone else. You can stay here."

"Really?"

"Yeah," she said.

He looked vaguely horrified by that.

"We're getting married. If you're going to be part of the family… I guess you better be part of the family."

She took his hand and led him to the front of the house. "Dad," she said. "Can Wolf stay with us for a couple of days?"

"Of course," Cain said, his eyes landing on Wolf, his expression far too cool. "We'll get a guest room ready."

She was going to argue, but then, if she was honest with herself, there wasn't a world in which her dad was going to be cool with her and Wolf sharing a bed under his roof. If they were lucky, by the time they were married he would be fine with it. She tried not to think about what she had learned about her dad and bakery tables since yesterday. But if she was just a little bit more brazen, she might mention it, but then, she imagined it wouldn't matter even if she did. Because she was his daughter, and he would unashamedly have double standards.

"I don't want to impose," Wolf said. "I can always stay with my cousins."

"Nonsense, son," her dad said, clapping his hand on Wolf's back. "It'll be good to get to know you more."

The words were friendly, but the tone was something else.

And she had a feeling that no matter how accepting her dad was, he was not going to be entirely on board or accepting of the entire thing for a while.

She sat on the edge of the bed in the guest room while Wolf put things away.

"So what brings you here?"

"You," he said.

She felt like she'd been wrapped in a fuzzy blanket and laid down on a cloud. In other words: she felt really warm and really good.

"Well, I like that." She lay back on the bed, looking up at him.

He arched a brow. "Don't start things you can't finish," he said. "I'm not about to get killed by your father. And before you say anything, he *would* kill me. He is clearly not actually all that thrilled that I'm here. Or that I exist."

"Oh, I wasn't going to argue," she said. "Because you're right. My dad would one hundred percent kill you. He's not actually all that chill."

Wolf snorted. "I noticed."

"I'll show you around the ranch."

"I'd like that," he said. "It's interesting. I like to see the way other people have their spread set up."

"You're a ranching geek," she said.

He laughed. "Is that a thing?"

"If it is, you are one."

"I like to just think I'm a professional in my field."

She stood up and he caught her arm, drawing her toward him. "How are you feeling?"

"Good," she said.

And what she wanted to say was, good now that you're here.

They walked down the stairs together, and the coast was clear of her family, which she found herself almost relieved by. They walked outside and stopped. And she took a deep breath, really luxuriating in the view. She had missed it.

"So you grew up here," he said.

"Well, not really. I was seventeen when we moved here."

"Right," he said. "And you hated it."

"At our ranch in Texas there were rolling hills and fields. All these bluebells. I pretended I didn't like living in the country, but I really did love it. And I didn't realize how much until we left. But I was... I was angry and resentful about everything then. And I had been for a few years. I know that my dad moved us here partly because of me."

"How long did it take for you to start to feel like this place was your home?"

"It wasn't a place, so much. Not the time here. It was the people who loved me. It was being with my uncles. Alison. Learning to bake. Getting really invested in that and falling in love with it. And gradually it became my home." She took his hand, and they began to walk down one of the well-worn paths that would take them to the main barn. Though it was quite a long walk.

"Do your dad and uncles all get along? I know something about sharing ranch land."

"Yeah. They all get along. More or less. Alex is more involved in Clara's ranch. He does things here, but they have their own place."

"That probably helps."

"Probably."

They walked along silently, and she let out a slow breath, watching as the air turned to a cloud and swirled away.

"So you were thirteen when your mother left."

"Yeah," she said. "We've talked about that."

"Tell me about the day she left."

She looked at him, and saw that his gaze was sharp.

"Why?"

"I'm curious."

"Well…" She realized that she had never talked about this. She had told people that her mother had left her. It was a thing that came up. She didn't have a mother. Not really. Hadn't for a number of years. That was easy to say. But the actual story? The actual time? That was something she just didn't talk about.

"As an adult I realize that relationships are complicated," she said. "And that there was a lot going on between my parents that I didn't see. And probably a lot of things my dad protected me from. A lot of red flags and things like that. But as it was… I didn't see any. I didn't know that they weren't happy. I didn't know my mother wasn't happy. And one day she was gone. I didn't realize it. I got up, and she didn't help me get ready for school. But she didn't always. Sometimes she slept in. My dad didn't say anything. It just seemed like a regular morning. But when I came back, well, then I realized something was different. I realized… And my dad said she left. And he said he didn't know where she'd gone. Just that she'd packed up all of her things and *gone*."

She took a shaky breath and shoved her hands into her pockets. "And I thought…she'll be back. Because my dad is a good man. Because I'm her daughter. And I couldn't imagine that she would stay gone. So I remember the day she left, but that wasn't the worst day. I was numb then. I kept thinking it was a mistake. I kept thinking she would realize. And then… Well, then I had to face the fact that that wasn't what was happening. That she had left on purpose. That she didn't want to come back. She didn't want to come back to me. Didn't want to come back to anyone."

Violet blinked hard. "It was a month after she left that I started to get angry." She remembered sitting out on the rope swing that hung off the tree in the middle of the field, watching the wind whip over that endless grass, creating a wave of green in front of her. It was so peaceful, so tranquil. And her rage boiled over. And she had screamed. And her voice had carried across the grass on the wind. A wave of fury.

She had wanted to uproot all that easiness. That lazy Texas day. And she had wanted to fill it with the kind of restless anger that had infused her veins. It was longer than that for her to cry. The sadness waited. And it was when she realized she wasn't going to get a chance to have a confrontation with her mother.

That was what had finally cooled her rage.

Because she had been clinging to it so that someday she could yell at her. Ask her what she'd been thinking. And in her angry teenage heart, it had been a speech filled with expletives, things that would shock her mother. She had honed her outrage to be something like a weapon. And it had protected her from the deeper, darker feelings that came along with the abandonment.

"It took me months to cry," she said. "And then when I did, I did it in my room. I didn't want my dad to see. I didn't want him to be worried. I didn't want him to be sad. But he knew. And then it just kind of calcified. And turned into something hard." She smiled. "You know, I tried rebelling."

"Really?" he asked, arching a brow.

"Yes. I had been here for just a couple of weeks. And I got invited to a party. And I got drunk. And there was this boy there… I don't know that I liked him. But I wanted somebody to like me. And he seemed to like me. As long as I kissed him."

"I don't like this story," Wolf said.

"Well, you'll like my dad's role in it."

"Get to that part."

"My dad and my uncles busted the party up. And my dad just about killed that guy. In fairness, I think he was over eighteen, and I was drunk. So my dad was furious. Like, shooting fire from the heat of a thousand suns furious." She laughed. "I realized I wasn't going to get what I wanted out of that. And then I really got involved with other things. And Alison did so much to get rid of my anger. And then I… I never wanted to do anything to mess up the security that I had. Because you can't… I know that my dad and Alison would never… They would never not love me. But you can't… You can't lose a parent like I did, like *we* did, Wolf, without wondering why. And worrying that it was you. That maybe there was something about you that…"

"I know," he said.

"Maybe it's a little bit easier to blame your dad when he chased off lots of women," she said.

He laughed. The sound cruel and hard. "I guess so."

"But nothing about it's easy, is it?"

"No. Nothing about it is easy."

"What about the day your mom left?"

"I cried like a baby," he said, grinning at her.

And she knew the grin was fake.

"Who was there for you?"

"My brother, Sawyer. He told me to pick myself up and quit crying. He said there was no point to tears. He was right."

"Wolf," she said. "That's not fair. You should've been allowed to cry."

"What was he going to do with the weeping little brother? Sawyer was strong. He was strong for me. He was strong for Elsie. He always was. Sawyer… I'm not surprised that he's a great father. I'm not surprised that it was easy for him to decide to be there for his baby. Sawyer is the kind of good that so many people think they are, but few people are. And yeah, it wasn't the most sensitive thing. He feels bad about it now. But it wasn't the wrong thing to tell me then. Because what was the point of dissolving? No one was going to take care of us but us. Our dad didn't give a shit."

"I'm so glad that I had my dad," Violet said. "I can't imagine just not having anyone. I mean, I chose to deal with some of my grief on my own. I chose to shut them out. But I got really scared. I got really scared about losing him, too."

"I wasn't scared of losing my dad. I knew he'd never leave the ranch. He had nothing else. But it was never about us."

"I'm so sorry, Wolf," she said. "I'm so sorry for what we both went through."

"Nothing to feel sorry about," he said. "We just do better, right?"

"I'd like to do better," she said.

"The bar is painfully low," he said, and she couldn't help but laugh, because he had a point.

"I think I'd like to do a lot better than our mothers. Than your father."

"We will."

They stopped walking. "Does it still hurt you?"

"What?"

"Your mom."

He shrugged. "I told you. No. I feel angry about it sometimes. But that's…"

"The only thing you let yourself feel?"

He laughed. Hard. "I let myself feel other things."

He wrapped his arm around her waist and looked at her, his gaze burning into hers. "You make me feel a whole lot of things, Violet."

"Do I?" She put her hand on his cheek. "What do I make you feel?"

He turned his head and bit the inside of her wrist. "What you make me feel I can't exactly show you right now."

And it made her hot. Because everything with him did. But it was just a sidestep. Because he didn't want to talk about actual feelings. And she remembered all the times she'd seen that sadness in his eyes. And she knew now that it was about grief. About what he'd lost. Maybe just Breanna, but maybe his mother, too. And there was anger there. It simmered. Banked heat that he couldn't fully hide. But there was more. And she didn't know how to get to it. She didn't even know how to get him to admit to it. Didn't know how to get him to let it out.

She showed him around the entire ranch, giving him a tour of the dairy facilities, and embarrassing herself by not really knowing what half of the things were called. But while she was comfortable with many aspects of living on a ranch, she was not enmeshed in the dairy life.

He met her uncles, and talked shop with them, which was sort of sweet, and not anything she would have ever thought she would… She had never really imagined bringing a man home to her family.

And here she was.

Bringing home a man she was marrying. Having a baby. Moving into this mysterious phase of life that she had always been a little bit afraid of. And she couldn't say that she wasn't scared now; it was just that Alison had made her feel like maybe fear wasn't something to be avoided. Not quite so much.

"Can you stay a few extra days?"

That question came from Alison late that afternoon.

"I… I guess so. Why?"

"Well, we're enjoying having you," Alison said. "I think your dad is enjoying having Wolf close at hand so that he can instill a little bit of fear in him."

Wolf was currently out in the barns, watching the various ranch proceedings.

"Wolf doesn't scare very easily," she said.

"I'm sure he doesn't," Alison said. "But your dad is a terrifying man."

Alison looked…pleased by that. Violet cleared her throat.

"Right," Violet said. "I mean, I'd like to. If he wants to."

"Also, I was thinking I could try and arrange an appointment for you with my OB. She was great with the boys."

"Oh," Violet said, her stomach going tight. "Yeah. I guess I do need to do that."

"Probably just to get your dates and all that."

"Yeah," Violet said. But it made her nervous. And it was something that she… She couldn't help but think she was avoiding it slightly. Because what if something was wrong? What if something was wrong and it disrupted this little pocket of happiness she'd created with him? And how would… How would she be enough to keep him around? If there was no baby?

"Great, I'll call her. I bet she can squeeze you in in the next few days."

Violet hesitated. "It's going to be really impractical for me to have my doctor visits here."

"Is there a doctor nearer to where you are?"

She thought back to the tiny town, and how she and Clara had basically explored the extent of it in an afternoon.

"I guess not. At least… I might as well go to somebody in Copper Ridge because I'm going to have to drive at least an hour, I'm sure."

"Right," Alison said. "I'll make arrangements."

When she passed Wolf in the hall that night, tension flared hot between them.

And after looking to see if anyone was around, she pushed him back against the wall and kissed him.

He was ravenous, and she loved it. And they were breathing hard when they pulled away from each other.

"I can't believe we have to have separate rooms," he grumbled.

"My dad is traditional," she said. "Oh. They want us to stay. For a few days? Alison made me a doctor appointment."

"Oh," he said. "A doctor appointment. Is everything okay?"

"Yeah. It's the doctor appointment that you go to just to make sure everything is okay."

"When is that?"

"Tomorrow. Actually."

"Okay. You and me, right?"

Pleasure flooded through her, along with a hefty dose of disquiet. "Yeah," she said. "You and me."

CHAPTER TWENTY

WOLF LIKED THE Donnelly ranch. And even more surprising, he liked the Donnellys. They were good people. Hard workers. They love their animals; they love the land. It was that sort of thing that mattered to him. They were all different from each other, half siblings, which seemed so close to his own family history, it was funny. But they were… They were functional. At least, they seemed it. Married with children and a thriving operation. It was… Well, it was not unlike Four Corners, he supposed. Except it was only Sawyer who seemed to have found his way to normal.

You're on your way.

Yeah. He had Violet. They were having a baby.

He ignored the pit of anxiety in his stomach. He didn't do anxiety. And more and more with this woman, with this… this whole future brewing between them, he felt uncertain.

Oh, not of what he would do. But there was such a host of things outside his control, so many people and so many… So many things had to come together for it to all work out, and Wolf just didn't possess the kind of trust in the universe that it took to take this kind of thing in stride.

The little clinic was on the edge of town, across the street from the ocean, and he remembered when the two of them had horsed around on the beach. It seemed like a lifetime ago. He'd been playing a different part with her then. And it made him ache just then. It made him angry. Angry that he couldn't be that for real.

Because she'd been *happy*.

It wasn't that she didn't seem happy enough. She did. She was affectionate with him. She smiled at him. She held his hand when they walked together. But she had been carefree with him then, and he'd felt the same thing—at least, he'd wanted to—and after he left, there had been a heaviness. And then there was the pregnancy. Yeah, he wished he could go back to that day at the beach. But instead, they were at the obstetrician.

He put his hand low on her back as they walked into the clinic. He wondered why the hell doctor's offices always had giant vases with fake reeds and shit. Was there anybody that actually liked that?

"This place is nice," Violet said.

Apparently, there were.

"Yeah," he said.

She went up to the front and checked in, getting a clipboard and the stack of paperwork, which she set about filling out. He felt like he shouldn't look over her shoulder as she filled in things like her Social Security number and medical history.

"What?"

"Seems personal is all," he said.

She gaped at him like he was an idiot. "Wolf, I could trace my Social Security number onto your back with my tongue and it wouldn't be the most intimate thing we've done."

He laughed in spite of himself.

After what seemed way too long, an employee ushered them into an exam room.

"Take your clothes off and put the gown on," she said. "The doctor will be with you shortly."

"Did you want me to go?" he asked.

Undressing in a medical context seemed different than the undressing they were used to. And he hadn't been with her that way in a few days, so it seemed…potentially invasive.

"I'm fine. Though you suddenly seem very concerned with boundaries."

"I'm being a gentleman," he said.

"False, Wolf Garrett. You are not a gentleman."

He sat down in the chair and rested his elbow on the desk that was just next to it. "Take your clothes off, then." He flicked the brim of his cowboy hat up, making a show of clearing his view.

"I think," she said, taking her top off slowly, and in spite of himself, in spite of the fact that they were in an exam room, and she was about to get… Well, he didn't know what the hell. He didn't know what happened at these things.

In spite of all that, he found himself getting turned on.

"I think," she said again, unclipping her bra and baring her breasts to him. He shifted. "That you're freaking out because this is all feeling very real."

"I'm not freaking out," he said.

"Oh, okay. I'm just suddenly supposed to believe that you were very concerned with my modesty. And my Social Security number."

She turned away from him and shimmied out of her leggings, and his eyes went to her ass. And it turned out that even in a doctor's exam room, he wanted to take a bite out of it.

She turned around, and he groaned in disappointment when she put the white hospital gown over her curves.

"See, not a gentleman."

He growled. "It's been too long since I've seen you."

And those words stuck in his head. They stuck in his throat. Because since when had he cared at all about one particular woman? He just hadn't. Ever. But ever since he'd met Violet she was the only one he wanted. It was her naked body that haunted his dreams. It was her naked body that he wanted. All the time. In front of him, on top of him. Draped over him.

That line of thinking was cut off when the doctor—a young woman with sandy blond hair—came into the room.

She looked way too young to be dealing with this kind of thing. And his irritation and arousal shifted to concern.

"I'm Doctor Peterson. I delivered your brothers," she said. "I think I remember you from then."

"Yeah," Violet said, smiling. "I was there when they were born."

Wolf was surprised by Violet's commitment to small-town pleasantries, even while naked lying on a table.

"Just going to do some basic exams today. And put the Doppler on you so that we can hear the heartbeat."

"Doctor Peterson," she said, looking directly at Wolf.

"Wolf Garrett," he said, sticking his hand out. She shook it. Surprisingly firm. And he decided that she was probably all right.

"And you're the father?" she asked.

"Yes," he said.

He was the father.

He was the father.

He knew that. It was why he was here. It was why he was in Copper Ridge at all. He knew that. But it was very strange to hear someone else say it. And quite like that. "You can come stand up here," she said, gesturing to a spot by Violet's shoulder.

So he did, those words still echoing in his head.

You're the father.

Eventually, she brought out a little machine and squirted some kind of jelly on Violet's stomach. Then she placed the wand on her stomach, and a watery sound filled the room.

Followed directly by a pulsing whisper, strong and steady.

"Is that...?"

"That's the heartbeat," she said. "Everything sounds good. And from everything you told me it sounds like the due date is probably July fifteenth. But that date may shift around as we do ultrasounds and get measurements. We'll have you back in four weeks, okay?"

"Okay," she said.

And just like that...he heard the baby's heartbeat. It was confirmed. It was happening. It was... It was a real thing.

And it felt heavy.

Violet didn't say anything as she got dressed, they walked out together and she made an appointment with the scheduler on the way out as she'd been instructed, and they didn't speak again until they were in the car.

"Are you okay?"

"Yeah," he said. "Everything went as expected."

Except, he hadn't actually known what to expect. Because he just didn't... He didn't know what the hell all this was about. And he didn't really know what to feel about it. What to think about it.

"It feels more real now," she said. "July fifteenth."

He cleared his throat and started the truck engine. "About when I was thinking."

He had not been thinking. Not at all. He hadn't projected any sort of math. He hadn't...anything. On anything.

"That gives us time."

"The cabin's not good enough," he said.

"The cabin is fine," she said.

"It's not. I got to start building an add-on. Hell, we gotta modernize the whole place. I don't know how the hell old the electrical is in that. Can't babies get electrocuted by chewing on wires?"

"Babies are not mice," Violet said. "I think it's from sticking their fingers into the sockets. But also, he isn't going to be born mobile."

"Doesn't matter. There's a lot of stuff to take care of. I should probably head back to Four Corners as soon as possible. I have to make some plans."

She put her hand on his thigh. "It's fine, Wolf."

"Look, I can't cook the baby. I don't have any control over that. But I can make sure that the house is ready. I can make sure that we have everything we need."

"Right."

"We should get married soon," he said.

"I agree. My mom… My stepmom… She wants us to have a real wedding. But it doesn't actually matter to me. I don't care about weddings. I just… I just want to get started with our life."

"Same."

"But let's just chill. We don't need to freak out. We can spend a few days here. My family is expecting us now. And I'm enjoying being here around Christmastime. I'm happy to spend Christmas with your family…"

"Well, as far as my family goes they don't really do much for Christmas. So…"

"You don't think it's going to be different now with your sister-in-law?"

"Oh, I'm sure it will be," he said.

"Well, maybe I'll enjoy that. Being there at the start of new traditions."

Traditions. And *babies.* And *family.* It was a hell of a thing.

It was a whole different set of vocabulary words to the ones he was used to.

Every night that week her entire family had been at dinner. Her uncles, her aunts, the little cousins, but tonight it was him sitting around the dinner table with her stepmother, her dad and the two little half brothers.

It felt… It felt as disconcerting as the doctor appointment, quite frankly.

"When Violet was really little," her dad said, "she used to hold her breath until she about turned blue if she didn't think she was going to get her way. And that is why I ended up calling her Violet Beauregarde the Blueberry. After Willy Wonka. And that's why she's Bo."

Her father was explaining the nickname that Wolf had heard multiple times over the course of the past couple of days, as if it made perfect sense. "But you'll know exactly what I mean in a few months, I guess. You just start calling them things. And every so often one is bound to stick."

"The baby is due July fifteenth," Violet said softly. Wolf tightened his hands around his fork and knife. "So the wedding will be sometime before then."

"Good," her dad said.

"That's exciting," Alison said.

"You should see some of her baby pictures," Cain said. "She was cute."

And that was how he found himself looking at family photo albums. Pictures of little Violet, skinny legged and spinning in those grass fields she told him about, surrounded by bluebonnets.

A window into a childhood that looked a lot happier than any portion of his own.

Before the cares of the world had touched her, too. Before her mother's abandonment had made her doubt whether or not there was something wrong with her.

He couldn't help himself. He touched that picture. That sunny smile.

"She was the cutest," Cain said.

He realized that Alison and Violet had slipped off to the kitchen, and he was just sitting there with Violet's dad.

"You know," he said slowly. "Protecting Violet is something I've done her entire life. But most especially after her mom left, I made it…the most important thing in the whole world to protect that girl. From as much as I could. The failure that I feel over not being able to protect her from her own parent is something else. It's painful. And it's something that I don't know I'll ever fully get over. Having to watch her grieve like that. So when I threaten you with bodily harm over hurting my daughter, you have to know it comes from there. From the fact that her happiness, her joy, is the thing I have spent my entire life trying to preserve in the face of some pretty shitty odds."

Wolf nodded. "I get that."

"You'll really get it when you hold that child in your arms. Because you might care about *my* daughter, I see that you do, but not like I do. That sense of responsibility, that sense of needing to protect? That's a different kind of love. Because no one else in this world is going to do it for you. It's on *you*. When you are the father, that is something that falls to you and you alone in a very specific way. You have to be hard. You have to be willing to fight battles. You have to be willing to slay armies. But you also have to be soft. You have to figure out how to be there for them, no matter what's going on. You have to figure it out. That's the thing. Because you are the one that they lean on."

Wolf didn't say anything. There was nothing to say. He

knew that he could build a house. He knew that he could protect. He didn't know how to do that other stuff. No one had ever done it for him.

"I know what it's like to be left," Wolf said slowly. "My own mother didn't stick around."

Cain's expression shifted. "I see."

"I feel sorry for Violet. That she has that in common with me. But we do have that in common. She has a great dad, though, from all that I've seen and heard. I personally don't know a hell of a lot about good fathers. Didn't have one myself. But... I know about bad ones. So maybe that's a start."

"Yeah," Cain said. "It's a start. But just remember that's all it is. That's all anything is. A start. You spend your life trying to get better. Trying to be better every day. To love the people around you better, and in the way they needed at the time. Because that's the other thing. The way that you love your wife, the way that you love your children, that will change. Because their needs will change. Right now loving Violet means not killing you, for example."

"Noted. You would really like to kill me."

"I wouldn't say *like to*," Cain said. "But I'm not opposed to it."

Wolf felt like the enormity of the day might crush him. And actually, his future father-in-law's threats didn't seem like the heaviest part. They seemed fair enough.

And maybe that was the most overwhelming thing of all. Seeing an inside look at her family. At the way they supported her still, all these years later. It wasn't as simple as just raising her and spitting her out to the world, which his own parents hadn't even managed to do. They had a lifelong commitment to her. To each other.

And it was more than just forcing their way through with

the sheer strength of their will and the determination to do the right thing. It was something deeper than that.

The way that you love them will change...

He shoved that to the side. And then, Alison and Violet came back into the dining room with trays that held mugs of hot chocolate with whipped cream and sprinkles piled high, and plates of cookies.

"Some specialties we're doing down at the bakery," Alison said, smiling. And she handed him a mug of hot chocolate and a cookie.

The almost maternal affection in her face made his heart clench uncomfortably.

"Let's go sit outside," Violet said, grabbing her own hot chocolate and taking his hand. He looked back at Cain, who had a strange, resigned look on his face, and then back at Violet, who proceeded to drag him from the room and take them out to the porch swing out front, draping a plaid blanket over their laps.

"It was a good day," she said, lifting her mug to her lips and looking up at him with an impish smile.

A good day. He had just been thinking how heavy it was.

"Good," he said.

"You seem less certain," she said, putting her hand on his cheek.

"It's not that I'm not certain," he said. "It's just a lot to take in."

"Yeah. Well. Things are changing. But I think I didn't realize how much I needed them to change."

"You looked like such a happy kid," he said, in spite of himself.

And he worried just then. If he would be able to make her as happy as she'd been in that picture. If he would be able to make their kid that happy. He didn't know that he could do either thing.

"Yeah, I was," she said. "Sometimes a sad kid. And sometimes an awful kid. Like all kids are."

"Were you happy after she left?"

"It took a long time," Violet said. "It took a long time to be happy again. But I am. I am and that's…amazing. It's amazing that any of us end up happy, isn't it?"

He nodded. Happy. Was that what this was? He didn't even know, but the feeling expanding in his chest felt sharp, and he was suspicious of it more than he was anything.

"I've been thinking a lot about that," she said. "About happiness. About what it is. And whether or not it's the most important thing. Well, about what it even means. When you're a kid, it's a feeling. Whether or not you want to smile. But it seems to me that everything good that happened to me in the last few weeks has made me want to cry a little bit, too. I just wonder if there's a point where happiness isn't that simple anymore. But I think it might be… I think it might be heavier, too."

Heavy.

That was the word he'd been thinking of. That was a word that resonated inside him. "It's just that I think when you're a kid, and you're spinning in the field, there's happiness, and it's real. It's like… It's easy. It doesn't cost you anything. And you're not afraid of what's going to happen next. When you're an adult, sometimes happiness is much harder won. But it goes so deep. And it becomes a part of who you are. Joy. And it can exist alongside fear. Sadness. All kinds of other things. It's more, and it's bigger, and it's…worth the cost, I think."

Heavy.

Yeah, he felt that. But he didn't know if he agreed with

her. Didn't know if it was the same. But he just didn't say anything. Instead, he just sat. They had hot chocolate and cookies. And she leaned her head against his shoulder as they rocked slowly on the porch swing.

"Wolf," she said, her voice quiet. "I love you."

The words were like a guillotine. Cutting off his breath. A clean slice that made it impossible for him to breathe or think or move.

And it threw him back. Right back.

I love you.

And silence.

A kiss on the forehead.

And the next morning she was gone.

I love you. He'd told her every day. Every single day. And it hadn't been enough to keep her there.

Breanna, I love you.

Wolf, it doesn't have to be that serious yet.

It doesn't have to be but it is. I would never have... I would never have slept with you if I didn't love you.

I... Wolf, I don't want to be this... It's been too intense.

Did we do anything you didn't like?

It's not that. I just... I didn't want to be in a relationship this soon.

Neither did I but I love you all the same. I love you.

And desperation had clawed at him as he'd said those words. Because abandonment was something he could *feel.* But she'd moved away from him.

And then a splash into the water, and no more sound. No more girl.

I love you.

But it hadn't been enough. It was never enough. It was too much and futile all at once. And the stars suddenly seemed like they were falling down around him. It was the quiet moments that hurt. These moments. When there were no expectations from her family. When there was nothing but them. And the feelings that grew between them. There was no sex to distract them, no noise. And he wasn't alone; damn but he wasn't alone.

He had cultivated being alone with someone next to him and made it an art, but he couldn't do it with her.

She'd gotten under his skin somehow. And it wasn't about Four Corners and how the Sullivans would judge him and Sawyer would disown him.

It wasn't about her parents and what they thought of him. Or about living up to some standard he'd never seen played out around him.

It was just her. And him.

It was terrifying. There was no range to ride, no fixed fence. She wasn't panting and writhing beneath him, begging for pleasure.

She was just sitting with him. Demanding nothing. Letting the feelings grow between them. Offering things to him that he had never asked for. And not even waiting to give them before she knew if he'd offer them in return.

"I love you."

And his heart stopped.

Because he knew this. He knew how it went.

I love you. And silence in return. *I love you*, and then they were gone. *I love you* and nothing but the broad expanse of stars, the terrible, silent water and Wolf alone.

It always ended with him alone.

He believed in the power of love. In the terrible, awful way that it reached inside you and rearranged everything that you were. In the way that it grabbed you and shook you like a ragdoll, left you broken and bleeding.

He believed that love could destroy you when you were in it alone.

And at the same time, he believed in its weakness.

Because a little boy who loved his mother with all he was hadn't been able to keep her from leaving. And loving Breanna… It hadn't been enough to keep her alive. To make her want him, to keep her happy, and it was all bound up in her loss.

Yeah, his love was powerful enough to chase people away.

There was no magic in it. It didn't make everything okay. Didn't make everything better. It was both, somehow. This wildly destructive force that cut through the heart of the landscape in his soul, and a powerless, weak emotion that left you devastated. That didn't hold people to you. Or hold them to the earth. That didn't guarantee happiness or success or anything at all.

It was a promise that couldn't be kept. And it chained you to people. And chained them to you forever.

While still not being enough. While still not lasting.

And he couldn't say it back to her. He couldn't do anything with it. He let it disappear on the air along with her breath. And all the while his blood boiled. The events of the day suddenly crashing in on him. The baby's heartbeat. The family dinner. The talk with her father.

The way that Alison had looked at him, like a lost little boy who needed a mother. Yeah, well, he had been. And he hadn't had one. It didn't matter. That was the thing. It just didn't matter.

And whatever Violet thought…

Love wasn't enough. And so he let it fade into the silence. Love wasn't enough, so he let it evaporate.

She didn't say anything more. She just rubbed her hand

over his, and he felt... He felt sick. He felt like every last shortcoming that he was.

They finished their hot chocolate, folded up the blankets and walked into the house. Alison and Cain were still up, sitting in the chairs in the living room.

"Good night," Violet said to her parents.

He nodded. And followed her up the stairs. He didn't say anything to Violet as he went into his room. And he did his best to just pretend that today hadn't happened.

Instead of replaying her words in his head, he just thought about his plans for the cabin.

Yeah. He would think about that. Because they needed a nursery. Yeah, there were two bedrooms, but it wasn't enough. They would need to do something better for the baby, and Violet probably needed a more modern kitchen.

He stripped his clothes off and walked through to the bathroom that connected to his bedroom. The shower was large, with dark tile and a big showerhead. And the amount of water it sprayed out was almost enough to drown out the thoughts inside him. So he would take that. He turned it on and stood beneath it, letting the heat burn it all away.

He felt a cool breeze and turned, to see the shower door open and Violet walk through. Naked.

"What are you doing?"

She looked at him, her eyes large and overly serious, filled with tears. "I wanted to see you. And you went to bed awfully quick."

"We're under your father's roof," he said. "He was pretty clear on this kind of thing."

"Yes, we are under my father's roof. But we are living our lives. And I needed to see you. Wolf, I just need you."

She touched him, and it was gentle. Everything about what was happening right now was gentle. And he didn't want that. He didn't know what to do with it. What would come next? More words of love? And what then?

No, he knew how to do certain things. He could be honorable. He could build her a house. He could be her husband. He could take her to heaven every single night in his arms. And he could keep on doing. Making his brother proud, working the ranch, building the legacy. Making her dad happy that he'd given permission for her to marry him. He could do that. It was the rest that he couldn't figure out. It was the rest that made him feel like he was dying.

So he kissed her. He kissed her, because he could do that. He kissed her because when he touched her, it drowned out everything else. It burned it all away.

He thought again of that day on the beach. Of the lightness there. And he thought about what she'd said about happiness. Dammit, had they been kids then? Because he didn't feel like he'd been a kid since he was six years old. But it had felt light then. It felt easy. And what had come on the heels of that?

Everything.

The baby and marriage, and *I love you*. And he couldn't feel the good side of that. He couldn't feel that joy that she was talking about. All he could see was an abyss. Dark and black, and pain that wouldn't have a bottom. Fiery, tearing, horrendous pain that would never ever find the end.

And the beast inside him took control. Because the beast… The beast was him. And it always had been. Desperate, needy. And pushing away everybody with the power of his love. That was what it was there for. To hold them all at a distance.

But it could do *this*.

It could hold her close. As long as they were naked.

So he kissed her.

And slid his hands over her water-slicked skin, luxuri-ated in the desire that he felt for her. And the fact that his cock was so hard it hurt. And the fact that he wanted her so much he couldn't see straight. He pushed his hands be-tween her thighs and felt how slick she was, felt how much she wanted him, too. Because she did. She might want love, she might want tenderness, she might want sweet words, but she wanted his body more.

She wouldn't hold this hostage for those words, because she couldn't say no to him. Silence… All that silence after *I love you.* All that space.

There was no space here.

She was looking up at him like she might die if she couldn't have him, and that was what he felt. If he couldn't be inside her…

Violet.

It was an obsession. It was an addiction. And it had been from the beginning. If he couldn't have her, then there was nothing. So where was the happy side to that? Where was the sweet to the bitter? Because he sure as hell couldn't find it, unless he was inside her body. The only thing he craved.

He would take the rest right along with it. But this was all he cared about.

He pushed his fingers inside her, thrusting in and out, watching as her eyes went cloudy, as her jaw went slack. And she moaned. "Quiet," he said. "Don't make a sound. Don't say a word. You want your daddy to know what you're getting up to in the shower?"

She bit her lip, shaking her head.

"You're a bad girl, Violet Donnelly. Letting me fuck you in your dad's house, against his wishes."

He backed her against the wall, and he wasn't the man

who had seduced her back at the bed-and-breakfast. And he wasn't the careful man who had promised to marry her.

This was *him*. All this darkness.

Let her love *that*. And see where it took her. Let her love this version of him and see how long she stayed.

She hadn't seen this side of him. He hadn't let him out. All the ugliness that had been building inside him for all these years. The anger, the hurt that he had never wanted to expand on anybody.

The anger over his mother leaving, which he had never done anything but bottle it up, because Sawyer had said, *and hell, he was right,* wasn't it something they'd all been through?

Dry your tears and move on.

He certainly hadn't wanted to get it on Breanna, who was sweet and innocent and lovely, and he'd wanted to have feelings for her that were just like that. Because he wanted to believe that he could have a different life than the one his parents had set him up for as a child. But he'd learned the hard way it wasn't true. And then he'd taken that and he'd bottled it up, too. Because how did he deserve to feel pain about it when she wasn't even here?

And he'd taken that wound and protected it. Never let it heal. Used it as a reminder.

His love was toxic.

It was wrong.

It killed everything it touched.

And inside him was a soul that was just filled with darkness. Never unleashed on anyone. And so it would be her. Because she said she loved him. Because she said she loved him, and Wolf knew how that would end. So he might as well push it there as quickly as possible.

"You want me, anyway," he said. "Even though it's bad. You were such a smart girl before you met me."

He kissed her again and felt her shudder beneath his touch. Felt her internal muscles clenched around his fingers. Then he turned her around, braced her hands against the shower wall and wrapped his arm around her waist, bending her there and pressing his arousal against her ass. "So pretty," he said. He pressed the head of himself against the slick entrance to her body, gripped her hips and thrust home. She gasped, and he reached around, clamping his hand over her mouth. "Quiet," he said.

And he began to fuck her. Because it was better than making love. Because what the hell had he been doing making love with her all this time? As if he had a right to that. As if it meant something. It didn't mean anything. Love wasn't strong enough. But this seemed plenty strong to him. It was like a fire in his veins. Like a monster.

You're the monster.

They sang countless songs about the power of love.

But the darkness in him was enough to destroy it every time, so what did that mean?

He knew what it meant. He knew.

He thrust into her, hard and fast, holding back her whimpers and cries with the force of his hand, clamped hard over her mouth.

But mostly, mostly, he just didn't want her to be able to say those words again. He wanted to drive them out of her with this. And when he uncovered her mouth, she wouldn't have anything nice to say at all. Not to him. It would just be silence. And he knew what came next.

He growled low in his throat, his climax overtaking him. And he spilled himself inside her, feeling her own release come to claim her. He straightened her up against his body, his hand still over her mouth, and he kissed her neck. Then slowly released her.

She was panting hard.

And she said nothing. They finished the shower, and he expected her to leave. She dried off, and he looked at the red marks left behind on her skin from where he held her so tight.

And he waited.

He waited.

But she said nothing. And then she slipped beneath his covers naked.

And he didn't want to speak, because if he did then she might. So he just got into bed with her.

Her hands drifted over his body, never stopping. And when he was hard again she climbed on top of him, put him inside her and rode him like she'd won something. And he couldn't resist her. All he could do was watch. The rise and fall of those beautiful breasts, and the glory on her face as she chased ecstasy.

And when he was shuddering out his orgasm she leaned over him and kissed his lips. "I love you."

And it made less sense than anything.

But he didn't have the strength to make her leave.

But it was all right. Because one thing he knew. She would be leaving.

Because that was how it always went.

CHAPTER TWENTY-ONE

THE NEXT MORNING Violet felt shaky, and she knew that she looked as exhausted as she felt. They needed to go back to Four Corners today, because she had to deal with Wolf on their turf and their terms. She'd said that she loved him. And he had said nothing. She would have been happier if he'd said *something*, even if it was something she didn't want to hear.

It was the nothing that was killing her.

"You know," Alison said while helping make sandwiches for them to take on the road. "If you are going to creep into your fiancé's room, in an attempt at blatant sneakiness, you might not leave *your* bedroom door open all night where I could see that you were not in it."

Her face got hot, especially remembering what had happened last night.

She cleared her throat. "Noted."

"I don't think your dad noticed. Or if he did, he is really pretending he didn't, and never wants to speak of it."

"Well, you know I'm attracted to Wolf," Violet bit out.

"I know," Alison said. "But you know, it's just things like that your dad doesn't need haunting his nightmares." Alison tilted her head. "You seem sad."

And it all crashed in on her. The way she'd told him she loved him. The way he'd been with her after. So rough and dark and desperate. It didn't scare her; it wasn't that. It was just the divide felt so big, the chasm between them, and she didn't know how they would ever...

She didn't know if they could ever cross it, and it terrified her.

"I don't know if I can love him through it," she said, her eyes filling with tears. "I don't know how to reach him."

Alison's brows crinkled. "You know you can stay here. You don't have to go back. You don't have to marry him."

"I have to go back," Violet said, sucking in a sharp breath, swallowing a sob. "I have to. Because I have to be brave. But it's really hard."

Alison put her hand on Violet's cheek. "The people that have been hurt the worst resist the hardest. I know. Because that was me. Learning to trust when you've been hurt badly is so difficult. But you're strong, Violet. You have so much of your dad in you."

A glow burned in the center of Violet's chest. "I do?"

"You are steady and faithful and hardheaded. And you care so much about doing the right thing. You love the people in your life so much."

"I like being like him," Violet said. "But I hope that I can be like you, too."

"Like me?"

"Because you're brave, Alison. You're really brave. And that is what I need right now."

She and Wolf drove separately going back to Four Corners, so at least now she had her car. But of course it gave him an easier time avoiding her.

They were welcomed back happily by his family that night. And he was... He was as cold and aloof as he'd ever been. Honestly, it was like a study in being a distant asshole.

He was abrupt to his family. He didn't even sit next to her at dinner.

"So Copper Ridge was good?" Evelyn asked quietly after dinner.

"Yeah," she said. "It was good. I had my first doctor appointment."

"And?"

"The baby is coming in July." She handed Evelyn some dirty dishes. "He wants to remodel the cabin. He wants to get married as soon as possible."

"Is that why he's being weird?" Evelyn asked.

"No," Violet said, but she didn't offer any more information. Because whatever was happening with her and Wolf right now…it was their complicated upsetting business. They went back to the cabin, and yet again, he was a beast in bed. Tearing her clothes off as soon as they walked through the door, carrying her back and pleasuring her until neither of them could breathe.

And then he was asleep before she could say anything.

He had gone someplace where she couldn't reach him.

He was completely shut off. However inaccessible she'd found him before…he was winning at it now. And this time without any of the charm.

"I hope you like lasagna," she said when he walked in that night.

"Who doesn't like lasagna?"

She was tempted to say *maybe you, because you are an unknowable creature*, but she didn't.

"I guess not many people."

"I was thinking," he said. "We need a new kitchen. You do a lot of cooking, which is nice. But I want you to have some better stuff."

"That's really sweet. Thank you." He wasn't being at all sweet and they both knew it.

"And we're going to need to sort out the bedrooms. Probably remodel the bathrooms while we're at it."

"Sounds almost like a new construction."

"I could do most of it myself. But it is going to take time. And you know, before the baby is born, it might actually work for you to go and stay with your parents."

"What?" Well, of all the things, she hadn't seen that coming.

"This place isn't going to be habitable," he said. "And I don't really give a shit. I'll sleep wherever. But you need a nice place. And you might as well be close to the doctor."

"Oh." It all made sense now. The creeping horror of it. "You... You want me to leave."

"It just seems smart," he said. "For you to go stay where you're comfortable during the pregnancy, and while I get this sorted out. The place is going to be gutted. While I'm at it, probably going to replace the roof. It's going to mean some camping for me."

"You are so full of bullshit, Wolf Garrett, it is unbeliev-able."

"What?"

"You want me to leave, because you want to be by your-self. Because you have been desperate to try and pretend like I'm not actually here for all this time. And don't think that I haven't noticed that. You are... You're incredible."

"I'm sorry, what asshole would ask his pregnant fian-cée to live in a hovel while it's being remodeled? How am I a bad guy for wanting you to be comfortable? How am I the bad guy for wanting you to have a nice place to live?"

"Because it's not what you want. It is not at all your goal. Your goal is to get rid of me."

"I am marrying you," he said. "I don't want to get rid of you."

"Right. So none of this has to do with me being in love with you?"

He stopped, his jaw turning hard. "No."

"Weird. Because I think it does. We were good. We were good and then you…"

"And then what? I quit pretending? I quit acting like a sweet, biddable boyfriend?"

"You were never that," she said. "No. You started trying to push me away. You're trying to push everybody away. You were even an asshole to your family."

"I'm sorry, if you can't handle living with me. I was on my best behavior when I met you, and I can't play that part for my entire life. Anyway, you like it well enough when I'm making you come."

"Yeah. You're good at that. We are good at that. That has never been our problem, Wolf. But the closer that I get to you, the more you want to use that to push me away. And I hate that. Because you know what, it's not pushing me away. It's like you're trying to scare me, and I don't get it."

"I'm not trying to do anything. But you know what? I did think about it. And the thing is, I can't play a part and wait to see what's going to happen for the rest of my life. If I'm going to live with you, then you have to live with me. And you have to deal with me. Which no one's ever had to do, Violet. My mother left. Breanna died. But not before adding to all of this. So congratulations. You can be the first person to successfully try to deal with me. But I don't know that you're gonna like it."

"You are pushing me away."

"I am not here to be psychoanalyzed. That is not my scene."

"Tough. This isn't your life anymore. It is our life. And I want it. I want that heavy happy, Wolf. I want it even if it costs. I am brave enough to push through this. Are you?"

"Push through what?"

"I asked Alison about this. About what to do with you.

Because I knew that I loved you, but that you love someone else. Because I knew that I loved you but that it was going to be a fight to try and figure out how to make you okay with loving me."

He just looked at her, his face blank.

"Do what you want, Violet. Call it whatever you want. But the fact of the matter is, it doesn't mean anything. And that's what you need to understand. We are attracted to each other. Great. That's good. We can choose to build a life together. Great. We can be committed to our kid. But you telling me that you love me... It just doesn't mean shit."

"It does to me. I am in love with you. I don't want to live in a marriage where you don't love me back the way that I love you."

"That's your decision, then. I knew it wouldn't last."

Almost as if he was waiting for this. As if he was glad to be able to say he'd known it wouldn't last.

"I said I don't want to. I didn't say that I wouldn't. I'm committed to you. I'm committed to us. That's why I decided to say yes to you before my second trimester. Because I can't go back to living life like before I loved you. I can't pretend that we were never us. You changed me. Loving you has changed me, and I am not interested in going back to before."

"But that's what happens," he said. "That's what happens. You love people, and they leave. You love them, they can't love you back, and I already know it, so I gave up. I loved her so much. I told her every day. I was... She was my favorite person. She was the sun and the moon and all the stars and I told her so. My mom, the prettiest woman in the world. The nicest. She smelled like vanilla. She left. I wasn't like you, Violet. I knew my mom was gone. I knew she was gone forever. I woke up in the morning and the house was empty. And I could feel it. And Sawyer said there's no use crying. None at all. Because that is what people do. They leave you. But I was an idiot. I was an idiot who thought maybe that wasn't true. I met Breanna and she was sweet and she was wonderful. And I thought that I could win. That's what I thought. The power of love, right? Big enough to heal all these wounds. I loved her, too. But she didn't love me back. And she died."

"She didn't die because she loved you."

"No, she didn't love me." The words were hard and flat. "I said I loved her, and she said...*let's not get so intense.* I said I loved her, and she... Hell, she basically ran away from me to her death, Violet."

"Wolf..." Horror stole over her. "What are you talking about?"

"She wanted to leave. After I said I loved her. She jumped off the dock to swim away from me. Me. And my love. Because that's how awful it is to be loved by me. Everyone runs from it eventually."

"No, Wolf, that's not...that's not what happened."

"It is what happened, Violet. If you can't look at me knowing that, I don't blame you."

"She didn't mean to die. I think you know she didn't choose death over you."

"I don't know that," he said.

"Wolf, of course she didn't."

"She still ran away..."

"She was a teenager. So were you. Would you have hurt her?"

"No," he said, drawing back. "I never..."

"She wasn't afraid of you. She was... She was just being a kid. And sometimes things happen. Accidents. And that's all."

"Maybe. But if I hadn't have been so…so hell-bent on being with her all the time. On redeeming all that pain inside me at her expense… I sure as hell wouldn't have taken her out to the lake in the middle of the damned night. I wouldn't have…told her I loved her like I have a stake in it, Violet, and I can't pretend that I don't. I failed her. I damn well did. Trying to keep her with me. Trying to be enough. I'm not doing it again. I am not doing it again."

"I love you," she said.

"I don't love you," he said. "I loved her. And that was the end. I don't love you."

Violet felt the sting of that like a slap. But she also knew that he was lying. Even if it was just to himself. Because this wasn't the grief of a man who couldn't get over his first love.

This was just a wounded animal, trying to hurt the thing that had backed him into a corner. Wolf was willing to be mean. He was willing to be hard. Willing to be cruel. She'd already seen it. He wasn't willing to be soft. He wasn't willing to be hurt. That was Wolf.

This was easy for him. These wild rampages were how he just pushed people away.

But she wasn't going to make it easy. She refused.

"Yeah, well, I love you, anyway. And I will be here. We will figure out the remodel. And we will make it work."

"Be reasonable," he said.

"You be reasonable."

"I'm going out."

He turned and walked out of the cabin, left her standing there. She ate lasagna by herself, and by the time she was exhausted and ready for bed, Wolf still wasn't home. And he didn't answer his phone. Didn't respond to his texts. She went to sleep, and woke up the next morning and he still wasn't there. In the afternoon he finally returned. He opened the door, and she was still there, and his expression went blank. "Why the hell are you still here?"

"Because I live here," she said.

"Why won't you leave?" he asked, his words fraying around the edges. "Why won't you leave now? Because we know that you're going to. Eventually. Do it now."

"I'm not the one who leaves. *You* leave. You left me. I'm still here. I'm so willing to give us a chance. But you… You're just trying to protect yourself. You don't want to love me because you don't want to get hurt. I am sorry that your mom left. I feel that pain, Wolf, I really do. I'm sorry that me knowing that pain, that your brother knowing that pain and your sister knowing that pain keeps you from being able to pretend that you are a special, uniquely wounded cupcake. Must be tough."

"It is," he said. "It's damn hard, no matter how you look at it. I'm not playing a game with you."

"You're just protecting yourself," she said. "Because here I am, ready to love you. Sawyer is married, he has a life, but you don't want that. What exactly are you trying to do? Push me away now so I don't surprise you with it later? Because that's stupid. I thought about that. I followed that path. And I asked myself, is there a point where losing you would hurt less? And the answer is no."

"You cannot possibly know what you're getting into with me. You cannot possibly want me."

"Why not?"

"Because *nobody* wants me the way that I am. I learned. After Breanna I learned. To play games. To be charming. To be less intense than I am. But I can't. I can't, and I know it. I could never have given her what she wanted. She would never have stayed."

"You don't know that. You're just… You're making up stories. Stories that let you hide. Because that's what you want to do. And I understand. Because I did the same thing. I told myself that if I put one foot out of line my dad and Alison would question whether or not I was worth it. I told myself that I had put so much into me, that I had to be careful and cautious and the right kind of good. But that was a lie. I could've come home pregnant at seventeen and my dad would've been on my side. He has always been on my side and he has never shown himself to be anything but on my side. I made it a precarious thing in my head because I wanted to be able to stay safe. I didn't want to fall for someone. I didn't want to be in this position. Because I knew that if I did I would fall deep. And that scared me. Because I felt like I'd already been hurt enough. So I do understand feeling that way. But it's too late. You already love me."

He practically growled. "I am willing to give you a life. I am willing to take care of you. Why can't that be enough?"

"Because why should we be what our mothers taught us? They weren't there to care for us. Why should we let them have a say over how much we get now? I want everything. I want to be loved. Forever. She tried to teach me that I couldn't be. And I refuse. You should refuse, too."

"It's too late for me. Because the thing is, I did try. And it didn't work then, either."

"It wasn't me. Try with me. Because I knew the minute that I saw you… I knew we weren't going to be able to walk away. I was ready to beg you back then, and I will beg you now."

"Then you didn't learn anything."

And then he turned and walked out again, leaving Violet broken a second time.

And while tears poured down her face she had to ask

herself how many times she was willing to break apart for this man's love.

She thought of their baby. She thought of the future they knew they could have.

And she thought of the man who needed so much to learn that not everybody would leave. And she realized that she would break herself apart as many times as it took.

And even while she sat in the depths of despair, she knew that in some ways she'd won a victory. Oh, other people might not see it. They might not understand it. But inside her heart, hope won.

Love won.

And she felt, for the very first time, like she was truly free of the pain in her past.

Like she was truly walking forward, being the woman she was meant to be, and not the one who had been created by loss and abandonment. And that was how she knew that no matter what, loving Wolf was worth it.

Because he was wrong about love. At the end of everything, the thunder, the lightning, the fight, it endured.

CHAPTER TWENTY-TWO

WOLF RODE HARD. He rode until he reached the top of the mountain overlooking the darkening valley below.

And he could see his cabin.

Could see the damned Christmas lights stretched around the roofline. And he wanted to forget her. He wanted to get away from this. He wanted to get back to who he'd been. All these years. This man who protected the wound in his core with deep, fierce intensity.

He couldn't get away from her. And that was… That was the worst damn thing about all of this. There had been a time when he'd been able to pull away. When he'd been able to be alone with people around, but he couldn't do that. Not with her. And he couldn't even be alone when he went away.

She had done something to him. She had changed him in a way that nothing else had.

And he wanted… He just wanted.

He was staring down the possibility of a future without this woman. And it made him mean. It made him hurt. It made him wonder what the hell the point of anything was.

What the point of safety was.

And here he was, out on this land, his family land, his family legacy. His family curse.

It wasn't that he wasn't happy for his brother. He was.

He was just so damned jealous. The realization knocked the wind out of him. Made it hard for him to breathe. He was jealous. Because he wanted that. He'd always wanted it. It was why he had gotten himself in deep at sixteen. Because he had hoped that he could find some way to have a life in spite of the fact that his family was supposed to be cursed. And he had decided he wanted it. And it hadn't worked out. He lost it. And Sawyer got it, anyway.

And it was why when Violet had said she was pregnant it was so easy to say he wanted to marry her. It was so easy. But it was the love part that was hard. It was the love part that made it feel like an impossibility. Like something he couldn't do.

He'd run far from it, and he'd run hard from it, but this was what he wanted.

And he wanted, more than anything, to be loved.

And that beast inside him howled. Because that was it. He wasn't grieving the loss of the woman he loved, loved so much he could never love anyone else. That wasn't it. It had never been it. He just wanted to stay hurt. Just enough. Just enough that he would never have to try again. Just enough that he would never get in so deep that he couldn't come back out. But he'd done it. He'd done it with Violet. And now he'd… He'd pushed her away.

And he'd…

He had it wrong.

Love wasn't weak. Love wasn't insufficient.

He'd loved his mother with his whole heart. And even though she'd left…she had loved him. Even though the words weren't in his memory, she'd been soft and kind. And it had left its mark on him. Enough to know he did want a family. To know he did want to fall in love. She had gone, but the impression of the love remained. For better and worse. Because it hurt. Because loving her and having her leave had caused a hell of a lot of pain. And he had loved Breanna. And yes, they'd been too young. Foolish in many ways, and in the end… Not the kind that would have lasted, he didn't think. But the experience of loving her had changed him, and it remained, too.

Bad, ugly and good all at once.

Because he had been a teenage boy who had been all in, even without having the maturity to understand that in the future things might change. He'd been intense, because he'd been honest about his feelings. That love might have been immature, but it had been real. It left an impression on your soul. And that was the other thing Violet was right about.

There was no good time to run.

Because in the end, it was too late. It was too late.

I love you.

And the silence was his.

This time he was the one who had run. He'd been running from the beginning. And she had been there. And he let his fear call her a liar. And she deserved a hell of a lot more than that. Violet had been brave. Violet had gone after what she wanted. Violet was fighting for them.

And what was he doing? Fighting to stay his own sad kind of safe. But this was what safe looked like. Being alone on the hill and looking down at the Christmas lights, being all by himself.

But when he looked down on himself, he only saw darkness.

And he wondered if he could possibly ask the woman who had brought all that light into his life to look past it and love him, anyway.

SHE *HAD* LEFT. But not because she was leaving him. She had left because it was Christmas Eve, and she wanted to be with her family. She didn't want to be sitting in that cabin, stewing in their separation. Stewing in their difference.

Alison clearly knew something was up. And her dad seemed to think so, too. But neither of them pushed.

Clara, on the other hand, was another story.

"He broke your heart again? That's it. He's on my last nerve."

"It's complicated," Violet said. "He's complicated. *We* are complicated."

"Sorry," Clara said.

They sat down to dinner, and nobody asked. And she was grateful.

She still had her ring on. She wasn't going to take it off. The fact of the matter was, they hadn't broken up. It was just that her heart was broken.

And the next morning, when they got up bright and early to open presents, she tried to smile at the excitement of her half brothers, tried to get in the Christmas spirit. She loved Christmas, after all. But she just wished that she was back home. Home at Four Corners. Because it wasn't the ocean that smelled like home anymore. It wasn't this house. It wasn't this town. It was wherever Wolf was. And he wasn't here.

"Violet," Alison said slowly. "I think…"

There was a firm knock at the door.

"I'll get it," Violet said.

She went to the door and jerked it open and stopped. It was Wolf. His arms laden down with gifts, a wreath slung over his arm. He was wearing a black shirt, a black cowboy hat on his head. He looked dangerous and filled with Christmas spirit all at once. Except his eyes were a storm. Because they were never anything else.

"What are you doing here?"

"Coming to my senses. Coming to you."

Her heart leaped. She couldn't breathe.

"Let's go outside," she said.

She brushed past him and gestured to the porch swing. "You can set your stuff down."

He did, all the wrapped packages in boxes, and the wreath, too. "I didn't figure I better come empty-handed. Not after that bullshit."

"Yeah." She crossed her arms. "It was bullshit. You are correct about that."

"Sorry," he said. "I'm sorry. I left you twice. And you have been nothing but faithful to me. You tried to show me. From the beginning. What we could have. I wasn't ready to see it. I was running scared. You were right. The thing is, Violet, I've never felt the way that I feel about you... ever. Never before. The strength of it terrified me. Because it wasn't like we could have sex and I could keep it separate. It wasn't like we could do any of the things that I was used to. I couldn't forget you. I couldn't write you off. I couldn't do anything but want you. And the more I wanted you the more I wanted to know you. Not just your body, but you. I wasn't prepared for it. It wasn't like anything I'd ever experienced. Because you were right. Happy like this, it's heavy."

She understood that. All too well. He continued, "Because it's weighted down with how much I want to love you the way you need to be loved. The way you deserve to be loved. And how afraid I am that I'm going to fall short. That I'm going to disappoint you. And yeah. That I'm going to lose you. And that it's going to be a pain I'm not going to be able to come back from. That's why I tried to stop. At sixteen I got so wounded I told myself I was never going to do it again. Not ever. Not because I couldn't, because I was afraid I could. Just like you said. Knowing… Knowing it could hurt that bad then, knowing that kind of loss could do what it did all those years ago, I never wanted to love anyone again. To love anyone with the kind of love that might be forever. But that's what I feel with you, Violet. That's what I feel about you. It is wonderful and terrible. And it is freedom. Because I'm not guarding anything or protecting myself or closing myself off. I'm just feeling. For the first time in…in a long damned time."

"Wolf," she said, throwing her arms around his neck. "I love you."

And he didn't let that *I love you* be met with silence.

"I love you, too," he said. "I love you."

He didn't get tired of saying it. He said it all through Christmas. And he said it when he decided he needed to ask her dad again if he could have her hand in marriage.

"Cain," Alison said. "There's a nervous young man that I believe has a question for you."

He wasn't nervous. He just thought maybe his heart was going to beat out straight through his chest.

Wolf Garrett didn't do nerves.

"I understand now," Wolf said. "I understand what I was missing. I wasn't as brave as her. But now… I hope I am. I hope to be. Because she deserves someone who loves as big and brave as she does. And that's what I'm aiming for. To be what she needs. Everything she needs."

"I appreciate that," Cain said.

"You know, I was tempted to say we did things backward," Wolf said. "I mean, a lot of people would say we did. But I don't think so. I loved her from the first minute I saw her. I just had to take some wrong steps to find my way to the right ones."

"Well, that I relate to."

And then he sat down and had a beer with his future father-in-law.

But later Violet snuck into his room. And he told her that he loved her all over again. And it was without a doubt the best Christmas he'd ever had. But he had love. And for the first time, hope, that things might just turn out right in the end, after all. And the last thought he had before he went to sleep was that he was genuinely happy for his brother. But he didn't envy him at all. Because he didn't want Sawyer's life. He wanted his own. And that was the miracle he hadn't known he'd been waiting for.

EPILOGUE

IT BECAME A running joke, the number of times that Wolf asked Cain's permission to marry Violet. And he was still doing it, every Christmas, five years later.

Thankfully, Violet's next pregnancy was a much less dramatic announcement. And their son was thrilled at becoming a big brother, even if he didn't know exactly what that meant. And once it had turned out to mean a lot of sharing of toys, the thrill of the younger sister had faded.

But the thrill of all of it never faded for Wolf.

He hadn't really known what unconditional love looked like. Not in his life. There had been nothing but time limits and conditions, and now he was surrounded by it. All day. Every day. He had Violet. He had the kids. He had her whole family. And hell, he even had his. Their Christmas had become a marathon. Because of course they had to spend time with Sawyer and Evelyn and their kids, though they saw them all the time, since they lived at Garrett's Watch. But they had to visit the Copper Ridge Garretts, which Hunter, Elsie, Evelyn and Sawyer joined them for. And then they had to do the big Donnelly thing.

He'd gone from being a loner to being anything but.

But his favorite times were still when he was alone. Alone with Violet.

Because that he had discovered was his very favorite type of alone.

Just the two of them. Just that quiet.

"I knew you were trouble," she said, touching his chin and lips right before they went to sleep that Christmas Eve. "Right when you first walked into the bed-and-breakfast."

"And you didn't run the other way?"

"No. Because you were the first time trouble ever looked worth it."

"Well, you were the first time love looked worth it."

"Good thing we were both right."

"Good thing."

"I love you," she said.

It didn't terrify him. It made him feel full.

He understood now. About why they wrote songs about this. This power. This feeling. Because it was everything. Because it could take a broken man and mend him, when nothing else could.

At least, Violet's love could. And had.

"I love you, too."

* * * * *

HER COWBOY
PRINCE CHARMING

CHAPTER ONE

JESSIE GRANGER HAD never been brave enough to go to the masked ball down in Mapleton. Well, *ball* was really stretching it. But it was what they called it. It was Christmastime, and everybody got a little antsy. A little sad maybe, a little drunk. And they liked to put on their fancy spurs, and some airs along with it, and pretend that Mapleton was some kind of big city.

She had never seen the point of it. It was a meat market. A place to hook up. And anyway, the holidays made her sad.

Her oldest brother did his best to make them not sad. Levi was a prince among men—if a bit too serious and a hell of a lot too overprotective. But she was twenty-three, and she was tired of being sad. And more than anything, maybe, she was tired of being alone. So she had put on the tightest dress that she had been able to find while still maintaining the ability to walk—and whether or not she was going to manage to keep her circulation going for the evening was iffy—a pair of high-heeled shoes unlike anything she'd ever worn before, a big, sparkly mask with feathers coming out of the top and a whole lot of red lipstick for good measure. Because well…it was kind of supposed to be a disguise.

But only kind of.

The problem with growing up in a town as small as Pyrite Falls was everybody knew who she was. And not only did everybody know who she was, they also knew who her older brothers were. And knew that they would kick their asses as soon as they looked at them if they were to fool around with her. She could have left Pyrite Falls, she supposed. But it just hadn't seemed right ever.

She was worried that Levi needed her—though he would swear up and down that he didn't. But her oldest brother had raised her and her siblings after their parents' deaths, and she could see how that had taken over his life. She worried he didn't have anything without them.

He swore up and down he was fine, but she just didn't believe him.

But there just wasn't...anything there. But there was Mapleton, the town over, where at least some things might be possible. And tonight she wanted to have the experience of walking into a room without everybody knowing who she was. Tonight she wanted to feel beautiful. Like a woman. Maybe she was looking for a Christmas miracle.

Maybe you just want to lose your virginity.

Whatever. Either way, she was feeling good.

When she had put on the short red dress that she had ordered online, she'd been surprised by how good her body looked in it. She was accustomed to seeing herself in baggy T-shirts and high-waisted jeans. The kind that gave a girl that particular Wrangler butt that some men liked, but in her experience men ignored her. Maybe it was the long, baggy T-shirts. But she'd been uncomfortable about her abundance of curves since she was a kid, and she preferred to wander around looking spherical rather than displaying the rather extreme hourglass she had.

But when she had put the dress on... Well, she felt like a different person. She felt like the kind of person who could do...damn well anything. The mask really helped. Because the mask made her feel like someone else entirely.

For the first time—especially since her crushing rejection two years ago—she felt beautiful.

The parking lot of the Evergreen ballroom was full. Normally, it was a place that hosted line dancing lessons, West Coast swing and the odd concert and special dinner. But once a year, she had been told, it was transformed.

She got out of the truck and crossed the gravel lot, and was surprised to find out there was a small line at the door. The women were wearing masks, and over-the-top dresses, though few men were decked out quite as grandly. Though they all had on masks, of varying degrees of severity, and definitely not the way the women did.

She bought her ticket at the door and got her hand stamped, and was ushered inside, where the whole space had been absolutely transformed. There were twisted trees covered in white Christmas lights all over the place, with blue light creating the feeling of a winter wonderland.

There was a dance floor, tables with champagne and appetizers. She was genuinely impressed. She hadn't actually thought anything in this area could be half so nice.

She was handed a glass of champagne and she smiled, taking a sip. She already felt like somebody else. Like she was somewhere else. And all right, it was just about forty-five minutes from home. And if Levi knew what she was up to he would probably have a coronary. But she would only have two glasses of champagne, and she would make sure to do it hours before she went home. She would be safe.

There was a giddy feeling in her stomach as she looked around. There were good-looking men everywhere, though most of them seemed to be attached.

But there was one man, standing in the corner, wearing all black. From head to toe. His mask was more like Zorro, bandit style, covering his eyes and most of his nose. His mouth was set into a grim line, his jaw square and arresting, even from where she stood across the room. He was big, broad shouldered, and he looked... Well, he looked kind of mean. He definitely didn't look like he was excited to be there. But she found she couldn't look away.

She imagined walking over to him. Imagined starting some kind of conversation. What would she even say?

Don't imagine. You're wearing a mask. You're dressed up.

Yes. She was. And for a moment she stopped, tried to see if there was maybe someone else. Somebody a little less dangerous. Somebody maybe a little bit less...everything.

Why are you here? Anyway. There's no guarantee anything will happen. But if it was going to... Why not make it a fantasy?

Yes. This was her chance to escape.

She didn't know why, but this year the approaching holidays had felt like a noose tightening around her neck. Like the grief of everything—the loss of their parents back when they'd been kids—had only gotten worse, instead of better. Like the passage of time made her miss her mother more than she ever had before. Made her miss her father's warmth and wisdom.

Their mother had been sick for several years before her death. Cancer that had just come back and back and back until she hadn't been able to fight anymore.

It had been devastating, and to a small child, as shocking as anything, because she hadn't fully been able to wrap her head around how sick her mother was. But the real shock had been her dad. Nine months later. A heart attack that had killed him right out where he was working on the ranch, and had killed him fairly instantly.

She felt like they had to be cursed. Like there had to be

something wrong with them, because how could that happen to them?

They had been such a happy family. And it had been up to Levi to take care of all the kids in the aftermath. And her oldest brother had.

So she had never wanted to say anything to him about just how difficult this time of year was.

But it was what had driven her here. What had made it feel unbearable now. Maybe it was that all of them were finally adults. Maybe it was Camilla's leaving to go to college. That probably wasn't helping. She didn't like endings. She didn't like change. Because she had lived through too much of it.

And so she would be bold. Because she wasn't here to be timid. At the end of all things, she was not here to be timid.

"Hi there," she said, making her voice a little lower, a little huskier.

The man looked her over, and she couldn't read his expression. His eyes were shaded by the black cowboy hat, his features obscured by the mask. The dark stubble of his beard made him look dangerous.

Her heart beat harder. Faster.

"Are you here all by yourself?" she asked.

His head tilted to the side. "Yes." And then she noticed. Noticed the way he looked at her body. And she felt a little bit of a thrill. She didn't think a man had ever looked at her body. Not like that. Slow and lazy, and interested. But then, she usually covered herself so that it wouldn't happen. So she sort of made her own invisibility cloak with those T-shirts.

"You?"

"Yes. I came alone."

"Surprising."

"I figured it was best to come alone since I didn't aim to leave alone."

Her own words made her tremble. She'd tried to proposition a man one other time in her whole life and it had not gone well.

He had, in fact, disappeared after.

Not that his leaving town for two years was directly connected to her, but it felt like it.

And it stung.

She'd had one serious crush in all of her existence. A long, enduring, *crushing* crush, fitting of the title because it made her feel like the air was being pressed from her body whenever he was around.

And when she thought of Damien Prince she… Well. It made her wish she were dead. Because she had wandered around mooning after him for most of her life. And he had never noticed her. Not once.

She'd checked.

Little girl, this is above your pay grade, believe me.

Bastard.

He didn't know what she wanted. She didn't believe in romance, anyway. She just thought he was hot.

The world had taken too much out of her to believe in fairy-tale endings.

When things were good, she knew they couldn't last.

The other shoe would always drop.

His thinking she was young and naive…it was offensive.

She didn't need to be thinking about him, anyway.

She hadn't even seen him in almost two years. He'd started some wine business up north. She had cried when he'd gone. Twenty-one years old and she'd been crying about a man who'd never seen her as anything other than a little sister. It was humiliating. But this wasn't humiliating. This was exciting. Electrifying.

Healing, even.

"I take your meaning just fine," he said.

"Do you want to… To dance?"

Because the woman she was tonight wanted to dance.

And the woman she was tonight didn't care if this mystery man turned her down. Sure. She would be disappointed. But she would find somebody else. She wasn't going to let it be singular or anything like that.

"If that's what you want."

He pushed back from the wall, and suddenly he was walking toward her. So tall, even in the shoes she was wearing. It made her dizzy to look up at him.

But they went out to the dance floor, and he pulled her into his arms. And she had never felt so… So delicate. So exquisitely aware of every part of her body as he pressed her against the hardness of his muscular form. She didn't know how long they danced for. Maybe fifteen minutes. Maybe two hours. Everything started to lose meaning. And she only had that couple sips of champagne.

It was like they were the only two people. And she couldn't see his face. But they couldn't see each other. They couldn't. Because it had to be like this. This fantasy. Where she was brave, and maybe a bit seductive, and not just Jessie, who was little more than Levi Granger's sister.

She didn't want to lose her grip on this moment. She didn't want reality. Not even a little bit. She needed the fantasy.

But then he kissed her. She'd never been kissed before. And it was like fire igniting her body. Igniting her veins.

And she was afraid. Afraid that now his mouth had

touched hers she wouldn't be able to stop kissing him. This man whose face she couldn't even see.

His beard was scratchy, and she loved it. She had never liked the look of a beard on a man before. And it really only added to how little she could see of his features, but she loved it all the same.

She pressed her body against his, melting into him.

And she could feel him getting hard, ready against her pelvis. "Come here," he said.

He took her hand and led her off the dance floor, out the door at the back of the room.

And then he pulled her into a very small storage room, closing the door behind them and propping a mop just under it to keep the door from being openable.

And then he was back to kissing her. Hard and deep.

She started to undo the buttons on his shirt, without even really thinking. This wasn't her. And not only was it not her, it was well above her level of experience.

She had thought to come to lose her virginity, but she certainly hadn't thought about doing it in a storage room, where there wasn't even a bed.

But she was past thinking. She pushed her hands beneath the fabric of his shirt, felt his muscles. Felt his chest.

And then she found herself being pushed back against the wall.

He kissed her neck, and she shivered. And then he pulled the top of her dress down, revealing the red lace bra she had on underneath, a bra that barely covered anything. "You're beautiful," he said, the awe in his voice giving her the strength to push on.

He pushed the bra cups out of the way and bared her breasts to him. He groaned, and suddenly big, rough hands moved up to cup her, his thumbs sliding over her nipples. And she let her head fall back as she gasped.

"Yes," she whispered, closing her eyes.

And then he was kissing her again, from her mouth, down her collarbone, to her breast, taking a nipple deep into his mouth.

And at the same time, his hands worked their way up her dress, between her legs. His fingers were stroking her, over the matching red underwear she had on, before he pushed them beneath the waistband, began to stroke her slick flesh in earnest. This man, the stranger, was touching her. And she thought she might die of pleasure.

And she thought dimly, it was the strangest thing, that for most of her life she had imagined that she could never want a man other than Damien Prince. And here she was, coming apart under the expert hands of a man whose face she'd never even seen.

It gave her hope, really. It gave her a lot of hope.

But right now it was about to give her an orgasm, and she couldn't think anymore.

Suddenly, he pushed two fingers up inside her, and she cried out her pleasure, desire raining down inside her like a storm.

Her hands were greedy at his belt buckle, clumsy and uncertain of what might happen next. But she managed to free his stiff arousal, and wrapped her hand around his heat. He was big. But then, she didn't really have anything for comparison. All she knew was that it was bigger than she expected. She had the vague feeling of being on a runaway train. She didn't know what she was doing. And she couldn't stop.

It was like her innocence was acting to make it even

more impossible to deny. Not as a barrier. Because she just needed to know what happened next. She needed to know.

He moved his hand down her thigh, gripped her leg and pulled it up around his waist, and then she felt the blunt head of his arousal testing the entrance to her body. She was powerless to do anything but roll her hips forward and accept the invasion. She was too hungry for it to do anything else. Too desperate for pleasure to be afraid of the pain.

And it did hurt. A cry was wrenched from her lips, and suddenly, his gaze met hers, fierce and almost angry.

"I'm fine," she said. "I'm fine." She put her hand flat on his chest and felt his heartbeat raging there, and then she kissed him. And he didn't resist anymore. He pumped deep inside her, and she was lost in the rhythm. Lost in the pleasure.

Then he lowered his head and bit the side of her neck, and her whole body spasmed, her climax shocking her, even as he found his own on a hard growl.

And suddenly she realized, she had just lost her virginity in a storage room two days before Christmas. She had just lost her mind. Utterly and completely. And all the boldness she had felt only moments before transformed into shame. How could it be anything else? Sickly, awful shame.

Tears filled her eyes, and she did her best to blink them back as she pushed away from him, and tripped on her shoes.

She started to fumble at the mop, trying to get it out from the door.

"Are you okay?" He didn't sound like the dangerous outlaw of moments before. He sounded concerned.

"I'm fine," she said.

"If you hadn't done that before…"

"I have to go," she said.

And she managed to right her clothing just as she wrenched the door open. She stumbled out into the hall, and saw an exit. Right out the back. It should be easy to take that, and go to the side where she had parked her truck. She ran down the hall, and he wasn't right behind her. Probably because he was still mostly naked. Her shoe came off, but she kept on running.

And then she went outside and ran to the left. She got in her pickup and jammed the key into the ignition, starting it as quickly as possible. And when she turned to look, she saw him. Standing there, his shirt still open, her shoe in his hand. Then she put the car in Reverse and went straight out to the highway. And she did not look in her rearview mirror.

CHAPTER TWO

HE HAD THE mother of all hangovers when he woke up the next morning. But Damien Prince had a feeling it wasn't strictly from alcohol. He had a high tolerance for alcohol, and anyway, working in the wine industry, it didn't excite him all that much. Alcohol was a professional hazard, and it was about refining and tasting, more than anything else. It was the woman. Whatever the hell that had been. He didn't… He didn't do shit like that. Not anymore. He was in his midthirties. He didn't screw women in storage rooms, much less take their virginity.

No. She could not have been a virgin. Except she'd acted like his thrusting into her hurt. And then she'd run away.

He rolled out of bed, in the small cabin he was staying in on his friend Levi's property. It was nice of his friend to invite him to stay for Christmas. It had been a last-minute thing. He'd called Levi on his way to last night's event, and Levi had said he ought to bunk with them, and it hadn't sounded half-bad, all things considered.

There was nothing for him to go home to, after all.

So he'd accepted the offer to come to the cabin after the event was over and stay through Christmas.

He hadn't been back to Pyrite Falls for two years. With good reason. A reason he didn't like to think about. A reason he sure as hell didn't want to think about with the mystery brunette's flavor still in his mouth.

He kept the shoe. That was dumb. He rolled out of bed, bare-ass naked, and went over to the table where he'd set it down. A sparkly, slip-on high heel that looked completely and totally impractical. And yet… She'd done things to him that no woman had done in a long damned time. His phone vibrated. He looked down at it, where it was sitting on the nightstand, and saw that he had a message from Levi.

Coffee's on.

Damn him and his rancher hours. Of course Levi kept rancher hours. Damien might have a vineyard now, but he was still a cowboy. In his soul, he always would be. It was why he was expanding to buy a property here in Four Corners. More land, not just for wine, but for animals. And anyway, Four Corners was home. No matter how long he'd been away. He got dressed and opened the door to the house. It was dim inside, and there was a collection of shoes by the front door. He started to kick his boots off, and then Levi came through from the kitchen.

"Hey," he said.

"Hey."

"Did the thing go well last night?"

"Yeah," he grunted. He walked away from the entry, and toward the kitchen. Toward the coffeepot.

"Must've been a late one."

"Those things always are." His friend poured him a cup of coffee and Damien nodded his thanks.

"You ever get tired of all the schmoozing you have to do for the wine industry?"

"Like your job doesn't require you to schmooze. It's not like beef isn't the same sort of business at the end of the day."

"Fair. But still… I prefer beef people to wine people."

"It's not about people. It's about the land," said Damien. And that much he meant.

"It's been too long."

"Yeah, it has."

He took a sip of the coffee and turned away from the kitchen, facing the entry door again. And something caught his eye. One of the discarded shoes. All sparkly and impractical. A slip-on.

Holy fuck. There was no way. There was no damned way that he had run away from her. That he had run away from her and…

He heard a thump on the stairs. And he knew. Without even looking, he damn well knew.

He looked up, and there she was, a tumble of brown curls, but wearing the kind of baggy shirt he expected from her.

"Good morning, Jessie," he said.

CHAPTER THREE

JESSIE WAS STILL HALF-ASLEEP. Jessie was half-convinced that she was dreaming. Actually, Jessie was pretty sure that she had been dreaming since about the middle of the day yesterday, because there was no way... There was no way that she had... And there was really no way...

Because there was Damien Prince. Standing in her house. Well. Her brother's house. And he was...everything she remembered except...he had a beard. He had not had a beard when he had left two years ago.

Something like panic burst in her stomach. It couldn't be. It could not be. Except he looked up at her, and their eyes connected. And she knew.

Last night she'd lost her virginity to Damien Prince. Oh, shit. She actually lived her teenage fantasy, and she hadn't even realized she was doing it.

Did you not, though?

She thought of how quickly she'd come apart under his hands. How greedy she'd been for him. How... Did he know?

His eyes flicked over to the corner, and she saw her shoe. Her damn shoe. And then he looked back up at her. He knew. He knew. Lord in heaven, he knew, and her brother was standing right there.

Oh, no. This was... It was impossible.

"Where were you last night?" Levi asked.

Oh, great. Leave it to her brother to make it weird. To make it *impossible*.

"I was nowhere," she said. "What I mean is… I was here."

Levi made a face. "You were not here. I looked for you. Anyway, I heard you stumbling around at midnight, so I know you got in late."

"I just went to Smokey's," she lied, hoping he wouldn't actually ask anyone if she'd been seen at the local tavern, since she absolutely hadn't been there.

"Really?" He narrowed his eyes over the top of his coffee cup.

"Yes," she said. "Really. I went to Smokey's. There's no law against that."

He frowned. "If I recall correctly, there used to be."

"Yes," she said flatly. "It was called me being under twenty-one. Which you may recall I'm not anymore."

"Yeah. Yeah."

It was difficult to maintain the casual conversation—which was also a lie—with her brother, when she was so extremely conscious of the way Damien was looking at her. So incredibly aware. And she wanted to run away. Or crawl out of her skin. But she felt like neither one of those things was a great option, all things considered.

"I've got to head out," Levi said. "The cows will not feed themselves. You coming out with me, Prince? Or are you soft?"

"I'm not soft," he said. "But it's not my ranch, and I had a late night. I'll meet you out there in a bit."

He sounded so casual. There was absolutely no weight to those words. Not a bit of heaviness. And that almost made it more ominous.

She couldn't guess what he was going to do or say or…

"Suit yourself. See y'all later." Levi drank the last of his coffee down, and nodded once before heading out the door. And that just left her and Damien.

"You were not at Smokey's last night."

Of course not. But she didn't want him to know that. Or at least, she didn't want to *admit* it. She wanted to make him question what he suspected.

"Sure I was," she said, her throat getting tight.

"Jessie," he said. "Did you know it was me?"

Well. That was direct.

She froze; that place between her legs was throbbing when she looked at him. She had always felt perfectly safe around Damien. Actually, to the point where it was sort of infuriating. She'd always thought he was beautiful, and she wanted to feel a little bit…like something had happened between them. But of course, he had never acted like that was a possibility. And the one time… Well. He rebuffed her pretty soundly two years ago. And her maneuver had been clumsy, and not even all that overt. But now… Now she could feel possibility between them. Because she'd had sex with him. That made her feel dizzy. Unsteady.

"I don't… I didn't… No. I didn't."

"You didn't?"

"For heaven's sake, Damien," she said, calling on all the spirit her brother had raised her with. "No, I didn't know it was you. Don't flatter yourself. I was there to have a good time. That's all."

"You've changed that much in the last two years?"

"People change. You grew a beard."

He reached up and touched his cheek. "So I did. Is that why you didn't know it was me?"

"Why didn't you know it was me?" she countered.

"Because," he said, and she knew by how flat and matter-of-fact his voice was when he said that word, that she was not going to like any of the words that came out of his mouth next. "I've never seen you with your tits out quite like that. Or on display to that degree. You normally dress like you're trying to flatter a snowman shape."

"What exactly are you saying?"

He gritted his teeth. "You looked different. You don't normally dress hot."

"Well, I was trying to dress to get a man. And you're all basic assholes, so there's only one way to do that. Anyway. Like I said. You've been gone. You don't know."

"You hadn't done that before."

"Sure I had. Do you honestly think that I went out and had my first time in a broom closet with a stranger?"

You did, though. You did. And even worse, it turned out it wasn't a stranger. It's just Damien. And you have to deal with the consequences.

"What the hell game are you playing?"

"What were you playing? Don't pretend that you weren't there to have sex."

"I wasn't," he said, his voice flat. "I was there because I sponsored the event with my wine. I'm trying to expand business. That's it."

Everything in her went hot. "But you knew right where to go to the storage closet. And you sure weren't hesitant."

"Fine. No. I wasn't going to question a beautiful woman setting her sights on me. Okay?"

Beautiful. He thought she was beautiful. That, she knew, was beside the point, but she kind of enjoyed the moment.

"Well, why is my moral character being called into question when you got into the exact same thing?"

"You said you didn't want to leave alone."

"All right. Maybe I thought… I just thought that…" She didn't want to tell him that she had seen him and had immediately wanted him so badly that all her inhibitions went out the window.

He walked closer to the foot of the stairs, went over to the doorway and picked up her shoe. "I have the other one."

"I know," she said. Then she shook her head. "I mean. I don't know. I... I did see you with it."

"Did I hurt you last night?"

"No. You didn't hurt me. I wasn't hurt. I... I was embarrassed. Because of this. Look how you're reacting. But I have just as much right to question your behavior as you do mine. It's either that or neither of us have a right, because we were both there."

"You didn't know it was me."

"Why do you care?"

"Because I said no to you, Jessie. You know that."

That hurt. And it made her feel guilty, even though she shouldn't. It hurt her, even if she shouldn't let it.

"Because you didn't want me?" she asked, pushing through the jagged pain that had risen up in her chest.

He looked away, and if it wasn't for the never-ending, abiding horror roiling in her stomach, she might've felt satisfied. Maybe that wasn't why he'd said no. Maybe it wasn't.

Just imagining that night two years ago hurt.

She'd really thought...

Damien was her favorite person in the world, and she'd been in love with him since she was knee high to a grasshopper.

She could remember when she'd thought he might feel the same.

At her twentieth birthday party he'd swept some frosting up off her cake with his forefinger and had gone to brush it on her face, and she'd...

It was embarrassing now.

But she'd caught his finger in her mouth instead and licked it, sucked his finger into her mouth. It had seemed like a funny idea in the split second between when she'd decided to do it and when she'd actually done it.

Then her tongue had touched his skin, fire had risen up in his eyes and something had gone so tight in her stomach she could barely breathe. And it hadn't seemed funny at all.

No one in her family had noticed that she and Damien had been caught up in an explosion.

So she'd thought maybe…maybe.

And it had taken her more than a full year after that to try and kiss him.

But he'd rejected her.

Hey, kiddo. Come on now. You don't want to do that.

He'd practically laughed.

Little girl, this is above your pay grade, believe me. You want romance, and that's not what you'd ever get from me.

"Believe me. After the last time we saw each other, I hadn't given you another thought. And I don't need to give you another thought now."

She moved up the stairs, and he caught her arm. And she… She felt like she was in danger of catching fire again. He was so close, and of course it was Damien. She felt like an idiot now. She'd been relieved, thinking that maybe… Maybe she wasn't hopeless for him. Maybe she wasn't a lost cause. But it was worse than that. She had walked into a room full of people wearing masks, and had zeroed in on her humiliating childhood crush, and he had been the only one she'd wanted. The only one she'd seen.

He smelled familiar. And she didn't know if that was from last night, or from all the years. She wanted to bury her face in his neck, breathe him in. She wanted to touch him again.

But she pulled away instead.

"I'm staying for Christmas." He released his hold on her.

"What?"

"Yeah. I'm down here looking at a piece of property, and Levi invited me."

"Oh, shit," she said.

"You're a pretty girl with a dirty mouth. Anybody ever tell you that?"

Her lips twitched. "You're a dirty boy with a pretty mouth. Did anybody tell you that?"

But that felt far too charged of a thing to say, and she regretted it the minute the words left her mouth.

Anyway. *Pretty* was the wrong word for any part of him. He was far too masculine for such a word. She was just grasping at straws. At the fences.

"Watch it."

"So what? It doesn't matter? You don't want me. It's not going to be any challenge for you to make it through Christmas without jumping me again."

Something in his eyes went flat. "Just so we're clear. I can't offer you anything."

"I didn't ask you for anything."

"You should've told me you were a virgin."

"I didn't even tell you my name. Why would I tell you that?"

"Because I didn't go slow enough, or make sure I didn't hurt you. It would have been fine if you were more experienced, but you aren't. I wish I would have known."

"That's the risk you take, Damien. When you have sex with strange women that you don't know."

And suddenly, the reality of all that expanded between them. Sizzled. She couldn't breathe. She was feeling warm. Far too warm. Oh, she wished she weren't. She really wished that she could draw a line underneath Damien Prince. She had given him her virginity; wasn't it enough? Couldn't that be it?

Apparently not. Apparently, it still…sizzled.

One thing was sure, though; this changed things. She'd been humiliated when he'd rejected her. Thinking that she'd imagined the heat between them that day over her birthday cake, that her fantasies had all been one-sided.

They weren't now.

He'd seen her naked, more or less, and she'd seen… Well, she'd been intimate with him. She'd felt him lose it. With her. In her.

That made her feel a lot more powerful.

She felt herself being drawn toward him. She took one step forward.

Suddenly, the door burst open, and in came Levi, stepping between herself and Damien. "Holy shit," he said.

Both she and Damien jumped back like scalded cats, and she had a feeling their guilt was written all over their faces. "What?" they both asked at the same time.

"Dylan is coming back."

Dylan, the second oldest Granger, had been deployed for nearly eighteen months.

"He is?"

"Yep. For Christmas," Levi said.

"No way," she said.

"Yeah, he's on his way back now. He's in Germany."

"Back for Christmas," she said.

She looked around the house, at the dearth of decorations. They really hadn't…done anything.

The holidays were weird.

"What?" Levi asked.

"We haven't seen him in so long. It just seems like…he should have a Christmas to come back to."

"That's true," Levi said. "I've got… I got a hell of a lot of work here on the ranch…"

"I can help," Damien said. "I actually love Christmas."

She turned to him. "You do?"

"Hell yeah," said Damien. "It was always a big deal in my family."

He got a little bit gruff then. And she felt... She felt bad. Because she knew that Damien's mother had passed away about nine months ago, but she hadn't really known her all that well, and... The thing was, both of her parents were dead. So that sort of thing often just felt like a sad fact of life. But now she realized he would be headed into the first Christmas since losing his mother. She had left Pyrite Falls when he did, moving with him. And he had certainly been taking care of her.

She had been a single mother for as long as they had known Damien. Which was a pretty long time.

"Well, hey, if you don't mind. We have Christmas decorations around here somewhere. And you're welcome to cut a tree off the property."

"Absolutely."

"Jessie will help," Levi said.

And Jessie felt tension creep up her spine.

"For all you know, I'm busy," said Jessie.

"What the hell would you be busy with? The work I gave you to do?"

"You're such an ass, Levi," she said.

"But I'm a *correct* ass."

"Get dressed," Damien said.

And something about that scraped along her skin. Well. She knew exactly what it was. It was the fact that last night she had been entirely undressed in front of him.

But she didn't want Levi to see that. Didn't want her brother to get wind of anything.

So she simply turned on her heel and ran back upstairs. And in her mind, she saw him standing there, holding her shoe.

CHAPTER FOUR

WELL, THIS WAS a fucking treat. He had screwed his best friend's younger sister. The same younger sister he'd been running from two years ago.

Yeah. He had tried for a while to reframe that. But the fact was… When she had leaned up against him, twenty-one years old and too pretty for her own good, in spite of how she tried to hide her assets underneath baggy T-shirts, she was clearly a beautiful woman.

Hell, he'd known it since her twentieth birthday, when he'd tried to do some childish older-brother nonsense, going to wipe frosting on her face, and she'd caught his finger in her mouth and…

Shit, he'd felt that all the way down to his dick and he'd wished he could unfeel that, but he couldn't.

She'd obsessed over him after that.

A year later she'd tried to kiss him.

He'd done the right thing. He had turned away from temptation. And the best thing was, he hadn't let her know she was one.

If she ever touched him…there would be no in-between. It would be forever, or an explosion that would destroy them all.

He wasn't going to risk it.

And then last night, when that woman in red had walked into the party, he felt like he'd been slugged in the gut. He hadn't known quite what had drawn him to her. It was clear now. He was responding to old chemistry. Dammit. So now he had taken his best friend's little sister's virginity, in about the sleaziest way possible, and all that was left to do was plan a Christmas party with her.

While the ghost of Christmas past dogged his heels. Fantastic. Fan-fucking-tastic.

"I'm ready," Jessie said, stomping back down the stairs, a black beanie over her brown hair, so low it covered her eyebrows. She was wearing a baggy sweatshirt and a pair of baggy camo pants.

And she was still sexy as hell because he knew what was underneath them now. She looked adorable. He hated that. He hated that quite a lot.

"Great. Let's get a move on."

They walked outside, and the ground was blanketed with snow. With that snow everywhere it just seemed harsh. Bright. Last night everything had been gauzy. Possible. And today in the broad cold snow and its reflected white light there was no hiding from what he'd done to Jessie Granger.

"How are you doing?"

"Oh, just fine," he said. "Contemplating all the ways that Levi might kill me."

"That isn't what I meant," she said. "I mean… I know your mom died. Sorry."

"Yeah," he said, swallowing. "Me, too."

He'd gotten pretty okay talking about it. It had happened. His mom, who had taken care of him, raised him all on her own, whom he had started to take care of in her later years, whom he loved, was gone. She wasn't going to make him enchiladas anymore. She wasn't going to ask him if he was working too hard. And he would've said no. No matter whether he was working too hard or not. He would never have changed his behavior. But she would have asked.

And it would've been good. Sometimes it hit him. That he really couldn't call her anymore. That she wasn't just down the hall. That nobody would ever care for him again the way that she had.

But most of the time, he was all right.

"I feel like I should've said something sooner."

"Oh, you mean when we were realizing that we had sex with each other? Because the fact that you didn't make me think of my mother right around that time is actually all right with me."

She snorted, and then clapped her hand over her mouth. "I'm sorry."

"No," he said. "If you can't laugh about it, what's the point of living through it? And by that I mean my mother's death and the fact that I screwed you."

"Levi doesn't need to know," she said. He took a big step over a fallen log, and stopped and watched as Jessie scrambled over the same one. "There's no reason to tell him."

"Sure," he said, gritting his teeth. "We need to swing by my place."

"Your place?" she asked.

"I just mean the cabin I'm staying in. There's an axe inside, and we're going to need it to cut down the tree."

"Oh. Good point."

The little cabin came into view, and he marched right in and grabbed the hatchet from the front room. And when he came out, she was standing about twenty-five feet from the entry, her arms wrapped around herself, her little nose cherry red. She was just so damned cute. And that was the problem. He'd thought that way back when, and he thought it now. And he was too old for her. Too jaded for her. Too everything for her.

But you had her now.

True. But he hadn't known it.

Like that makes it better. It makes you a bigger ass, actually.

His self-awareness could take a hike as far as he was concerned.

"You look like you're afraid I'm going to bite you."

She laughed. It was a strange and almost frantic sound. "To be honest," she said, "I'm actually slightly more afraid that I'll bite you."

"Don't be so honest, Jessie."

Her words caused a kick of lust to hit him in the stomach.

"Why not? You've seen me naked. What's the point of lying?"

"For sanity," he returned.

They continued walking through the snow, with Jessie shambling behind him, taking two steps to keep up to his one.

And there he saw it. A big, glorious pine tree. Exactly the kind that his mother would've loved. And that mattered. It just did. Because he wasn't in his own place for Christmas.

"I like this one," he said.

She stood back, wrinkling her cherry-red nose. "I mean… It's okay."

"What's the matter?"

"I'm not a huge fan of Christmas."

"The girl who was at the masquerade ball last night is not a huge fan of Christmas."

"No."

"So why throw a big Christmas for Dylan?"

"I don't know. I guess it's the thing we do. We perform for each other."

"Why?"

"Because what else is there to do? We care about each other. And so sometimes that means going through the motions even when it's not easy."

"What, just in case one of you likes Christmas?"

"I dunno. But what I do know is that my brother has been deployed through two Christmases. And I think that he should have something special for when he gets home."

"That's awfully nice of you."

"Well. We are all each other has."

He related to that a little better than he would like to. Except for him... It had been him and his mom.

"Yeah."

He swung the hatchet decisively, and took a big chunk out of the tree. Then he swung it again, and again. And let it fall where it was.

"I'll help carry it," she said.

He looked at her out of the corner of his eye. "I'm good."

He picked it up by the center of the trunk and hefted it up over his shoulder, letting the tip drag as they walked back through the snowy splendor.

He could hear her feet crunching in the snow behind him, and it was just the damnedest thing that he was so physically aware of her. But it wasn't new. Jessie had been a problem. And as far as he was concerned, relationships were too valuable for him to screw them up.

Levi had always felt like a brother to him. And he knew Levi had enough brothers, so his friend didn't necessarily feel the same, but Damien didn't have any. And growing up, a fatherless child in a very small town, Levi had been a buffer between him and a whole lot of judgment.

He could remember clearly when Levi's parents had died. He'd been seventeen, Levi had been eighteen. He'd done his level best to be there for his friend.

But it was tough. And now... The empathy that he felt was pretty off the charts.

It had been such an abstract thing to him then. And he had thought of it more in terms of how Levi was supposed to care for all those siblings. But now he wondered how the hell his friend had weathered losing two people who mattered as much as his mother did, in such a short span of time. And taken all that responsibility on board on top of it.

They arrived back at the main house, and he left the Christmas tree propped up against the wall outside.

"Do you know where the decorations are?"

"Well, it might take a trip to the attic. But I think we can find them."

"Lead the way."

She did, up the stairs, and to a spot in a hallway with wood paneling that was a slightly different color than the rest of the ceiling. She reached up, but her fingertips fell immediately short of taking hold of anything.

"What was your plan, Jessie?"

"I don't know," she said, looking grumpy.

"I've got it," he said. "Lucky you that you had me around."

"Yeah. Well. It definitely makes a difference compared to the last couple of years."

He stopped for a moment, then reached up and found the rope that was stuffed up in a hole in the ceiling, and tugged down the little trapdoor. He could see a wooden ladder folded up that was likely attached to the opening. He grabbed the end and yanked it down. And when he turned to look at her, she was staring.

"Do I need to answer that? I mean, answer for it? I had a business to build. I bought into a mature winery, because I didn't want to sit around and wait for things to grow. Now I'm expanding, so I'm coming back."

And he realized that she did want a deeper answer than that. That she wanted more. She was looking at him with irritated expectancy.

"That's it," he said.

"You know, it just always felt like you left because of what I did."

"Oh, hell, Jessie. I did not uproot my entire life because you tried to kiss me."

Her cheeks turned scarlet, and she scrambled up the ladder ahead of him. He followed behind, more slowly. And he realized it was a mistake. Because for all the attic was dim, inhospitable and possibly filled with mice, it was also a small enclosed space. And the memory of the softness of Jessie's skin, and the tightness of her body, made the idea of mice just not such a big deal.

"I just felt... It felt like a pretty full-body rejection," she said.

"Well, it was," he said. "Because Levi means the world to me. And you know what he would think if..."

"I know. I guess I just thought that... I thought that we were something. Even if it wasn't romantic. But you just left and you didn't talk to me again."

And there was something unspoken in the way her eyes shone in the darkness of the room.

It was like death. He knew it well. That wall of silence where a person had once been.

"Right. But I'm still here," he said.

"But you weren't. Not for me. And what you saw last night... That was me trying to move on. That was me trying… I was trying. I was trying this. I was trying to be better. To be easier. I was trying to put all that behind me. To lose my virginity. But it wasn't with a stranger. It was with you. And you know how relieved I was, when I walked into that room? I saw a man standing up against the wall, and I wanted him. And I just thought…" Suddenly, her whole face went red again.

"You just thought what, kiddo?"

"I just thought that maybe you didn't own my desire. I thought that maybe I could just want another man, and the reason I wanted you so much for so long was that you were there. You were around. That was it. But no. You, Damien Prince, were it. You were him. So now I'm back to square one. Well, I'm probably on square two. But it is still way closer to the beginning than I wanted to be. I wanted to vanquish my demons. But all I managed to vanquish was my hymen."

He winced. "Sorry about that," he said.

"Yeah. Yeah. I'm not. I knew what I was doing."

"Did you? Because it seems like here we are in the middle of a whole lot of unintended consequences. And I didn't get the feeling that was the idea of this whole thing."

"Well. Maybe not. Maybe not… But I…"

And suddenly, she was far too close to him. Smelling like lavender he suspected came from laundry detergent, and her skin, which he had never taken note of the smell of before, but now that it had been under his hands, under his mouth, he had opinions about it. And it was just there. So apparent.

"Let's look for the decorations," she mumbled, moving past him and rummaging around.

He saw two boxes. One labeled *Memories*. Another labeled *Trauma*. And there were sharp-toothed monsters drawn on it.

"Who's responsible for that?" he asked.

"I think it was Camilla," she said. "But I would not be surprised if Dylan had some involvement in that, too."

"And what's in it?"

"Like life insurance stuff? Medical records. Just all the shit that we kept because it was necessary to document certain things. But all related to the losses. So…"

"Got it."

"Like you said. If you can't laugh about it…"

"What's in the memories?"

"Family photos. Some other things. I don't look at them very often."

"Right."

"It really could all be labeled trauma. Let's be honest."

"It's tough." He shrugged. "Not that I'm comparing. You were kids. It's different."

She looked thoughtful for a second, and then moved quickly to the next stack of boxes, twisting and turning them to check the labels. "I don't know that it is. We might need different things from our parents at different ages. But let's face it. We need them. Loss is loss."

"That's true."

"I've lost both of my parents."

"Hey. I managed to lose my dad before I ever found him."

"Right. Well. I guess what can you do but laugh about that, too?"

"That's fine with me. I don't give a shit about my dad. He never wanted me. He didn't take care of us. He doesn't matter."

He felt a fierce regret at the center of his chest.

If he had his dad, he wouldn't be alone right now. So there was that.

"Victory," she said. "I have ornaments. And a tree stand. Oh, and there's a tree skirt. And rolls of Christmas lights. And some of this is probably from 2003. So…"

"Ancient," he said, his tone dry.

"Super ancient," she said, grinning.

He reached over to help her, and she grabbed the same spool of lights at the same time, and that brought her toward him, where she froze, only an inch of space between their faces.

"Damien…" she whispered.

"Let's get this out of here," he said, jerking away, and grabbing what looked to be the heaviest box, the tree stand and a spool of lights. He would figure out how the hell to get down the ladder with all of this in a minute.

He just opted to jump down. But he needed to get the hell out of that attic with her.

Otherwise, he was going to do something very stupid. Again.

CHAPTER FIVE

SHE STILL COULDN'T BREATHE. They had been so close up there and…the attraction really burned between them. But it was even worse. The conversation. Feeling like she… understood him.

She had felt close to him before he left. Close enough that that wild summer night when they'd been the only two left at the bonfire that they'd been having in honor of them all being in one place, had seemed intimate.

And it had seemed…like it was theirs. Like there was no reason she shouldn't try for the things she wanted most. The thing she had wanted most when she was fifteen years old and had noticed that his muscles might just be the most perfect creation on the earth.

Yeah. That.

And as if on cue, he walked through the front door just then, holding the tree up on his shoulder, his forearms shifting as he moved, and she couldn't help but stare at the way his biceps curled, bold.

She'd touched all those muscles. But not enough to satisfy her. And she hadn't known it was him.

Did you not, though?

Well. She hadn't. And maybe there had been some thoughts of Damien. Maybe deep down she had known… something. But she hadn't been able to openly, consciously enjoy his body.

And you still don't get to.

Why not? The barrier to what happened two years ago was that he didn't want Levi to be upset at him. And she'd been roaming around being hurt by him not wanting her all this time. But he had wanted her last night.

Maybe he didn't want her now. Maybe now that he knew, it didn't matter that he'd seen her naked and wanted her then.

Maybe just being her was enough to turn him off forever.

She watched him set the tree down. She knew she was staring.

"Help me with the lights," he said.

She did, and he took the end of it, beginning to wrap it around the large evergreen.

"So. Do you still want me?"

He froze. He arched one brow, looking at her with frosty eyes. "Why the hell would you ask that?"

"Because I'm trying to get a gauge on this. Are you just… Is it me? Is it me? Am I fundamentally a turnoff? Is it because I'm in a baggy shirt? Is it just the me of it all? Because you only see me as a child, and only when I was a disembodied pair of tits could you get excited about me."

"Please don't say anything like that to me ever again."

"It's a valid question."

"We are in your living room. And Levi could walk in at any moment."

"So what? I don't care what Levi thinks."

"Because Levi is your brother no matter what," he said. "And Levi could go from being my friend to my enemy pretty damn quick. If you don't think your brother would absolutely kick my ass for this, you don't know him very well."

"He doesn't own me," she said.

"No. He doesn't."

"I bet if you quizzed him, he would think that I'd probably had sex already."

"Oh, I don't doubt that. And I'm not suggesting that your brother thinks that you're never gonna have sex. But I do think he figures his friend who is twelve years your senior is not the one doing the honors."

"What does it matter?"

"I've known you since you were a kid. It matters because I'm supposed to protect you."

"Why? Because I'm a woman? That's bullshit."

Him and his overprotective nonsense. He thought that he knew more because he'd had more sex than her?

"It's not bullshit," he said.

"The orgasm felt good. How was it harming me?"

"Because you could get hurt. Because I knew what my limitations were, and what I was interested in and what I wasn't."

"You're making a lot of assumptions about me."

He rubbed his hand over his face, and he looked tired. "Am I wrong about them? Do you want a family, Jessie?"

"I don't know. I wanted you. I didn't really think about what else there was."

She felt really stupid having said that.

"Well, I was never headed toward family life. What I wanted was to build a business. That's my focus."

"You're assuming a hell of a lot about me. That I can't just have sex for fun."

"I'm not sure if you can because—"

And suddenly, they heard the front door open, and mutually froze.

And heard footsteps.

Then Jessie started to hurriedly run circles around the tree, wrapping the lights, as if demonstrating a little bit more progress might make it believable that they hadn't just been talking about sex.

And there was Levi, looking exhausted from the day.

"Nice," he said.

"Yeah," Damien practically grunted.

"I was thinking maybe we could have pizza?"

"Such a long drive," Jessie said.

"No. I order it, and have them deliver it to a friend of mine's address that's on the outskirts of the edge of where they deliver. And it cuts my drive time in half."

"That's brilliant," Damien said.

"A country boy can survive," Levi said. "I'll put the order in, and be back in about an hour."

"Sure," they both said.

And then when Levi walked out, they were assured that they had the house to themselves for the next hour. And that suddenly felt weighted. And very, very dangerous. "We better make progress on these decorations," she said.

Yes. They would do decorations. As if every single one would be evidence of the fact that they hadn't been lusting over each other. Or that she hadn't been lusting over him.

"I don't find you unattractive," he said, once they hung the last decoration on the tree. "But it doesn't matter. Because the fact is, you're you. And I'm me. I've already lost my family. I can't lose you all, too."

Of all the things she'd expected, it hadn't been that. And it made her feel...hopeless and sad, and deeply honored, all at once.

It made her want to draw closer to him even as she knew he was trying to push her away.

She just didn't understand why Damien had to make her feel so much.

CHAPTER SIX

LEVI ARRIVED WITH PIZZA, and by then, the youngest Granger, Camilla, was home, too.

And he and Jessie had turned this house into a winter wonderland. As if it was evidence that they hadn't been thinking about stripping each other's clothes off. But that was all he'd been thinking about. The only thing. And he felt… Well, he felt a bit like the liar that he was. Both to her and to Levi.

Because it had happened. That was the thing. And he knew why he had resisted two years ago. She had been twenty-one years old, and he'd been about to leave. He hadn't wanted to take advantage of her. Her innocence, the fact that she'd had a girlhood crush on him. He hadn't wanted to take advantage of any of that. She was too important to him. Not just Levi.

But now… It had happened, and he was going over excuses that sounded more and more asinine the longer he tried to stick to them. But it was this. This family thing. Sitting around eating pizza together. It mattered. With the Christmas decorations all around him that he never would've had if it wasn't for them.

"Dylan is flying into Portland at like two in the morning," Camilla said, reaching to the center of the table and pulling an olive off one of the pizzas.

"Don't do that," said Jessie, slapping her sister on the hand. "Nobody wants your feral fingers all over their food."

"Jessie," said Camilla, her tone measured. "If there is a ferality scale, you are far more at the robust end than I am."

And it was all this family shit. It just felt like a lot. Like something different than he'd experienced in his life, and it made him even more determined to protect it. This moment made him want to double down on what he already knew.

But then he looked at Jessie, and he felt something inside himself rise up and roar. He wanted to protect her. And that was the problem. He didn't see a way to have her and protect her, and protect this. She looked up across the pizza, her eyes caught his and he felt lightning go straight down to his gut.

"I am not," Jessie said. And he realized that she was talking to Camilla. But she was still looking at him.

And here it was, Christmas Eve, and her brother would be here in the morning. And they would all gather and do the Christmas thing. And then Damien would go. He would go because it was what he had to do. He'd wrap things up on his own piece of land, and then he would go back up north. It would take some time for him to move down here. And then what? That was the question. Then what would happen?

She was forbidden to him. And always had been. It hadn't been a problem until recently. And that was why... That was why it had been easier to go. And coming back... She ended up right in his path.

Well. There was one way that he could have this family, and protect her and have her.

They finished eating and Jessie melted away, leaving him at the table with Levi.

"So you're really going to move back?"

"At least on a part-time basis."

"It will be good to have you."

But there was weight to that, even if he and Levi would never really be able to acknowledge it. Levi had lost enough, and their friendship was important. Damien knew that. And right now... Sitting with his own loss, Damien felt like all this mattered more than it ever had.

"You did good," he said. "With everybody."

"Almost done," he said. "Camilla is going off to college, and that'll be that. Empty nest."

"Except for Jessie," he said.

"Yeah. I guess. Though, she's an adult. I don't ask for an accounting of her whereabouts. Jessie can do whatever she pleases."

He regarded his friend closely, not certain if there was something underneath his words or not. "Can she?"

"I mean, within reason. But you know... I realize she went to that masquerade the other night. I realize that she came home and left one shoe sitting in the entryway." He leaned back in his chair and made his focus level as he regarded Damien. "And I saw the other one down in the cabin you're staying in."

"Shit," Damien said.

"And that response tells me you're not really confused about how it got there."

"She didn't leave it there," he said. Because that was true.

"How'd it get there?"

"I... I had it."

"Right. So..."

"Is this the part where you throw me out in the snow?"

"No," Levi said, rapping his knuckles on the table. "It's not. Because God knows she's not a kid. She's not stupid. And she's been in love with you since the dawn of time."

"If you knew that, why didn't you say anything?"

"Because I figured… I figured you didn't feel the same. Anyway, it's not really my ideal scenario. I don't think my sister should necessarily be with somebody the same age as me who has never once acted like he wanted a commitment. But then I also figure…she's gotta make her mistakes. And if she chose to be with you… Well. It's her mistake."

"Maybe I'm not a mistake."

"Maybe," Levi said. "I'm open to that."

"I don't really know what to do with this conversation. I was expecting threats of violence."

"I'm only going to commit acts of violence if you get out of pocket. Like I said. Jessie is twenty-three years old. I don't have shit to say about who she sleeps with. Never have and never will."

"Well," Damien said, the words leaving his mouth before he could think better of them, "that's because she'd never slept with anybody before."

His posture straightened slightly, and Damien saw a lick of fire in Levi's eyes. And he could feel danger.

"Well, that changes the complexity of things slightly."

"It's complicated. And it's probably not a story you want to hear."

"Oh, I guarantee you that I don't. But what I wanted to make sure was… Don't hold anything back on account of me. That's it."

"Well, I was," Damien said.

"If being with her is something that you want, if it's something that makes you happy…then be with her. I mean, assuming she wants to be with you."

"That's the question," Damien said.

Levi's blessing was the first step in being certain this

wouldn't ruin the only family he had left. He couldn't control what Jessie would do.

But he could change himself. Make real, firm decisions about what he wanted.

He didn't have any excuses left.

He was the one who had to take this step.

Jessie had done it first. Tried to kiss him. Been the honest one about the attraction between them.

Now he was the one who had to take the risk.

CHAPTER SEVEN

JESSIE WAS STANDING in front of the Christmas tree, staring up at the lights. She just… She ached. And she couldn't quite put her finger on why. It was this season. Because it was so full of hope. Because every song promised that if you let your heart be light your troubles would be out of sight. Because the world acted as if Christmas was a giant antidepressant, when for her… Perhaps it was that. The glitter over the top of the darkness. It just didn't seem to make it better. It often made it worse. And she had wanted to do something, to feel something, that would make that desperate weight go away, and all she'd done was stepped into a further complication.

And then suddenly, she felt his presence behind her. And she knew it was him. Like she knew the snow was falling outside even though she couldn't hear it. Knew it was him just like she knew that tomorrow, even when the sun lit up the world, and Dylan walked through the door, they would be together, but never really quite together.

Because she knew that no matter how much glitter, there would always be darkness.

She turned to face him. "What do you want?"

"I want to talk to you."

"Why?"

"Because. It's Christmas Eve. And you were beginning to look a little bit sad over dinner."

"Christmas always makes me sad. That's why I dressed up. And put all that makeup on and went to the masquerade."

"Because you wanted something to make you feel better?"

"And another memory for Christmas."

"What's your bad Christmas memory?"

"It's not really a bad memory. It's just a bad feeling. Like it's supposed to do something that it can't. And that's worse than every other time. Like a whole season of birthdays, but you don't want to get another year older. Something like that. And it's always being shouted at you. Relentlessly, in songs and movies and commercials, that it's the season to be joyous. But it's often when I miss my family the most. Often when I feel the biggest ache. Gratitude toward Levi, and pain over missing my parents. All of it. That's the problem. It's just… It's just so hard."

"Hey," he said. "I know."

"I know."

"Take a walk with me."

"It's cold outside."

"I guess that's like Christmas," he said. "Because here we are, standing in front of the tree, but if we go outside it's going to be cold. The snow is still there, even though it's warm in here. Just like the glitter doesn't take away the grief. It's just there. Like it's always been. Like it always will be. So you might as well walk in the snow. For a little bit."

"I'm not sure if that made no sense or…more sense than any damned Christmas carol I've heard."

"Let's find out."

She looked around, checking for Levi. Damien didn't seem to be concerned at all. He took her hand, and they went outside. The air was light and cold, sharp. White flakes tumbled down through the air, landing with absolute silence onto the snowpack that already surrounded them. It was dark, except for the moon, which shone valiantly through a hole in the clouds. Now that she was thinking of it all like a metaphor, she really couldn't unsee it that way. It was just all there. All the time. A fire inside if she needed to get warm. The moon, to guide her way even in the darkness.

And Damien was there. And he was warm and solid standing next to her. They started to walk, and she didn't think too deeply about where they were walking. She just listened to the crunch of their footsteps in the snow. She just enjoyed being beside him, because she had wanted that. She had wanted that for a long time. And it was Christmas Eve. And if the songs could promise that there was something magical about it, she didn't know why she couldn't have magic in the moment. She was desperate for it, in fact. Hungry for it. So when she reached out and let her fingertips touch his, she waited. For him to respond. To see if he felt it, too. To see if he was caught up in it. And then he wrapped his fingers around hers, and walked along the darkened road with her, holding her hand. Like they were something more than two people who had quick sex in a broom closet. Like they were something more than two people who had known each other with a whole other person between them.

She was Levi's younger sister. He was Levi's best friend. But Levi wasn't there now. It was just Jessie and Damien. And what they were to each other. Which seemed to shift and change with each step forward. Which seemed to grow with each deep breath she took in, as if she could feel her lungs just slightly more each and every time. With the air. With promise. With hope.

They were headed toward his cabin. That much was apparent now. It was small and cozy, and he'd left a fire going in the woodstove. It was one room, and she knew that there was just an outhouse out back. And her shoe was sitting on the table right there in the entryway.

"Sit down for a second," he said.

"Why?"

"You'll see."

So she did, and he knelt in front of her, beginning to untie the laces on her snow boot, slowly and painstakingly. And she couldn't help but laugh. "Damien," she said. "You're being ridiculous."

"Maybe," he said. "But it seems like the thing to do, Cinderella. In fact, it doesn't really seem like there's any other point."

Then he slipped her thick boot sock off her foot, and she wiggled her toes. And he took the sparkling high heel and slipped it right on her foot.

"It's a perfect fit," he said.

"You just needed to be sure?"

"Yeah. I just needed to be sure. And it's kind of a magical thing. To see you. You, Jessie Granger, wearing that shoe. Because I know you were the woman that I saw walk into that space. But ever since then, you look like the you I've always known. And it doesn't make you less beautiful. Don't mistake me. It's just that it was easy to think of you as two different things. But this is you. It's all you. The girl in the snow boots and the sweatpants, and the girl in the red dress."

"And you're just the same. It's just you don't have a Zorro mask. And now I'm getting used to the beard."

"Stand up," he said, grabbing her hands and pulling her up into a standing position. She was lopsided because of the high heel and the snow boot. She had a beanie on her head, and he grabbed the top of it and lifted it off, letting it fall down to the ground. Then he cupped her chin, tilting her face up. "You're beautiful," he said.

"Thank you," she said.

"I'm not saying it just for my benefit. You're beautiful, and I want you to know it. You're beautiful, and I want you to know that I mean right now. I want you to know that that night… It wasn't the first night that I thought so. I had to leave, Jessie, because when you tried to kiss me, you damn near lit my world on fire. You were hotter than that bonfire, and it scared me to death. Because I knew if I didn't kiss you, then we couldn't go back. And I knew you were too young, too inexperienced…"

"Well, I wasn't, though. Because when we… When we actually did…"

"Exactly," he said. "When we actually did, when all my own doubts were stripped away. When it could be nothing except just seeing where the chemistry went, well, then… I was wrong. You weren't mismatched for me. You were perfect. And you always were. I just…couldn't see it when I looked and saw Jessie. And it wasn't anything to do with you. It was to do with everything…"

"Everything surrounding me," she finished.

"Yeah. I remember. I remember when your parents died, Jessie. Your mom. And then your dad… And it felt so unfair. I remember just wanting to be there for you. For all of you. I certainly never wanted to be the reason that you cried."

"Well, you were. Just so you know. After the bonfire. I was so embarrassed I'd…"

"Yeah. But that was a fitting trade. Just a little bit of sadness for all the hurt I could've caused you. That's all." He took her hand and brought her close, led her out to the center of the cabin. And her with her one high heel and snow boot clocked after him. Then he pulled her into his arms like it was a ball, and swayed back and forth with her. She laughed, and he twirled her, before bringing her back up against him. "No masks," he said. "Just us."

And that was when she kissed him. With all the pent-up desire inside her. For the very first time in her life, she looked up into his eyes, knowing it was him, and she closed the distance between them. Claimed his mouth with hers, and the best part was, he kissed her back. Harder. Deeper. Longer than she could've imagined. She was lost in it. In him. In tidings of comfort and joy that she hadn't even believed in before this moment. And she could understand. The glory in being wrapped in the glitter of the season and letting it sweep you away. Because sure, the darkness and snow were still out there. Sure, there was still grief. But there was this. There was this, and they were them, and it was more than she ever dared hope. "I need to get that shoe off," she said, kicking the high heel away. And then he lifted her up off the ground, wearing one boot and the rest of her snow clothes, and carried her over to the bed in the corner.

"Say my name," she said, feeling needy and desperate, hungry for the acknowledgment that it mattered to him as much as it did to her who they were. Exactly who they were in this moment.

"Jessie," he said. "Jessie Granger."

"Yes," she whispered, before he kissed her again.

He lifted her foot, put it in his lap, began to unlace her remaining boot, getting it loosened and pulling it slowly from her foot, along with her sock.

He paused for a moment, and dealt with his own shoes. Before drawing her close on the bed and kissing her again. It was a stark difference to that frantic coupling in the broom closet. It was a stark difference to everything that had come before. Because this was Jessie and Damien. Making a decision to do this. Making a decision to be together.

They were meeting as equals, here in this bed. She wasn't a virgin anymore.

Close enough.

But still. Still. She pushed his coat off his shoulders, began to work the buttons on his shirt. He pulled her sweatshirt up over her head, and before she knew it, they were stripped down to their underwear. And she was lying in bed with him, watching as her fingertips trailed over his muscles. Watching as her palm skimmed over the well-defined pecs and abs. His hair tickled her fingertips, and she luxuriated in the feeling. Of all that masculine heat and warmth.

He kissed her neck, down her collarbone, down to the edge of her bra. And she ignited. This was what she had wanted. Since that night. It had been hell. Being around him, trying to pretend it hadn't happened. She was just so relieved they weren't pretending that it hadn't happened anymore.

She wanted him. She wanted this.

She wanted everything that came with it.

And that thought scared her. Because the truth was, no matter how warm it was in this cabin, it was still cold outside.

And the metaphor was good for all the rest of life.

Don't think about it. Don't think about anything past now. You wanted a Christmas miracle, and this is your damned Christmas miracle. So just take it. And don't ask any questions.

She listened to her stern inner voice, because what else was there to do? She listened to that voice because she was powerless to do anything else. So when he unhooked her bra and cast it to the floor, lowering his head and taking her nipple deep within his mouth, she gasped, arching against him.

And she let there be nothing. Nothing but the warmth. Nothing but the pleasure. Nothing but the touch of his mouth, his tongue, his teeth, his hands. Nothing but the pleasure that he brought her as he moved his big hands up her body, skimming his thumbs over her nipples before taking one into his mouth again. It was impossibly intimate, and it was Damien.

This is Damien.

It was Damien, and it was her fantasy made reality. And this was the miracle she hadn't thought to ask for. So she would simply take it. Allow it to exist at face value, and ask for nothing more.

She couldn't afford more.

That was a damned fact.

His hands moved down, his fingers sliding beneath the waistband of her underwear, as he pushed them down her thighs, trailing them past her ankles and onto the floor. She wasn't embarrassed. She hadn't been fully naked in front of him that first time. And she also hadn't known that it was him. Everything was different about this. About this moment. About this desire. Everything was different.

But her need was just as intense.

He moved his hand between her legs and began to stroke her, finding her wet and hot and ready for his touch.

But it wasn't enough. She wanted more. She wanted him.

It was her turn to strip him entirely naked, and this time she gloried in him. The look of him, the feel of him. The knowledge of who he was.

She had wondered, occasionally, when her fantasies

about Damien had heated up, if it would actually be uncomfortable to be with him. Given how well she knew him. Given who he was. But no. It wasn't. It was everything, and so was he. Like she had been made for this moment. And if that felt weightier, more terrifying than it should, she wasn't going to examine it. She wasn't going to do anything but enjoy the sparkle. Enjoy the warmth.

'Tis the season.

She wrapped her hand around his hardened length and pumped him. Then she lowered her head, slowly, taking a tentative taste of him with her tongue.

He groaned, his hand coming up to grab her hair, holding her fast as she took him in deep. Her body shuddered as his did. His response to her the sensual boost that she needed, and she was lost in it. In the way she could make him growl. In the way she could make him lose himself. She was lost in everything. And she loved it.

"My turn," he growled. And she found herself lifted bodily away from him, flat on her back on the bed, her thighs parted.

And then he forced them apart, holding her knees wide with his hands before lowering his head and swiping his tongue across that sensitized bundle of nerves there. "Mine," he said, before burying his face between her legs and consuming her in the white heat of desire.

She clutched his shoulders, her fingers digging into his skin.

And his word echoed between them.

Mine.

Mine.

What did it mean to belong to somebody? Could you even trust such a thing?

In this life, in this world, where things could be ripped

tremendously away from you, how can anything ever truly be yours?

She didn't know the answer. And right now she didn't want to try and figure it out. Right now all she wanted to do was luxuriate in the feel of him.

It was all she could manage.

So she arched against him and silenced her mind, riding the wave of pleasure that was beginning to crest inside her. He pushed a finger inside her, and then another, pumping them in time with the movements of his tongue. And her orgasm broke over her like a stunning tsunami.

It left her spent, breathless, lost. With no way to find the shore. But she didn't have time to mourn that. Because he was there. He was there, so she couldn't really be lost.

He was there. So it would all be okay.

He was there. And he was everything.

He gathered her close, kissed her on the lips, kissed her until her need was at a fever pitch. Then he positioned himself between her thighs, and thrust home.

She gasped, lifting her hips up, her internal muscles gripping him tight as he claimed her.

It was perfect. He was perfect.

She wrapped her legs around his waist, held his face in her hands and kissed him as he claimed her over and over again.

Mine.

She wanted to be his.

She wanted to be his more than she wanted anything in the entire world. And if she could gift herself, and know that it would last, then she would. Without a doubt. Unequivocally.

But it was Christmas. And gifts given on Christmas

were beautiful right at the time. And then they were worn and faded, forgotten about before next year.

They went in boxes labeled memories. Or boxes labeled trauma. But they didn't last.

She pushed that thought aside as another climax reached its peak, and she clung to him, crying out her pleasure in tandem with his, as she felt him pulse inside her.

And it was silent. Nothing but the crackling of the wood in the fireplace. And the knowledge of the snow falling outside.

"Merry Christmas," he said.

"Merry Christmas," she agreed.

And he put the covers over her and brought her close to him.

It was a far cry from a quickie in a broom closet that ended with her running away.

But she would let herself be held. Tonight she would let herself be held, because tomorrow would come quickly enough. And it felt like a reckoning. Or maybe just a resounding clang of a silver bell.

But tonight there was this. Tonight there was maybe miracles.

And that felt good enough to her.

CHAPTER EIGHT

IT WAS CHRISTMAS MORNING. And the morning dawned bright and cold in the cabin, because the fire had gone out sometime during the night. But the fire had never gone out between himself and Jessie.

Damien looked at the woman sleeping in his arms.

It was such a funny thing. He'd never seen a real marriage. A good marriage, at a close vantage point. His mother had always been single, and the way that she had acted about the very idea of a nuclear family had just made it something that he didn't consider of extreme importance. But now he could see it. He could see a life with her, stretching before him. He could see hope and a future in a way that he never had before, the potential for it, with her. Yes. He could see that. All of that.

And he wanted it with such a ferocity that it nearly scared him.

And not much scared him.

But he had never been in a situation where he had anything to risk. Jessie had lost a lot in her life. A whole lot. She lost so much, and so he supposed she had always seen life as a risk. And he could appreciate fully that she had put something on the line when she tried to kiss him and he'd rejected her. He felt like an ass. Because he just hadn't known. He did now. Now that he'd experienced loss. And now that things felt precarious. Like they were on the edge of something. Something he might not be able to get back. He kissed her forehead, and she opened her eyes, looking at him sleepily. "Damien?"

"Yeah. I'm right here."

"Merry Christmas," she mumbled.

Then her eyes flew wide. "What time is it?"

"I don't know."

"Well, hell," she said. "Hell and damn. Hell and damn and shit."

"There's that dirty mouth again."

"It's Christmas morning. And Dylan was supposed to get here bright and early. And it's..." She looked outside. "It's gone sunup."

"Yeah."

"Well, Levi is going to be a little bit suspicious if he goes upstairs to wake me up for Christmas morning and I'm not there."

"Levi knows where you are."

"He's going to kill you. He's going to murder you, and then..." She stopped. "What?"

"I said he knows where you are."

"No. He can't. He can't know where I am. Because that would mean..."

"He came in here yesterday. He saw the shoe."

"What?"

"You're starting to sound like a broken record, sweet pea."

"But there's no way he can know. Because if he knew, you would be dead."

"It turns out not. It turns out he respects you as a woman, and respects what you want."

"No way. Not my brother. My brother is an old-fashioned hard-ass."

"I had a talk with him."

"So what, he just knows that we are sleeping together?" She winced. "I mean, that we slept together. Not that we are sleeping together. We just… We did the one time again. Because it was Christmas Eve. And it was the magic of the season and all of that."

"That wasn't it for me. And I made that pretty plain to Levi last night. Jessie… I was wrong to reject you back then. And I didn't really do it to protect you. I thought I did. I did it to protect myself, because I knew that if you ever touched me…that would be it. I knew that it could never be a casual thing. And I was right. It can't be. Not with you and me. This is real. This thing. And it was… I was on the verge of going out and really trying to make something of myself. And now I have. And you're not twenty-one. And… I care about you. I always have."

"No," she said. "We can't do that. We can't do this."

"Why the hell not?"

"Because," she said, almost sounding panicked. "Because that's not… That's not what it was supposed to be. And it can't be that, anyway."

"So when you tried to kiss me, you figured what? That I was going to sleep with you and walk away?"

"I hadn't thought it through. I hadn't… I hadn't really considered it. I just knew that I wanted to kiss you. I didn't want…"

"You didn't want what?"

"I can't do it," she said. "Because it's Christmas, and Dylan is coming back and everything is sad. Everything is always sad. And life is sad, and you can't trust it. And Christmas songs are never going to heal the world. They're never going to fix your life. The season isn't magic. And even if it was, it's over. Christmas is over. And we have to be, too."

"I just told you that we don't."

"I can't do it," she said. "I just can't."

And she got her things together quickly, putting her boots on, and running out the door. Like she wasn't headed to a place just a few feet away.

CHAPTER NINE

BY THE TIME Jessie got to the house, everyone was sitting in there. Around the Christmas tree. And there was Dylan. Her breath left her body in a whoosh, and she launched herself across the space. "Dylan," she said, wrapping her arms around his neck, like she always did. Trying to make sure that all of him was here. She had always hated that he had joined the military. She knew that Levi hated it, too, but that he didn't oppose it, because he didn't oppose choices they made as adults.

The fact that he had apparently proved when it came to her relationship with Damien.

Damien.

He was acting like he wanted this to be something. And she just wasn't brave enough to do that.

"Hey," he said. "Where have you been?"

"Just overslept," she said. Which was stupid, because she had clearly just come in from the cold. He looked behind her, and she could feel that he was exchanging a meaningful glance with Levi.

"Good to see you," he said, opting not to make a comment.

"But," Camilla said, opening her mouth. And Levi reached down and grabbed a cookie off the tray next to them, and shoved it in her baby sister's mouth.

"Just chill, Camilla," he said.

"But hnm ummh nrrrrrrh," she said, her words completely unintelligible.

"It'll keep," Levi said.

There were presents, and she opened them. And there was also a little stack of presents that was untouched. Because they were Damien's. And he just didn't show. Of course he hadn't. She had rejected him, except that maybe her having the power to hurt him in some way seemed... unlikely. Ridiculous. But maybe she had. Maybe she had actually devastated him.

She pressed her fists to her eyeballs and tried to take a breath.

As soon as they were done opening presents, and they moved with Levi heading out to start grilling the meat that they would have for dinner, him knocking snow off the barbecue and arguing with Dylan about how they were going to prepare things, Camilla zoomed in toward her like a little gnat to a lamp. "What did you do?"

"What do you mean?"

"Where were you?"

"None of your business," she said to her little sister.

"Really? None of my business? What were you doing?"

"I just..."

"Did you sleep with Damien?"

"Camilla," she said.

"That's my name, not a *no*."

She sniffed. "You don't understand. You are a virgin."

"And you aren't," she said. "Which means something changed, because Lord knows you have just been hanging around hung up on him for years..."

"Nothing," she said. "It was just...a fling. And then... Now it isn't a thing."

"Did he dump you on Christmas Eve?"

"No. I dumped him."

"What?"

"I don't want to talk about it," she said to her little sister.

"Why are you insistently emotionally constipated?" she asked. "Like, come on."

"You come on," she said. "You barely remember what life was like with Mom and Dad. But I do remember. And it's been hell without them. And it was hard to lose them. And…"

"So you all go and make your own lives more lonely. Look at Levi… He's… He's basically a grumpy old man and he's just in his thirties. You were wearing baggy clothes, all ready to be an old maid because Damien wouldn't give you the time of day, and now he is, and what? You want him to go back to being an untouchable object because it was easier? Easier than admitting that you want him? That you love him?"

"Well, he didn't say that he loved me," she said. "What he said was that he wanted to try. And I don't… I can't do it. Because…"

"Because you're always waiting for the other shoe to drop. I get that. Because we lost Mom, and it was terrible. But we figured we had had our fill of bad things. And then Dad."

"Yes," she said. "It's waiting for the other shoe to drop."

"You can't live that way."

"You're a child," she said. "You literally don't know anything about anything."

"That's what you keep saying. Except I know I'm going to go to college. Except I know that I didn't choose the bad things that happened to me, and I'm not gonna choose extra bad things just because."

"You make it sound easy. But you don't know what it's

like. You don't know what he makes me…feel. What he's always made me feel. I have had feelings for him since I was a kid. When I was brave enough to act on them he rejected me."

"And now you're rejecting him? It just seems like you're creating your own issues."

"No, I just… I wanted to know that I was going to be okay if things didn't work out between us. I went… I went to that Christmas party. The mask one in Mapleton. I wanted to hook up with a guy that I didn't know. I wanted to prove to myself that I would be okay if Damien Prince never cared about me. But what I found instead was Damien. So I can't prove it to myself. I don't know if I'm going to be okay. And Dylan isn't done in the military and…"

"I hear what you're saying," Camilla said. "But no. You don't know if you'll be okay. I'm sorry. But that's just how it is. You don't really get to know."

She stared at her little sister, who said all these things so very matter-of-factly. It was maddening. Infuriating. And she just kept thinking about last night. About the way he had put that shoe on her foot. About the way he had danced with her. Awkwardly, with that one shoe and the one boot and…

She turned away from Camilla and found herself drifting toward the entryway, where her other high heel was still sitting, laying oddly in a pile of shoes in that doorway.

And it hit her then. She had the other shoe. She was the one holding it. And there was something about that revelation, that realization, that gave her a sense of power. A sense of determination. She was waiting for the other shoe to drop like she had no control over any of this. Like she had no control over what she did. How she changed and what she learned. What she decided to fight for. As if the other shoe was simply fate. That would fall from heaven one day and crush her beneath the weight of it, because that was how it had felt to lose her father after her mother when she'd been just a child.

But it wasn't a trend. It was just life. And there were things that had happened since then that were…up to her. This was up to her. "I'm an idiot," she whispered.

"That's what I've been saying," Camilla said.

"I mean… I really am."

She picked up the shoe by the door, and without bothering to put on her coat, she ran outside. She ran all the way down to Damien's cabin. And she knocked on the door. He didn't answer. She opened it, and she found it empty. "Dammit," she whispered. She looked around and didn't see his truck anywhere. He was gone. He was gone.

She went back into the cabin and looked again. His belongings were gone and so… So was her shoe.

And she stared down at the one in her hand, and she realized then and there, it was up to her to put that pair back together.

And so she went back up to the house and got in her own truck, and took off down the road with her glittering high heel in the seat beside her.

She was on a mission. And she was going to find Damien.

CHAPTER TEN

DAMIEN HAD DETERMINED that the better part of valor was to let her get on with her Christmas. He felt... Hell, he didn't really know what he felt. Heartbreak, he supposed, though he never had an experience of it when it came to love. Romantic love.

Had he really fallen in love with her in just a couple of days?

No. He fell in love with her years ago. *You just didn't know how to let yourself in on it.*

But she didn't want to do it. And hell, he couldn't blame her. The world was a cold and unforgiving place. And she'd seen a lot of bad shit.

He didn't want to be just another terrible thing that had happened to Jessie Granger. He cared way too much for that.

Suddenly, in his rearview mirror, he saw a blue truck. Hot on his bumper, and driving pretty dangerously considering the weather.

It took him a minute to realize. It was Jessie. He put his blinker on like a good Oregonian and pulled to the right side of the road, and Jessie pulled swiftly after him.

"What the hell are you doing?" he asked, getting out of the driver's side and shutting the door firmly behind him.

"I had to find you," she said, getting out of the truck,

holding a high heel shoe in one hand. "I have the other shoe."

"Yeah."

"I am afraid of the other shoe dropping. But I have the other shoe. It's… It's me. I'm the one who's making a bad choice here. I'm the one who's sabotaging us. And I have to quit acting like everything is fate. I have to quit being afraid. So I…" She started to unlace her snow boot, out there in the freezing cold, and kicked it off, then she started to work at the boot sock. "I am putting the shoe on myself. Because it fits me, and I want to wear it."

"Jessie…"

"You can get the other one now," she said, breathing hard, as she bent down to start the endeavor of pulling the other boot off.

"This is a little much," he said.

"It's too much," she said. "It's all too much. This is without a doubt the most too much anything has ever been. But I want you. And I love you. And I'm deciding to be in it. Without being afraid. This is my choice. And the terrible things that have happened to me before don't get to decide how happy I'm going to be now."

"You love me, Jessie Granger?"

"Yes, you dumbass. I have. For my whole damn life."

"That dirty mouth…"

"You like it. You like me."

He turned around and walked slowly back to his truck, emotion expanding in his chest. And he grabbed the shoe that he had brought with him. "You're right," he said, making his way slowly back to her. "I do. I like it a whole hell of a lot. But I love you."

He got down on one knee, holding the shoe in his hand. And she slipped her bare foot into it. And it felt every bit like an engagement ring. There she was, in her snow pants, and her high heels. And it felt like this undeniable truth. She was the Jessie he had always known. And the Jessie who had changed his life forever at the ball.

They were the same. And she was his.

"I love you. I think we ought to get married. And live on the big property here together."

"I want that," she said.

"You are so brave," he said. "And just so damn special."

She kissed him, like her whole life depended on it. Like their new life depended on it.

"You know," she said. "I guess I was wrong. About Christmas. Or maybe just about life. I kept thinking that just because bad things happened, it meant the good wasn't real. But it's more real, isn't it? It sparkles brighter because of the darkness."

"I think so," he said. "At least, it's true when I'm with you."

* * * * *

Get 4 FREE REWARDS!

We'll send you 2 FREE Books plus <u>2</u> FREE Mystery Gifts.

FREE
Value Over
$20

Both the **Romance** and **Suspense** collections feature compelling novels written by many of today's bestselling authors.

YES! Please send me 2 FREE novels from the Essential Romance or Essential Suspense Collection and my 2 FREE gifts (gifts are worth about $10 retail). After receiving them, if I don't wish to receive any more books, I can return the shipping statement marked "cancel." If I don't cancel, I will receive 4 brand-new novels every month and be billed just $7.24 each in the U.S. or $7.49 each in Canada. That's a savings of up to 38% off the cover price. It's quite a bargain! Shipping and handling is just 50¢ per book in the U.S. and $1.25 per book in Canada.* I understand that accepting the 2 free books and gifts places me under no obligation to buy anything. I can always return a shipment and cancel at any time by calling the number below. The free books and gifts are mine to keep no matter what I decide.

Choose one: ☐ **Essential Romance**
(194/394 MDN GQ6M)

☐ **Essential Suspense**
(191/391 MDN GQ6M)

Name (please print)

Address _____ Apt. #

City _____ State/Province _____ Zip/Postal Code

Email: Please check this box ☐ if you would like to receive newsletters and promotional emails from Harlequin Enterprises ULC and its affiliates. You can unsubscribe anytime.

> **Mail to the Harlequin Reader Service:**
> **IN U.S.A.:** P.O. Box 1341, Buffalo, NY 14240-8531
> **IN CANADA:** P.O. Box 603, Fort Erie, Ontario L2A 5X3

Want to try 2 free books from another series? Call 1-800-873-8635 or visit www.ReaderService.com.